CONTENTS

Couch Potato Chaos: Gamebound by Erik Rounds

ISBN: 9781718049277

Edited by Crystal Watanabe
Cover by David Debaene.

COUCH POTATO CHAOS

Book 1: Gamebound

Written by Erik Rounds

Edited by Crystal Watanabe

Cover by David Debaen

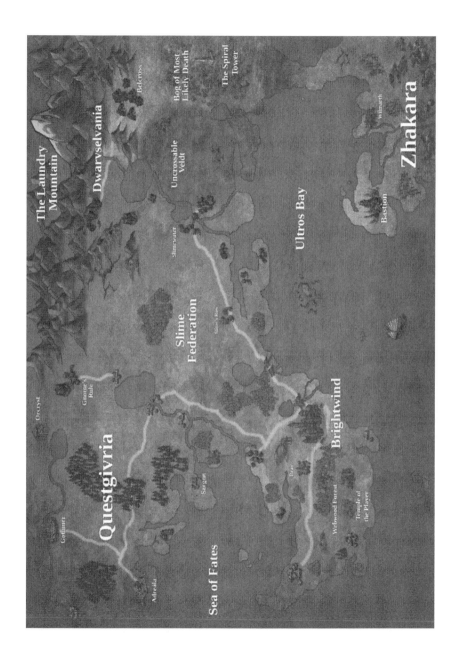

CHAPTER 1

Catalyst

Consider the couch potato. Sedentary creatures, they spend their days transfixed by the warm, iridescent glow of their screens for hours at a time, passively consuming entertainment while producing little of value or merit. They avoid most forms of physical exertion while subsisting primarily on a diet of cupcakes, microwave lasagna, and caffeine.

Tasha was the embodiment of the couch-potato archetype. She had spent the better part of her childhood sitting on the floor in front of her TV, either enjoying the campy serialized science fiction of the day or watching her father play poorly translated Japanese role-playing games on their 16-bit gaming console. Back then, she would sometimes read the character's dialogue aloud, using funny voices while watching him play.

Those were some of the best years of her life. By the time her father died, she'd inherited his taste in both video games and cringeworthy television.

It was her love of gaming which led her to pursue a career in the video game industry. Her studies led her to be a decent enough programmer, but after college she quickly learned that landing her first job in the industry was easier said than done. Most game companies ignored her resume entirely, and those few who did respond turned her away, suggesting that she get more industry experience before bothering them with an application.

When she was finally called in for an interview, she was over the moon. They had asked her some simple questions in vector math and programming, as well as some math-based logic puzzles that wouldn't have felt out of place in a Professor Layton game. When they offered her a job with an insultingly low annual salary, she had thought herself lucky. It was way below the industry average but not entirely unreasonable for someone just starting out.

For the first few years, the job meant something to her. The company put actual effort into making their games entertaining. Times had been better then. The first game they developed was a mid-core action platformer. Sure, it was a tad derivative, but the game had character, and she enjoyed working on it.

She was used to working long hours of unpaid overtime, but at the beginning she didn't mind as much. It was a labor of love, and the office was filled with laughter and the occasional impromptu Nerf-gun fight. But things had changed since then. The job no longer had a sense of purpose, and the comradery was no longer there.

In an attempt to increase short-term profit, the company had switched to flooding the market with minimal-effort pay-to-win mobile games. Most of their projects were just re-skins of the same game with small cosmetic changes.

Most of her colleagues had the presence of mind to move on to other companies, but not her. Tasha hated change. She sometimes daydreamed about quitting, but it never went farther than that.

One fateful Friday evening, Tasha was riding home on the metro after a day of especially pointless and mind-numbing work. The company was always crunching these days. The hours had grown longer and the weekends had grown shorter.

As the bus came to a stop, she made her way to the front and stepped onto the sidewalk. The driver closed the door behind her without a word, and the bus pulled away.

She was about to start walking toward her apartment complex when her smartphone began to vibrate in the pocket of her jeans. She took it out and glanced at it. It was her boss.

Why is that horrible little man calling me now? This was supposed to be my weekend off.

She let the call go to voicemail, thinking if she ignored him, he'd leave her alone. She'd worked weekends for three weeks without rest. Enough was enough.

The sky was already growing darker as the sun made its daily descent into the western horizon. A single drop of rainwater touched her cheek, followed by another. Thick storm clouds had gathered in the distance and were approaching rapidly.

She picked up her pace, planting one foot after another in rapid succession. She'd need to move quickly to reach her apartment before the storm hit.

She neared a familiar fork in the road, which split off to the left and right. Having walked this path on a daily basis, she knew that both paths would converge at her apartment. To the left were rows of shops and restaurants, including a pizza place that she rather enjoyed, and the right touched upon a residential area filled with houses and apartment complexes. Experience had taught her that neither path would get her home more swiftly than the other.

Today, however, she saw something out of the ordinary: a dimly glowing blue rectangle hovering in the air. She approached it slowly, tilting her head in curiosity.

The box floated unsupported. It just sort of hung there in stubborn defiance of the laws of gravity. It was a bit like a partially visible TV screen, but it didn't appear to be connected to anything.

Naturally, Tasha did the first thing that any halfway reasonable human being does when confronted with the unknown—she poked at it with a stick. There was a nice pointy one on the ground beside her, so she picked it up and jabbed at the screen a few times. The small twig made contact with the rectangle but continued through it without resistance as though the screen wasn't there.

She extended her arm and found that it went straight through the ghostly projection. It was like one of those holograms from any number of science fiction shows... or maybe a UI element from a video game.

Circling around the strange apparition, she found that it looked nearly the same from the back. Observing it from the back revealed that the text was inverted, as if being seen through a mirror.

She regarded two lines of text written on the screen. The first line was an arrow pointing to the left accompanied by the word

"Adventure." Below that was an arrow pointing to the right with the word "Safety."

Tasha took a step away from the glowing blue box. The arrows were pointing in the two directions that the road branched into. There was nothing notable down either path, save for the rapidly increasing rainfall.

It was like a signpost. One way for adventure and the other for safety.

What a convenient gamelike mechanic, she thought. *If this were a game, taking the path to the left would trigger some sort of scripted event.*

As a professional game developer, she was used to thinking about things in terms of video games. But there was a world of difference between video games and reality.

On reflection, she didn't consider herself an adventuresome lady. She would often dream about going on adventures, but those were just fantasies. Real-life adventures were scary, involved the risk of bodily harm, and made one late for work the following day.

For several long minutes, she just stared at the glowing screen as it floated unmoving in the air. One way for adventure and the other for safety. Perhaps this was the universe's idea of a practical joke. Or, more likely, this was nothing more than a stress-induced hallucination.

After a moment of contemplation, she mentally chided herself and took the path to the right, the direction indicated by the word "Safety." The rain was picking up, and she didn't have time to indulge in this sort of meaningless nonsense. Not if she wanted to avoid the bulk of the storm and remain marginally dry.

As she stepped up the pace, lightning arced across in the horizon before her. The flash momentarily highlighted the shape of the oncoming storm clouds followed by a report of thunder. As she passed rows of houses on the street to her left, several of their outdoor lights switched on, providing modest illumination to the darkening street. The storm was very nearly upon her.

Her right foot splashed into a newly formed puddle as she walked. She had tarried for too long at the crossroads, and the trickle of rain had turned into a downpour. Some of the water from the puddle entered her shoes and filled her socks so that every time she took a step, they made a sloshing sound.

She continued for nearly five minutes before she reached the door to her apartment complex. It was a large twelve-story brick building lined with balconies. This apartment building featured a security box at the front entrance to deter the uninvited. Upon typing in the four-digit code, she heard a click indicating that the door was unlocked and that she could enter.

She reached out her hand to turn the handle and open the door but didn't actually touch it. Some inner doubt caused her to hesitate, and her hand remained suspended in the air right before the handle. It was as though there was a finality to the act of opening the door.

Why had she chosen safety over adventure?

Hesitating, she considered her earlier actions. Surely the floating screen thing was just a figment of her imagination brought on by stress, but even if that were the case, she still could have indulged the fantasy and chosen adventure. She had made a deliberate choice, and it was one that she had repeated many times throughout her life.

Her refusal to leave her job was only the most recent example of this. She hated her job and remained only because she was used to being there and it supported her couch-potato lifestyle. She lived her entire life in the path of least resistance.

Her hand stubbornly refused to touch the door handle, and she remained there, transfixed. She couldn't bring herself to do it. Why hadn't she chosen adventure?

A low click sounded. The electronic lock had grown bored of waiting for her to get on and do something and had relocked itself. If she wanted to enter the building, she would need to reenter the code to assure the lock that she really did want in.

As she turned around, she looked back the way she had come. She stood sheltered under the apartment building's entrance as a curtain of rainwater rushed inches from her. The rainfall had grown into a mighty torrent.

"This is stupid," she said aloud. "Just open the damn door."

Instead, she turned away from the potential warmth of her home and ran back into the storm. Seconds after she passed through the curtain of water, she was soaked from head to toe. The cold wetness of her clothes pressed against her, and her denim jacket became heavier in the deluge. Water dripped from her hair and into her eyes, forcing her to blink away the rainwater.

She took off running down the street beneath the dim glow of the streetlights. Minutes later, she reached the place where the two roads diverged.

The glowing screen was a beacon in the storm. It was still there. She could make out its shape and dim glow between the lines of rainfall.

She picked up the pace, but this time she took the road to the left, following the path marked "Adventure." A flood of cold rainwater enveloped her body, sending fresh shivers through her body.

The rain-filled night was illuminated by a brilliant flash of light. At the same time, there was a thunderclap as a lightning bolt struck a nearby deciduous tree. A tree branch struck her as it fell, knocking her to the asphalt and earning her scratches to the face and knee.

Fear and pain overtook her for a moment. As she got back to her feet, she found that the large tree had fallen into the road, blocking her path. There didn't seem to be a way around it, so she pulled out her smartphone and turned on the flashlight app to light her way. The only way around it was through a large pool of water, so she found the best point to climb over the tree.

Although she was out of shape and shunned any form of physical exertion that didn't involve a remote control, she nevertheless climbed over the tree and stood on the other side. She returned her phone to the pocket of her jeans.

Pellets of water beat against her as she made her way along the path. It was as though the wind was alive and trying to force her back the way she had come. Gritting her teeth, she pushed against it, her feet sloshing the rainwater one step at a time.

Finally her apartment building was once again in sight, and what a sight it was. Lightning struck the top of the apartment building once, only to strike the same location a moment later. Seconds passed, and a third bolt struck the same place. Each time she heard and felt the thunderous sound of the impact.

Although she was understandably hesitant to approach the building after such a phenomenon, she did so. Fighting against the wind, she forced her way step by step to the door. Finally, she was standing under the safety and relative dryness of the apartment's awning once again. Exhausted, she collapsed onto the ground, leaning against the brick wall.

After a moment, she got to her feet and entered the code into the security box. This time she didn't hesitate and grabbed the handle, opening the door. Stepping inside, she let the door shut behind her. She stood upon the base of the stairwell as water dripped from her hair and clothes, forming a small puddle on the thinly carpeted floor.

Her jeans were torn at the knee where she had hit the pavement. She was wet, frozen, and bleeding from the knee and elbow as she began her ascent. Each step sent a small shudder of pain to her leg. When she finally reached the third floor, she unlocked the apartment door and stepped inside. She closed the door behind her and fastened the door guard. She desperately wanted to take a hot bath.

At first it appeared that nothing had changed. Her home was a small-budget single-bedroom apartment. It wasn't much, but she didn't need much space. With her work schedule, she barely spent any time at home anyway.

There was a small kitchenette that doubled as a dining room and tripled as the foyer. It opened up into a modest living room. The living room had a balcony, but Tasha rarely used it, not being the outdoorsy type. A raggedy old couch took up the bulk of the living room while a ten-year-old plasma TV occupied a small table in the corner.

Her exercise bicycle sat in the far, unused side of the living room. Lately it had been accumulating cobwebs. She'd been meaning to give it a good dusting and clean off the cobwebs, but she could never seem to find the time.

There was a narrow hallway which led to her bedroom and a utilitarian bathroom. She proceeded past the bathroom and entered the bedroom.

The bedroom sported a twin bed and her desk, where she kept her computer—a pink anime cat-themed Windows 98 netbook. Her infrequent visitors and even more infrequent boyfriends would try to get her to upgrade to a more modern PC, and maybe one just a bit less pink, but she'd resisted the temptation thus far.

She would prefer to spend the money on video games rather than an updated laptop, but that was only a small part of the reason. The netbook had been a gift from her father, and it had become a keepsake—something to remember him by. Her father had died nearly ten years ago, and the netbook was one of the last things that he gave her.

She was about to get undressed in preparation for a bath when she noticed a light emanating from the pocket of her jeans. She pulled out her smartphone. She had neglected to turn off the flashlight app from earlier. As she was about to switch it off, she spied something amiss.

On the cell phone face, where it normally showed the current time of day, the numbers 99:53:05 appeared. Now it read 99:53:04. 99:53:03. For some reason beyond her understanding, her cell phone's clock had been replaced by a countdown. She shut down her phone's flashlight app and set it face up on the computer desk.

She looked up at the round analog clock that hung on her bedroom wall. It had also undergone a change. Where there used to be twelve numbers there were now ten, ranging from 0 to 90 in increments of ten. The hour and minute hands were pointed up, and the second hand was ticking down in a counterclockwise rotation. Her netbook indicated that the current time was 99:52.

She took a moment and considered her options. In the last half hour, she had witnessed floating translucent dialogue boxes, had a transformative moment of self-discovery, been nearly killed by two lightning bolts and a falling tree, and now all of the clocks in her apartment seemed to be ticking backward. Upon further analysis, panic seemed to be the most reasonable option available to her.

The clock's second hand continued its counterclockwise journey. When it reached the 00 number at the top, the minute hand ticked backward ever so slightly. It had to be some sort of countdown, but a countdown to what? Was she expected to do something before it reached zero? If that were the case, there was just under one hundred hours left.

She couldn't write this off as a trick or delusion. Whatever was happening now was a consequence of her decision at the crossroads. She had chosen to go on an adventure, and now it seemed that one had found her.

CHAPTER 2

The Inverted Clock

Tasha spent several minutes transfixed, staring at her wall clock in wonderment and confusion. Its second hand continued to tick backward along its slow counterclockwise rotation.

She was roused from her stupor by a sharp buzzing sound. It took her a moment to realize that the sound was from the door buzzer. Someone was outside the building and wanted to be let in. She made her way back to the entrance and touched the button on the speaker linked to the box outside the building.

"Hello?"

The box replied in a staticky male voice, "Delivery service. I have a package for Tasha Singleton."

She hesitated. Who would be making a delivery at this hour, and through the storm? She pressed the button on the box, allowing the man entry to the building. After a few minutes, there was a knock at the door. Keeping the security chain fastened, she opened the door a few inches. It was indeed a delivery guy carrying a brown cardboard box. The man smiled at her. She closed the door, undid the lock, and opened it the rest of the way.

"Tasha Singleton?" the man said. "I've got this package for you. Could you sign for it?"

The first thing she noticed about the man was that he was completely dry. If he had been out in the storm, his clothes ought to have been dripping wet.

"Uh... yeah. Sure thing. So... I guess the rain has stopped?"

The man looked at her quizzically and said, "I don't know what you mean. It hasn't rained a bit all week. You must be mistaken."

She scribbled her signature on the man's tablet and received the small brown parcel. While doing so, she snuck a surreptitious glance at his digital watch. It read 99:48.

"Hey, can you tell me what time it is?"

The man glanced at his watch and said, "It's 7:23. Good evening, miss." With that, he turned away and left.

After closing the door and securing the lock, she placed the package upon the kitchen counter. It was a plain brown cardboard box. Turning it around in her hand, she found the label and saw who it was addressed by.

The sender was her father, Jak Singleton, who had died ten years prior. She considered the box for several moments in bewilderment before noticing that the label indicated it had been sent seventeen years ago, seven years before his death. This package was a time-delayed delivery.

That shouldn't be possible. She had only moved into her apartment a few years ago, so logically her dad wouldn't have known where to send it. Somehow her father had pulled a *Back to the Future II* and sent her a package almost two decades before he could have known where she would be living.

Well, the mystery wouldn't solve itself. There was nothing for it but to open the package and see what was inside. She dug around in her utility drawer for some kind of cutting instrument. There were scissors somewhere, but she couldn't find them, like usual. Finally, in desperation, she pulled out her apartment key and used the sharp pointy edge to cut through the tape. Having opened the box, she found one of those metallic static-proof bags. Setting the box aside, she carefully removed a single object from the bag.

It was a Super Nintendo video game cartridge. The label on the cartridge featured a crossed sword and staff against a black background. The words "Legend of Etheria" appeared below them in bold red lettering.

Both she and her father had been avid video gamers. It had been one of the few things that they had in common while growing up. After his death, she had inherited his rather sizable collection of video games, but she'd never heard of this one. Why had her father sent this to her?

She decided to postpone the luxury of panic until after she took a shower. She was still cold and dripping wet. She set the game on the counter and headed to the bathroom.

CHAPTER 3

The Gamebound Traveler

Her body was wet and chilled to the bone. What she really wanted was to take a long, soaky bubble bath with her favorite rubber duck, Mister Quackers. Regrettably, she felt that she couldn't afford to take any more time than necessary. Nothing inspired haste more than an impossible and mysterious countdown.

After the all too brief shower, she bandaged up the cuts on her knee and face. They had already stopped bleeding on their own, but it wouldn't do to let them get infected.

Her favorite PJs were sitting on top of the laundry pile in the hamper. They weren't technically clean, but in her personal estimation they still qualified as clean-adjacent. She threw them on and donned her comfy red bathrobe. The bathrobe was old and worn out, but she still liked it. It was warm, and she would occasionally use it as a makeshift blanket while vegging out on the couch. The finishing touch to her ensemble was her trusty bunny slippers. She slipped her feet into them and returned to the living room.

She was distracted by a low buzzing sound coming from the kitchen. Her cell phone was vibrating in place on the counter. The front surface of the phone indicated another incoming call from her boss. She reluctantly hit the answer button.

The voice that came over the speaker was harsh and abrasive, not unlike the caller himself. It was her boss, Hubert Stensly.

"Tasha! Why didn't you answer the phone earlier?"

Because I was trying to avoid having to talk to you.

"Hey, boss. I was taking a shower. What do you need?"

"Next time, bring your phone with you into the bathroom. I don't like having my time wasted. Listen, Tasha, we lost some people, so I'm going to need you to work this weekend to take up the slack."

"What do you mean you lost some people?"

"The entire programming team quit except for you. It was right after you left the office."

"You mean Harvey and Lenny both quit at the same time?"

"Apparently they both got hired by some startup on the east coast. Can you believe that Harvey complained about the working conditions and mandatory unpaid overtime? Those ungrateful traitors. Don't worry, though, we'll just hire some fresh meat right out of college. But until that happens, you'll need to work weekends."

"But you said I could have this weekend off. We talked about this."

"Listen, sweetheart, do you have the first clue how privileged you are to work in the game industry? Let me mansplain this to you in a way that you'll understand. Eighty-hour weeks and unpaid overtime is an expected part of life as a game developer. You've been in the industry for long enough to know this."

"Maybe if we made games people actually wanted to play, your employees wouldn't mind putting in the extra hours," she said. "Besides, if we're behind, it's only because we overcommitted."

"That'll be enough of your sass, woman. I expect to see you at work tomorrow morning. This game isn't going to write itself. So unless you want to be begging for scraps out of a cardboard box on the sidewalk, I better see you in here early tomorrow morning. No sleeping in will be tolerated. Good night!"

After her boss ended the call, she let out a short string of profanities as she put the phone into her bathrobe's single pocket. She had really been looking forward to having a weekend off.

Hopefully she could deal with this metaphysical crisis in time to get to work in the morning. She turned her attention to the other object on the kitchen counter. The game cartridge loomed ominously where she'd left it. With no small amount of trepidation, she picked it up and examined it from all angles. It appeared to be no different than any other Super Nintendo game in her library.

She brought the game cartridge to her bedroom, fired up her netbook, and pulled up Netscape Navigator. A Google search for "Legend of Etheria" brought up no positive results. There were a number of books with that title, but nothing that looked like a video game. "Etheria SNES" and "Etheria game" both came up negative as well.

Having exhausted her other options, she decided that there was nothing for it but to plug the game in and see what happened. She kept all of her video game stuff that she wasn't using in the closet across from the bathroom. It was the same closet where normal people kept towels, bedsheets, and washcloths. Her Super Nintendo was stashed in there somewhere. She finally found it sandwiched neatly between her Colecovision and OUYA.

Out of the corner of her eye, she spied the clock. It was now 99:12 and still ticking backward. Clearly she was on a time limit. Whatever it was that she was expected to do, she had better get on with it.

She carried the game system back to the living room and set it on the coffee table between the plasma TV and her cushy sofa. Fortunately, her TV was old enough to still have the composite video inputs needed to use the system.

She threw herself onto the couch and searched through the cushions until she finally uncovered the remote control. After the TV finished its ten-second warmup cycle, she reached over and hit the power switch on the game system.

There were none of the company logos or splash screens that normally appeared on these games. Instead, after a moment, she was presented with a highly pixelated vista showing an ocean backdrop, which scrolled by via a Mode-7 effect. Epic-sounding game music played, setting the tone. The view settled and panned upward to reveal clouds that surrounded the game title "Legend of Etheria." An animated serpent coiled itself around some of the letters.

The Mode-7 effects weren't bad, and the music was nice, but so far it didn't seem much different from the multitude of the other games of that era. Certainly nothing that would explain this situation.

Two options appeared at the bottom of the screen: "New Game" and "Continue." The word "Continue" was grayed out. She pressed the A key, but nothing happened. Apparently this was one of those games which used the B key to select and A to cancel. She pressed B, and the screen faded to black.

The words "Enter your name" appeared at the top of the otherwise black screen. Using the controller's direction pad, she entered the name "Tasha," taking care to use lowercase letters where appropriate. She liked to imagine herself as the protagonist, so she used her own name when video games gave her the option. With luck the protagonist would be female or gender neutral, otherwise the name wouldn't make much sense.

Having entered her name, she selected confirm and pressed the B key. The moment her finger depressed the controller's button, she was overcome by a rush of dizziness and vertigo. Her vision faded, and everything around her was shrouded in blackness.

Her body was stuck in a standing pose and resisted any attempt at movement. She tried to inhale, but the air was thin and it was difficult to breathe. She thought she could hear tense music playing. Was someone there?

"Help! Someone! Anyone!" she called out, but her voice sounded muffled.

Her body seemed to be encased in something. There was pressure pushing against her arms, legs, and chest, holding her in place. A well of panic rose up as she realized that she was facing the very real danger of dying. She had to get out! She needed air!

She struggled to breathe, but the air wouldn't come. After leaning forward, she felt a momentary sense of motion. She leaned forward again and felt the same sensation of motion. She began to rock back and forward, pushing her weight against whatever was holding her. Her center of gravity abruptly shifted to her abdomen as she fell forward. For a moment she seemed to be falling, but that moment came to a sudden halt as she hit the ground.

There was a jarring sensation of pain as whatever had been confining her shattered into fragments. At least she could breathe again. She took in several desperate gasps of air but then erupted into a coughing fit, having inhaled dust.

Rubbing the dust out of her eyes, Tasha looked around and tried to ascertain her situation. It seemed that she was lying prone on the ground in a dimly lit room. Clay fragments lay scattered around her body. It was too dim to see them properly, but they were pieces of what had been confining her.

Slowly she removed the last of the clay pieces that covered her and got to her feet. She was in a large chamber and was surrounded by walls lined with intricate carved designs and murals.

Along the walls were tall pedestals that displayed statues of different people. There were dozens of men, women, and children. Six of the pedestals were empty and had fragments at their base. One of them was the pedestal that she had fallen from. Had she been inside one of the statues? That would explain why she couldn't breathe and was now surrounded by clay fragments.

She could still hear the music but couldn't place a source for it. The melody was coming from all around her. The music was less intense and more atmospheric now. It didn't seem to be coming from any external source. It actually sounded like the music was playing inside of her head.

There were several dimly glowing objects that she hadn't noticed before. They floated in her view and looked suspiciously like a heads-up display from a video game. There was a compass floating at the bottom of her field of view, and three red hearts at the top. One of the hearts was empty, and the one in the middle was only half full. There were several other status bars that she didn't recognize right away.

Her heads-up display aligned with her torso rather than her head. As she turned her body, it remained right in front of her. She found that she could turn her head without it getting in the way. Although there wasn't any visible surface, it seemed as though the HUD was projected onto a curved screen that centered around her. Finally, there was an animated green arrow growing upward right in front of her on the inside of the HUD.

After she swiped her finger upward along the green arrow, the arrow vanished. A floating blue curved rectangular screen appeared in its place, similar in form to the one that she'd seen at the crossroads earlier that day. On the left side of the screen was a rough stylized portrait. The portrait showed her dark skin and frizzy hair, though the lips seemed a bit off, and Tasha never looked anywhere near that wistful in real life. The words "Tasha Singleton (Level 1 Couch Potato)" appeared alongside the image of her face.

At the bottom right of the screen was a clock. It read 99:03:14 but wasn't ticking downward.

Along the right side of the floating screen were options for Items, Quests, Stats, Abilities, Map, Tools, and Options. When she reached out and touched the screen, it resisted her touch. It was actually there, and she could interact with it. She tapped on Stats, and a second screen appeared:

Tasha Singleton (Level 1 Couch Potato)	
Race	Human (Player)
Subclass	None
Weapon	Unarmed (ATK 1)
Armor	Cozy Bathrobe (DEF 0.25)
Heart Containers	1.5/3
Mana Containers	3/3
Amusement Index	5.1
Strength	2
Intelligence	8
Agility	2
Precision	4
Charisma	4
ATK	2
MAG ATK	7
DEF	2

MAG DEF	6

This was clearly a menu from an RPG video game. What else could it be?

"Hey," she complained to nobody in particular, "what's the big deal giving me an agility of 2?"

At least she had a reasonably highish intelligence score, but her strength and agility were just embarrassing.

There was a Super Nintendo controller hovering just below the screen, but she decided to ignore it for the time being. She was only capable of dealing with so much weirdness at a time. She closed the stat page and dismissed the menu by tapping the red X in the corner of each screen.

Just as that screen vanished, another appeared in its place.

Quest: Welcome to Etheria
Class: Main questline (Compulsory)
Welcome! You've been summoned to Etheria and are trapped in the Temple of the Player. Find a way to escape. Beware, for monsters lurk in the darkness. Good luck!
Conditions for success: Find a way out of the temple.
Conditions for failure: None
Reward: 50 XP

Well, that settled that. It was now an inescapable truth that Tasha had been sucked into a video game. Just then, the thought occurred to her that she may well have gone mad. Considering the events of the past few hours, that did seem to be a reasonable hypothesis.

Well, if I have gone mad, the very least I can do is take my madness seriously and find a way out of here.

The walls were covered in a faintly glowing bioluminescent moss. It wasn't enough to fully light the vast hall, but at least it offered some indication of the room's boundaries. The statues formed a wide semicircle, and there was a large door at the far end of the room.

Tasha began walking toward the door but only made it a few paces before tripping over a step that she hadn't seen in the darkness. Breaking the fall with her hands opened up some additional scratches.

She got to her feet and pulled out her cell phone from her bathrobe pocket. Fortunately, it appeared to have made the journey with her and was undamaged. Like most city dwellers, Tasha was lost and confused without her phone. The screen said that it still had 69% of its remaining battery life, so hopefully it would last long enough for her to find a way out. The time on the front read 99:03:12, but it was no longer ticking downward as it had been doing back in her apartment. She watched it for a moment longer to make sure, but the time didn't change. Hadn't it been higher before?

She flipped on the phone's flashlight app and had a proper look at her surroundings. She was in a vast circular chamber. There were several flights of stairs from where the statues were arranged. As she approached the great door at the far end of the chamber, she began to question her earlier assumption that it was a door. Doors tended to have keys or knobs or some other mechanism to open them. The only thing that distinguished this door from the wall was a slightly darker shade of stone.

Circling the room, she came upon a raised platform along one side of the door. Curious, she stepped onto it and heard a loud grinding noise followed by a short musical tune. A horizontal sliver of light appeared from the base of the doorway as it lifted up. A few seconds passed, and the entire door opened, revealing a hint of the chamber beyond.

Grinning, she took a single step toward the door. The moment her foot left the pressure plate, the enormous stone door slammed against the ground with a loud bang.

Huh. Tasha had solved this exact puzzle dozens of times in video games. Clearly she just needed to put a heavy object on the plate to hold it down while she passed through the door.

She searched the room for something that she could use to hold down the plate. For the briefest of moments, she considered using the stone debris from her statue, but the clay fragments barely weighed anything and most likely wouldn't do the job.

She discovered some ornamental spears on display against one of the walls. She examined one, and a small blue box appeared just above it with the item's details:

Low-Quality Blunt Spear
Class: Weapon (spear)
A basic pole with a pointy bit at the end.
Damage: 0.75
Durability: 10

Snatching one of the spears, she gave it a practice thrust into the empty room. In the bottom corner of her vision, a message faded in:

Ability Unlocked: Spear Weapon Proficiency (Level 0)
Type: Passive weapon proficiency
Represents your experience using spear-based weapons. When using spears, accuracy is increased by 1% and damage is increased by 0.5%

Although her spearmanship clearly left much to be desired, she still felt more comfortable holding a weapon in her hands. The bit in the earlier quest notification about monsters lurking in the dark concerned her.

Spear in one hand, phone in the other, Tasha slowly made her way to the far side of the chamber to the left of the door. There she found what she was looking for: a large metal box with handles built into each side. It was slightly larger than she was tall. The handholds clearly implied that the box was meant to be pushed or pulled.

She returned her phone to her pocket and moved to the other side of the box. After putting her weight against it, the massive box only budged a few inches. She took a step back and threw herself against the box. The box only slid another foot, and Tasha's shoulder felt the pain from the impact.

How does Link make this look so easy? Guess my strength score might be deserved after all.

It would take hours to move the box to the plate at this rate. She tried pulling the box, but that ended up being even less effective than pushing it. She made an effort to lift up the box to turn it over onto its side, but all that earned her was a sore back.

I'm not using my head. There's gotta be some other way to move this besides brute force.

It was time to put her intelligence of 8 to work. Maybe she could use the spear as a lever to lift it. Unfortunately, there was nothing around that she could use as a fulcrum.

Instead, she removed the spearhead from the pole. After some experimentation, she discovered that it could be separated by detaching the rivet that bound the spearhead to the shaft. After repeating this process for the other spears, she laid them down in a series in front of the metal box. Finally, she lodged one of them underneath the box. This required a small amount of elbow grease, but she made it happen.

Moving to the far end of the crate, she pushed with all of her might. The box moved slowly at first, but rapidly picked up speed as it moved onto the pole and transferred its weight to the next one.

In this manner, Tasha was able to move the large metal box to the pressure plate. After she pushed the crate the final few inches, it pressed down against the plate, causing the door to side open.

She reattached one of the spearheads to one of the poles so that she wouldn't have to face the next room unarmed. Spear in hand, she approached the doorway and entered the next room.

CHAPTER 4

Resurrection

Tasha found herself in a wide hall with a closed door at the far end of the room. Weapons of all kinds lined the walls, each upon their own pedestal. Floating in the center of the room was a faintly glowing glass sphere.

Another quest dialogue appeared before her as she entered the room.

> **Quest: Violence is Always the Answer**
> **Class: Subquest (Compulsory)**
> **It is dangerous to go alone. Take one of these with you.**
> **Conditions for success: Select a weapon and find a way to the next room.**
> **Conditions for failure: None**
> **Reward: 5 XP, one weapon of your choice**

Dismissing the quest message, Tasha approached the strange floating orb. The sphere resisted her attempts to move it. It wasn't being suspended by any cords or other mechanism; it was simply floating in place. Tasha had witnessed dozens of impossible things in the last few hours, so she wasn't as freaked out by the glowing sphere as she otherwise would have been.

Experimenting, she put her weight against it, and it moved ever so slightly. As it moved away from its original position, she noticed that the glow darkened just a bit. When she let go, it moved back, regaining its previous glow.

This must be another puzzle. She reasoned that if the orb was hit with enough force, it could trigger the door to open. Sure, she was using video game logic, but it felt appropriate. She would choose one of the weapons lining the walls and hit the orb with as much of an impact as she could.

One by one, she inspected each of the weapons. Each time she examined a weapon, a small translucent dialogue appeared, listing the weapon's name and stats.

In a group along one wall were throwing axes, battle axes, and hatchets. A short distance off were several varieties of bows, crossbows, and slingshots. They were tempting, but Tasha didn't see herself as a projectile-weapon user.

There was a small selection of firearms as well.

If there are guns in this world, why would anyone use a sword or a bow?

The answer became apparent when she read the description for one of the rifles.

> **Cheap Imitation Boomstick**
> **Class: Weapon (firearm)**
> **A low-quality Zhakaran-made firearm with low damage and poor aim. This is a cheap imitation of the higher-quality dwarven-made boomstick of the same name. Requires ammunition, which can either be crafted or purchased from NPC merchants.**
> **Damage: 1.5**
> **Aim: -2**
> **Cooldown: 2 seconds**
> **Durability: 190**

The damage stat was only slightly higher than other weapons, and the cooldown and accuracy was low. On top of that, she would have to worry about ammunition. It was possible that other guns might have better stats, but if she was fighting close range, it would make more sense to use a sword or spear.

Tasha passed right by a set of steel knuckle gloves and examined a row of staves and wands. Being able to cast spells was an appealing possibility. She picked up an oaken staff and pointed it at the wall, saying, "Magic missile!"

Nothing happened. Maybe there was a way for her to acquire spells. While holding the staff, her Magic ATK increased from 7 to 9. But without any spells, it was little more than a walking stick.

On one table was a set of throwing stars, some nunchucks, an umbrella blade, and two metal war fans. She picked up the war fans and examined them. The item stat window said that it was called a tessen and dealt 1.25 damage. If she chose the metal fan, she could be stylish, fight like a samurai, and be able to cool herself off if it got too hot.

After accidentally cutting herself with it twice, she returned the tessen to the table. In the right hands, it might be an effective weapon, but without the needed martial-arts training, she was more likely to injure herself than anyone else.

If this was going to be her adventure, she wanted a sword. Swords were cool. She made her way to the section of the wall that held blades of various types and sizes.

While it was true that Tasha had a measly two strength points and two agility points, there was no reason to believe that would always be the case. This was a point that she was firm on. She'd always wanted to fight using a sword. She had even practiced in her apartment using a wooden practice sword. She even had the busted lava lamp to prove it.

There were swords of varying lengths and styles. Tasha picked up a curved piratey sword that one might reasonably expect Redguards to use. It was light and she could swing it easily. It might be a smart choice, but it wasn't speaking to her, so she returned it to its pedestal.

Mounted on the wall was an enormous buster sword that was actually taller than she was. She attempted to lift the large metal weapon from its pedestal, and it crashed onto the ground, very narrowly missing her good foot. She tried to pick it back up but could barely lift it a few inches. There was no way that Tasha could fight effectively using a weapon that she couldn't even lift. Not having any way to return it to its mount, she left the enormous blade on the ground where it had fallen.

Just as she was about to try the katana, something else caught her eye. It was a long sword with a mahogany handle that sported a trigger as though it were a gun. Since the handle was designed to resemble a gun, it wasn't completely parallel with the blade. This was it. This was her weapon, it just had to be, even though she had no idea how gunblades were actually supposed to work in a real-life sense. The weapon had a trigger, but no barrel.

Beginner Gunblade
Class: Weapon
A low-cost gunblade used for training.
Damage: 1.0
Durability: 300

There was a small question mark icon next to the weapons stats, so she tapped it.

> **Gunblades are a specialized form of sword with a trigger**
> **handle that allows you to rapidly invoke gun actions. Different**
> **spells can be selected by flicking the selector switch with your**
> **thumb. Both right and left handed gunblades are available for**
> **purchase.**
> **The Beginner Gunblade is prebuilt with the following spell:**
> **Firestorm**
> **Spell class: Enchantment**
> **Increases damage by 30% and adds fire element for 0.91**
> **seconds.**
> **Cost: 0.11 mana**

Grasping the gunblade by the handle, she gave it a few practice swings. It had weight to it, but she could swing it around easily enough. The angled handle would take some getting used to, but the weapon just oozed with style.

Making her way to the floating sphere, Tasha assumed the familiar sword stance that she'd seen in countless Japanese cartoons and had practiced in front of the mirror when nobody was watching. The gunblade swept through the air and impacted the sphere, hitting it and causing it to darken for a moment. As the sword impacted, two hearts floated above the sphere, one of them emptying in response to the damage. The orb darkened slightly, but after a few seconds it returned to its original color as the hearts refilled.

> **Ability Unlocked: Gunblade Weapon Proficiency (Level 0)**
> **Type: Passive weapon proficiency**
> **Represents your experience using gunblades. When using gunblades, accuracy is increased by 1% and damage is increased by 0.5%**

So apparently a single hit wasn't strong enough to dislodge the orb. She took another look at the weapon's description. It said that if she pulled the trigger, it would deal extra damage, but only for 0.91 seconds. If she timed her downswing, she might be able to get the damage boost with her next attack.

Deciding to try it out first, she extended the gunblade and pulled the trigger. Immediately the sword began to vibrate, and then the blade was wreathed in flames. She very nearly dropped the gunblade in surprise. Heat radiated from the fire, but the flames didn't come in contact with her hand. A second later the vibration ended, and the flames vanished. One of the two mana containers on her HUD was ever so slightly reduced. With her two mana containers, she should be able to use the ability just under twenty times.

All right, it's time to put this to the test. She raised the sword above her head, pulled the trigger, and slammed the sword onto the sphere. The glass sphere blackened and fell to the floor, shattering into pieces. The door at the far end of the hallway opened in response.

Before Tasha could advance into the next room, two smallish humanoid creatures entered through the now open door. They were short, skinny, mostly bald, greenish men wearing loincloths and carrying large knives with curved blades. She focused on one of them, and a description appeared alongside the creature in her field of view.

"Boblin A (Level 1)" floated in the air above the creature, along with two heart containers. Tasha glanced at the creature's partner and similar text and hearts appeared above it. Scan data appeared in a small window in her battle HUD:

Boblin (Level 1)
The weakest monster at the outset of any adventure.
ATK 1   Mag ATK 0
DEF 2   Mag DEF 1

Beside the scan data and at the bottom of her HUD was her combat log. The text was big enough for her to read without having to turn her head.

2 Boblins appear! Combat started.
Boblin A fingers his sword menacingly.
Boblin B attacks Tasha.

The moment she read this text, one of the creatures rushed at her. Before she could react, the creature plunged its cold metal dagger into her midsection. As the metal blade met flesh, it sank into her belly. She could hear the sound of her muscles and tendons being ripped apart by the foreign object. For several seconds, the creature held the knife there before pulling it out and backing away.

The gunblade fell from Tasha's hands and hit the stone floor at her side. For just a moment, she didn't fully comprehend what had happened, but then waves of burning pain overwhelmed her senses. Tasha had never experienced this level of raw pain before.

The sound of her screams of pain and agony filled the air. Her hand instinctively went to the wound in her belly and came away dripping with a wet, sticky substance. She looked down at them and saw that her hands were coated in blood. Tasha wanted to say something, to beg for mercy, but her mouth was already filling with blood.

Her vision began to blur. She could barely make out the second grinning creature as it slashed her throat open with a single crosswise cut. She collapsed to the floor, her life essence draining away. Tasha tried to breathe but was unable to draw in air. Her awareness of the world around her diminished, and seconds later was gone.

Tasha's body had died, but she was still aware and fully conscious. She had no eyes to see with and everything was black as pitch. Panic flooded her mind as she tried to breathe but found that she could no longer do so. Her mouth and lungs were both gone, but the impulse to draw in air was no less urgent.

Am I dead? she wondered. *That asshole creature must have killed me. What the hell kind of afterlife is this?*

For a long while, she was overcome by the constant need to breathe. She had the urge to scream but couldn't. Tears would have been welling up in her eyes, had she the tear ducts to produce them. Desperation and a sense of terror overwhelmed her. Tasha began to fear that she would never experience anything again, that she would just linger in a world of senseless nothingness.

It took time, it might have been minutes or hours, but eventually she became accustomed to not being able to breathe. There was no discomfort, no active sensation at all. No hunger, no thirst, and no pain. Her discomfort gradually diminished.

She distracted herself by focusing on her memories. Time she'd spent with her father growing up. She remembered how angry she was with her mother after the divorce. She'd barely spoken with her since then, even after her father's funeral. In this place of death, Tasha wished that she had been more forgiving.

She thought about her job. She was going to be late for work, permanently. She'd never really done anything useful with her life. She had never worked on a video game that she could be proud of, not really. She didn't have any close friends or family to remember her. She would die unaccomplished and unremembered.

It was too late to do anything about any of that now since she had died and this was surely Hell. It wasn't like any sort of hell that she'd read about in *Dante's Inferno*, but the thought of spending an eternity without sensory input was just as terrifying.

It was easy to lose track of time in that place devoid of dimension. Tasha had no idea how long she had lingered there. As the procession of moments went by, they blended together, and her awareness of the passage of time became less defined. For a long while, nothing happened. Nothing at all. Then, despite not having any ears to listen with, Tasha heard something. It was a voice in the darkness, calling out her name as though from a great distance.

"Tasha."

Then she heard it again, this time louder, more distinct, and with her own voice. She could sort of see something now. It was an unclothed woman with her own body looking back at her.

"Tasha."

The woman in front of her said her name a third time, her lips matching up to the sounds. She was so close. Tasha felt like she could reach out and touch her...

Her eyes snapped open, and she drew in a deep breath. Tasha was alive and had a body again. She could feel sensation once more. She could feel the air against her bare legs and arms and the course feeling of stone beneath her bare feet. The sound of her own breath filled her ears, and for a moment she reveled in the simple joy of filling her lungs with air.

Tasha was standing on a stone platform in a dimly lit room. Her legs were like wobbly noodles as she stepped down off the platform and onto the main floor. She was barefoot and clothed only in a plain sleeveless white shirt and a simple pair of short cloth pants.

A message hovered in the air in front of her:

You have died and respawned.

Time elapsed in Oblivion: 1 hour, 9 minutes

You have lost 5% of your level progress, bringing you to 0 XP.

She dismissed the message by tapping it away. Respawned? As in being reborn after death in a video game?

Tasha felt different. It wasn't clear how, but she didn't feel the same as before. It was as though she'd changed somehow, that she wasn't the same person anymore.

Taking in her surroundings, Tasha quickly realized that she was in the same starting room that she had appeared in earlier. At her feet, clay fragments littered the ground. The large metal box was where she had left it: on the pressure plate. Light shone through the large door at the far end of the room. It was the room with all of the weapons where that... thing had killed her.

A rush of anger overcame her. Anger at herself for dying so easily. Without pausing to think about what she was doing, Tasha headed toward the door. Picking up one of the spears, she peered into the room and saw the two creatures wandering about in repeating patterns. They hadn't noticed her. She waited patiently until they both had their backs to the door.

The moment the boblins' backs were turned, Tasha ran into the room and thrust the spear, impaling one of the creatures in the back.

2 Boblins appear! Combat started.

Backstab – critical hit – Tasha deals 2 damage to Boblin B.

Boblin B dies.

The boblin let out a scream of pain and vanished. Its body dissolved into a purple cloud of particulate vapor that dispersed into the room. The spear that impaled the creature was covered in blood.

The second boblin rushed to attack her, but Tasha extended her spear in an attempt keep it at bay. Her attacker tried to move past her spear but was unable to dodge past her defense, so it returned to its earlier position.

Tasha quickly scanned the room. The gunblade was lying on the ground next to her corpse, which still lay unmoving. Her corpse's dead, unblinking, unseeing eyes locked on the ceiling above.

No time to get all weirded out and introspective now, Tasha. There are monsters to kill.

She reached down with her free hand and picked up the gunblade from where it lay on the stone tile, dropping the spear. With no small amount of trepidation, she approached the boblin and slashed at it in a downward motion, and the blade opened a diagonal cut into its skin. The boblin didn't even try to dodge her attack.

Tasha deals 1 damage to Boblin A.

The creature lunged at her in response, but she backpedaled, losing her balance and falling backward to the floor, causing her to land right beside the corpse. The boblin rushed her, so she stabbed toward it. The creature's own momentum drove it right into her blade. She pulled the gunblade's trigger, causing the blade to vibrate and ignite, tearing the boblin apart from the inside.

Tasha deals 1.5 damage to Boblin A.

The creature's body vanished, fading into the same purple haze as its companion and rapidly dissipated into the surrounding air.

Victory! All enemies have been vanquished.

+10 experience gained (90 to next level)

6 GP found.

Boblin blood coated her white shirt with splotches of red. As a wave of nausea set in, she started to retch, but since her new body had never eaten anything, she had nothing to throw up.

Getting to her feet, she backed away from the woman's body in the center of the room. It was her body, still dressed in the bathrobe and bloodstained PJs. There was a smattering of blood pooled on the ground, and her pajama top was soaked red.

Upon seeing the wound in the corpse's belly, Tasha's hand went to her own belly sympathetically. But Tasha had no such wound. Her skin was smooth and without any injury.

The air was frigid, causing her teeth to chatter. The simple cloth garments that she had respawned with provided no real protection from the cold. She gazed at her corpse's bathrobe longingly. It looked warm and inviting. She found herself actually considering looting her own body.

She couldn't quite believe what she'd done to those boblins. Knowing herself, after respawning she should have curled up into a fetal position. Instead the first thing she'd done after coming back to life was to kill two creatures. Now she thought about killing more boblins and was excited by the idea.

The old Tasha hated violence of any kind. She wouldn't harm a fly. She literally captured flies in bottles and set them free outside. That's how much of a pacifist Tasha used to be. How had she changed so much in such a short period of time?

Gathering her determination, she moved to her former body and carefully removed the cell phone from her bathrobe pocket. She then drew out her arms from the bathrobe. The body was limp and didn't resist movement. The body was still warm to the touch. Ignoring the unfortunate smell as best as she could, Tasha removed the bathrobe and dragged the body to the corner of the room. She wished she could bury it, but that didn't seem practical in her current situation.

It seemed somehow appropriate to offer a short prayer over her corpse, just in case.

Tasha opened her menu by swiping up and accessed the inventory page. She pulled out her phone and touched the button to store it away. Her phone was currently the only object in her inventory list.

She wanted to explore the menu system and learn more about the world that she had been transported to. Right at that moment, however, Tasha was more interested in finding mobs to kill.

CHAPTER 5

The Pugilist and the Thief

Two travelers stood upon a hill overlooking the valley. The man and his adopted daughter had spent the last two months trying to reach this place. The latitude and longitude they had been given matched up; they had made it without a moment to spare.

The girl wore a tunic, trousers, and a brown cloak that partially hid her brown hair. She was short, and her frame was almost painfully thin. She couldn't afford a true invisibility cloak, but her cloak was enchanted with an unnoticeability enchantment, which was nearly as good. Monsters were less likely to target her and people's eyes naturally slid off her as though she wasn't there when the ability was in effect.

She adjusted her glasses and tapped at a translucent glass-like panel, which hovered before her in the air. To anyone who might have seen her, it would appear as if she was just tapping at the air. Menu screens were only ever visible to their users.

After a few taps, a spyglass materialized out of thin air and into her hand. She dismissed the menu with a gesture and regarded the spyglass.

Her name, Pan, was etched into the spyglass using stylized lettering. It was both elegant and functional, designed to allow the user to see long distances. It was spelled to increase magnification, but doing so cost the user mana points, and Pan needed to conserve the small amount she had left. Even without using mana, the spyglass was a useful tool.

Her father had given it to her for her fifteenth birthday a few months past. In only two years' time, she would be considered a full-fledged adult. This concerned her for a moment, but she put her worries out of her mind. She needed to remain alert. They were traveling through the wilderness, far from the safety of civilization and the protection offered by well-traveled roads.

Her hands were trembling, but she steadied them as she brought the spyglass to her eye. Peering through the spyglass at the valley below, she could discern the outline of an ancient structure. She pulled up the map screen from her menu, and the familiar translucent pane of ethereal glass revealed the area map. Her map could only show places where she had already visited and was expanding as she traveled. She had plotted the longitude and latitude coordinates into her map, and a navigation point appeared at their destination.

"Ari," she said, pointing. She handed the spyglass to the man, and he took it from her trembling hands.

"Don't call me Ari," the man said. "It's Dad, remember? You're supposed to call me Dad."

Ari was several feet taller than Pan and was wearing a heavily worn set of travel garments. His tattered cloak was in desperate need of either repair or replacement, but he had made it a rule to avoid towns and the services they provided. As long as Pan wore her hood up and Ari wore his hat, onlookers from a distance might mistake them for elves. Advertising their status as human refugees would be an invitation for trouble.

Since setting out, they had been assaulted twice by angry natives. The war with the humans was still too fresh in elven memory, and the law was liable to turn a blind eye whenever humans were the victims. Fortunately, they had very nearly reached the end point of their journey.

He took the spyglass from her and inspected the distant structure. There was evidence of some of the ruins of an ancient city. Dozens of stone columns stood like sentinels on the grassy field. The columns were the only complete things, so much of the structure had crumbled to dust, ravaged by the ages. Some of the stone columns were partially collapsed, but a few held their vertical form. A maze of dilapidated walls indicated where buildings used to be.

"I can see a structure," Ari said. "I think that area with the pillars might have been a castle. Or maybe a temple. What do you think? Should we head there first?"

Pan waited for a moment and offered a shallow nod.

"Good," he said, returning Pan's spyglass to her. "If things go well, we should be able to reach our destination before nightfall. Let's get moving."

They descended the hill toward the structure. Ari took up the lead, and his daughter trailed several paces behind.

After traveling for about twenty minutes, a notification appeared in Ari's log:

Entering new zone: Temple Ruin – Northern Outskirts
Recommended level: 12 – 15

They both came to an abrupt stop. This could be problematic. Ari was a level 11 monk and Pan was a level 6 thief. If multiple level 15 mobs appeared, it could be trouble. Level wasn't everything, of course. High-level equipment could bridge the level gap, but neither of them were burdened with an overabundance of good gear.

Mobs weren't truly sentient, and that was their main weakness. If you learned their attack patterns, it wasn't impossible for a low-level adventurer to defeat a much higher-level monster. Things became more complicated when fighting multiple opponents, however.

"Go around?" said Pan, drawing a circle with her hands.

Ari shook his head. "We could try to circumnavigate the zone, but we don't know its shape or extent. Mapping it would take time, and according to Libra's prophecy, we need to be there by tonight."

He pulled out the small slip of paper that he had received from the Libra, the Eidolon of Prophecy. The text written on it said: "To find a cure, travel to longitude 33.285947, latitude -96.572767 by sundown on Catuary 29th."

There was still plenty of time to make it by nightfall, but only if they traveled in a straight line. If they were killed, they would respawn at their last save point nearly a hundred miles to the east.

Death in Etheria was not permanent, but resurrection came at a cost. The person who died would lose 5% of their level progress, whatever equipment they didn't have in their inventory would remain with their corpses, and they would lose any distance they had traveled since saving. There were also less tangible costs to resurrection.

While a person's spirit and memories survived the transition from one body to another, something ineffable was lost. The new body was not simply a copy of the old one but an approximation. There were always differences between the old body and the new one, including significant deviations in the brain's makeup. Those differences led to changes of personality. When someone resurrected, their memories survived but their personality was lost forever.

Pan had died three times in her short life, and although her autism had survived each of her rebirths, something was lost each time it happened. Her tastes, preferences, and behavior changed radically every time she died. She didn't feel that she loved as deeply now as she had in her first life and often thought about that version of herself.

The XP loss was painful and could mean days or weeks of lost experience grinding, but that wasn't the main reason that people avoided death. It was the loss of self that people feared the most.

"I don't think we have a choice," said Ari. "We'll have to cut straight through. If we get attacked, we'll run rather than fighting. Otherwise, just be careful and try not to draw aggro. We can't afford to take any risks."

It wasn't in Ari's nature to run from a fight, but experience had taught him to be pragmatic. Now he had someone he cared about to protect, and this quest was important to them both.

Descending the hill, they continued their journey toward the temple ruins. Just under an hour later, a purple mist-like cloud began to form around them. Occasionally specs of light emerged and drifted to and fro on the wind before flickering out. The misty substance that surrounded them was known as ethereal mist. The fact that they could see it was the telltale indicator that they were about to face a random encounter.

"Time to suit up," Ari said, tapping at a quick-slot on his HUD. His travel clothing was replaced by a white martial artist gi that marginally boosted his defense and speed-derived stats. As a pugilist, he fought unarmed and didn't use weapons. Some pugilists used brass knuckles or claws, but use of those weapons would have precluded the use of certain abilities. Also, they cost money, which was in short supply.

Pan tapped at her HUD interface, and a crossbow materialized in her right hand, her weapon materializing in her outstretched hand. Her travel clothing was replaced by a set of studded leather armor.

It simply wasn't practical to travel while wearing leather armor due to the oppressive summer heat, so she only equipped the armor when she expected to be in combat. She had her combat equipment set to a quick-slot on her HUD so she could change between travel clothing and combat attire in a matter of seconds.

A pouch of bolts appeared on her belt. Her choice of the crossbow made sense given her weak strength stat, but she dearly wished she could switch to firearms. Unfortunately, quality dwarf-made guns were expensive, and the cheaper Zhakaran and elven-made imitations weren't worth it. The crossbow was a reasonable compromise.

She had experimented using a classic compound bow, but she lacked the upper body strength needed to fire it with sufficient force. The amount of damage that a bow dealt was derived from the user's strength, and she would never be strong. She considered the crossbow a more elegant weapon, as it improved her aim significantly. Of course, the drawback to the crossbow was its reload time. Reloading a crossbow took several times longer than a regular bow.

She used the wooden cocking lever to arm the crossbow. Her hands were shaking, so she closed her eyes and counted backward from ten. When she opened them, her hands were steady. Just a little further; she was almost there.

She chose to go with a standard bolt with an iron tip. This variety of ammunition could be recovered after firing, saving valuable GP. If she needed to swap it out for a more expensive explosion, freeze, or poison bolt, she would be able to do that before firing. She'd have to read the situation to know what was appropriate.

The mist continued to swirl around them. The random encounter would trigger as they started moving. Pan took a position a dozen feet behind Ari. She was a ranged fighter and needed to keep her distance from the fight if possible.

Once again, Ari started walking, his legs displacing the mist with every step he took. Pan followed at a safe distance. They proceeded in this way for about a minute before the mist abruptly pulled together to a point in front of the pair. It gathered into coherent shapes, revealing the outline of two creatures. As the purple cloud coalesced, it solidified, and two fully formed mist monsters (colloquially known as "mobs") stood before them. One of them was a towering ogre and the second creature was a snake woman.

Pan's HUD was replaced by the combat HUD. Scan information for the two monster types appeared in a separate window beside her combat log.

Grogre (Level 14)
A towering mass of muscle and body odor, a grogre is kind of like an ogre but with more grrr factor.
ATK 26 Mag ATK 0
DEF 18   Mag DEF 12

Lamia (Level 8)
Part snake, part woman, all deadly. The woman part is in the top half, not the bottom half.
ATK 12   Mag ATK 8
DEF 12   Mag DEF 8

1 Grogre and 1 Lamia appear! Combat started.
Grogre (Level 14) attacks Ari.
Lamia (Level 8) attacks Ari.

The level 14 grogre stood several feet taller than Ari. Shaggy brown pants covered its green bark-like skin. The large mob held a club as large as a tree over its head as the creature prepared to bring it down.

Over the grogre's head, ten heart containers appeared beside its name and level.

Pan was standing a safe distance away. If she had been too close, she would have gained aggro, meaning that the mobs would have attacked her rather than Ari.

Noticing the small pouch on the grogre's belt, Pan held out one hand toward it and invoked her thief ability, shouting, "Steal!" The knot keeping the pouch secured to the creature's belt came untied, and the pouch flew through the air and into her outstretched hands.

When mobs died, they vanished into mist along with anything they might have been carrying. For that reason, it was necessary to use Steal during battle in order to gain extra loot.

The moment the pouch appeared in her hands, Pan dropped it into her inventory without even looking at it. She would have time to inspect whatever it was once the battle was over.

"I don't think running is an option," said Ari. "Grogres are faster than they look. Don't worry Pan, we can take them."

Beside the grogre, the level 8 lamia spit a poison attack at Ari. Ari dodged the attack, but doing so moved him closer to the grogre's downswing. The grogre's club smashed against Ari, knocking him back. The hit had cost him four hearts, bringing him down to eight from his original twelve. The attack timer for both monsters began to refill.

Pan couldn't risk attacking the grogre. His most recent attack seemed to do four hearts of damage, and that was against Ari, who had a higher defense stat. She only had five hearts to work with. A single hit dead on from the grogre might be enough to finish her off. Instead she took aim at the lamia and pulled the trigger. The bolt left her crossbow and impacted the lamia in its shoulder, taking one heart and leaving it with five. The lamia abruptly changed targets, moving toward her.

Without hesitating, Pan again began cocking and rearming the crossbow. By the time the reload was complete, the mob was right in front of her. Pan took aim and shot the lamia in its head, dealing critical damage. It recoiled in pain but recovered quickly, moving in for the attack.

The lamia still had two hearts left. Having closed the distance, it bit down on Pan's shoulder, drawing blood.

Lamia deals 3 damage to Pan and inflicts Poison.
Pan is poisoned and will lose 0.5 hearts per minute.

Pain in her shoulder and a feeling of nausea overtook her. She drew the dagger from its sheath and plunged it into the lamia's neck. The lamia screamed in pain and writhed on the ground for a moment before its solid form dissolved into a purple cloud of mist. By the time Pan fished out an antidote, she had lost half a heart from poison, leaving her with only one and a half hearts. Her nausea faded, but the pain from the injury remained.

While this was happening, Ari was squaring off with the grogre. Its attacks were slow but powerful. Ari invoked his Stone Fist ability, hardening his hands and allowing him to break through tough armor. He focused on dodging and landed quick jabs on the monster as opportunities presented themselves. Due to the level difference, each jab only took off half a heart.

When Ari had brought the grogre down to seven hearts, it let out a great roar, adding a momentary paralysis debuff to Ari. The giant drew back its club, readying to bash Ari's head in. An attack like that would be enough to finish him.

Pan took one of her expensive ice bolts and loaded it into her crossbow. As the grogre brought the club over its head, she let the bolt fly. It arced through the air and impacted the grogre's chest, dealing no more than ¾ of a heart in damage. The beast suffered from the paralysis effect, but it wore off after only a few seconds. There was too much of a level difference between Pan and the grogre, but she had earned its enmity.

As the creature broke free from its momentary paralysis, it turned away from the still-paralyzed pugilist and charged at Pan. Pan was already down to one and a half hearts, but it didn't matter. Even at full strength she wouldn't survive a single hit from the monster.

There wasn't enough time to reload the crossbow, so she dropped it to the ground and took off running. Daring to look back, she saw the grogre chasing her at a mad sprint, gradually closing the distance.

Despite its slower body movements, its larger legs gave it a decided advantage in speed, though it suffered from an inability to make rapid changes in direction.

Pan used this to her advantage, making sudden right-angle turns every time it got too close. Her shoulder continued to burn with pain from earlier. She wanted to stop and heal, but the grogre wouldn't give her a moment's rest.

Pan was doing her best to lead the lumbering monster toward Ari, whose paralysis debuff had finally worn off. Despite her stat-augmented agility, her poor legs were getting worn out from the constant sprinting.

Ari was running toward her, and as they passed each other he invoked his Stone Foot ability, leapt into the air and dropkicked the grogre in the head, dealing a full three hearts of critical damage. Before it could react, Ari kicked the creature an additional two times for half a heart each, bringing it down to just under three hearts.

The grogre ignored his attacks and continued chasing Pan. Its targeting algorithm considered the girl's low level, which made her a preferred target. The mob's simple clockwork brain forced it to ignore Ari's attacks in lieu of a softer target.

Pan was still running, but her mad sprint had slowed to a jog. The grogre would have no trouble catching up with her now. In her exhaustion, Pan collapsed to the ground. She threw her knife at the monster, but it simply bounced off the grogre's tough skin, dealing no damage.

The grogre raised the club over its head once more, making ready to smash it into the poor girl's body. Before it could do so, Ari wrapped his hands around the grogre's waist and planted his feet into the ground. He quickly invoked his God Strength ability which would double his strength stat for the next ten seconds. Its ten-hour cooldown meant that it was a one-shot ability.

Pushing his muscles to the limit, he lifted the grogre into the air and allowed himself to fall backward, slamming its head into the ground.

Ari uses Suplex on Grogre, dealing 4 damage. Grogre dies.

As the grogre crashed into the ground, its body exploded into a purple cloud.

Victory! All enemies have been vanquished.
Ari: +12 experience gained. (325 to next level)
Pan: +3 experience gained. (110 to next level)
30 GP found.

Ari walked over to the girl and produced a health potion. She took it from him and downed it quickly. The injury to her shoulder vanished to be replaced by unbroken skin. The only evidence that she had ever been injured in the first place were the splatters of blood and torn fabric.

"You were amazing," said Ari. "That's one of the toughest battles we've fought since we left home. You need to be more careful, though. In battle, it is more important for you to protect your own life than to risk it protecting mine. You should have run as soon as you finished off the lamia. That would have been the smart thing to do."

She wanted to say how grateful she was that he saved her life. If she had died, she would be too late, and then her dream would never come true. She wanted to explain that she didn't want him to sacrifice his life for hers, even if it seemed like the rational move. Instead, she simply nodded, her face an unreadable mask.

She pulled out the pouch that she had stolen from the grogre and handed it to Ari. Ari smiled and dropped the contents into the ground. There were several ten-piece GP coins and a hand grenade. Grenades were small consumable devices charged with single-use explosion spells. They were useful in combat but far too expensive to use regularly. They would most likely sell it next time they were in a city. Pan picked up the grenade and Ari scooped up the coins, adding them to his inventory.

There were no other drops, so Pan retrieved her crossbow, and they resumed their trek toward the structure. Fortunately, they only faced one more random encounter—three level 8 lamias who posed little challenge for the two experienced travelers.

When they finally reached the ruins, the sun was already brushing against the western horizon. All about them was a maze of ruined buildings covered in moss. Vegetation had long since claimed this ancient place. They traveled between broken stone walls where long ago there might have been a cobblestone street.

Finally they reached the great pillars that Pan had seen hours earlier through her spyglass. They passed under a great stone archway that had somehow weathered the ravages of time. The shape of the walls was more or less apparent by the line of collapsed stone.

After ten minutes, they had finally reached the waypoint. They were standing at the precise latitude and longitude described by Libra's prediction. It was a grass clearing surrounded by the remains of the ruined temple.

Pan watched Ari explore the small room. Its boundaries were roughly defined by the imprints from where the walls had once stood.

She wanted to help with the search but found herself unable to focus. Her hands had begun shaking, and there was nothing she could do about it. The air was full of dust and caught in her throat, prickling her like dozens of tiny needles.

The lines of her shirt were like razors against her skin, and her shoes were sandpaper against her feet. She hated having to wear shoes; they were so constraining and uncomfortable. She tore them off and threw them away as far as she could. Her wristband was crushing her arm, so she tore that away too, scratching the skin as it came off.

There were insects everywhere, and she scratched at several bug bites with annoyance, slapping herself to get the bugs off. She was vaguely aware of Ari saying something to her, but she couldn't focus on his words; the sound of the insect life was deafening. He was too close too; she didn't like people being this close. It made her feel vulnerable.

She screamed and scrambled back against an ancient stone wall, scanning the area for somewhere to hide. She wanted to run away, but when she tried to stand she lost her balance and collapsed against the wall.

This was happening now. Why did this have to happen now? She was supposed to be doing something important. This was no time for her to lose control. She hadn't had the time to release her stress, and now she was paying the price.

There was a dull pain on her head, and she realized that she had been slamming her fists against her skull. How long had she been doing that? She felt something being placed on her head.

Her eyesight became blurry, and there were yellow dots at the periphery of her vision. Her body began trembling. Someone had covered her with a blanket. Her eyes were swollen with tears, and her throat was scratchy from the screaming. Eventually she lost consciousness.

Ari covered his daughter with the blanket where she was lying against the stone wall. There wasn't much he could do to help her other than leave her alone and make sure she didn't injure herself until the meltdown had passed.

He took out a small bag that had a picture of a tent on it and placed it on the ground. He pulled the cord that held it shut, opening the bag and invoking the campground spell. Campgrounds were single-use items that repelled mobs and wild animals for a twelve-hour period. A lightly glowing blue circle appeared above the ground, indicating the boundaries of the spell. Even with this economy campground there was still enough room to set up several small tents and a campfire.

First, he removed the collapsed tent from his inventory and began setting it up. It was little more than a few metal rods and some worn fabric to keep out the rain, but it was sufficient to grant them both shelter for the night. He had been meaning to purchase a new tent, but GP had always been tight for them.

Once the tent was ready, he took out some wood and kindling and started up a fire. It was hard for him to focus with the sound of his daughter screaming and crying, but they needed fire to stave off the cold of night. He removed a matchbook from his inventory and lit the kindling.

Pan's autistic meltdown had grown worse. She was hitting herself on her head over and over. Ari had already removed a padded leather helmet from his inventory that he used for these situations and secured it on her head. That would limit how much she hurt herself until the meltdown passed.

Pan would occasionally have these meltdowns in response to anxiety. When she did, she would become unresponsive until she wore herself out. Trying to stop her would be useless and even counterproductive. She hated being touched, so he didn't try to comfort her. Instead he gently carried her into the tent where it was dark and didn't have as many distractions.

Their homeland of Zhakara was not kind to people with disabilities. In Zhakara, the weak were dominated by the strong, and most people saw autism as a critical weakness. Leaving their homeland was the best decision they could have made.

His daughter could function normally most of the time. She could work, play, and even fight with Ari against the monsters of the mist. She was a decent marksman for someone of her level. She could even carry on a conversation, though her sentences tended to consist of short, simple phrases. Rather than speaking aloud, it was often easier for her to write down what she wanted to say in her notebook.

Her screaming and crying went on long into the night until she finally fell asleep. Ari removed her helmet and bundled her up into her sleeping bag, then returned to the fire and heated up some coffee. He would stand watch. He would be fine without getting any sleep.

This was where Libra had sent them, and the eidolon of prophecy was never wrong about anything. He had made thousands of predictions and was never wrong about any of them. Not even once.

Ari opened his menu and checked the time. It was 6:10 a.m. The sun was rising, banishing the starry night. That's when Ari noticed something peculiar on the northern horizon—a dark field of clouds in an otherwise empty sky. It didn't drift gently like clouds tended to do;

instead it sped with deliberate purpose. It was moving in their direction against the wind.

Flashes of light were soon followed by roars of thunder. The clouds were closer now, and there was a rapid change of air pressure that caused his ears to pop.

Pan appeared from inside the tent. There was a bruise on the side of her head where she had been hitting herself, and her hands were stained with blood. "Ari? I'm really sorry."

"It's okay. It doesn't matter now."

"But... last night I..."

"Pan, just forget it. Look."

Ari pointed at the oncoming storm clouds. "There."

"Headache. So loud."

He handed her a healing potion as she watched the anomaly. The bruises on the side of her head vanished as she drank it.

The sky darkened, and droplets of rain quickly formed pools in the campground. The wind stirred, causing the fabric of their tent to flap. As the minutes passed, the wind increased and the rain turned into a wild torrent.

"We need to find shelter," said Ari. Pan looked at the tent, but it had already been ripped out of the ground and was flying off into the air. That was their only tent!

Pan shook her head. There was nowhere to take shelter. None of the ruins would provide them the least bit of protection. Her anxiety from before was diminished to manageable levels, she could deal with this.

Something significant was happening, and she needed her wits to deal with it.

The storm was now directly overhead. The storm clouds swirled above them in a spiral pattern. Normally that would indicate a forming cyclone, but no tornado emerged from the clouds.

From the center of the vortex, a singular bolt of lightning struck an empty place in the air directly above the two travelers. Pan screamed and covered her head with her hands.

There was no ground at the point of impact. Instead, a wave of purple mist formed at the bolt's terminus. The mist grew downward, forming the outline of a great building, following the lines and contours of the brickwork. The wave continued until it hit the ground several seconds later.

A second bolt of lightning struck the same location, and again a wave of purple mist formed the outline of the temple. A third bolt struck, and then a fourth.

Pan pointed at one of the partially destroyed pillars. As the wave of purple mist passed over it, the unbroken part of the pillar was revealed.

Through the rain, Ari said, "This must be Catalyst... the goddess of change. She's said to take the form of a storm cloud."

As lightning continued to strike the air above them, the outline of the pillar became more and more pronounced. Above them, lines of mist began to form into a stone ceiling. Bricks formed walls. The translucent mist solidified, and the two travelers found themselves inside a stone room. The light, wind, and chaos from outside vanished, and they were in a room with dark walls covered in bookshelves and a single exit.

"What just happened?" asked Ari, "You saw that, right?"

"T-T-Temple?" asked Pan.

"I think you're right. For some reason, the goddess of change has reconstructed this ancient temple."

Pan pulled up her menu and checked the zone information. It read "Temple of the Player – Small Library." In the corner of her menu, the clock caught her attention.

"Ari, the c-clock is broken," she said.

Ari pulled up the menu and confirmed that the clock read 99:03:14.

"You're right... I see it too."

They both remained silent for several minutes. Pan was the first to recover. "L-Let's explore."

"Yeah, good idea," agreed Ari.

The two of them left the library and entered the bottom floor of the temple in search of answers and possibly the cure that they had come to find.

CHAPTER 6

Denver

Tasha had just left her corpse behind in the room with all of the weapons. As the door shut behind her, a prompt appeared:

Congratulations!
Quest Completed: Violence is Always the Answer
5 XP awarded.

Dismissing the prompt, she took in her surroundings. It was a hallway that branched off to either side. The HUD's map had filled in the shape of the room as she moved. Taking the path to the left, Tasha encountered another three boblins. They saw her right away, so backstabbing was out of the question. They were standing in a line, apparently waiting for her to make the first move.

Deciding to hold back, Tasha studied their attacks. She found that they each had their own ready progress bar in the combat menu and would wait until it was full to attack. When Boblin B's timer filled up, it left the formation and jumped at her. She slashed her gunblade horizontally, slicing the creature before it could reach her. Before she could follow up, Boblin A was already on the offensive. Tasha wasn't able to dodge in time and took a minor hit on the side, costing her one heart.

When Boblin C approached, she was ready and stabbed at it, impaling the creature before it could reach her. Once impaled, Tasha pulled the trigger, sending a wave of fire into the monster, killing it.

Just as the other two boblins had, this one dissolved into purple mist upon its death. A rush of satisfaction overcame her as she killed it.

It was Boblin B's turn to attack again, but she had already studied its pattern and dodged to the side just as it reached her. Slashing horizontally, Tasha cut the creature's throat, killing it instantly. After that, Boblin A wasn't much of a challenge.

Victory! All enemies have been vanquished.

+15 experience gained. (70 to next level)

9 GP found.

On the ground where the last boblin had been lay a small capsule-shaped container. She picked it up, and it slid open. It was a loot drop. Opening it, she found that it contained three beef tacos wrapped in nondescript white paper and a plain white aluminum can with the word "cola" written on it. So as long as she kept killing these creatures, she would be given food to eat. She focused on one of the tacos.

Beef Taco

Class: Food

Calories: 161

Restores 1.13 mana and heart containers over 10 minutes.

This was fortuitous since she had not eaten since lunch. Seeing tacos and cola in what she had assumed to be a medieval setting was a bit of an anachronism. Maybe she had been assuming too much about this world. Any society that had an appreciation for tacos could not be truly thought of as primitive.

The food tasted good, and over the next ten minutes, her empty heart container refilled. The bloody wound at her side diminished and was replaced by smooth, unbroken skin, though the blood remained. It seemed that food had a restorative effect in this world. Tasha wondered if she would be stuffing her face with tacos during battle. She shook her head and smiled. That was just silly.

This was like one of poorly-thought-out video game tropes where the hero finds an entire turkey dinner just lying on the dungeon floor and eats it for 100 HP. Well, Tasha refused to eat any floor turkey.

She did realize that eating during combat wouldn't be effective since it took nearly ten minutes after eating to restore a single heart.

Her belly full of yummy tacos, Tasha got back to her feet and followed the corridor to a large chamber. An altar lay on the far side of the room to her left. Multicolored lights shone through stained-glass windows, creating patterns of color along the long pews. The room vaguely resembled a mega-church, only it was crawling with dozens of murderous fiends. In other words, it was exactly like a mega-church.

Let's see. If each boblin is worth three XP and I need seventy XP, I'll need to kill twenty-four boblins to reach level two. Sounds easy enough.

"Come here, you wonderful little bundles of experience!"

She picked up a loose stone and threw it at an isolated group of boblins. Of course, her throw missed completely and didn't even come close to reaching them. Fortunately, it landed close enough to get their attention.

Two groups of boblins reacted and attacked her at once. She ducked back into the room that she had come from and allowed them to come to her. In an enclosed space like the doorway, Tasha could kill them one at a time. This was a tried-and-true tactic that she commonly employed in video games. If she were to fight a large group of enemies all at once, they could surround and overpower her, but in a confined space, she only had to deal with them one at a time.

It took her five minutes to finish off those seven boblins, and she was only hit once. Their attack patterns were, for the most part, predictable, and she was able to foresee and avoid their attacks, but one of the strikes got through her defense, opening a shallow cut into her leg.

A bleed debuff appeared, which drained one half of a heart container every thirty seconds. After finishing off the boblin, she tore off a piece of her shirt to use as a makeshift tourniquet. She tightened the piece of cloth around the cut, which reduced the blood loss and caused the debuff to vanish from her HUD.

The next time she sniped a boblin, she didn't miss, and killing them in a small group was easier. Over the next half hour, Tasha completely cleared the room of boblins and only lost one more heart container. An annoying *beep beep* tone began to play, a warning that she was down to her last heart container.

Fortunately, her condition of low health didn't last for long. Just as she finished the final boblin off, a message appeared:

Victory! All enemies have been vanquished.
Level up!
You have reached level 2.
200 experience to next level.
You have 4 unassigned stat points.
Choose either a heart container or mana container.

A red heart container and blue vial floated in the air in front of her, waiting for her to choose.

Tasha decided to pick the heart container. She could get more mana later once she figured out how to use it.

Tasha reached out and touched the heart container, but nothing happened. *Huh.* She picked it up and held it in her hands. It seemed to be made out of some sort of tough glass.

"Heart container, I choose you!" she said aloud. Nothing happened.

Momentarily at a loss as to what to do next, she tried to add it to her inventory but received a message saying that the object could not be stored. Surely she wasn't expected to carry this thing around with her. What would Link do in this situation?

Realizing the answer at once, Tasha lifted the heart container above her head for the world to see. The normal background music stopped, replaced by a fanfare. When it completed, the object in her hand vanished and a fourth heart container appeared on her HUD.

"Okay, then. Now to see about my stat points."

Opening the menu with a flick of her finger, Tasha pulled up the stat screen. She had a general idea about what stat points were supposed to represent in RPGs but thought that it would be best to confirm before making any decisions. Tapping on each one brought up a new window that described the stat and allowed her to assign the points.

Strength: The amount of physical strength you have. Higher
strength values deal more damage for each attack and allow

you to carry heavier objects. Contributes to ATK and DEF
values at rates depending on class.
Agility: Determines your speed and ability to dodge incoming
attacks. Agility also determines how quickly you can attack and
perform other physical actions.
Precision: Determines your accuracy and likeliness to hit an
enemy. Affects the aim of projectile weapons. Also affects
abilities that use precise actions, such as needlepoint and
breakdancing.
Intelligence: How intelligent you are as measured by neural
activity. Affects the power of magical spells. Contributes to
Magic ATK and Magic DEF values at rates depending on class.
Charisma: Affects how attractive, compelling, and charming
you are. Doesn't affect battle but can open new dialogue
options with NPCs and affects the cost of goods from NPC
merchants. A high charisma score will make it easier to
influence others.

She decided to place three stat points into agility and one stat point
into strength. Despite having low starting agility, it made the most
sense. As a swordswoman, she would need a high agility score to land
attacks on her enemies and dodge incoming attacks.

Setting the agility points, Tasha tapped on "confirm." The result
was instant and staggering. At the very moment the confirm button
was touched, she was engulfed in a cloud of mist, and her body
transformed. The extra baggage that she'd been towing around her
thighs and stomach vanished and was replaced by muscle.

For the longest time, Tasha just stood there admiring her newfound
unflabbiness. Removing the phone from her inventory, she snapped a
selfie. Several dozen selfies, actually.

Couch Potato Tasha was now a thing of the past. Though come to
think of it, her character class was still listed as "Couch Potato." She
touched it on the menu, and a description of her class appeared.

Couch Potato:
The Couch Potato class is one of the most unique classes and
also one of the most difficult to play. As a couch potato, you

have an extra stat added to your HUD labeled "amusement index." This number ranges from -10 to +10. At level 1, a 2% adjustment is made to all stat points such that when the amusement index is 10, all stat points are increased by 20% and when it is at -10, all stat points are lowered by 20%. The unadjusted stat is shown in parentheses. Higher levels yield greater adjustments.

When the amusement index is less than 0, you receive an "unamused" debuff where you will begin to lose max hearts and MP at a rate of 10% per negative point on the amusement index. The MAX hearts and MP are restored when the amusement index is brought back to 0.

Every forty minutes, you will lose one point from your amusement index. The only way to recover amusement points is to passively consume entertainment. This can be in the form of reading books, watching a play, listening to a story, playing a non-physical game, or any other form of low-interaction entertainment. Forty minutes of entertainment consumption will restore ten points on the amusement index.

Based on the type of entertainment consumed, relevant abilities may become temporarily unlocked. For example, if you were to read a book about an underwater city, you might gain the ability to breathe underwater. Only one such ability can be active at a time, and the ability is lost if you receive the Unamused debuff. While the learned ability is unlocked, you can practice it to raise your proficiency at that ability. Once it reaches proficiency level 1, the ability is unlocked permanently.

There is a 50% penalty applied to sources of entertainment that you have already consumed. Consuming the entertainment while in the presence of someone who hasn't consumed that entertainment negates the penalty. Bonuses are awarded for certain conditions, including sitting on a couch, eating snacks, and sharing the entertainment with three or

more people. This bonus applies to stat proficiency as well as the amusement index.

Time spent sleeping does not cause the amusement index to fall.

NOTE: You can change classes by visiting the Job Change NPC at any large settlement. Subclasses become available at level 10.

Having finished rereading the class description, she closed the window. It was certainly an interesting class. If she wasn't constantly reading or watching TV, she would lose stat points. Since she was stuck in what seemed to be a medieval-style fantasy realm, she wasn't likely to find a TV. Of course, she might be wrong about the era; too many things were out of place.

She pulled out her phone. Even if she didn't have a TV available, she could still play games and watch movies on her phone, at least until the batteries ran out. It was still at 69%, and she'd been in the temple for several hours already. Her amusement index was down to 2, which meant that she was only a few hours away from receiving an "unamused" debuff.

She took a seat on one of the pews and started up her favorite plumber-based platform game. When she started up the game, a notification appeared in her HUD's log:

Couch Potato Mode Active

After about half an hour, her amusement index reached 10. She closed the app and noticed that the cell phone's batteries were still at 69%. A game like that should have drained the battery considerably.

Once she put the phone away, a prompt appeared.

Couch Potato Mode Ended

Ability Unlocked: Double Jump (Level 0)

Type: Acrobat ability (unlocks at level 2)

Grants the ability to jump once while already airborne. Ability resets when you touch the floor. Height of second jump is increased by 5%.

Would you like to set this as your current ability? Yes/No

She tapped yes. Double jumping was a staple in platform video games. But while the ability felt perfectly natural in a video game, it made no sense in the context of the real world. How could she jump when there was nothing solid for her feet to push against?

She returned the phone to the safety of her inventory and resolved to give it a try. She crouched down and jumped several feet into the air. While still airborne, she pushed her feet downward and was surprised to find that it connected with something solid. A blue platform had formed at her feet and then instantly dissolved into blue mist, allowing her to jump while airborne.

She hadn't actually expected it to work, and therefore she missed her landing, sending her tumbling to the ground. Her fall had cost her a quarter heart container.

She got back to her feet and tried it again, this time with more success. A progress bar momentarily appeared on her HUD, indicating that her Double Jump ability was 2% unlocked.

She would have to practice double jumping later. It was time to get back to exploring the dungeon. Or temple. Whatever it was.

Apart from the way that she'd come in, there was only one other exit from the room: a large wooden doorway. Light shone through a stained-glass window adjacent to the door, which implied that the door was the way out.

Grabbing the handle of the door, Tasha pushed outward. Nothing. She tried pulling with a similar lack of progress. There just wasn't a lock or any obvious mechanism to open it. She did briefly consider breaking the window but ruled that option out right away. Tasha liked stained-glass windows. They were pretty. The thought of smashing one didn't seem right. Besides, she didn't want to get into the mindset where property damage became an option of first resort.

Above the doorway was another window, but this one was already broken. She couldn't reach the window from where she was on the ground. She even tried double jumping, but it remained out of her reach. Tasha could get through if she was above the doorway. The question was how to get up there.

She considered stacking up the pews, or maybe angling them to form a ladder, but they seemed to be built right into the floor and couldn't be removed without destroying them.

So she searched the room for anything suspicious, leaving no candelabra unturned. Eventually she discovered that the altar at the front of the room was not stuck to the floor. She pushed it out of the way and found that it had been covering up a pressure plate. When it was no longer covered, a large metal crate fell from the ceiling and crashed into the ground right next to her.

Okay, so now she had a metal crate. Yay? How was this useful to her? Scratching her head, she took a good look around in an attempt to find something useful. Situated right above the crate was a ledge that she could climb to reach the rafters. If she climbed up there, Tasha could circumnavigate the room along the roof until she reached the exit.

In stark realization, Tasha came to appreciate the entirety of her situation. Not only had she been sucked into a video game, she'd been sucked into a badly designed video game. How did the temple's worshippers normally get out? Was the congregation expected to climb along the rafters to reach the broken window above the clearly useless door? Why even have a door if the worshippers were expected to display their athleticism as a condition of being allowed to leave? How did the high priest get the metal crate back into the rafters after everyone left?

Grumbling to herself about the total lack of narrative consistency, Tasha climbed up onto the altar and jumped from there to the metal crate.

Ability Unlocked: Climb (Level 0)
Ability Unlocked: Jump (Level 0)

Surprisingly, it worked. Her newfound agility allowed her to jump between the altar and the crate. Standing on the crate, she jumped and reached upward with both hands, grasping the ledge.

As she hung on the edge of the platform with both hands, Tasha realized that she would need to perform an action that had eluded her over her many years of living a sedentary lifestyle—she would need to perform a pull-up. With all her might, she pulled her body up to the ledge. Though her muscles strained from the effort, it was easier than she expected, and she was able to raise her body onto the ledge.

Standing on the high platform, she turned around and jumped toward a beam, catching it with one hand. There wasn't enough room to stand up on the horizontal beam, so she Prince of Persiaed herself along the beam until she reached a rafter that was large enough for her to stand on.

Amazed at her newfound acrobatic talent, she gradually edged across the wooden rafters. That's when she spied a treasure chest balanced on one of the wooden supports. Even though a treasure chest just lying around on the rafters didn't make logical sense, she knew that she needed whatever was in that box. Her gamer instinct wouldn't permit her to leave an exposed loot chest unpillaged.

With deliberate slowness, she took one step at a time over the narrow wooden beams. The floor beneath her was far away. So very far away. Taking a deep breath, she continued toward the object of her desire. There was only just enough width on the support beam for a single foot and nothing to hold on to, so she held both arms outward to balance herself. When she finally reached the chest, she grabbed the nearby vertical beam for support and undid the latch on the wooden chest with her free hand. As she did so, light emerged from within, and a short fanfare played in her head. When she peered inside, the light vanished, and she retrieved the single item from the chest.

It was a metal wristband. As she looked at it, a description appeared:

Iron Bangle
Class: Armor (accessory)
A stylish iron wristband.
Armor: 1
Magic DEF: 1
Durability: 300

That was a cool find. Somehow this thin circle of metal offered four times the armor rating as her bathrobe. Chalking that up to video game logic, she slipped the thin metal band onto her wrist. Checking the stat screen revealed that her DEF and Magic DEF stats both jumped to 7.

Turning around, she made her way along the horizontal supports toward the door. She moved across the support beam closest to the door. The broken stained-glass window was still several feet beyond what she could reach. She would have to make the jump. Taking several minutes to gather her determination, she pushed off the wooden rafter with one foot, leaping toward the open windowpane. She was off by just a little, so she double jumped to correct her aim.

As she flew through the air, it occurred to her that there might not be anything to catch her fall on the other side. Too late now.

Either by luck or by stat-augmented skill, her aim was spot on. She sailed through the open window and fell crashing to the ground far below. The impact with the stone floor shattered Tasha's leg and cost her three hearts. Why, oh why did she ever think that this was a good idea?

Waves of pain shot through her leg, and for several moments she was unable to focus on anything else. When she finally looked around, Tasha realized that she was outside at the bottom of a flight of stairs that led to the purposeless doorway. No wonder she had fallen so far. She was in an atrium garden at the base of the stairs. Above her, the sun shone brightly. Before her was a glowing white circle set upon a flight of steps a dozen paces away. Above the circle floated the translucent image of a blue rectangle that looked suspiciously like a floppy disk.

Her leg was broken, so she couldn't walk toward whatever the glowy white thing was. Nobody was going to help her. She would have to put on her big-girl suspenders and pull herself up by her nonexistent bootstraps. If only she'd saved one of those tacos from earlier, she might have gotten her hearts back.

Over the course of the fifteen minutes, she somehow managed to crawl the distance, her hands clawing the ground toward her. She dragged herself up the stairway and reached her hand out toward the white circle.

Save point registered.
Health and mana restored. All status conditions removed.

Her pain diminished as she touched the glowing circle and the rotating floppy disk vanished. A cloud of ethereal mist flowed around her body, healing her injuries before dissipating. Her leg no longer hurt. In fact, the bones had healed in just a few seconds. Tasha decided then and there that save points were amazeballs and that she would never pass one by without availing herself of its curative properties.

Tasha stepped off the save point and walked to the edge of the atrium. A vast landscape extended to the horizon in all directions. Glancing over the cerulean railings, she found the ruined remains of a city far below. This must be the highest floor in the temple. There was nothing but grassy fields in any direction as far as she could see. Even if she managed to get out, where would she go?

Well, one thing at a time. She would escape the temple and then figure out what to do once she made it outside.

As Tasha explored the atrium, she came to the realization that she wasn't alone. On the far side of the atrium from where she'd entered was a cage with an animal inside. Once she got close enough to make it out, she immediately recognized it for what it was.

Trapped inside the cage was a velociraptor, a kind of small dinosaur about as big as she was. Thankfully it was caged. After seeing *Jurassic Park* as a child she had nightmares for weeks, and she hadn't bothered going to the newer sequels. If the monster were free, it would surely rip a poor girl like her to tasty bite-sized pieces. It was probably hungry, and she was the only source of food nearby.

As she inched closer, she expected the creature to snap at her, but instead it just looked at her with sad, pleading puppy-dog eyes. This dinosaur was messing with her mind. It was more reminiscent of a caged dog than a vicious monster. She liked dogs, but her apartment manager would never let her keep one, and she was too lazy and cheap to move to a better place.

There was something on the floor of the cage that she hadn't seen earlier. Thin pieces of clay littered the cage floor. They looked familiar. Then she remembered. When she'd woken up in this world, she had been contained in clay pieces just like this. Had this dinosaur been trapped in a clay statue the same way she had?

Tasha didn't really think that it would respond, but maybe talking to it would help.

"Umm... hiya. I'm Tasha. So, hypothetically speaking, if I were to let you out, would you tear me to little nummy bits and gobble me up?"

No response. Based on internet memes, she half expected it to answer in a British accent while wearing a monocle and sipping Earl Grey. That didn't happen, though. Instead it made an adorable yelping sound. In that moment, she wanted to adopt the velociraptor and take him home and cuddle him and squeeze him lovingly while Netflixing.

Tasha wasn't the sort of person to just leave a hungry animal in a cage to die. It wasn't in her to do that. There never really was any choice in the matter. The cage was shut with a simple latch from the outside. Even if the raptor had opposable thumbs, which he didn't, there was no way for him to reach the locking mechanism from within the cage.

"Just so you know," she said, "I'm told I taste terrible. Trust me on this."

Hoping that she wouldn't regret the choice, she lifted the latch, causing the cage door to inch open. Instantly the raptor sprang outside and leapt on her, locking her to the ground. She got a nice good look at a full set of razor-sharp teeth and knew that she was done for. She wished that she could say that she hadn't screamed her lungs out at that moment, but sadly that did not comport with the truth.

Fortunately, rather than tearing her to tiny bits, it stuck out a forked tongue and proceeded to lick her in the face. It really was like a big puppy dog. A big puppy dog with razor-sharp fangs and claws. Above him was the text "?????" That must be where his name is supposed to go.

"So, I guess you aren't going to eat me after all. I think that'll be good for our long-term relationship. Erm... Do you have a name?"

He let Tasha get to her feet and looked at her questioningly.

"Okay, let me think of a name for you. How does Yoshi sound?"

There was no response.

"Really? Because I kind of liked that name, though it might get me sued by Nintendo. Okay, in that case, how about Cringer? No? Spot?

Okay, not Spot. That's dumb. Who names a dinosaur Spot? Dino? What about Barney? No, wait! Forget that last one. I'm not calling you Barney."

The animal continued to stare at her in apparent confusion. If she was being honest, Tasha was glad he hadn't responded to the last one. Turns out that she sucked at naming dinosaurs. Who knew?

"Okay, how about Denver? Do you like that?"

He looked at her happily and made a few yelping noises. It seemed that Tasha had found his name. The "?????" next to his name was replaced by "Denver (Level 1)."

"Great! Pleased to make your acquaintance, Denver. Now that we're besties, let's get the hell out of this place."

A few minutes of searching later led her to discover a flight of stairs leading into the temple's bottom floors. Humming a little ditty, Tasha led her newfound friend down the stairs and into the lower levels.

CHAPTER 7

Boss Fight

U pon descending the stairs, Denver and Tasha proceeded through a corridor filled with boblins and proceeded to kill them with relative ease. It was good not to have to fight alone. When she pulled up the menu, it showed that he was now part of her party. It showed his current level and progress to the next level, but his stats were hidden. His portrait appeared beside hers, though his was an artistic rendering rather than a photo. Tasha wondered who drew it.

At the far end of the room was a locked steel door that she wasn't able to get open. There were also side rooms attached to the main hallway that each had their own mini puzzle. Sometimes Tasha would need to push blocks onto pressure plates. She found that to be slightly easier thanks to the extra stat point, but it was still hard work.

One of the rooms she explored contained a toilet and a sink. That was fortuitous because she felt the call of nature. She was about to use the toilet, but she hesitated.

Hold on a minute, what if this is a trap? What if the toilet is actually a mimic? She shook her head. *Nah, what self-respecting mimic would impersonate a toilet? On the other hand, it could still be a non-self-respecting mimic. Oh, whatever shall I do?*

Finally, she settled on a tried-and-true tactic that humanity had developed over the ages to deal with the unknown mysteries of the universe: She poked the toilet with a stick. It didn't respond. Ultimately, she discovered that it was a regular toilet. It was good to know that this world had developed indoor plumbing. She supposed that it made sense that whoever built the temple didn't want their worshippers doing their necessary business in the hallway.

After completing her bathroom business, Tasha and her trusty dinosaur, Denver, returned to exploring the dungeon. In another room, she encountered a new type of monster. It had four legs, furry red skin, and a funnel-like nose. It strongly resembled Q-Bert.

Schnozrok (Level 3)
He has a belly full of rocks made ballistic through the process of rapid nasal decompression.
ATK 5   Mag ATK 0
DEF 4   Mag DEF 3

It would project fist-sized stones out of its schnoz at Tasha and Denver. Tasha wondered how the biology of such a creature worked. The first one that hit her cost an entire heart container. Once she knew what to expect, Tasha learned to dodge their attacks until she could get in close to finish it off. Either two slashes with her gunblade or one firestorm-boosted attack was enough to finish it off.

Once she finished off the schnozroks in that room, the door to the next room opened automatically. The next room contained a number of pits that fell to the level below, which separated the entrance from a platform at the far end of the room. Two schnozroks stood upon the far platform and shot rocks at her from a distance.

Hanging from the ceiling atop each of the pits was a batlike creature with one eye.

Keekee (Level 1)
Gets its kicks by dive-bombing people right when they are jumping over pits.
ATK 1   Mag ATK 2
DEF 1   Mag DEF 1

She carefully approached the edge of the first pit and measured the distance to the other side. Thanks to her newfound agility, she could probably make the jump without difficulty. She regarded the keekee suspiciously but had no way to attack it from so far away.

Stepping back to give herself room, she darted forward and leapt over the pit. When she was halfway across, the keekee swooped down and rammed into her, redirecting her flightpath into the pit below. The keekee's impact only cost her a quarter heart, but the fall to the next level brought her down to half.

She chamber she had fallen into was being patrolled by several boblins. One of them got a hit on her, slashing her arm before she was able to scramble back to her feet. The boblins weren't difficult to defeat as she had already studied their movement and attack patterns, and she made short work of them. The room was otherwise empty, save for a ladder that led back to the entrance at the upper level.

Her injured arm pulsed with pain as she climbed up the ladder back to the second floor. When she ducked her head out, a schnozrok fired a rock at her. She just barely ducked in time. She quickly scrambled up the stairs. The keekees remained motionless on the ceiling, waiting for her to attempt her jump over the open pit.

There has to be some way to take the dumb bat thing out. She needed to trigger its dive attack and kill it when it came close enough. Assuming this was a normal video game NPC, it probably triggered the dive based on how close she was to it.

She reached her arm across the pit as far as she could. The keekee didn't move.

Just a little more...

Finally, as she was leaning as far over the pit as she dared, the keekee dived at her. She slashed at the keekee as it passed, but her gunblade only tasted empty air. The bat landed on the roof behind her and immediately dove at her a second time.

I must still be within range. This is my last shot to hit it.

She slashed at the keekee and hit it, knocking it to the ground, where it exploded into mist. Her attack score of 3 and the mob's low defense of 1 allowed her to deal three hearts of damage, which was more than enough to kill it.

Her way unimpeded, she leapt across the first pit and repeated the process with the second keekee. All the while, she dodged intermittent projectile attacks from the two schnozroks at the end of the chamber. Finally, she made the final jump and dispatched the two schnozroks.

One of them dropped a key when it died. Stuffing it into her pocket, she made her way back to the main hallway and used it to unlock the far door, which led to a mid-sized chamber filled with large green monsters that resembled a familiar toy from her childhood. The creatures moved from place to place by turning from one side to another, head over tail.

Slinker (Level 2)
What haunts your dreams and hatches schemes and eats
everything that it sees? A thing, a thing, a monstrous thing,
oh, everyone knows it's a slinker.
ATK 1   **Mag ATK 2**
DEF 3   **Mag DEF 2**

The slinker was covered in a furry green membrane. They were actually sort of cute. Tasha imagined herself with a nice cuddly pet slinker monster.

She approached one of the slinkers, and it promptly leapt into the air and swallowed her whole. One moment she was standing right next to it, and the next she was engulfed in darkness, suffocating and being pressed in from all directions. She would have died a second time if Denver hadn't come to her rescue. Less than a minute after she'd been swallowed, the slinker monster vanished into a cloud of purple mist. For the next ten minutes, she lay on the floor trying to clean as much of the slinker's digestive juices out of her hair as possible.

Deciding to take a short break, she removed her cell phone from where it rested in her inventory. The time on the lock screen read 98:58:49.

I must have been in this temple for hours. The message from before said that she had died and was in Oblivion for at least an hour. How had only twenty minutes passed?

The time remained the same down to the second. This was a mystery that she would have to solve at another time. Who knew how much time had passed since she had checked her social media. Just as she pulled out her phone, she realized the absurdity of what she was trying to accomplish.

I'm in another world. Of course my phone isn't going to work. There wouldn't be any cell towers or Wi-Fi hotspots to connect to.

She pulled out her phone, and just to verify her suspicions, she fired up her web browser. In stark contradiction to the logic of the situation, her phone had a strong 4G connection. She went to several of her favorite websites, and they worked perfectly. When she tried to pull up Twitter, however, it wouldn't connect. So she could perform web searches but couldn't leave social media posts. Her email wasn't working either.

Tasha so distracted testing her phone that she didn't notice the hooded figure who had appeared atop a flight of stairs at the end of the room. The figure held one hand out toward Tasha and yelled, "Steal!"

Without warning, Tasha's phone came loose from her grip, flew through the air, and the cloaked figure caught it in her outstretched hands.

"Hey! Hey, what the hell! Give that back!" Tasha cried, getting to her feet. She saw the face of the cloaked figure for the first time. It looked like it might be a little girl, but she couldn't be sure. The figure darted away through a door at the top of the stairs.

Not wasting any time, Tasha darted up after the figure through the door, leaving Denver behind her. The next room was filled with roving puddles of acid that moved in seemingly random patterns. There were two doors, and the girl ran through the door to the right. Tasha dodged between the puddles and opened the door, following the cloaked figure.

Around her was a hallway with doors on either side. One of the doors was swinging closed. She rushed down the hallway and threw the door open, stepping inside. The room was a small library with only a single entrance. There were two people within, a tall man with pointy hair in a martial-arts outfit and the cloaked girl hiding behind him. The man had been absorbed in some book.

He was taller than most men she had met, and his spiky hair would have fit right in at an anime convention. His uniform only partially covered his otherwise bare torso. He wasn't unattractive in a chiseled-from-steel sort of way. Not that Tasha was into that sort of thing. She normally preferred her men to have some extra padding, and this guy did not qualify in that respect.

The man had turned to face the girl and hadn't noticed Tasha come in. "Pan, you stink. What happened?"

The girl pointed at Tasha. He turned and saw her for the first time.

"Hello, miss. I thought we were alone here."

"Sorry about the smell. I was just swallowed by a slinker, and I'm afraid I'm still covered in its digestive juices."

"I understand. It happens to the best of us. Here, let me clean you up."

The idea of a man cleaning her caused her a moment of trepidation. "That's okay, mister, you don't have to—"

Ari held out his hand and performed a simple gesture while saying, "Cleanse." When he did this, the slinker's internal digestive fluids lost its grip on Tasha's skin, clothes, and hair, sliding off and pouring onto the ground. Sweat, dirt, and other detritus came loose from her body as well. When the spell was complete, she was as clean as she had ever been. Even some of the blood caked on her bathrobe came loose, though the fabric was still stained red.

"Was that magic?" she asked.

The man nodded. "Of course. It's just a simple cleansing spell. You don't need to be a mage to use simple magics like it. Sorry, I guess I assumed that you didn't want to smell like that."

She looked between the two of them, "No, I'm happy that you did that, so... thanks... I guess."

He extended his hand. "I'm Aralogos, but most people just call me Ari."

"I'm Tasha. I didn't realize that anyone else was here. Actually, I don't really know where 'here' is."

He closed the book and set it on the table's surface. His daughter hid further behind him. "I can help with that. You are in the Temple of the Player. My daughter and I were exploring the area, and the temple sort of appeared around us during a thunderstorm."

"The Temple of the Player?" Tasha said, "Well, I'm a player. I was just playing a video game when I found myself in the statue room upstairs. I've been trying to get out for hours now."

Ari frowned. "Really? You're a player? Are you quite sure about that? Your scan data says 'Couch Potato,' not 'Player.'"

"There's nothing confusing about that. Most players are also couch potatoes, after all. What, are players a big deal or something?"

"Yeah," he said, "they're mythical figures from history. There have only been five somewhat credible reports of players in the three thousand years of recorded history. The arrival of a player always heralds great change or catastrophe.

"Not to be rude, but can you show me any proof that you are truly a player?"

Tasha shook her head. "I don't have anything like that. I don't feel like any kind of legendary figure, though. I'm just a girl who likes playing games."

"Well, don't worry about it. We did meet in the Temple of the Player, so it isn't that outlandish a possibility," Ari said, "I see you've already met my daughter. Don't be offended; she's shy around new people."

Tasha crossed her arms. "But not too shy to steal from them? Your daughter took something that belongs to me."

He brought out his daughter from behind him. "Oh no, not again. What did you take from her?"

The small girl showed Tasha's phone to Ari.

"I've told you before, only use your Steal ability on monsters, not on people. Other people don't like it when you take their things. Now return the magical glowing rectangle to our new friend and say you're sorry."

The girl protested, pointing at the pile of digestive fluids on the ground, "But... I thought... she was a m-monster."

"Hmm. You probably shouldn't say that about someone. Most people will think it's rude. Anyway, give the nice lady back her rectangle."

She outstretched her arm, handing the phone to Tasha. She looked at the ground, her face an unreadable mask.

Tasha took the phone from her, and the girl's hand went back to her side. "It's okay, no harm done. How about we team up and find a way out?"

Ari shook his head. "We can't leave yet. We need to search the temple for something. Don't worry, though, we'll help you find a way out first."

The girl was completely covered by her cloak. Tasha was only able to see her face.

"Hey, no hard feelings about the phone, okay? What's your name?"

A look of abject terror appeared on the girl's face. She opened her mouth, and Tasha thought she was going to say something, but no words came out. After several attempts, she said "P... p..."

She pulled out a notebook and scribbled something on it with a pencil, handing to Tasha. It read, "My name is Pan. Sorry about before."

"Pan?" Tasha said.

The girl smiled and nodded, sighing in relief.

Tasha said, "You don't talk much, do you?" Pan just shook her head while looking at the floor.

"Listen," said Ari, "did you eat yet? Why don't you join us for lunch? At least I think it's lunchtime. The menu clocks don't seem to be working like they should be, which is concerning."

Tasha's mind filled with thoughts of food, and happy thoughts flooded her. "Yeah, I could eat."

Ari tapped at an unseen surface in the air in front of him, and a pizza in a nondescript brown cardboard box materialized in his outstretched hands.

"Where did you get that?" asked Tasha.

"This pizza? It's a fairly common monster drop if you know where to hunt. I hope you like pineapples and ham on your pizza. Pan gets anxiety when pizzas don't have pineapples on them." Ari looked apologetic.

Tasha didn't actually like Hawaiian pizza but had the good sense not to say so. She took a seat and grabbed a slice. "So... Mr. Aralogos. What brings the two of you to this temple?"

"Just call me Ari. The two of us have been searching for something, and our search led us here. We weren't expecting a temple to appear all around us."

"What are you looking for, exactly?"

Pan hesitated before answering. "A cure."

"A cure for what?"

Pan just remained silent. Maybe she meant a cure for her condition. It seemed like she was more than just shy. She might be autistic, but Tasha couldn't say for sure.

She decided not to pry any further, and their conversation quickly turned to other topics. Tasha's health and mana had been gradually recovering as she ate. By the time the pizza was done, her health had been fully refilled and she felt refreshed.

"Ari, can you tell me about magic? That cleaning spell you cast on me before, can anyone do that? I've been focused on increasing my number of hearts, but I was wondering if I should think about increasing my mana supply instead."

"Sure," Ari said. "Anyone can cast spells, but caster types deal higher amounts of damage and can use more complicated techniques. Spells consume mana containers that slowly refill over time outside of combat, so the number of mana containers that you have decides the number of spells that you'll be able to cast in a single battle. It is possible to cast multiple spells with the same container, depending on the spell."

"So how would I cast spells?"

"You'll need to write them yourself, or transcribe them from a spell book. I found this simple fireball spell book here in the library." He pulled out a scroll and held it out to her. "Take it. Pan already knows the spell ,and I have no need of it."

She thought about the tabletop and video games where spellbooks vanished once they were read by the caster. "Will the book disappear if I copy the spell?"

He handed the book to Tasha. "Disappear? Of course not. It's just a book with some script on it. Go into your menu, click on magic, then 'create new.' That'll bring you to a spell designer. Just copy the script exactly as it is written."

Tasha opened the menu and tapped through it, bringing up the spell designer. A floating QWERTY keyboard appeared in the air in front of her. She took a good long look at the spellbook, flipping through the pages.

The first page described the fireball spell and where it should be used as well as the potential dangers of misuse. The spell itself began on the second page. She read the first entry and recognized what it was immediately.

"I know what this is. I mean the language and syntax is different from what I'm used to, but it's definitely source code. There's a class definition, event handlers, conditional statements..."

She kept turning pages. "This seems to be a list of commands to manifest a projectile and an event handler to compress the air at the end point, transmute the gathered air into hydrogen, and ignite it, creating an explosion.

"So... magic is basically computer programming, and mages are all programming nerds. That makes so much sense."

"I don't know what a computer is," Ari said, "but yes. All magic spells are scripted programs. The script is just half of the process, though. Once you are ready to invoke a spell, you need to gather the mana within your body to feed to the spell."

"How do I do that?"

"It will automatically happen when try casting the spell, though there are techniques you can use to purify your mana, amplifying its effects. For now, just focus on casting the spell."

Tasha spent the next half hour transcribing the code from the spellbook to the menu screen while Ari went through the rest of the books. It was unfortunate, but there didn't appear to be any way to transfer spell scripts other than copying them by hand.

"Now this is interesting. When I added the part that creates the projectile, a red marker appeared, indicating mana cost offset. Same thing for the end-point explosion. The script that describes how to cast it has a negative cost."

"That's so you can see how much spells cost," Ari said. "You can offset the mana cost by adding elaborate and complicated methods of invoking the spell. So if you see a mage dancing a jig while chanting, he might be trying to cast an expensive spell without needing to consume too much mana.

"I've never met a gunblade user, but I think you can change the invoke script to allow the spell to cast when you pull the trigger."

"Oh, yeah," said Tasha as she tapped away at the invisible keyboard. "The code completion feature is showing me a list of API commands. If I just change this slightly... and done."

She tapped on "Save," and the fireball spell was added to her list of available spells. "Let's try this out."

Raising the gun, Tasha flicked the switch to spellcasting mode, brought it to eye level, and pointed it at the back wall.

"No wait!" yelled Ari, but it was already too late. When Tasha pulled the trigger, energy rushed through her entire body, starting from her feet and shooting into her abdomen, her chest, and into her head. It wasn't painful, more like a tingling sensation that ran through her body.

Red light filled her sword ,culminating into a fireball that emerged from the end and crashed into the wall. Tasha was knocked backward against the opposite wall by the recoil. Fortunately the fireball explosion didn't hit any of the books.

"Sweet!" she exclaimed in triumph. There were burn marks on the wall. Pan was watching happily with a big smile on her face.

Ari facepalmed. "Tasha, are you insane? We are in an enclosed space surrounded by books that are made out of extremely flammable paper."

She lowered the gunblade. "Oh, right. My bad. I'll be more careful with that from now on. So... are there any other spellbooks in the library?"

"No, that was the only spellbook. There are some other books you might be interested in, though."

Tasha began to peruse the library's selection. It wasn't a large library by any means, but there were several dozen books that caught Tasha's attention. One was titled *A Brief History of Questgivria*. She leafed through *A Treatise on the GP Based Economy*, *A Bozo's Guide to Effective Inventory Management*, as well as *Gods, Eidolons, and Aire: Who They Are And How Not To Piss Them Off*.

One book that caught her attention was titled *Complete Magic-System API*, which would surely come in handy when designing spells. Ultimately she took all of the books and added them to her inventory for later perusal. Each book took up a single slot in her inventory— presumably because they were each unique titles and therefore didn't stack. She had two hundred slots, so she was fine for the time being.

As she was removing everything from the room that wasn't nailed down and adding them to her inventory, she asked Ari, "So do you know anything about the couch potato class?"

"Just a little," he said. "It's a difficult class to be. Most people go for the more straightforward fighter and caster classes."

Tasha frowned. "So you're saying it's a crappy class?"

"Not at all. Most classes unlock new abilities automatically by leveling up. The couch potato class is different. With couch potato, the only way to unlock new abilities is by reading books, watching plays, or listening to music or stories. Each book offers a different ability, and there's no way to know what ability you'll get until you actually read the book. The same book might teach a different ability to different people with the couch potato class.

"Once you actually learn a new ability, it only remains unlocked until you replace it with a different ability from another book. The abilities unlocked in this way are at level 0. If you can raise them to level 1 before switching abilities, it remains unlocked permanently."

Tasha smiled. "So I can get any ability from any class just by reading books, playing games, or watching movies?"

"Movies?" Ari said, looking at her strangely. "I have no idea what that is, but yes. You can unlock any ability from any class. The catch is that you wouldn't know which book to read to gain that ability. You might spend a lifetime just trying to find the right book to give you the skill you're looking for. With other classes, you know ahead of time which abilities you'll get at which level. Also, the abilities are still level locked. So if you receive a level 10 pickpocket ability that belongs to the thief class, you wouldn't be able to use it until you reach level 10 in couch potato."

"It still sounds like I'll be able to get more abilities as a couch potato."

"That's true, though you need to put much more effort into finding and mastering those abilities."

"Is there anything else I should know about the class?" she asked.

"The class-based stat bonuses are more complicated. A fighter class might offer bonuses to strength, and a mage class might offer bonuses to intelligence, but the couch potato class is trickier. As a couch potato, you'll receive a bonus to every stat after reading a book. That bonus decreases over time."

"So, the stat bonus is only really useful for a few hours after I read a book or watch a movie?"

"That's right. It gets worse, though. The bonus can go negative, and when it does, you lose stat points, and the number of heart containers drops by half. Don't get me wrong, the couch potato class is a powerful class. In fact, it is common among crafters and merchants. It is, however, one of the hardest classes to master."

"Thanks, Ari. How do you know so much about this?"

He shrugged. "I do a lot of reading."

Having taken everything of value from the room that wasn't nailed to the floor, they made their way back to the room that Pan had found her in. The same room that used to hold carnivorous slinkers. Denver was curled up on the floor, taking a catnap. He looked up and got to his feet as he saw his mistress approaching.

Before Tasha had a chance to introduce him to the two newcomers, Pan had already gone up to Denver and started petting him, and he licked her face in return. It turned out that the girl liked dinosaurs.

They continued exploring the temple. Pan and Ari had already cleared out most of the lower level. Finally the party reached a large room that appeared to be the entrance. There was a large doorway with stained-glass windows shining multicolored light into the room. On the floor against two opposing walls were four pressure plates.

Ari looked the room over. "I believe that if we stand on all four pressure plates at the same time, that the door will open. That's how these sorts of puzzles usually work."

Pan and Ari each stood on two of the plates on one side. Unfortunately, Pan wasn't quite heavy enough to weigh it down, so she removed some of the heavier items from her inventory to increase her weight. It seemed that when items were stored in a person's inventory, they ceased to exist until they were removed. Tasha would have to inquire about that in the future since the disappearance of objects appeared to violate the law of conservation of mass.

Getting Denver to stand on the pressure plate and not move wasn't easy. Eventually she coaxed him to lie down on the plate by luring him there with a slice of pizza. Fortunately he stayed there for long enough for Tasha to reach her own pressure plate. As she stepped on the plate, the room started to rumble, and a hole opened up in the center of the room. High tempo orchestral music began to play in her head. She recognized the style of music as a video game boss battle theme. Rising to fill the hole was a circular platform containing an enormous iron glove that ascended into the room.

Words appeared in the air above it in a fancy script:

The Master Glove – Dungeon Boss

In her HUD, scan data appeared for the temple's boss monster:

The Master Glove (Level 6)
Boss monster who guards the Temple of the Player. The Master Glove is a floating disembodied white glove... of DOOM!
ATK 7
Mag ATK not applicable
DEF not applicable
Mag DEF not applicable

Thirty small hearts appeared in the air above the towering figure.

Tasha staggered backward. The monsters she'd fought against so far had been small and manageable. This floating glove, on the other hand, was nearly as large as her living room.

Pan brought out her crossbow, aimed it at the floating iron glove, and pulled the trigger. The bolt left the crossbow, hitting the glove but deflecting off its iron surface, dealing no damage.

Ari turned to Pan. "Don't waste your ammo. Don't forget that this is a dungeon boss. You'll only be able to hurt its special weak point. Just watch its attack patterns for any openings."

The fist formed into a palm and swept across the room, pummeling Tasha's body and slamming her into the wall, knocking her breath out. The battle had just started, and she was already down to three hearts.

The palm slammed into the ground in three different places across the combat arena. It drew back into the air and pointed, thumb up and index finger pointed toward Tasha. Light coalesced at the edge of its finger. Tasha dodged out of the way as a bolt of lightning stormed toward where she had been only moments before. A small crater appeared in the wall.

In the palm of the hand, an eyeball opened. Tasha's video-game-fu told her that this must be its weak spot. Traditionally, eyeballs and glowing squares indicated points on a boss where they could take damage. She aimed her gunblade at the eyeball and shot a fireball. The shot was off and hit the palm to the side of its eye, doing no damage and consuming half of her mana in the process. She wouldn't be able to cast that spell again during this battle.

After that, the giant metal glove repeated the same set pattern. First it would sweep across the room, then slap the same three places in the ground that now had impact marks, did a projectile attack at one of the party members, and then opened up, revealing an eyeball. The entire cycle took less than half a minute. The second time it appeared, she missed as well. Tasha clearly needed to boost her precision stat.

"Pan, I need you shoot the eyeball when it appears."

The girl nodded and quickly reloaded her crossbow while Ari and Tasha dodged the monster's attacks. Denver had wisely run off somewhere.

When the eyeball was finally revealed a third time, Pan fired a bolt right into the hand's eye. Tasha cringed sympathetically despite herself. The hand collapsed to the ground, eye pointed upward. Tasha ran to the hand and stabbed it over and over. Ari's fist appeared to turn to stone as he pounded against the eyeball over and over again. Once they had dealt ten hearts of damage, it closed its eye and began the cycle all over again.

This time it added another attack to the cycle. After the projectile attack, it spun its index finger around in a circle, blasting the ground open as the end point of its beam hit the floor. Tasha took a hit from its finger bullet, and that brought her down to two hearts. Pan missed her opportunity to fire since she had to dodge its circle attack. Finally Pan did manage to hit it the next time around. Ari and Tasha beat the crap out of the collapsed glove, bringing it down to ten heart containers.

After that attack, the Master Glove continued its cycle but at double the speed that it had been attacking with before. When the eye opened, it was only for two seconds. Due to the increased speed, the finger bullet hit Tasha again, bringing her down to one heart and wounding her left leg. It was dodging too quickly, and Pan couldn't make the shot. Tasha looked to where the impact marks were on the stone floor.

Right before the glove slammed into the ground, Tasha dove into the center of the impact crater and held the gunblade straight up, propped vertically against the ground. She flicked the switch on her gunblade to the default setting and pulled the trigger just as the palm slammed right into her sword, impacting its eye.

The hand fell to the ground, and Ari scrambled to finish it off. His fists were a blur as he pummeled the eyeball one hit after another. Finally, the Master Glove flew up into the air and spasmed, flying this way and that. Purple rays of light burst from it as it shattered and finally dissolved into mist.

Victory! All enemies have been vanquished.
+750 experience gained. (371 to next level)
870 GP found.
Level up!
Level up!
You have reached level 4.
You have 4 unassigned stat points.
Choose either a heart container or mana container.

Choose either a heart container or mana container.

Pan was tapping at the air in front of her. Tasha couldn't see anything, but it was plain that she was using a menu. "I leveled up. Level 7."

Tasha dismissed her battle log. "Congrats! I just gained two levels. I just made level 4."

"I'm halfway to level 12," said Ari. "This just simply isn't possible."

"I don't see why not. That was a pretty tough boss. Isn't it normal to level up after a fight like that?"

He shook his head, tapping at the air in front of him. "No, it isn't normal. Pan spent nearly a year going from level 5 to 6. I didn't think that it was mathematically possible to gain two levels at the same time. That boss gave me 550 experience. I would have expected maybe forty or sixty on the outside."

Tasha thought about that. "Ari, just assume I know nothing about how experience points work. Because I don't."

"I suppose I can give you a quick overview," he said. "Every person on Etheria has one or more character classes. You can only have one character class at a time, though it is possible to set a subclass to receive half of its stat and class modifiers."

Tasha opened up her menu. "You mean like how my class is couch potato?"

"Yeah," said Ari. "My class is pugilist and my daughter's is thief. Each class has its own level, a special number that describes how far you have progressed in that class. When you gain a level, you receive four stat points and the ability to increase either your health or mana reserves."

Tasha thought back to the multitude of Japanese RPGs she'd played that did the same thing. "Yeah, multiple classes with their own levels is a pretty common trope."

"I thought you told me to assume you know nothing."

"Sorry, please continue. I was just wondering how experience is calculated."

"I'll just explain that, then, though the mechanics of leveling is common knowledge. So each level requires a different amount of experience points, or XP, to progress to the next level. Just take the level number and multiply it by one hundred to know how many experience points you'll need to reach the next level. So going from level 1 to 2 would take 100 XP, reaching level 3 would take 200 XP, level 4 would take 300 XP, and so forth.

"There are many ways to earn XP, but the fastest is by killing mobs. The amount of experience is based on different factors, including level difference, class and racial modifiers, the number of people in your party, and so forth. Fighting weaker monsters than yourself will result in much less experience, while a bonus is awarded for fighting higher-level monsters. The most optimal strategy is to fight monsters several levels above your own but not far enough that you face a high chance of dying. Boss monsters give a bonus amount of experience as well."

The leveling system sounded just like some MMORPGs she'd played in the past. Some aspects of this world seemed to take after classic console games while others more closely resembled online RPGs. The boss battle was clearly patterned after a Japanese action RPG, while the leveling system was closer to an online game. It seemed like stat growth and damage calculation was linear rather than exponential, which made it more similar to a classic tabletop RPG.

Ari continued. "Still, even with the boss and level bonus, we shouldn't have gotten anywhere near that amount of XP from a single battle."

Pan had stopped listening and was rapidly tapping at the air in front of her.

She must be assigning stat points. Since Tasha had eight unassigned stat points, she decided to do the same thing.

Her intelligence was already fairly high, so that stat seemed less important, at least for the time being. Tasha desperately needed to raise her strength and agility score since they both played a large role in melee combat. Eventually she would need to add points to precision to improve her aim and hit rate.

Charisma didn't seem to play a role in combat, but there was more to a typical RPG than just combat. Traditionally, a higher charisma score would open up new quest options and improve prices at shops. She resolved to put some points into charisma at the next level up.

For now, she elected to assign three stat points to strength, three to agility, and two to precision. The moment she confirmed the stat assignment, her body transformed, just as it had earlier. The remainder of her excess body fat vanished, and her body felt lighter. As she felt her arm, Tasha discovered something that had never been there before—actual, factual muscles. She opted to add two more heart containers.

She opened the menu and checked her upgraded player stats:

Tasha Singleton (Level 4 Couch Potato)	
Race	Human (Player)
Subclass	None
Weapon	Beginner Gunblade (ATK 1)
Armor	Cozy Bathrobe (DEF 0.25) Iron Bangle (DEF 1)
Heart Containers	6/6
Mana Containers	3/3
Amusement Index	8.5
Strength	5
Intelligence	8
Agility	5
Precision	6
Charisma	4
ATK	5
MAG ATK	7
DEF	8
MAG DEF	6

As long as she had the stat window open, Tasha thought that she would go through her abilities. They had been piling up. In fact, every time she had performed an action since arriving in Etheria, there had been a constant stream of messages saying that she had unlocked new abilities.

She scrolled through her list of abilities. Most of them were simple things like weapon proficiencies, jumping, climbing, running, sneaking, conversation, eating, going to the bathroom, listening, spell design, and even one for being digested by a monster. She wasn't sure that was one she should be happy about. She hadn't reached level 2 in any ability yet, but some of their progress bars had begun to fill.

There was an ability called Stat Shuffle, but it was grayed out. There was no ability description, only some accompanying text which said that Stat Shuffle wouldn't be unlocked until level 6. She would have to wait until level 6 to learn more about it.

The ability at the end of the list was one that she didn't recognize.

Rapid Leveling – Level MAX
Player-specific ability. Player and all party members gain experience points and learn abilities at ten times the normal rate. Only applies to the first six party members, including the player.

"Uh, Mr. Ari, I think I know why we've been leveling up quickly."

Tasha read the description of the rapid leveling ability to him out loud.

"Well, I guess that settles that," he said. "There's no longer any question that you are a player. You've just saved us years of level grinding. So... where will you go from here?"

"I'm not sure. Until now I was just focused on getting out of the temple."

"Then I suggest you see the high-elven king. If you travel to the north for about thirty miles, you will find a road. Follow it to the west, and once you come upon a town, you can hire a caravan to take you the rest of the way to Brightwind Keep, where King Questgiver dwells. The elven king is wise, and according to the legends, he gave advice and direction to earlier players."

Tasha wanted to write all this stuff down but didn't have any paper or writing things.

"So... there are other players beside me, or am I the only one?"

"There hasn't been a player in Etheria for many centuries. Like I said before, until I met you, I'd not really believed that they existed. If the myths and legends are to be believed, there have been five players before you. The first was Taj the Wanderer. He aided the first elven king and helped found the save-point network that prevents death. Then there was Erik the Incorrigible, followed by Scott the Questionable, and then Charles the Not Quite As Incorrigible As Erik. The most recent player was Jak, Slayer of the Lich Queen."

Did he say Jak? As in her *father*, Jak? If her father was a player as well, that would explain why he possessed the game cartridge to begin with. He had never said anything about Etheria before. What else didn't she know about him?

Ari continued. "Every player has had a drastic effect on this world, either for good or ill. I wonder what your legacy will be, o Tasha the Couch Potato. I wish Pan and I could come with you, but we've traveled for months to reach this place."

"You've done more than enough," she said, "without both of your help, I never could have gotten past that freaky eyeball hand monster. So, I just need to travel north and turn left when I get to a road? Got it. Just one question... Which way is north?"

Pan was pointing at something in front of and below her.

After a moment, Tasha realized what the girl was trying to tell her. "The compass on my HUD. Got it."

They said their goodbyes, and Tasha walked through the now open temple doorway with Denver in tow.

Quest Complete: Welcome to Etheria

50 XP awarded.

The quest had been completed, but a new one hadn't appeared to take its place. It seemed that the quests weren't going to hold her hand. The temple was truly beautiful when seen from the outside.

Tasha turned in place until the letter N on her compass was in the center of her HUD. With the temple at her back, she started walking. After taking no more than a dozen paces, there was a harsh grinding noise coming from behind her. The temple was shimmering a dim purple. The building itself began to fade away, turning into a purple cloud of mist. For a moment, Tasha could actually make out the shape of the floors and walls as the temple vanished.

The building's dematerialization took but a handful of seconds, and once it was gone, Ari and Pan were left standing alone in a field of crushed grass and dirt amidst some ancient ruins.

Ari clapped his hands together. "Change of plans. On second thought, Tasha, we'll accompany you after all."

The save point that had been on the temple roof now lay amidst the temple ruins. After Ari and Pan touched it, Tasha set off with them on her journey with her newfound friends.

CHAPTER 8

The Jester and the King

The citadel of Brightwind Keep sat at the heart of the capital city deep within the borders of the elven kingdom of Questgivria. The central pillar was as tall as a skyscraper. If a person stood ᴀ e courtyard at its peak on a cloudy day and looked upon the city, they would see the clouds from above.

Surrounding the central pillar were half a dozen shorter spires that towered above the city. Thick stone walls connected them to one another and guarded the castle interior.

A mesh of circular glass rings connected the shorter buildings at odd angles, arcing between the seven spires. These were lifts, which served as the only entrance to the spires and allowed the elven nobility, guests, and servants to travel between them. Points of light traveled along these glass halos as they transported their occupants to different areas of the castle.

If one were to look at the castle when the sun was highest in the sky, glimmers of light would reflect off an invisible magical wall that protected the castle from attack from above. The only access to the castle was through three doors in the front wall connecting the southernmost pillars.

The largest of the three gates remained closed, except to let in giants and dragons, and during events, when large numbers of people were allowed entry. It took a great deal of strength to open it and could only be opened by multiple giants or dragons working together.

The second gate was to admit royalty and their guests, while the third gate let in workers and supplicants.

Brightwind Keep was not only one of the tallest artificial structures in Etheria, it was also the best defended. An army of dragons wouldn't be able to penetrate the walls or magical wards. The sorceress queen of Zhakara might be able to break its magical defenses, but it was guarded by a small army of high-level elven archers and warriors.

And then there was *him*. No, the king didn't like to think about *him*, but today he didn't have any choice. The need for knowledge and understanding trumped his normal dislike of the man.

The elven king, Iolo Questgiver, paced in circles around the courtyard.

"Where is he? I summoned him an hour ago."

King Iolo Questgiver was tall for an elf. Though he was over two thousand years old—as measured in Etherian years—to human eyes he would appear to be in his midthirties. He brushed away his long black hair, revealing pointed ears, and resumed pacing.

A harried elven servant emerged from the stairs below and stepped into the courtyard.

"My king," he said, "we found him. He was performing in the city square. It seems quite a crowd had assembled."

Behind the servant, a man followed. Most people thought he was a goblin, or perhaps a deformed dwarf. He was about half of the king's height, had an elongated nose that ended in a sharp point, eyes the shape of wide slits that never fully opened, and a mostly bald head that was covered in but a few rogue hairs.

His skin was clay white. Most people thought that his face was painted, but it wasn't. He didn't wear any kind of makeup.

By far his most distinctive physical characteristic was his grin. It was unnaturally wide and ever present. This wasn't a simple smile that anyone would reveal in response to some minor amusement—it was a deep, pervasive contortion of the face. An expression of sublime regalement at everything around him. A momentary smile might be reassuring, but this was just the opposite.

His clothing was loud and boisterous. Atop his head, he wore a hat with three prongs, each a myriad of colors and a jingle bell at the end. His pants were striped, and he wore a shirt of red and green that alternated colors on either side. His socks were mismatched, and he wore cloth shoes with an upward twirl at the end.

The elven servant spoke. "Now comes Snickers the Bumble, jester and advisor to His Majesty King Iolo Questgiver."

"O rapture and joy, what a marvelous day!
Has the king some concern that I might allay?"

"Yes, Snickers. Good of you to ask. Surely by now you know about the menu clocks. They've changed to some kind of countdown. What does this mean?"

"Be not confused and don't misconstrue,
'Tis the god Entropy taking his due."

"Entropy? The serpent god of destruction? What do you mean his due?"

"He will encircle the world and give a great squeeze,
he'll squash out all life and crush it with ease.
Naught will remain when he is all through,
when the god of destruction has collected his due."

"So the past has caught up with us at last," the king said. "When will this happen?"

Snickers replied gleefully.

"All this will happen, oh Questgiver King,
when the timer runs dry,
the world he will wring.
He'll draw closer and closer till the clock is all done,

then he will crush, kill, maim, and destroy. Oh, what
fun!"

"Don't tell anyone else about this, Snickers. I don't want to start a panic. I'll make an announcement when we have a plan of action."

The creature's smile grew wider.

"I deeply regret that when this begun
in the courtyard below, I told everyone
that the world would soon come to its terminal end.
I didn't forestall telling the truth or pretend.
If you had but asked me to keep myself quiet,
I wouldn't have told them and started a riot!"

The elven king started to feel a headache coming on. He looked at Snickers, annoyed. "Don't go anywhere. I'll have more questions for you later."

Snickers the Bumble took out a bouncing ball and some jacks from somewhere buried in his pocket, sat on the floor, and started playing. King Questgiver turned to the servant who had escorted Snickers in.

"I need you to send swallows to our allies in the slime kingdom and to the dragons of Dragonholm. Have them send their representatives as soon as possible. Send a messenger to every member nation of Questgivria as well. Tell them that I have information about the menu clocks."

"Yes, Your Highness," the elf said.

"Oh, and where is my daughter? Where is Kiwistafel?"

The servant thought for a moment. "She is currently fighting mobs with Prince Hermes and Sir Slimon. They've been away for three weeks but should still be in the vicinity of the castle."

The king nodded. "It might be best for her to return to the castle for the time being. Have her found and brought back."

King Questgiver pulled up his menu. The clock read 99:11:10. The timer diminished slowly; it had gone down less than a minute in the last hour.

He looked out into the night sky, not knowing that the ancient god who lived there was staring back at him.

On the 29th of Catuary, at precisely 2:25 p.m., an unprecedented phenomenon occurred. Throughout the whole of Questgivria, to the best of this newspaper's knowledge, all citizens had their menu clocks replaced with a bizarre countdown. The countdown appears to be ticking backward from one hundred hours. It has been confirmed that the time is diminishing at irregular intervals. Much of the time it remains stationary, and at other times it is reduced by entire minutes. There is no obvious rhyme or reason as to why it is behaving in this strange manner.

Shortly after this phenomenon took place, Snickers the Bumble, who is advisor to high king Iolo Questgiver, made a statement in the town square of Brightwind City. According to Snickers, the countdown heralds the return of the eidolon known as Entropy. At the time of this printing, the crown has declined to comment. Expect late editions of this paper as this story develops.

—Special Edition of The Brightwind Tribune, *Catuary 29th, 3205 3E*

CHAPTER 9

Random Encounters

In order to understand ethereal mist, we first must define it. The mist can be best described as the omnipresent medium through which the divine beings known as aire regulate the balance of our world. Ethereal mist particles are shapeshifting organisms capable of assuming whatever form is required of them.

Ethereal mist can shape itself into both solid and gaseous forms. When a mob spawns, a sufficient quantity of mist draws together to form the material of the monster. During its transitory form between a gas and a solid, it appears as a purple mist-like cloud. When the monsters are killed or despawn, their solid form dissolves, dissipating into its original gaseous state.

Mist is also present in our own bodies. When a person levels up and assigns stat points, mist particles affect changes in the body, improving muscle tone, bone strength, and physical appearance as well as the brain's level of neural activity.

A person with a high strength stat will have bones that are as hard as steel and muscles to match. Someone with a high intelligence score will be able to perform differential calculus in their head. Someone with a high charisma score will always know the right thing to say to sway others to their point of view. Etherians shape the people they are through the allocation of statistic points.

In addition to a person's primary stats, there are also derived stats based on what sort of armor and equipment a person has equipped. A piece of armor with a high defense stat will cause mist to form a light, invisible barrier at the point of impact, reducing the amount of damage to match the calculated amount.

Ethereal mist is a necessary part of everyday life. In fact, it is safe to say that life could not exist without the presence of mist. Deep thought requires at least some points be allocated in intelligence. Without strength points, nothing would stop a person from being killed by the first wild animal they meet.

An existence without mist is absurd to even contemplate—the only way people can truly improve themselves is through stat allocation. The absurd concept that intelligent life could exist without mist should be relegated to the confines of speculative fiction and has no place in serious academic study.

—On the Behavior and Composition of Ethereal Mist *by Jarl Lorren*

A s a hardcore couch potato, Tasha was thoroughly unaccustomed to doing so much walking. It was fortunate that her augmented agility and strength prevented her from getting easily worn out. Of course, it would have been nice if she had something to wear. Something other than bunny slippers and a bathrobe.

After walking for what must have been close to an hour, she could feel a change in the atmosphere around her. The air pressure seemed thicker, and there were multicolored swirls dancing about.

She stopped and turned to her new friend. "Mr. Ari, what's going on? The air around me looks all funky."

"Don't worry, Tasha. It's nothing to be concerned about."

"Well, that's good," she said, relieved.

But Ari continued, "It's only the mist trying to kill us."

Tasha flung out her arms, exasperated. "And just how is that nothing to worry about? What is this 'mist' stuff, anyway?"

He pointed at one of the eddies that formed in the air. "Do they really not have mist where you come from? I suppose I can explain it to you. Mist is an ever-present miasma that stretches across all of Etheria. It's in the very air we breathe. There are living intelligent beings who live within the mist."

"You mean like that glove monster back at the temple or those boblins that tried to kill me?"

"No. Those are merely artificial constructs designed to fight us. They are mindless beings that can only follow preprogrammed attack patterns."

"They're artificial? Then who designed them?"

"They are designed by the aire, the beings I was talking about earlier. They exist as part of the mist without physical bodies that we are able to see."

She looked around at the swirling patterns of color. Tiny drops of light floated in the air amongst the swirling clouds. "How many of them are there?"

"We don't actually know. We only have information about the handful who choose to interact with us. There are two major types of aire that we are aware of. First there are the developers. Tasha, why don't you open up your options menu, then scroll down and tap on 'Credits'?"

Opening the menu, she did as he asked. Then she tapped on the "Credits" menu option. The first line read "Lead Producer," followed by static. After that there was Associate Producer, Art Director, Concept Artist. Further down was Lead Programmer, Behavior Programmer, Lead Designer, Tech Artist, QA Lead," and so forth. Each line was followed by a line of unreadable static.

"Those are the gods of Etheria," he said. "They design the dungeons, program the monsters, set up quests, and maintain the economic balance."

"Wait a minute," Tasha said. "Let me get this straight... Are you telling me that the gods that you worship are game developers?"

"Well, not me personally, but Developerism is the main religion on Etheria. It's understandable, I suppose, since they did literally create the world we live in.

"Like I said, there are two kinds of aire that we have knowledge of. The other kind are the godlike beings known as eidolons, and they only number in the dozens. They actually appear in physical form within our world, and each has a unique archetype. Before you ask, yes, some people do worship them."

"Have you ever met an eidolon?" Tasha asked.

"I saw one right before I met you. Catalyst, the goddess of change, appears as a great thunderstorm. Immense thunderclouds appeared above the temple, and a series of powerful lightning strikes brought the temple into being.

"Besides her, there is Entropy, who appears in the night sky. He takes the form of a great serpent, but he is so far away from us that to the naked eye he seems to be nothing more than a bright spot in the sky.

"There is a trickster god who resides at Brightwind Keep with the high king. He's taken the form of a clown. He's one of the few eidolons who communicate with humans using the spoken word."

The clouds of mist continued to swirl around them. "Do we need to worry about them?" she asked.

"The eidolons? They aren't dangerous as long as you take great care in your dealings with them. The eidolons are governed by a set of rules, which keeps them from harming us, at least not without our consent. One of the things we know about the eidolons is that they can't do anything to us without our permission. The eidolons are like players, and this world is their playground. They follow strict rules in order to keep the game fair. If an eidolon ever offers to make a deal with you, exercise great caution. There are many legends about eidolons who trick mortals into entering foolish agreements."

Tasha's mind went back to the floating sign that appeared at the crossroads. Could that have been Catalyst, the eidolon Ari had described?

Had she inadvertently entered into an agreement with one of these godlike beings? Her taking the path of "Adventure" might have constituted consent for an eidolon to bring her here. By bringing Tasha to Etheria, the eidolon had delivered on the promise of adventure.

"Thanks for the info," she said, "So what about this mist? Why is it surrounding us now?"

"It's surrounding us as a warning," said Ari. "We're about to be attacked by mobs."

"*What*? Why didn't you say so sooner?"

"They won't attack until after we start moving. You should equip your weapon. We're in a higher-level area, so let me do most of the fighting. Even if you don't fight, you'll still get a smaller portion of the gained XP."

"Got it."

Pan had already equipped her crossbow, fully cocked it, and loaded a bolt into the barrel.

After removing her gunblade from her inventory, Tasha proceeded onward, following Ari half a dozen paces behind. The mist continued to grow thicker as they advanced. After a few minutes, the mist coalesced into a fearsome beast and three larger-than-ordinary frogs. Her battle HUD appeared.

Grass Wumpus – Level 11
A fearsome smelly beast. If you see him, it's already too late to get away.
ATK 21   Mag ATK 0
DEF 16   Mag DEF 7

Giant Spotted Frog – Level 6
Used to be a giant spotted prince.
ATK 10   Mag ATK 4
DEF 6   Mag DEF 4

1 Grass Wumpus and 3 Giant Spotted Frogs appear! Combat started.
Grass Wumpus attacks Tasha.
Giant Frog A attacks Tasha.
Giant Frog B attacks Tasha.
Giant Frog C attacks Tasha.

Tasha balked when she read the notification and looked up to see a giant beast and all three frogs bearing down on her.

What? Why is everything attacking me? That's not fair!

Fortunately, Ari was able to pull the wumpus off her with a spin kick to its bark-like abdomen, and Pan took out one of the frogs with a well-placed headshot. Denver had tackled another of the frogs, distracting it and allowing Tasha to focus on the single remaining enemy.

Tasha slashed at one of the frogs, injuring but not killing it. She had mistimed the trigger action and failed to deal fire damage to it. The oversized amphibian jumped at her. She attempted to dodge, but was able to avoid its attack.

A situation like this called for a witty pun. "Prepare to croak!" She groaned inwardly at her horrible and not-at-all-witty pun. After two more strikes, she was able to finish it off.

After all three of the frogs were killed, Tasha, Pan, and Denver turned their attention to the battle between Ari and the wumpus. Ari hadn't taken any damage, but the large furry creature was still at over twenty hearts.

After Pan finished reloading, she leveled her crossbow at the wumpus and fired a bolt that took out one of the creature's eyes. It screamed in pain, losing two and a half hearts, but then it abruptly stopped paying attention to Ari and began rampaging toward the girl.

Reacting to some misguided instinct, Tasha placed herself between the enormous mob and the girl. It wasn't a smart or strategic decision, but she did it nevertheless.

Tasha stabbed the wumpus in the belly, dealing three-fourth hearts of damage. Pulling the trigger caused her sword to ignite and vibrate, dealing an additional half heart of damage. The wumpus swung at her and would have killed her, but fortunately she was too close for its giant arms to have enough leverage to deal much damage.

Pan hit it with another headshot, and Ari hit it with a barrage of heavy punches and kicks. It was already down to seven hearts. Even so, it remained fixated on Tasha, ignoring everyone else's attacks. It must have been because she was cute. That's what Tasha told herself, at any rate.

It was doubtful that Tasha would be able to survive even a single hit from the massive creature. It moved faster than she did, and she was lucky that Ari and Pan were able to finish it off before it reached her.

Victory! All enemies have been vanquished.

+170 experience gained.

13 GP found.

As the victory music played, Ari helped her to her feet. "Tasha, I thought I said not to engage these enemies if you could avoid it. That monster is far too high level for you. You could have been killed."

"I know," Tasha said, "but it was attacking Pan, and I just sort of reacted."

"And I appreciate that, but she's twice your level. Pan knows how to take care of herself."

As he said that, Tasha felt two small arms wrapping around her. Pan was giving her a hug, but she didn't say anything. The hug only lasted a moment as she backed away and picked up a capsule that the monster dropped.

"She doesn't normally like being touched," said Ari. "I guess she likes you."

"I guess so."

Tasha looked at her gunblade and said to it, "And now I will give you a name. And I shall call you... Kermit the Frog Cleaver."

Her traveling companions simply looked at her like she was some kind of idiot.

"What? You guys don't name your weapons?"

Aralogos shook his head. "I don't use weapons. I specialize in unarmed combat, and I'm not naming my fists. Because that would be weird."

"C-can I name my crossbow Josephine?" Pan asked.

"Trust me," Tasha said, "all the best weapons have names."

The capsule contained some hand soap and three rolls of toilet paper. Well, at least that solved her bathroom related concerns for the immediate future. She added them to her inventory.

After the fight, they decided to break for lunch. Ari handed out some cheeseburgers in paper wrappers from his inventory along with some French fries and strawberry milkshakes. Tasha thought that this was odd. She didn't recall passing a Wendy's in their travels. The burgers and fries were still hot and delicious, as though they had been freshly made, and the milkshake was chilled. It appeared that items that were placed in a person's inventory went into some kind of suspended animation.

"Mr. Ari, can I ask you something? It's something that has been bothering me."

He nodded. "You can ask me anything. It's just Ari, by the way."

"So... in this world, what happens when someone dies? I died once and was in a place of darkness for the longest time. Then I came back to life and I was... different somehow. I'm changed... more violent and more decisive than I used to be. What happened to me?"

He hesitated. "I'll try my best to answer. When you die, your essence spends some time in Oblivion while a new body is prepared for you. The new body isn't a copy of the old one, but it is very similar. Your spirit and memories are installed on the new brain, but since the new brain isn't simply a copy of the old one, there will be some changes in how you think. Most people avoid death in order to preserve their personality and identity."

"I see," she said. "So I'm not the same person I was before I died."

"No, you aren't," he said, "But it's best not to overthink it. People constantly change over time. I'm not the same person I was when I woke up this morning. I've changed some since I met you. The only difference between that kind of change and resurrection is how abruptly the change happens."

She thought about that. What constituted Tasha as a person? was it just her memories, or did her personality play into it?

"So... I'm a new person, similar but distinct from the Tasha who died."

"That's an enlightened viewpoint," Ari said. "We Etherians are used to the concept of resurrection and the death of personality that accompanies it."

"Is there any way to bring someone back from death to their old body so they don't lose their personality?"

Ari looked thoughtful. "There have always been rumors of such an ability, but I think that's all they are, just rumors. To my knowledge, there are no healing spells or abilities that can bring people back from the dead."

They cleaned up the picnic and continued on their journey. As they walked, Tasha repeatedly jumped into the air, invoking her Double Jump ability. After a few minutes of this, Ari asked, "Tasha, what are you doing? You look ridiculous."

Tasha stopped jumping. "I'm trying to level up my Double Jump ability so I can keep it. My class gave me this ability, but I can only keep it if I level it up. It should just be another half hour or so."

He shook his head. "Whatever you say."

She did finally achieve level 1 in Double Jump and collapsed to the ground, exhausted. Ari handed her a canteen and helped her to her feet. They took a short break before continuing.

After about an hour of walking, she received a notification that they had entered a zone of level 5 to 8 mobs. The monsters seemed to be mainly boblins and imps. Between the four of them, the creatures that spawned did not present much of a challenge.

While walking, Tasha noticed a herd of elk grazing in the distance. They might have been deer or antelope. She hadn't watched enough *Animal Planet* to be able to properly discern the difference.

"Those are elk right?" Tasha said. "Don't they have to worry about being attacked by mobs?"

"N-no," said Pan. "They c-can't see monsters."

Pan seemed to have opened up and was becoming more verbal around Tasha.

"Most people believe that wild animals don't even see monsters," said Ari. "Animals usually run from humans when we engage monsters, but that's just because they see us swinging swords around and shooting fireballs and stuff."

"What about Denver?" Tasha asked.

"When an animal is domesticated, they stop being wild animals and can see monsters. They also gain the ability to resurrect at save points. Remember in your earlier battle, Denver helped you by attacking the giant frog. If there were any wild animals nearby, they would have just seen you swinging that gunblade around."

Pan was standing in front of her. It seemed like she wanted to say something, but she averted her eyes.

"Pan, is there something you want?"

Finally she said, "R-rectangle... p-please."

"Rectangle?" It took Tasha a minute to realize that the girl was talking about her phone. She pulled it out and showed it to Pan. Tasha explained how to use it and agreed to let her borrow it until she needed it back. The girl was fascinated by the small handheld computer.

The remainder of the day alternated between walking and fighting mobs. That afternoon, Tasha must have faced a dozen random encounters. Even without any formal training with the sword, she felt that she was doing quite well. Each time a set of enemy mobs was defeated, her XP bar inched just a bit higher.

By the time the sun began to set, Tasha had made it to level 5. She put two points into charisma and another two points into agility. Again Tasha felt different after allocating the points. She wondered if her speech had improved along with her charisma stat.

Tasha Singleton (Level 5 Couch Potato)	
Race	Human (Player)
Subclass	None
Weapon	Beginner Gunblade (ATK 1)
Armor	Cozy Bathrobe (DEF 0.25) Iron Bangle (DEF 1)
Heart Containers	4/4
Mana Containers	7/7
Amusement Index	6.1
Strength	5
Intelligence	8
Agility	10

Precision	6
Charisma	6
ATK	5
MAG ATK	7
DEF	8
MAG DEF	6

The party didn't make camp until the sun was almost touching the horizon. Tasha helped set up the campsite while Aralogos built a fireplace from pieces of wood that he had stored in his inventory. He said he was going to cook up a beef stew for supper, which sounded great.

As much as she'd enjoyed the hamburger for lunch, Tasha wouldn't want to eat that at every meal. It was good to know that homemade cooking still existed in a world where monster drops included fast food.

CHAPTER 10

Immortal Coil

"You seem to be getting the hang of combat," Aralogos said. He was cooking up some stew over the campfire. It smelled amazing.

"Yeah, thanks," Tasha said. "I feel much more powerful than before. I'm pretty confident fighting these monsters."

"Have you ever fought before this?"

"Not really, no. When I was a kid I got into a few fist fights and got my butt handed to me and... that's about the extent of my fighting experience."

"Your... butt handed to you?" he said. He shook his head. "You players have some of the oddest expressions."

"So how far is it from here to the castle?"

"It depends," he said. "If we take the direct path, we could reach the main road tomorrow, and travel will be much faster. It would mean cutting through a region of level 11–16 monsters, though. At only level five, you wouldn't stand much chance against them. They would be mostly targeting you since you are the lowest level in the group.

"On the other hand, we could circumvent that area by traveling three days to the east. The monsters would be similar in level to the ones you've fought today. This would add about five days to our trip. Once we reach the road, we should probably hire a caravan to take us the rest of the way. We could reach the castle city two or three days later."

Tasha nodded, and with that, supper was ready. She ate her fill of yummy stew and relaxed by the fire with Ari. They engaged in idle conversation while Pan remained transfixed by Tasha's phone. Based on the sounds the phone was making, she was probably playing *Fruit Ninja*. Tasha had played the game earlier, and it unlocked the ability Lament of the Kumquat, which provided bonus damage against fruit-based enemies. She didn't think it would be a useful ability at the time but began keeping notes to track which TV shows and books offered which abilities.

As Tasha lay back on her hands, she looked up and for the first time really saw the star-filled night sky of this foreign world. Specifically her attention was drawn to the moon. Set directly above them, it was larger than the moon that she was used to. Was this world's moon actually larger, or did it just have a smaller orbit?

"Are you looking at the moons?" Aralogos asked.

"Moons?" Tasha said. "I only see the one."

"There are two moons," he replied. "The big one that fills the sky is called Perm. This is the larger and closer of the two moons. But there is another, and it brings me to the legend I promised to tell you about and the reason people come back to life after dying.

"Do you see that line of four stars?" he said, pointing. "Look just to the right of it. That small dot is the god Entropy. He orbits Etheria as the smaller of our two planetary satellites."

"I think I can see it. The dim one, right? Are you telling me that moon is a god?"

"Let me tell you the story. The ballad of Lorien the Deathslayer."

"Y-you mean you're going to sing?" Tasha asked hopefully.

"Daddy c-can't sing!" Pan joked. "Anything but that!"

Aralogos looked annoyed. "There is a popular ballad based on his story, but I wouldn't want to traumatize my daughter by attempting to sing it. I'll just tell it to you as best as I can remember it."

Tasha nodded, and Pan went back to her game.

"In the early days of Etheria, there was no resurrection. When someone was killed, they remained dead.

"That was before the elves immigrated to Etheria. We don't know how or why they came to this world, but after they arrived, they established a grand civilization. Among the sentient races, elves are considered the fairest, wisest, and most resilient. They don't age the way we do and are not prone to disease.

"In Etheria, the only way to survive and prosper is to challenge the creatures who dwell in the mist. Despite the great strength and resilience of the elven people, it wasn't long after they arrived before some of them were killed by the creatures of mist.

"The first king of the elves, Lorien Questgiver, was deeply concerned by this. He was responsible for the welfare of all elven folk. So for decades he researched how to fend off death and keep his people safe from it, but no answers were forthcoming.

"One day, he was approached by a man. It wasn't an elf or a human or dwarf or any of the other known races, but was still clearly a man. He was short with pure white skin, and he wore brightly colored clothes. He had a sharp, elongated nose, and when he spoke, it was only ever in rhyme. They said that he was always smiling with an uncommonly wide grin.

"The man sought an audience with the elven king. He claimed that he was but a traveling priest, a devotee of the great god Entropy.

"Now, the serpent god, Entropy, is the embodiment of chaos and destruction. As such, he would not speak for himself because he considered speech a form of creation. With words, we create ideas, and even that small amount of creation was antithetical to his existence and offensive to him. And that is why Entropy would only speak through an interpreter.

"The mysterious priest spoke for Entropy, saying that he had grown tired of dealing out small bits of destruction at a time and yearned to destroy the entire world and all life at once. For you see, the life of a planet is measured in billions of years, but the age of men and elves is short by comparison.

"Even gods had to follow their own rules, and the Etherian gods had all agreed not to interfere without the express permission of the people who lived there. The other gods wouldn't allow Entropy to destroy a single thing without his victims' permission.

"Recognizing the elven king as the representative of all sentient life on Etheria, he offered to make a deal. Through the interpreter, Entropy promised to stop claiming the souls of those who died of anything but old age. This was the origin of the save-point network, which allows people to be reborn after death. In exchange, after three thousand years, Entropy would return to destroy the world in its entirety.

"The elven king considered this offer. He would be able to completely free his people from death, and they would once again be fully immortal. Before the three thousand years were up, the elves could leave this world and return to their homeland, escaping Entropy's final destruction. He agreed to the offer, and at once, all violent and accidental deaths became non-permanent. People who died came back to life at the save points. The elven king Lorien Questgiver had put an end to death itself.

"Entropy was overjoyed, because he would only have to wait for what, to him, was a short amount of time. The doom of Etheria was inevitable, or so he thought.

"Be he was deceived. For you see, his mysterious priest was in truth a trickster god in disguise. When the trickster revealed himself, he took on the name of Snickers the Bumble and offered a new deal to the king.

"The trickster god, Snickers, desired the throne for himself. I have no idea why a god would desire such a thing, but he offered a way to nullify the deal before the three thousand years were up. There would be a one-hundred-hour period of time when nullification would be possible. In exchange, Snickers would take the throne when the bloodline of high-elven kings ended. Snickers has served the line of elven kings ever since. The current king, Iolo Questgiver, is a direct descendant of Lorien Questgiver so his line lives on."

"The humans can't have been happy with the elven king for making that deal on their behalf," Tasha said. "It sounds like the elves got the better part of that arrangement if they can just leave before the three thousand years are up."

"Indeed not," he said. "Though all races benefited from the near abolishment of death, none of them were happy with the cost. The nations that had lived in peace until that point began to war with one another. The abolishment of death ultimately led to the bloodiest wars in our history.

"The elven nation of Brightwind, which we now know as Questgivria, the human nations, and the dragon-dwarf alliance, all warred with one another. Since their soldiers would return to life upon dying, the war lasted hundreds of years with no side ever gaining any significant advantage. Hundreds of thousands of people died millions of times before the war ended.

"But eventually, the war did come to a close. The elven king who had originally forged the agreement left this world in the way that only elves can. The new king, his son, King Lakuruel, sued for peace, and eventually all three nations agreed.

"Is that true?" Pan asked, looking up from the phone.

"I suspect much of it is exaggerated," said Ari, "but at least part of it is true. The elven king we are traveling to see has an imp-like advisor working for him who isn't elven or human and speaks only in rhyme. Most people believe that he is the trickster god who spoke for and betrayed Entropy.

"There is a reason I'm telling you this story. It has been about three thousand years since the events of the story were alleged to occur. A few years ago, there was a celebration because three thousand years had passed, but Entropy hadn't returned.

"I assumed that it was just a myth—until you appeared, and the countdown appeared on our menus. That's why we need to see the king. Because if the myth is true, your arrival might not be an accident, and the king might be able to tell us more. There's only one way to know for sure. We need to meet with him as soon as possible."

Tasha looked back up at the dot in the sky. It seemed that it had moved across slightly from where it had been.

> **Ability Unlocked: Measure of Entropy**
> **Provides knowledge of the level of disorder in the target system.**
> **Classless ability, unlocks at level 1.**
> **Would you like to set this as your current ability, replacing Double Jump? Yes/No**

That looked to be a specialized ability that was completely useless to her, so she tapped "no."

For the rest of the evening, they engaged in idle conversation and avoided talking about serious affairs.

Pan handed the phone back to Tasha, and she checked the time. It said 98:26:55 and was unchanging. Its behavior still confused and vexed Tasha. That and the fact that her phone had barely used any of its battery and still had a perfect 4G connection while in Etheria. Staring at her phone did nothing to unravel the secrets behind her present situation.

Without a tent, the three travelers had no choice but to sleep under the stars. Luckily, the weather that night was fair. She fell asleep to the sound of Pan snoring. She found it strange that a girl so small and normally so reserved could snore so loudly but wisely decided to keep that observation to herself.

CHAPTER 11

The Webwood Forest

"It's time to get up," Ari said, standing over Tasha's sleeping roll.

Tasha briefly opened her eyes but then turned over to the other side and fell back asleep. The sun was just barely peeking out over the horizon. Why did Ari have to be a morning person? A few minutes later, the smell of coffee roused her from her slumber, and she groggily sat up. She was still wearing her bathrobe and resurrection clothing—she didn't own anything else to wear.

This was her first morning in this world, and Tasha wasn't accustomed to waking up so early. Ari handed her a cup of coffee and a jelly doughnut, and that helped take the edge off waking up at such an unnatural hour. It was about twenty minutes and a bear claw later before she was ready to set out.

They traveled for several hours over the wild grass. Every thirty or forty minutes, a random encounter would spawn. The enemies weren't difficult, and Tasha got fighting giant frogs down to an artform. They attacked using predictable patterns, and the timing of their attacks was advertised by the battle HUD. So long as she was careful, Tasha was confident in her ability to bring them down.

As they were walking, Ari turned to Tasha. "So, this 'second breakfast' that you describe. Does everyone from the world of players eat breakfast twice a day?"

She swallowed a piece of her peanut butter sandwich. "Yes, everyone on Earth has second breakfast. Especially couch potatoes. By the way, Ari, I've been meaning to ask... How do you make your hair all spiky like that? At first I thought you used lots of hair gel, but I don't think that's it."

He ruffled his hair. "What do you mean? My hair is naturally spiky."

"Really? Because in my experience, hair grows out in strands and then either extends outward straight or in curls. I've never seen strands of hair that could self-organize into acute triangles like that."

"Discussing my admittedly majestic hair will need to wait for another time, for behold!" Ari swept his hand majestically. "We stand before the Webwood Forest. Within we will face much higher-level monsters than you've seen so far. If I were to guess, most of them will be spider based or possibly bug based. We should be able to reach the other side by nightfall if we keep up a quick pace. Take care not to lose your life in this dark place."

Tasha nodded. "Good to know. Don't die. I'll make a note of it."

Tasha's last and only save point was at the ruins, where she had arrived in Etheria. She certainly didn't want to lose that travel time or experience death again. She was still getting used to the new version of herself and wasn't ready to let go of her new personality.

As the forest surrounded Tasha, her view was obstructed on all sides. There wasn't a clear path to follow, so they forged their own path between the trees in a generally northward direction.

Pan and Ari were on high alert, and the carefree banter from the previous day had vanished.

The trees themselves had tall trunks with bunches of leaves at the top that filtered the sunlight and cast leafy shadows. The sound of wildlife was all around her. Small creatures like rabbits and squirrels scampered along the ground, and birds darted between the trees overhead.

At one point she actually crossed paths with a small tiger. The tiger growled at her menacingly but kept his distance and eventually was lost from sight in the woods. Pan had her crossbow nocked with a bolt, but she lowered it when the animal retreated.

"There is no need to be concerned," Ari assured her. "Wild animals know not to mess with adventurers. Still, it's best to be on guard."

It took about an hour of traveling for the first mob to appear. The mist formed into twenty great spiders. Her battle dialogue indicated that they were level 12 opponents, and they were all targeting her. At level 5 Tasha wasn't even sure that she could damage them. Each of the spiders had only eight hearts. The real problem was their sheer number.

Before they had even formed completely, Pan had her crossbow out and readied a blue bolt. The head of the arrow wasn't pointed but started to glow blue. Pan released the bowstring, and the bolt sailed through the air, striking a spider. Rather than piercing it, the bolt formed into a great ice spike that encased several of the spider's legs. The ice bolt immobilized it and dealt four hearts of damage.

The other nineteen spiders were making a beeline for her, ignoring Ari and Pan completely. Ari had told her to avoid fighting, but Tasha wasn't sure that was a viable option. She pointed her gunblade at one of the oncoming spiders and pulled the trigger, hitting one of the spiders dead on with a fireball. It didn't even flinch as it took one heart of damage.

She couldn't fight with any effectiveness. Was she supposed to run? Not seeing any other option, Tasha took off, sprinting through the clearing, away from the spiders. She cried out at a sharp pain in her leg and fell to the ground. One of the spiders had hit her with a paralysis attack.

She had already lost two hearts from that hit alone. Though her vision was obstructed by the ground, she could see a debuff indicator reporting that the paralysis would last another ten seconds.

She felt something crawling on her prone body. When she was a kid, she used to have nightmares about spiders crawling all over her while she was unable to move, and it had terrified her. That wasn't her anymore, though; that was the original Tasha. She was still frightened, as anyone would be, but she wasn't panicking.

Fortunately a moment later she heard Ari's voice, and the feeling abated. Once the paralysis left her, she scrambled to her feet and saw Aralogos land a drop kick on one of the spiders, killing it. He grabbed the legs of one of them and threw it across the clearing, but it got back up a moment later.

Pan nocked another bolt with a green end and aimed it directly at her. She fired, and Tasha felt a blunt impact from the hit. As the bolt hit her, she was surrounded by a warm glow. The pain in her leg from where the spider had shot her was gone. The combat log said that Pan had hit her with a healing arrow.

Three spiders were still focused on her, and one of them spat poison. She twisted out of the way just as the slimy mass of poison shot through the air past her.

Another one dived at her, and she swung at it, dealing half a heart of damage while knocking it away. Tasha clearly couldn't harm them, but at least she could use her blade to defend herself. Other than being used as bait, she wasn't much more than a liability during this battle.

A steel-tipped arrow hit one of the spiders in front of her, and it died screeching in pain before vanishing into mist. Tasha checked the combat window, and it showed that only six of the enemies had been defeated, but several had taken damage.

She focused on defense for the rest of the battle. The remaining spiders were focused on her and attacked her with poison shots and physical melee attacks. It was all she could do to avoid being hit.

Pan was firing a barrage of steel bolts into the same enemy, slowly draining its health until it eventually died and faded into ethereal mist. It only took her about seven seconds to reload each bolt, but in battle, seven seconds was a lot of time. While Pan was doing that, Ari was attacking another one with a flurry of kicks and punches. The one Ari was fighting targeted him but was quickly defeated.

Pan and Ari finished off the remaining spiders, and the battle ended. Tasha drew a deep breath, relieved that the danger had passed. A moment later, a window appeared before her:

> **Victory! All enemies have been vanquished.**
> **+340 experience gained. (597 to next level)**
> **63 GP found.**
> **Level up!**
> **You have reached level 6.**

You have 4 unassigned stat points.

Choose either a heart container or a mana container.

Pan smiled and said, "Level nine."

Tasha held out her palm for a high five, but Pan just looked at it, confused. "You're supposed to hit it with your own palm. It's means victory!"

The small girl carefully touched her palm to Tasha's. They would have to work on that.

"Anyway, looks like I'm level 6 now."

A magic vial and heart container floated in front of her. So far she'd focused on health, but maybe she should invest in magic. As it was, she couldn't get more than three fireballs off before running out of mana.

She chose the mana container and put four stat points into agility. She decided to focus on intelligence the next time she leveled up. Right now, Tasha needed to be able to dodge enemy attacks, and a higher agility would help with that.

As she did this, her muscles became more toned, and she felt more vibrant. Tasha wondered how high she could jump.

Well, there's only one way to find out.

It was time to test out her new agility. Crouching down, she leaped high into the air and saw the ground race away from her. A moment later, she slammed her head into a branch of the tree above her, flipped through the air, and slammed into the ground. Naruto had always made it look so easy.

Getting back to her feet, she rubbed the bump on her head where she'd hit the branch. That branch was at least three meters above her. She tried again, this time looking above her before taking the jump. She reached up and grabbed the tree branch, pulling herself up with ease. Tasha wondered if she might be able to jump through the trees ninja style with a few more agility upgrades.

"So... is this going to be a thing?" asked Ari. "Every time you level up, are you going to show off jumping and acrobatics?"

"Yeah, most likely," Tasha admitted, jumping back to the ground and landing safely on her feet.

The next random encounter didn't spawn for just over an hour. Tasha still wasn't able to do more than one or two points of damage to the spiders and left most of the work to Ari and Pan. Honestly, she felt like an NPC in an escort quest. She had managed to get her Dodge ability to level 3.

By that evening, Tasha had made it to level 7. She took another mana container and socketed two more points into agility and two into intelligence. She didn't feel especially smarter, but she couldn't be sure. Her attempts at doing some long division in her head were unsuccessful. She would need to put many more points into intelligence before getting that Mensa qualification. Pan had reached level 9 and Ari said he was just a few fights away from reaching level 12.

Upon reaching level 7, an additional ability unlock prompt appeared:

Ability Unlocked: Stat Shuffle (Level MAX)
Type: Active ability (Player specific)
When invoked, all earned stat points may be reallocated. 15%
of earned stat points are lost for the duration of this effect.
After five minutes, all stats are returned to their original state.
Cooldown: 12 hours

Now this was kickass skill. It would let her min/max her stat points to fit the situation. It was a double-edged sword, though. She would lose 15% of her stat points, making her weaker than she would be without it. On top of that, there was a twelve-hour cooldown, which would severely limit its battle effectiveness. Maybe there was some way she could use it to her advantage in the future.

She still couldn't deal enough damage to the enemy to contribute in a useful way, but she was able to dodge the spider's attacks with relative ease thanks to her high agility stat and her level three Dodge ability. The battles were exclusively against spider-type creatures of varying size.

Each battle yielded experience points, GP, and the occasional cylinder that contained loot. Most of the loot were common dropped items. One of the capsules contained several packets of instant coffee, for which she was greatly appreciative.

Denver hadn't been participating in the battles. Considering his low level, that was probably for the best. Whenever battles started, he ran off into the woods and rejoined the group when everything was clear.

There was one unfortunate incident. During one of the battles, Tasha shot a fireball at one of the spiders, but the creature dodged, and the fireball instead hit up some foliage behind it. Fortunately, they were able to get the fire under control before it burned down the entire forest.

After their fire-fighting episode, Ari suggested that Tasha hold off on shooting fireballs while in the forest.

"Yeah, I get it," Tasha said. She made her voice deeper. "Only I can prevent forest fires." Pan and Ari didn't acknowledge her joke.

The forest was beginning to darken with the setting of the sun.

"How much more f-forest?" complained Pan.

"We should be almost there," Aralogos said, consulting his menu. "But the sun is going to set soon. If we don't make it before then, we'll have to make camp. Trust me when I say that we don't want to face forest monsters at night. They are much higher level and from what I hear, more terrifying."

"But we'll be fine if we set up camp, right?" Tasha said.

"Yeah, the campground spell will protect us from monsters and animals alike. We'll need to find a large enough clearing to set up the camp, though, and this forest has been pretty dense lately."

"You mean we might not even be able to camp in the forest? What kind of monsters show up here at night?"

"Probably something spider based, though I've heard stories about creeper trees and daemon wolves spawning in forests at night."

"Let's just get through this forest as fast as possible," Tasha said as she began speed walking.

Finally she cleared the forest, leaving a line of trees behind her. The western sky was already tinted red, but the sun was little more than a sliver on the horizon. In the distance was a row of dim lights that highlighted a dirt road. She thought she could see the faint glow of campfires in the distance.

Ari pointed at one of the lights. "Those lights are from the waystones, which protect travelers. Monsters can't spawn near them."

"I bet we could reach it in ten minutes if we hurry," she said.

"No," said Aralogos, "look around you. The mist around us is thick. We're about to be attacked by monsters, and the sun has almost set. If we move, we'll be attacked before we reach the road and the protection that it offers."

She could tell that this was true. The telltale swirls of purple were surrounding them. How had she not noticed it before?

"We could just make camp here and go the rest of the distance in the morning," she said.

Ari looked uncertain. "Campgrounds aren't cheap. They cost money. That's why I wanted to reach the road by nightfall. We can set up camp by the waystone without wasting one of the mobile campgrounds. They cost 200 GP each. That's money that we could spend on food or weapon maintenance."

She wondered for the first time just how badly off Ari and his daughter were. A pang of guilt stung her; they had been taking care of her, and so far all she'd been to them was a burden.

"What if we ran? We don't try to fight whatever monster appears, we just run as fast as we can to get to those lights."

He thought about her suggestion. "That might work, but it's risky. If the mobs can move quickly or are projectile users, they might kill one of us before we reach safety."

Pan pointed at the sunset. "Sun isn't g-gone."

"If we start running right now," Tasha said, "we might be attacked by mobs before the sun is fully set. Then we'll be attacked by enemies that we can beat."

Ari made his decision. "All right, let's go now. Everyone run!"

They broke into a sprint, making for the road, and after about five minutes they were attacked at the halfway point. Unfortunately it seemed that the sun had already set and the creature that formed around the party was an enormous spider, only this one was as large as a house. It raised its razor-blade arms and let out a paralyzing screech.

Tasha glanced at the combat window. The enemy's name was Spider Queen and her level was twenty-nine. It had fifty heart containers, and her name appeared red in her HUD.

"Run!" cried Aralogos, and he and Pan darted for the lights in the distance. Tasha stood, momentarily frozen in fear. For several long moments she couldn't drag her gaze away from the terrifying creature. It screeched at her and approached. Finally she came to her senses and turned around, running away from the horrific monster as fast as she could.

The Spider Queen fired some webbing at Tasha. The sticky webs caused her to collapse and pinned her to the ground. She squirmed against the webbing, but the spider silk vines were pliable and stuck to her skin. She couldn't snap them or break free. Her gunblade was still in her hand at her side, so she pulled the trigger, engaging the gun's trigger action "Firestorm." The effect only lasted a moment, but it caused the webbing to catch fire, and she tore herself free. Some of the burnt webbing reached her left leg, scorching her flesh.

She stumbled back up and hobbled on her good leg as rapidly as she could. In the distance, Pan and Ari had almost made it to the safety of the road.

The Spider Queen spit at Tasha while she was running and hit her in the back with some kind of corrosive spit. Tasha didn't stop running, but the acidic liquid burned through her bathrobe and into her back. Even so, she didn't stop running. If she weren't hobbling she might have been faster than the spider, but as things were, it was only a matter of time before it caught up with her.

The light post along the road was only a few dozen meters away. Tasha looked back and saw the enormous spider looming over her. She wasn't going to make it. The monster shot more webs at her, wrapping her body in strands of spider silk. Her gunblade slid from her hands and fell to the ground. The Queen stuck Tasha with a stinger, paralyzing her and causing her body to go numb. After a moment, the pain from the acid eating away at her back receded, replaced by the panic of not being able to move.

The Spider Queen lifted Tasha into the air and began to spin webbing around her in a cocoon-like web. Tasha weakly tried to struggle, but it was to no avail. Her hands wouldn't respond to her commands, and her awareness of the world around her was fading.

A bolt of fire flew through the air above her, and the webbing broke from the Spider Queen's hold, causing Tasha to fall to the ground.

As she started to fade out of consciousness, Tasha saw Pan and Ari racing toward her. Her eyes started to shut of their own volition. For a time she faded in and out of awareness. She felt hands lifting her, and someone placed her upon Denver's back.

Moments later, she was moving away from the battle. Aralogos was fighting the Spider Queen on his own, landing kicks and punches on the creature. Her eyes shut, and when they opened again, he had been impaled by one of the Spider Queen's blade-like appendages. Blood dripped from where he was stuck as he was raised in the air. His body went limp in the Spider Queen's grasp, and she threw him to the ground.

Tasha saw nothing else before her consciousness faded.

CHAPTER 12

A Song of Bacon and Pancakes

Light shone through a thin curtain, casting rays into the dust-filled hotel room. Tasha blearily blinked her eyes open. It was still far too early in the morning for rational thought. Slowly her memories of the previous night's events began to trickle back.

Her heart sank as she remembered the previous night's encounter with the Spider Queen. How it had poisoned her and wrapped her up in webbing. How Ari had been impaled, saving her from what she imagined to be a fate worse than death.

She sat up in the bed and found a tear was trailing down her cheek. Other than her parents, she couldn't imagine anyone caring about Tasha enough to give their own life, but Ari had done so without hesitation.

She took in her surroundings. She was alone in a small room with two beds and a single exit. Her bloodstained bathrobe was folded and placed on the dresser. Someone had brought her here.

There was commotion coming from beyond the room's single door. She stood up, but as she was about to open the door, the handle turned and the door opened. Aralogos stood framed in the entrance.

"Ari, you... you're alive."

"Yes, of course I am," he said.

"But... I don't understand. I saw the Spider Queen impale you. Your heart containers were drained. I saw you die."

He shook his head. "Do I look dead to you? You... must be mistaken about what you saw. I'm okay. I fought her long enough for you to escape, but she didn't impale me. After we escaped, Denver carried you to the inn. It was fortunate that the town of Bray was less than a mile up the road."

Tasha wiped away a tear and hugged him. "I'm so glad that you're okay."

Ari hugged her back. After a moment, he pulled away. "It's okay, Tasha. I'm not hurt. We all made it away safely."

"Nobody has ever saved my life before. I'll never forget it. From now on, you're my hero."

Embarrassed, Ari actually blushed. "It's nothing, really. Listen, why don't you come out and join us? They're serving breakfast."

Thoughts of food quickly changed Tasha's mood. "I'll be right out."

Ari nodded and closed the door. As she retrieved a bathrobe from the dresser, another article of clothing caught her eye. It was the martial-arts uniform that Ari had been wearing the day before. It sat neatly upon the table beside his bed. She picked it up and unfolded it to reveal a large hole through the front and a matching hole in the back. Blood was caked to the fabric around where it was ripped.

It had all been a lie. Ari said that he hadn't been stabbed, but the evidence was right in front of her. She hadn't imagined it. Why was he keeping this from her? Didn't Ari trust her with the truth?

It was time to confront him and get to the bottom of this. She slammed the door open and walked out into the dining room. Ari and Pan were sitting together at a table. Tasha marched up to Ari, stuck out her index finger, and regarded him sternly.

"Ari, there's something I need to ask you, and I want you to be completely honest with me."

Ari looked nervous but tried to meet her gaze. "Okay, Tasha. What is it?"

The smell of freshly cooked bacon and pancakes assaulted her, and she hesitated. "Um... where did that bacon and those pancakes come from, and how can I get some?"

Damn! That wasn't the question that she meant to ask. Her willpower had been broken by the overwhelming power of bacon.

Ari pointed at a buffet-style breakfast table. "Oh, that's what you wanted to know. It's over there. It's a buffet, so take as much as you like."

So hotels in Etheria had breakfast buffets. Neat.

Tasha filled up on pancakes and bacon, allowing cardiac-arrest-inducing levels of butter and syrup to run off the pancakes and onto the bacon. She washed it down with several cups of coffee.

Pan was eating eggs, bacon, and what looked like grits, each of which sat in their own pile. None of the different foods on her plate were allowed to touch each other. She even used different pieces of silverware for each dish to make sure they didn't mix.

By the time breakfast was finished, Tasha had all but forgotten about the Spider Queen and the bloody garment. She wouldn't think about it again for some time.

Aralogos took a sip of his black coffee and said, "After breakfast, I'm going to purchase some provisions and see if I can find a caravan heading to the capital. Pan, why don't you take Tasha to the armorer? Those cloth rags aren't helping you much in combat."

"Shoes?" Pan suggested.

Tasha nodded. "I couldn't agree more."

Her fuzzy slippers were not meant for cross-country travel. Her feet would thank her when she replaced them with footwear optimized for walking long distances over uneven terrain.

Aralogos went off on his own while Pan and Tasha headed into the outpost. Bray was little more than a small walled-off village with an inn, an armorer, and an item shop. A smattering of houses dotted the perimeter.

She was able to easily identify the shops based on the logos inscribed on signs above the stores. The armor shop had the engraving of a shield. The inn that she just left had two engravings—one of a bed and another of a mug since it doubled as a tavern. The item shop that Ari went off to had the engraving of a flask.

One wall was lined with a row of outhouses. Tasha groaned. If there was one thing that she missed from Earth, it was consistent access to indoor plumbing. There were no lines, so she picked one and went in.

Unlike the outhouses she'd seen from her own world, these consisted of a basin that was only a few feet deep, the bottom of which was completely clean and didn't seem to have any obvious mechanism to use to dispose of the waste. It was nowhere near as cryptic as three seashells, but it wasn't quite what she was used to.

There was also a kennel area. Tasha stopped there after her bathroom adventures, wanting to check on Denver. The kennel was surrounded by walls designed to keep the raptors from wandering away. An angled roof covered one side and provided the animals some limited protection from the elements.

About a dozen raptors were lazing about inside the kennel. A few of them were playing, taking turns chasing one another, but most were of them were resting. For a moment Tasha was afraid that she wouldn't be able to recognize Denver amidst the multitude of dinosaurs, but she needn't have worried. As she approached the kennel, Denver got to his feet and ran up to the edge of the fence to meet her.

She patted him gently. "Hey, fella. You really helped me out yesterday."

"Buy a saddle?" Pan asked.

"You mean I can ride Denver like a horse?"

"What is... horse?"

She thought back to yesterday and how he carried her away from the battle. If Tasha attached a saddle, she would be able to ride him much more effectively.

"How much? Do you think they have one at the item store?"

A dwarven man approached from inside the kennel. "Oy, human! Get away from the raptors, ya blistering idiot! If ya mess with the beastie, he's liable to bite yer arm clean off!"

"But this one is my raptor. He's never bitten me."

"Oh, this is yur raptor, is it? And just what manner of digestibles have ya been feeding 'em? He looks like he hasn't had a proper meal in weeks. Raptors can't survive on whatever tree bark and dandelions ya've been givin' him."

"Mostly pizza and cheeseburgers," Tasha admitted. "At least for the last day or so. I don't know what he had before that. I only just got him. You see, I found him in the reconstructed remnants of an ancient temple. He was encased in a magical layer of stone and—"

"Cease yer prattling on, ya senseless dolt. If I had a GP for every fanciful story adventurers bring to me... Well, I figure I'd have at least several GP by now. Listen, ya need to feed yer raptor a more sensible diet. Either let 'em hunt fer his own food, or buy some raptor food. But listen to me: No more bread and no more cheese. Raptors are meat eaters and canna properly digest it. Freshly killed game is best."

"Okay, no more cheeseburgers. Got it."

Pan seemed to have vanished. Tasha could see her hiding ineffectively behind a tree, trying to shield herself from the clearly mentally unsound dwarf. Tasha wondered if the girl might have had the right idea.

"Listen, is there somewhere I can buy a saddle?"

"A saddle?" the dwarf said, somehow personally affronted. "Ya want a saddle? Ya have the look o' someone who's ne'er ridden before."

"No, I haven't," she admitted.

"Better come wit' me, then, an' I'll give ya a quick lesson."

> **Quest: Driver's Ed**
> **Class: Sidequest**
> **A seemingly insane dwarf has offered to teach you how to ride.**
> **Conditions for success: Learn to ride a raptor.**
> **Conditions for failure: Don't do that.**
> **Reward: 40 XP, right to purchase a saddle**
> **Accept or Decline?**

Who the hell was writing these quest descriptions? It must have been one of the Game Designer gods that Ari had told her about before. She tapped "accept," since she had planned to do that anyway.

The dwarf led Denver out of the kennel, and Tasha followed him to an open field enclosed by a wooden fence.

The dwarf attached a saddle to Denver, and she got on. One of her horrible exes used to take her motorcycle riding, and mounting Denver wasn't much different. Denver even helped by lowering his body as she tried to mount him.

She took the reins and said, "Giddy up!" Nothing happened. "Hi-ho, Denver, away! Yip yip? Warp one, engage?"

The dwarf sighed and told her that she was holding the reins completely wrong. He taught her how to use them to steer Denver's head, which would control the direction the raptor moved. She could use the reins to adjust Denver's speed.

At the end of her half hour lesson, she had the basics of riding down. There was surely much more to learn, but this was enough to get her started. The quest completed, and Tasha happily accepted the free XP and paid 140 GP for the saddle. The dwarf assured her that she was getting a bargain, but truth be told, she had no idea what the value of money was in Etheria.

Tasha checked her menu. It showed that she had 510 GP remaining. She wasn't really certain how much that was in relation to anything. What would the GP-to-dollar exchange rate be? Once she got an idea for the cost of things, Tasha could start making some sensible money decisions.

Pan led her to the armor shop. There was a small clothier in the area, but she ignored it, deciding that protective clothing was more important. She also passed by an NPC merchant. Tasha was curious about the NPC, but Pan dragged her past as though the NPC wasn't there. Apparently she'd have to investigate the NPCs of Etheria at another time.

Tasha wanted something that would ameliorate her combat ability and maybe provide some protection. She was getting more than a little tired of just barely surviving enemy encounters on a day-to-day basis.

As they walked, she regarded her torn and tattered bathrobe and sighed to herself. She loved that bathrobe. Well, Tasha had been Arthur Denting it up for long enough. It was time to buy some proper armor. Some chainmail with good full-body coverage would be nice.

Pan led Tasha into the armor shop. The room was filled with different styles of armor hanging on racks set against the walls. She spied a suit of ornate heavy armor set atop a display pedestal. There was a glass display case that housed bracelets, chokers, and other various accessories.

Finally, Tasha found what she had been looking for. Rows of footwear sat upon several rows of shelves. There were heavy iron boots, leather shoes, sandals, as well as a selection of more ornate shoes with high heels. Definitely not those. She would need something that she could move around in quickly.

A beautiful black-skinned elven woman with ghost-white hair was reclined at the checkout counter, reading a book. This was the first elf that Tasha had seen in Etheria, and she did her best not to stare.

Tasha couldn't quite make out the title of the book that the dark elf was reading, but it seemed to be some sort of romance novel, if the images on the cover were any indication. The cover art depicted a bare-chested over-muscled elven man posing majestically with his hair blowing in the wind. She could only guess where the wind was coming from, since he looked to be indoors.

The beautiful elven woman looked up for a moment and locked eyes with Tasha. She screamed "Hey, Ramon! Customer!" and went back to reading her novel.

Tasha turned back to the display and picked up a pair of leather shoes. They looked like they would be comfortable while allowing for some freedom of movement. As she looked at it, an info window appeared above it.

Standard Running Shoes

Class: Armor (shoes)
Speed +3
DEF +1
Style +3
Cost: 40 GP

She turned and looked at a pair of women's iron boots. Another info window appeared:

Standard Iron Boots
Class: Armor (shoes)
Speed +1
DEF +8
Style +1
Cost: 190 GP

She wondered what the stat "Style" was. Maybe it worked in conjunction with her charisma score? Perhaps she needed a certain amount of style to get into fancy clubs.

The other items seemed well outside her price range. But since she was presumably going to be meeting a king, she should at least look halfway presentable. Her funds were limited, so she chose the leather shoes and put the iron boots back on the rack.

There was a section marked "Clearance," but none of the items looked like they would suit her. There was some heavy armor and some gauntlets. There was also a green shirt. Tasha scanned it by focusing on it.

Green Shirt of Translucency
Class: Armor (shirt)
Def +1
Style −2
Cost: 20 GP
Effect: The shirt is partially translucent, causing the covered area to be see-through.

Perhaps this had been a failed attempt at a shirt of invisibility. Whatever the case, it seemed to have no practical value whatsoever.

As she examined the other items, a large elven man with a wide face and shoulder-length hair, presumably the lady's husband, emerged from a back room.

"Yes, sweetie?" he said.

"Don't sweetie me, Ramon," she said. "We have a customer, and you're just lounging around doing who knows what!"

"I was forging armor for us to sell, my beautiful honey bunny," he said.

She held out her hand, silencing her husband. "Nope, don't care. Just see what this human needs. I think it wants to buy some shoes. And remember to mind your manners in front of the customers."

Upon saying this, she leaned against the counter and went back to reading her book.

"Yes, dear," Ramon said and turned to Pan and Tasha. "How can I help you? I see you've picked out some shoes. Would you like to try them on?"

Tasha tried on the shoes, and they fit her feet perfectly. They felt so much more comfortable than her poor bunny slippers. She felt as though she could actually run in them.

Agreeing to the sale, she removed the 40 GP from her inventory by selecting the amount in her inventory screen. Four small silver ten-GP coins appeared in her hand. Being able to take out the exact amount she needed was certainly convenient. Each coin had a GP symbol on one side and the number "10" on the other. She handed the four coins over to Ramon, completing the sale.

For a moment she wondered if she should have bartered for a better cost. Tasha had never been good at bartering, but maybe if she had a higher charisma score she could have worked out a lower price.

"Can you show me some armor?" she said. "Something I can move in easily but offers some protection."

Ramon looked her over. "Ah, you're gunblade user, huh? Hmmm... and a couch potato to boot. I would suggest light armor for you, but I'll let you make that decision."

He pulled out a measuring tape and started taking her measurements. This made Tasha feel mildly uncomfortable, but she let him finish.

"I think we have a few pieces that might work for you." He exited through a door toward the back room to retrieve the armor.

Pan was looking intently at a bracelet under the display case. Tasha walked up to the counter and took a look.

Thief's Copper Bangle
Class: Accessory
Chance to steal +25%
Style +3
DEF: 5
Magic DEF: 3
Cost: 600 GP

Tasha could understand why the girl would want that. It would certainly be useful given her profession.

The man returned a moment later with two suits of armor. He set them both upon a counter and showed her the first piece. The first item was heavy armor that would hamper her movement speed, so it wasn't really an option. She examined its stats:

Heavy Plate Iron Armor	
Class:	**Armor**
DEF:	**+24**
Speed:	**-4**
Fashion:	**+12**
Cost: 410 GP	

Having a defensive boost like that was appealing, but she had already decided on an agility build and wanted to be able to move about quickly. "This one's not for me. How about something that doesn't slow my movement speed?"

"No problem," said Ramon. "We've still got one more item that meets your class and level requirements." He brought out a second suit of armor and placed it on the counter.

"Now, this piece of light armor is designed with agility-type builds in mind. It'll improve your movement speed while offering a modest amount of protection."

She examined the item, and a moment later the stat window appeared above the item:

Light Chainmail Armor
DEF: +8
Speed: +2
Fashion: +20
Cost: 340 GP

So the armor somehow improved her movement speed? It didn't make logical sense, but she wasn't about to complain.

The armor was a collection of several pieces of chainmail, which had to be worn together as a set. The elven proprietor handed her the armor, and she took it from him. With her other hand, she opened her equipment screen and replaced the tattered bathrobe and PJs with the armor.

It was certainly convenient and time saving not having to change her clothing manually. Purple threads of mist formed around her as her bathrobe vanished to be instantly replaced by her armor. At least there wasn't a magical girl clothing-change dance sequence. One moment she was wearing her bathrobe and plain white shirt and short pants, and the next moment she was wearing a suit of chainmail armor. Spying a full-length mirror against the wall, she went over and looked at herself.

For several minutes, she just stared at the armor in disbelief. Tasha had not properly seen the shape of the armor before equipping it so didn't really know what to expect.

She described the armor out loud. "It's a chainmail bikini with a single piece of shoulder armor and several pieces of decorative lace."

She didn't normally wear revealing clothing because of her natural body type. She had never been confident in her appearance, but with her stat-augmented body, she was able to make the outfit work. Female body armor in games was a bit of a pet peeve for her, though.

It wasn't actually uncomfortable—there was an inner lining that prevented her bare skin from coming into contact with the metal chains, but she couldn't imagine wearing this for extended periods of time. She couldn't even imagine wearing this monstrosity in public. It had the stats she wanted, and she could afford it, but why did it need to look this ridiculous?

Pan was blushing. "You look f-fine."

"Thanks, Pan, but that's not the point. The purpose of armor is to protect the wearer from being injured. What if the monsters decide to hit me anywhere but the chest area? This armor doesn't make any sense!"

"Of course," said the elven proprietor, "we do our very best to minimize the armor's body coverage while maximizing its stats."

This didn't make the least bit of sense to her. Was there something that she was failing to understand?

"Can you explain that to me? How can the armor protect me if it doesn't cover the areas I'm likely to be stabbed in?"

"By increasing your defense stats, dear lady," he said. "Consider this logically. Were the armor to cover the area where monsters are apt to hit you, the armor might get damaged. I pride myself in creating pieces of armor with high durability, and the only way I can do that is to ensure that it doesn't get hit."

"I... see. So, you design armor specifically designed not to be hit," Tasha said. "I suppose makes a bizarre sort of sense. It's a bit... drafty, though, and it chafes just a bit. What if I catch a cold? Also, I don't see men walking around wearing armor as revealing as this."

As if on cue, the door behind her opened, and an elven man walked in. He was wearing what could only be described as a pair of tight fur underpants that barely covered his private bits and featured a tiny plate chest piece held together by leather straps.

"I stand corrected," Tasha muttered, unsuccessfully trying to purge that image from her mind, but she couldn't unsee it.

The man who had entered walked over to them. "Fair day, friend Ramon. I have come because I wished to compliment you on this armor and perhaps pick up a matching headpiece."

"Of course," Ramon said. "Let me take care of this customer first."

The dark-elf woman who was still buried in her romance novel said, "Don't forget to take the human's money. That's the most important part of any business transaction."

"Yes, dear," said Ramon. "I was just about to do that."

She removed the 340 GP from her inventory, and three large golden coins appeared in her hands along with four smaller silver coins. She handed them to the man.

"Thanks for your purchase, miss," Ramon said and turned his attention to the scantily clad elven man who wanted to buy a hat.

Tasha and Pan left the store and stopped at the clothier, using the last of her meager supply of GP to purchase a set of traveler's clothes and a pair of boots. At least this way she would only have to wear the armor during combat. The menu interface made it easy for her to change clothing simply by using the equip function, or she could set an armor loadout in one of the quick-slots on her HUD.

Having finished her shopping and having run her GP supply dry, Tasha and Pan made their way to the item shop. Ari was waiting outside and came over once he saw them.

"Hi, Pan. Tasha, I've got our provisions and found a caravan that can take us within twenty miles of the capital. It leaves in about an hour. We can ride in the back of one of their wagons if Denver can help pull. We'll also need to pay forty GP per head. Denver will need a harness. Can you pick one up?"

"I picked one up already," Tasha said, "so we should be good. I kind of spent all the rest of my money on clothes, though..."

Ari sighed. "It's fine. I'll cover you. I've still got enough left over."

"Thanks, Ari, you're the best!" She kissed him lightly on the cheek.

Ari blushed. "Don't give it another thought."

She had nearly an hour before the carriage would be ready to leave, so she listened to a random music station on her phone. Eventually "Chariots of Fire" played, unlocking the Sprint skill.

Ability Unlocked: Sprint (Level 0)
Type: Active acrobat ability (unlocks at Level 4)

When invoked, you can run at 200% of your normal speed for 5 seconds. Higher levels will increase sprint speed and duration. Cooldown: 1 minute

Huh, that skill would have been nice to have yesterday *when I was fleeing from the Spider Queen.*

An hour later, they met up with the caravan. It was made up of several dozen carriages riding together, each being pulled by one or more raptors. Once Denver was secured to a harness, Tasha, Ari, and Pan sat in the back of one of the carts, and the caravan departed from the outpost.

CHAPTER 13

Ninja Attack

Princess Kiwistafel was being hunted. She had been traveling with two companions—a dwarven prince named Hermes and the man she had fallen in love with, a paladin named Sir Slimon. The three of them had been close childhood friends, but both of her companions had been killed by the riders in black. The battle window identified her enemies as Human Ninja x34. There had been well over forty, but her companions had managed to kill quite a few of them before falling.

She knew her friends would respawn in a few hours at the castle save point, but she also knew that they would never truly be the same. For the time being, she was on her own, being pursued by a large band of shinobi.

Her raptor, Bessa, was racing away from the oncoming horde at full speed. The sun was setting to her left, and soon it would be too dark to run at this speed. She could see the shadow of Brightwind Keep in the distance, set against the darkening horizon. It was unlikely she would make it before being overtaken.

She leaned in to Bessa, trying to reduce her frame and buy just a little more speed. She pushed her long green hair out of her face and focused on the terrain before her. The legion of shinobi were still gaining and were barely out of spitting distance.

Her eyes began to glow a brilliant white. She held her right hand behind her, toward her oncoming enemies and rapidly wove a pattern with her hand.

"*Fraisha á Krâllinísh!*" she cried, and showers of liquid fire rained down from the sky upon her pursuers. Unfortunately they moved out of the spell's area-of-effect range before taking much damage.

Again her eyes started glowing, and she made another hand pattern. Maybe her explosion array spell would slow them down.

"*Thórbash á Timdâ!*" A torrent of lines arced from her fingertips and formed a line of fiery explosions between her and her pursuers. This time, the impact hit many of them. Her battle notification window showed that the number of enemies had decreased by two and was now down to thirty-two. There was no way she could kill the remaining thirty-two human ninjas on her own.

Less than a minute later, Bessa was struck by one of the enemy's kunai. The raptor collapsed, causing Princess Kiwistafel to smash into the ground, tumbling over and over until coming to a stop. She'd lost two heart containers. Her vision blurred, but she got back to her feet and hobbled over to Bessa. The raptor lay prone on the ground but was still breathing.

The shinobi rode in circles around Kiwistafel. Bessa tried to stand back up, but half a dozen kunai struck her, knocking her to the ground. The raptor gave off one last painful cry and died in the princess's arms.

The ninjas dismounted and started to close in. The princess wiped away the tears that had started to form and opened her eyes, revealing that they were glowing a brilliant white. She tapped something on her HUD, and her oaken staff appeared in her hand. She still had enough mana for her most powerful spell: a wide area-of-effect wind spell designed to be used against armies.

The amount of mana that the Tempest spell called for was high, but she managed to bring it down by several mana points by increasing the casting time and complexity. It would take seven seconds to cast and required her to perform a complex dance as part of the casting ritual.

Her body moved through the dance, flowing in rhythm to the power of her spell. She surrendered her body to dance, her body moving with a clarity of purpose. Her body flowed with a staggering grace that captivated the onlooking shinobi.

One of the ninjas came to his senses and yelled, "She's casting a spell! Stop her!" But it was already too late. Her invocation dance ended in a flourish, and the Tempest spell was invoked. "*Mâhlûr Pendarshî Kaluhûr.*"

The bulk of her remaining mana vanished from her HUD, only a single point remaining. It wouldn't be enough to kill all of her enemies, but she hoped she could take out at least some of them.

The wind rose and spiraled clockwise around her, forming a violent cyclone. Several of the smaller ninjas flew into the air by the sheer force of the wind, and many of the raptors fled or were killed by the storm.

Kiwi checked her combat window. The enemy count was down to twenty-nine enemy ninjas. Now twenty-eight. Twenty-six.

Seconds later, the Tempest came to an end. Twenty-six of the enemy ninjas still remained, and she only had enough magic left for a small spell. She'd killed six of them, but it wasn't enough.

The ninjas weren't trying to kill her; if they were, they would have killed her before now. The fact that they were trying to subdue her rather than take her life indicated that this was a kidnapping. Someone wanted her captured, and she couldn't see any way to escape.

If only she'd died along with her friends, she would have respawned back in the city. As a different person, perhaps, but at least she would be free. As a hostage she would only be a burden to her kingdom and her people, and that was the last thing that she wanted.

One of the ninjas approached her. "It's all over, Princess. You've lost. Just give up, and I promise you won't be hurt."

She looked around her at the devastation. Her friends were dead, her raptor killed, and she was in a battlefield surrounded by a legion of her enemies. There was only one escape from this situation. She checked the battle HUD and saw that she still had six heart containers.

Her eyes again began to glow. The ninjas stepped back and readied their weapons. Princess Kiwistafel held forth her staff and placed her right hand at her own chest. If she couldn't kill her enemies, she would take her own life and escape them through resurrection. There was a massive level cost for an act of suicide, but it was still preferable to being a hostage.

"You shall never have me... *Tétha Lishkâ!*" She cast the only attack spell that she had enough MP to afford.

A bolt of electricity surged from her fingertips and into her chest, filling her body with electrical energy that arced through her and into the ground. The wound in her chest was a blackened patch of skin. Pain rent at her body as she struggled to draw in breath.

The blast had hurt her but hadn't killed her. She had somehow missed her own heart. How had she missed? Even through her blurry vision, she could see her battle HUD clearly. She had gone from six heart containers to half of a single heart container. She was just barely alive.

She fought through the pain. One more shot should do it, but she had no more mana to spend. She tried to raise her hand to bludgeon her own head, but her arm wouldn't respond to her commands.

She could hear laughing coming from the male shinobi who had spoken to her before.

"You lost, Princess," he said. "It's all over. Tie her up and heal her wounds. Take her staff as well; it should be worth a good amount of GP. And our promise not to hurt you? You've just rendered that null and void with your suicide attempt."

She felt hands on her, restraining her hands and legs and binding her legs together.

"We were going to go easy on you, but you just *had* to resist," the voice said.

She had to think of a way to damage herself. In desperation, she bit down hard on her tongue. Through the pain, she watched as the damage indicator went from half a heart to a quarter heart. There was no blood damage.

One more time. She was about to take another bite, but then she felt a warm glow fill her as her health was restored. One of the ninjas had cast a healing spell, restoring her self-inflicted damage. Someone gagged her and covered her eyes.

"Goodnight, Princess," a female voice said in a mocking tone.

The ninjas lifted her limp form and tied her to the back of one of the surviving raptors. Kiwi looked around as best she could. They had lost over half of their raptors and more than a quarter of their shinobi. Getting back to their patron wouldn't be easy, but it was clear the first part of their assignment was done.

A needle pricked into the back of her neck, and she fell into unconsciousness.

CHAPTER 14

Road Trip to Brightwind

Tasha sat on a small bench inside the covered wagon. Pan and Ari sat across from her. Through the window in the back, she made out a line of nearly a dozen raptor-drawn carriages similar to the one she was in.

Each of the carriages was drawn by raptors. Tasha hadn't seen any horses in Etheria yet—it appeared that velociraptors were the primary form of transportation. She couldn't see Denver from where she was, but knew that her raptor was drawing one of the carriages ahead of her.

The driver was an elven man in what Tasha considered to be sensible travel clothing. Tasha, Pan, and Ari were the only passengers, though the rest of the space in the carriage was being used to transport goods, so there wasn't an abundance of leg room. After a few minutes, the gates of the outpost behind them disappeared from view.

Pan looked at Tasha expectantly, so she shrugged and handed over her phone. Pan started up some game and phased out everything else.

The dirt road wound through hilly terrain. Every few miles there was a waystone along the side of the road. The stone pillars were engraved with a rune that emitted a dim glow, visible even during the day. These waystones warded off the mobs, and the caravan didn't spend enough time between them for the random encounters to occur.

This was how the roads provided protection against monsters. Occasionally the carriage passed groups of travelers resting at these waystones. Sometimes there would be tents or merchant stalls set up as well.

Tasha decided to spend some time fine-tuning her fireball spell. As a programmer, she quickly grew familiar with the code syntax and the logic involved in spellcraft. The API manual that she had found in the Temple of the Player enabled her to learn the language quickly.

As a programmer, she was able to quickly acclimate herself to the syntax, and the API reference guide familiarized her with the commands and event handlers that she would need to create simple spells. While she didn't have any other spellbooks, she was able to augment the fireball spell to create guided and higher-yield versions of the spell.

Through her studies, Tasha came to understand that one of the advantages of a gunblade was how it could propel a magic spell at high velocity toward a target. This reduced the mana cost of the spell since most spells expended energy toward the target. The gunblade, as well as other forms of magi-guns, reduced that cost and offered swift delivery of spells.

The only disadvantage to using a gunblade rather than a stave or wand was that gunblades didn't offer any magic-attack boost. In order to deal more damage, she would have to make a spell that consumed more mana points, and for her those were in short supply.

There were ways to reduce mana cost, but those involved increasing the complexity or time spent in casting. She could perform an elaborate dance, recite a series of complex words, or make elaborate hand gestures. Tasha couldn't dance worth a damn, but her many evenings spent reading Tolkien books and watching *Star Trek* had given her the ability to memorize and recite long strings of nonsensical words.

She designed a number of different spells, each of which were triggered by a phrase combined with a gesture. It seemed that the harder it was to perform the spell, physically and verbally, the more mana points it reduced from the cost of the spell.

After some experimentation, she developed a powerful AOE blast that would deal heavy fire damage to anyone in range while knocking people away. The spell would have cost seven mana, but she was able to bring it down to three by giving it a ten-minute cooldown, reducing the projectile's travel speed, increasing the cast time to five seconds, applying a damage penalty for casting it in any direction but north, and by requiring the recitation of a phrase and certain body movements.

She chose to use the body movements and syllables used for the Kamehameha attack in *Dragonball*, one of her favorite animes. During one of the infrequent breaks in their journey, she used the spell interface to record her body movements and voice triggers.

Those restrictions made the spell incredibly inconvenient to use, but it let her cast a more powerful fireball than she would have been able to afford given her limited mana pool of four points.

The couch potato wasn't a caster class, so she was limited to only three active spell slots. There were also API commands that she didn't have access to due to class and level restrictions. She could design as many spells as she wanted but could only bring three of them with her to battle, and swapping them out mid-battle would be too time consuming.

Ultimately she settled on two variants of the fireball spell, which would be triggered by her gunblade in addition to the one high-powered fireball spell. One of the variants was slower but more powerful, and the other did less damage but shot out at a higher speed.

After the first fireball accident back at the temple, she was unwilling to test her work while riding in the carriage. There were infrequent breaks from travel when she could test her creations, but the high-powered fireball spell consumed all but one of her mana points, so she was only able to test it once.

She also added a Fire Line illusion to the two gunblade-triggered spells. These would serve as an aim assist to attenuate her lackluster aim. Whenever she put her finger on the trigger, a red line would extend from the end of the gunblade in the direction it was pointing. It was an idea she got from a popular Keiichi Sigsawa anime she'd been watching. While in use, it consumed only a minute amount of mana.

Her Spell Design ability had been steadily increasing in level as she worked on the spells. By the conclusion of the first day, she had managed to achieve level 3 in Spell Design.

Spell Design (Level 3)
Type: Passive ability
Represents your ability to program spells. Spells that you design yourself receive up to an 8% power bonus and 1.4% cost reduction as a function of the spell's originality. This bonus does not apply to unmodified spells copied from spellbooks.

As evening approached, the caravan made camp around one of the waystones. Tents were set up just off the road around the waystone. Tasha, Pan, and Ari didn't have a tent, so they slept under the stars. Tasha enjoyed it, at least until it started to rain. By the time morning came, she had only gotten a few hours of sleep, and the clothing that she'd slept in was drenched. Getting a quality tent would have to be her next priority.

After learning the fundamentals of illusion magic, an idea for a new spell struck her. It wouldn't be useful in combat but could be of great use for a couch potato like her.

It was a simple magnification spell—an illusion that showed a magnified version of the small object behind it. It also amplified the sound coming from that object. It took her a while to prevent audio feedback, but by that evening she had a fully working version of the spell. Since it was only an illusion, worked in a single direction, and had no effect on enemy mobs, the cost in mana was nominal. She could keep the spell running almost indefinitely so long as she had something to eat or drink every hour or so to replenish her mana.

It was time to put her spell to use. She unlocked her phone and loaded up a video for *The Princess Bride*. Propping her phone upright against a rock, Tasha cast the magnification spell, creating a larger illusion of the phone. The effect of this was that she had turned her phone into a big-screen TV.

She spent the evening Netflixing with Ari and Pan. They started with *The Princess Bride*, which in Tasha's estimation, was the best action comedy ever written. After it was done, a prompt appeared:

Ability Unlocked: To the Pain
Type: Passive barbarian ability (unlocks at Level 14)
Improves aim by 25% when attempting to slice off an
opponent's limb.
You will not be able to use this ability since you do not meet
the level requirements.

She couldn't use the ability yet, but made a note of it in her notebook. After *The Princess Bride*, she played *Labyrinth* followed by *Star Wars: A New Hope*. Partway into each movie, a new ability was unlocked, its description appearing on her HUD. She didn't keep any of them, but if she needed one of these abilities in the future, she could simply watch the associated show beforehand. She added the details of each ability to one of the empty notebooks that she'd acquired in the temple library.

Star Wars: A New Hope – Mind Trick
Type: Active illusionist ability (unlocks at Level 11)
Chance to put an idea into the mind of target with an
intelligence score of 50% or less than the caster.
Cost: 1 mana
Cooldown: 20 minutes

Labyrinth – Gravity Shift
Type: Active time mage ability (unlocks at Level 41)
Allows you to change the direction of gravity subjectively,
enabling you to walk on walls.
Cost: 1 mana per 10 seconds

They were both impressive abilities. After some experimentation, she found that she only needed to watch either show for twenty minutes for the ability to be offered.

On the third day of travel, Tasha was watching the landscape go by when she saw a strange outline in the skies above. If this were Earth, she would have assumed it to be an aircraft, but that wasn't possible in Etheria, was it?

She got Ari's attention and pointed at it. "Ari, is that what I think it is?"

He squinted at it, trying to make out its features. "It is if you think it's a dragon. It's rare to see them this far to the south."

The dragon lowered its altitude and passed right over the caravan. It was now close enough for Tasha to make out some of its details, including its red scales and long tail. It passed right over the caravan and continued on its way, disappearing into the distance a few minutes later.

Ari turned to Tasha. "Did it seem like he was looking for something? The way he flew in close."

Tasha had no idea how dragons normally behaved, so she had no opinion on the matter. After the abrupt appearance and subsequent departure of the dragon, the rest of the morning was largely uneventful.

That morning was spent watching *The Matrix* on Tasha's phone. This unlocked a new ability, which Tasha quickly accepted.

> **Ability Unlocked: Bullet Time (Level 0)**
> **Type: Acrobat ability (unlocks at level 6)**
> **When projectiles are flying toward you, you become aware of them and your perception of time slows down subjectively to 50% speed, allowing you to react.**
> **Duration: 5 seconds**
> **Cooldown: 15 seconds**
> **Would you like to set this as your current ability, replacing Sprint? Yes/No**

She tapped "yes," as an ability like that could come in handy when dodging incoming arrows. The next half hour was spent with Pan throwing crumpled-up pieces of paper at Tasha in order to set off the Bullet Time ability. By the time Brightwind Keep appeared in the distance, Tasha was over a third of the way to unlocking it.

The keep itself was a shimmering skyscraper at the top of a hill in the center of a walled city. The central pillar was tall and imposing, and it was surrounded by half a dozen shorter pillars. Connecting each of the towers was a mesh of circular rings.

After detaching Denver, the trio continued on foot toward the city. They traveled along the road, but Tasha looked longingly at the grassy plains that surrounded the city. It had been days since Tasha had been able to kill anything, and she was beginning to feel the itch. She was also excited to try out some of her new fireball spells in battle.

While she enjoyed returning to her couch-potato roots, some new unfamiliar aspect of her thirsted for combat and the blood of her enemies. Her level growth had stagnated over the past few days.

"Hey, Ari, how about we go off the main road for a while? I was hoping to fight some monsters. I'm starting to feel out of practice."

He shook his head. "I would advise against it. I'm unfamiliar with this area, and it would be bad if we encountered monsters beyond our ability. Once we reach the city, I'll see if I can get a map that we can use for level grinding in the future."

"All right, fine," Tasha huffed.

"Besides, we haven't registered with the local save point. If any of us died, we would have to travel here all the way from the outpost we last saved at."

"That's... also a good point," she agreed, albeit reluctantly.

They continued walking down the paved road toward the castle. Traffic was rather heavy as all manner of people went about their business. Most of the citizens were elven, which made sense as this was an elven kingdom. Humans were clearly in the minority. Tasha passed a party of dwarves all decked out in heavy armor. She hadn't yet seen any female dwarves, though. Maybe their females didn't travel? Alternatively, it was also possible that female dwarves had beards and she'd already seen them without realizing it.

Slimes were fairly common travelers on the road leading to the castle. These creatures had animated, generally smiling faces, and each one was somehow distinguishable from the next either by their shape, color, or the style of hat that they wore. Slimes never wore any clothing apart from the occasional headpiece. Each of them had glowing cores surrounded by a layer of animated goo. They traveled mainly by hopping from one place to another, but she did witness one of them extending a tentacle to pick up a piece of fruit at a vendor's stall.

A bunny woman was traveling with a party of sheep. Tasha thought she might be a shepherd until one of the sheep engaged her in conversation.

A giant, nearly as tall as a house, walked right by Tasha. She looked up and waved at him, and he tipped his enormous straw hat politely.

Eventually the trio of adventurers reached the gates of Brightwind City. A line had formed at the entrance. It was over half an hour before they reached the front of the line.

The elven customs agent at the city gate addressed them, his head resting on his arm. His posture exuded boredom and indifference.

"Oh, great. More human refugees. Just what this city needs. State your name and business, humans."

He adjusted his glasses and took a drink from his latte.

"She's the p-player," said Pan.

Ari actually facepalmed when Pan said this. Maybe they should have agreed on a plan beforehand.

"Just ignore her," said Aralogos. "She thinks her friend is the reincarnation of *the* player. It's just a game they're playing. We're here for work. My name is Aralogos Branford, and this is my daughter, Panela Branford."

Tasha looked at him, surprise evident on her face. "Your name is Panela?"

"Pan," the girl corrected. "Don't like Panela."

Ari continued. "This lady is our friend Tasha Singleton, who is most certainly not a player."

"And what manner of work do you seek?" the elf asked, his face the very embodiment of disinterest.

Tasha took this moment to assert herself. "You know, adventure work. Killing mobs, delivering small packages, rescuing damsels in distress. That sort of thing."

"There be plenty of work to be had given the recent trouble," the customs agent said.

"What recent trouble?"

"The king's daughter was kidnapped several days ago. There haven't been any ransom demands. There's a reward for her safe return or any information leading to her captors."

"Do we have any leads?" Ari asked.

"Make your inquiries at the castle. Off with you," he said, waving them away.

Tasha passed through the large city gates, her friends in tow. The interior of the city was both vast and crowded. It made downtown Manhattan look sparse by comparison. People of a great multitude of races filled the streets, and the foot traffic had no sense of order from what she could discern. Pedestrians had to fight the crowd to get to wherever they were going.

At this rate it would take hours to reach the castle. Movement was slow and arduous. Eventually, they left the main streets, and they could traverse with relative ease. Occasionally Tasha encountered waystones along the city streets.

That must be how they keep monsters away from settlements like this one. They weren't everywhere, though. There were signs that warned against intentionally hunting monsters within the city limits.

It took the better part of an hour to reach the castle entrance. The door itself was immense both in breadth and height. She wondered what kind of creature would need a door that large.

As if in answer to her internal query, a great screeching sound filled the air as four winged dragons emerged from behind the castle and landed at the entrance. Tasha instinctively pulled out her phone and snapped a photo.

The largest dragon grabbed a great cord with his mouth and pulled the great door open. Upon entering, he pulled the door shut behind him. Tasha marveled at the sight and wondered if such fantastic events were commonplace in the city.

"Well, we made it," said Ari. "Let's go in and meet the king."

He didn't seem overly fazed by the dragons.

Tasha passed through the large gate into an open courtyard which was walled off from the rest of the city and served to provide ingress to the keep. The large door that the dragons had used loomed before her on a platform out of reach. A smaller set of doors were set in the wall before her.

She led Denver to a small stable by the courtyard entrance and left him there, promising to return soon.

Statues and island gardens adorned the interior of the open courtyard. There were marble statues of elves, dwarves, dragons, and even slimes. There were no human statues, however. Tasha stopped to take in one of the more prominent elven statues. It read "Princess Kiwistafel Questgiver." The statue was of a beautiful elven woman wearing an elegant gown. Her arms were outstretched to her sides, her palms open. The most distinctive characteristics were her smile and welcoming eyes.

Turning away from the statue, Tasha found several elven guards standing at attention around the courtyard. Ari led the way past the guards toward the smaller set of doors. The stoic guards didn't acknowledge her presence or show any sign that they noticed the party of humans.

Standing at the entrance was a guard wielding a polearm. Tasha focused on him, and his scan results appeared as a small translucent blue box.

Kellarus Evergreen (Level 45)
Guard

There were forty hearts above his name, neatly organized into four rows of ten. If there was any trouble, she wouldn't stand a chance. Not that Tasha was planning on making trouble, of course.

As she was about to pass through the entrance into the castle, the guard named Kellarus moved to block her entrance.

"State your business, humans."

He said the word "humans" with an air of derision.

"We're here to meet with the king on a matter of great urgency," Ari said.

Kellarus smirked at them and narrowed his eyes. "The royal family is not seeing supplicants at this time. Particularly not with human refugee beggars such as yourselves. Maybe you're aware of the oncoming apocalypse, or the kidnapping of the princess? His Majesty has other concerns beyond listening to the troubles of human rabble."

Tasha decided that this would be a good time to add her two cents. "Actually, we're not supplicants or beggars. I need to see the king regarding the menu countdown. I have some information for him."

It turned out that was the wrong approach. For some reason, this guard had it in for humans and was more than willing to take it out on the three newcomers.

"A human beggar has information that is of interest to an elven king? I think not. Now get out of my sight before I decide to arrest all three of you for disturbing the peace. Maybe a few days in a cell will teach you respect for your betters."

"She's the p-player," Pan interjected.

The guard laughed. "A player? Are you serious? I'll give you this, human, that's the most original attempt to gain entrance that I've ever heard. To start with, the player who defeated the Lich Queen is a man, and this is a woman.

"Besides that, someone as important as the player wouldn't be human. Your species barely qualifies as sentient. Now get out of my sight. Your stench is fouling the air."

Ari started moving away, pulling Tasha by the arm. "Let's go. This is getting nowhere."

After moving a safe distance from the guard, Tasha came to a stop. "What was that guy's problem? Is this how humans are always treated in this country?"

Ari hesitated before answering. "For the most part, yes. Most of our kind who reside in Questgivria are refugees from Zhakara, a country that these people have been at war with for many decades. When they see us, they only see the enemy."

"That doesn't excuse his behavior," Tasha said. "I'm not leaving until I get us into the castle. We didn't come this far just to back down now."

Ari just shook his head. "Tasha, trying to force our way in would be tactically unsound."

Tasha let him see her angry face. "Ari, I don't need that kind of negativity."

"Well... okay, Tasha, what do you want to do?"

She thought for several minutes, and slowly the beginnings of an idea took root in her mind. A wicked smile grew across her face.

"Follow my lead," she said. She pulled up her menu and invoked the Stat Shuffle ability. It was time to try this ability out. Properly used, Stat Shuffle could give her the advantage she needed to gain entrance into the castle.

When she invoked the ability, a new window appeared, allowing her to reassign her stat points. There were twenty-four unallocated stat points. Without wasting any time, she put everything into charisma, bringing her up to twenty-eight charisma points.

She would need each and every point of charisma in order to pull off the level of bullshit artistry that she had in mind.

Her body changed again as a result of the stat allocation. She felt taller, more confident, her skin was smoother, and her breasts increased in size and firmness. She hadn't expected that last bit, but it could work to her advantage.

A timer appeared at the bottom of her HUD, letting her know that she had five minutes remaining on her Stat Shuffle ability. Once it elapsed, her stat allocation would return to normal. Not wasting any time, she walked back up to the guard.

"Hey, what are you doing back, human? I thought I told you to get lost. Or are you going to insist that you're a player again?"

Tasha shook her head. "I'm obviously not a player. A player would surely be a strong elven man like you, not a human woman. That's assuming players even existed to begin with."

"Right you are." He nodded. "Which brings me back to my question: Why did you come back?"

"You've been very helpful, but I sense some unhappiness in you. You don't really enjoy this line of work, do you?"

"Well..." he started, "now that you mention it, not really."

He frowned. "It gets rather tedious standing here day after day, hour after hour."

"That must be terribly boring."

"Oh, it is! The highest point of my day is when I get to verbally abuse humans, but even that gets old eventually. I mean, the position pays well enough, but the endless tedium would wear on anyone after a while."

She frowned back. "Why, that sounds just horrible. I take it things weren't always this way for you? You have the look of someone who's seen the world and done great deeds."

He nodded proudly. "Well, you're right about that, human. I once was a great adventurer. It took me centuries of training to reach my current level. I wandered the world seeking adventure and glory. But then everything changed."

Tasha waited a moment for him to continue, but he said nothing.

"Did... you take an arrow to the knee?" she prompted experimentally.

He glanced at his knee. "What? No, of course not. Even if I had a knee injury, a healing potion would have cured it right up. What happened is that I got married. Ah, my dear Gabby. I would do anything for her. Even trade in a life of carefree adventure for a stable income. Mob hunting isn't as lucrative as you might think."

Tasha continued. "But as an adventurer, you would get to see new sights. You wouldn't need to stand in the same place all day. You could fight in glorious life-or-death battles against fierce opponents."

"What you say is true. If only..." he said with a faraway look on his face.

"Well, then, why don't you? Just tell them that you want to quit and follow your dreams. Battle and glory awaits you, brave elf. Gabby would surely understand."

He shook his head vehemently. "Oh, you don't know Gabby! She would drive a knife through my heart if I quit. I mean that literally, you understand. And then when I respawned at the save point, she would do it again for good measure, just to make sure that I learned my lesson."

Tasha could feel herself losing control of the situation. "Maybe Gabby doesn't need to know. Just make sure you get back home before it gets too late in the evening, and she won't know the difference. Once she sees how happy you are, it won't matter what job you've been doing. You can tell her then."

For half a minute, he just stared at her as if deep in thought. Finally he came to a decision. "You know what... you're right! I'm wasted on guard duty. I'll go tell the captain of the guard tomorrow."

"Why not right now?" Tasha prompted. "Time and tide wait for no man— ELF! I meant elf."

He was about to leave but hesitated. "Oh, but I can't leave my post."

Tasha smiled. "Don't worry, friend, I'll take over and guard this entrance while you are away."

He looked her over and said, "A human guard to the elven keep? Well, as long as it's only for a short amount of time, I think it would be okay. Just no sneaky letting people into the castle while I'm gone."

"I wouldn't dream of it," she assured him.

"Thanks. You know, you aren't so bad for a human."

The guard entered the castle and a moment later was out of sight.

> **Ability Unlocked: Bullshit Artist (Level 1/50)**
> **Type: Passive ability**
> **Your lies will now be 5% more creative and people will have an additional 2% chance of believing them.**

Ari came up to stand beside her. "I can't believe that actually worked."

Tasha shook her head in disbelief. "That makes two of us."

"I wonder just how many times Gabby will kill that guard."

"Oh, at least twice. Maybe three times," Tasha said, gesturing for them to proceed through the now open door. As she did so, Stat Shuffle wore off, and her body returned to its previous state. If Ari or Pan were confused about her rapidly shifting body, they didn't say anything.

Tasha had made it into the keep of King Questgiver. Perhaps now she would finally get some answers.

CHAPTER 15

Snickers the Bumble

The castle entrance hall was a large chamber, with more open space than an aircraft hangar. In truth, an aircraft hangar wasn't that far off the mark. She'd seen dragons entering the castle, and this room was large enough to contain many of them. Mighty pillars were spread across the vast room, providing structural support.

After several minutes of walking, Tasha entered the throne room. The throne itself sat upon a platform above a row of stairs. There were actually three thrones: a large one in the center and two smaller ones at either side. The room itself was empty save for a single person sitting upon the large throne. Tasha couldn't make him out, so she approached cautiously.

When Tasha was finally close enough, she realized that this couldn't be the elven king that she had come to see. The man sitting on the throne wasn't an elf or a human. His elongated nose, his loud clothing, and his pure white face all led Tasha to one conclusion: This was the king's jester.

"Um... hello? Who are you? Is the king available?"

The jester looked at her sadly, his eyes drooping and a forlorn look cast upon his misshapen face. He fell back into the king's throne.

"Oh, perchance to be a king,
upon my head a golden crown,
to sit and rule and dance and sing,

151

yet I am nothing but a clown."

Tasha looked to Ari, who just shrugged.

The creature who sat upon the throne noticed her for the first time. His sad expression was quickly replaced by one of unbridled glee. He gave her the largest smile she'd ever seen in her life, an unnatural smile that framed his entire face.

"And now comes a player to visit the king,
what query or portent does this fine lady bring?"

"Who are you?"

He put his feet up on the side of the throne and leaned onto the chair's arm.

"Oh, I'm not but a jester and ever so humble,
well known to the people as Snickers the Bumble!"

Snickers the Bumble? Tasha's mind ran back to the story that Ari had told her days before, the tale of Lorien, the first elven king. He was said to have a servant who only spoke in rhymes. Could this be the same person? If this jester was truly a divine being, she should be careful about what she said.

"Listen, Snickers, I need to see the king. Can you get him for me?"

Snickers stood from the king's throne and said,

"The king is disturbed, distracted, and distraught,
the quiet of solitude is what he has sought.
His daughter was kidnapped by ninjas most vile,
so His Highness will be rather engaged for a while."

"The princess was kidnapped by ninjas?" she said. "The guard did say something about a kidnapping. Ari, if we rescue the princess and return with her, getting an audience with the king should be easy."

"Us, rescue Princess Kiwistafel?" said Aralogos, "I thought you were joking about the rescuing damsels bit earlier. We're not heroes."

Tasha shook her head. "If there is one thing that my many decades of playing video games has taught me, it's that the player's job is to rescue the princess. Snickers, do you know where the princess is?"

> *"I have not the faintest whiff of a clue,*
> *so I'm afraid you will just have to make do.*
> *You could ask her companions, the slime and the dwarf,*
> *they've been searching for clues at the fisherman's wharf."*

"Ask a slime and a dwarf down by the wharf. Got it," Tasha said, turning to leave.

Tasha led her companions in silence through the corridor leading to the castle entrance. Once outside, Ari turned to her. "I don't see how we can rescue the princess. King Questgiver surely has warriors much more experienced than us on the job. This isn't something that people like us can do."

"I'm not sure how we'll find her," Tasha said, "but let's at least try. We can start by finding these friends of hers that the jester mentioned."

"So do we just head down to the docks and look around for a dwarf with a slime?"

"We have to start somewhere," she said.

The elf guard Kellarus chose that moment to appear through the gateway with another guard in tow.

"Well," he said, "I'm off on my life of adventure. Thanks for holding my place, human."

"Don't mention it," Tasha said. "Go forth, young elf. Fame and fortune await you."

The elf proceeded through the courtyard with a smile on his face, carrying a small cardboard box.

CHAPTER 16

Rumble at the Market Square

After leaving the castle, they spent the next half hour walking to the docks. The capital city was set up against a wide river that fed into the ocean.

When Tasha arrived at the harbor, she got her first look at one of the riverboats as it arrived. It was a steam-powered cargo vessel with a large circular paddle at the fore, which cupped the water and propelled the vessel upriver. It was crewed by people who she assumed to be orcs, judging by their green skin, long fangs, and bulging muscles. In their company was also a short lizard woman with grayish-blue scales where there should have been skin. Maybe she was a kobold? It was never clear to Tasha whether kobolds were lizard-like or dog-like in appearance, as that tended to change based on the fiction. They were transporting a number of large wooden crates that were secured to the deck.

After a moment, Tasha realized that she was staring at the vessel and returned to the matter at hand. The docks were massive and sprawling with people. These were people in the most general sense of the term. There were elves all over the place but also orcs, gnomes, humans, slimes, dwarves, bird people, fairies, bunny people, and quite a few other races that she couldn't recognize from any of the fantasy tropes that she was familiar with. There had to be dozens of different races all living and working together under the elven kingdom's protection.

How were they to find two people who they'd never met before in a crowd like this? All she had to go on was that it was a dwarf and a slime—but there were dwarves and slimes everywhere.

"Maybe we should split up," Ari suggested. "Keep an eye out for any slimes and dwarves traveling together. I know it seems rather vague, but that's all we have to go on."

In Tasha's opinion, splitting the party was never a good idea and always ended badly. It also complicated the DM's task, making him grumpy. On the other hand, they were in a friendly city rather than a dungeon. What could go wrong?

"All right," Tasha said, "I'll meet the two of you back here in half an hour."

Tasha then realized that she had no way to tell when half an hour would have passed. Her phone and the game menu both read the countdown at 96:50, and they weren't moving. She would just have to head back when she thought half an hour had passed.

"Bye," Pan said as she ran off into the crowd.

Tasha watched her leave. "Will she be okay by herself?"

"Yeah," said Ari. "She's much tougher than she appears and probably a higher level now than most people in the crowd. She wouldn't have gone off on her own if she felt a breakdown coming. I'll see you in thirty minutes."

As Tasha started walking in the direction of the taverns and shops, she saw a large number of dwarves and quite a few slimes. None of them walking together as a single party, however.

After walking for another ten minutes or so and not seeing anything that looked like the object of her search, she caught sight of something interesting. A cat girl in a black leotard was running down an alley, and she was being chased by a band of brutish orcs. Her face and hands were covered in brown and white fur.

The girl fled from her pursuers, leading them between stalls in the marketplace, right toward the square where Tasha was standing. "Please, someone help me!" cried the cat girl.

In pursuit were five orcs weaving between the market stalls. That's when Tasha saw it. Right beside a bomb seller's stand was a barrel painted red with a black flame outline insignia and the word "EXPLOSIVE" written on it in big bold lettering.

Three potential plans of action sped through Tasha's mind.

1. Attempt to learn more about the situation before acting.
2. Walk away since this clearly has nothing to do with you.
3. Shoot the explosive barrel with a fireball.

Tasha's video game upbringing instinctively led her to choose the third option. Rescuing a cute cat girl from a horde of orcs seemed like a legitimate excuse to try out her new high-powered fireball spell in a combat situation. Besides, she was itching for some combat and hadn't had a chance to fight since Webwood Forest.

She decided to start the fight by going all out while she still had first strike. She checked her compass to confirm that she was facing northward. She began the motions and syllables used in the Kamehameha wave from *Dragonball*. She would have to time the movements and sound cues perfectly. Fortunately, she'd practiced this multiple times in front of the mirror when nobody was watching.

She stepped forward with her left foot and adjusted the placement of her right foot while lowering her center. Both arms went to her right side, and she cupped her hands as she chanted the syllables of the spell.

The cat girl ran straight past her as the orcs began to close the distance. A speck of light appeared in her cupped hands and grew in size and intensity. This part of the spell was just an illusion, but making a good impression was key in any encounter.

The orcs had come to a stop right next to the explosive barrel. One of the orcs pointed at her. "Watch out! I think that human is spellcasting."

As her incantation completed, she put both arms forward toward the gathered orcs. A ball of energy wreathed in blue flames emerged from her outstretched hands and flew at the gathered orcs. The summoned projectile was slow moving, taking over a second to reach them, but even so, it struck one of the orcs head-on. The resulting explosion hit the gathered orcs, and the splash damage caused the barrel to explode, dealing even more damage. The heat wave from the explosion reached her even where she was standing. The orc who had been struck lay dead on the ground, killed by the fiery impact.

Quest: A Meow-nificent Rescue
Class: Sidequest
Help the mysterious cat girl escape from the attacking orc horde.
Conditions for success: The cat girl escapes pursuit.
Conditions for failure: The cat girl is captured or killed by the pursuers.
Reward: 80 XP

"I've got this, just run!" Tasha said.

"Thanks, stranger. You're saving me from being captured. I won't forget it," the cat girl said and ran off.

They were trying to capture her? Maybe they were somehow connected to the princess's disappearance. Tasha had expected ninjas, but for all she knew these could be hired hands.

"She must be an accomplice." The orc who was leading the chase pushed himself back to his feet. "Get her!"

The remaining four orcs charged straight at her. They were all large, angry, heavily armed, and each had excessively manly facial hair. Tasha instinctively took a step away but knew that if she didn't stand her ground, the orc kidnappers might still catch the cat girl. They needed to be stopped here.

Her eyes were drawn to the corpse of the dead orc on the cobblestone floor. This was the first time that Tasha had killed someone who wasn't a product of the ether. She'd just killed an actual *person*, and his body wasn't vanishing. She hadn't felt guilty about killing mobs since their bodies vanished and they didn't look or act like real people. This orc had a look of fear on his face when she'd killed him, something no mob had ever displayed.

She froze, shocked by what she had done. The dead orc stared at her in judgement with dead eyes. In her hesitation and inaction, she was very nearly hit by a thrown axe. She managed to dodge just in time.

Now isn't the time to lose your nerve, Tasha. I just need to think of these as any other enemy.

Gathering her determination, Tasha lifted her gunblade and aimed it at the nearest orc's head. She pulled the trigger, but nothing happened. A tone indicated that she didn't have enough mana. That one high-powered fireball spell had left her with under a single mana point, and it wouldn't refill until she had something to eat. She should have enough left over to use the firestorm trigger action a handful of times. For the rest of the battle, she would have to rely on her sword skills and her wit.

There were four orcs still before her. Tasha checked her battle window. Three of them were level 5, and one was level 6. Her surprise fireball attack had damaged each of them, but they still outnumbered her four to one. She had made it to level 7, which only gave her a slight level advantage. Each of her opponents were disoriented.

The nearest orc was holding axes in both hands. He swung one of them at her in a downward arc, but Tasha successfully deflected it. She tried to dodge his other axe, but the blade hit her in the left shoulder. When the axe hit her, there was a momentary barrier that slightly reduced the axe's velocity. She only lost three quarters of a heart container from the impact.

It hurt like hell, but Tasha was surprised that it hadn't done more damage. Was this because of the defense stat on her chainmail bikini? She had just been hit with an axe by an expert fighter with more muscles than anyone she'd ever met, but the blow had barely scratched her. The pervy armor salesman had been on point about how actual body coverage didn't matter in terms of damage absorption.

She jumped back, putting some distance between her and the orc who had struck her. The other three orcs had formed a circle around her. This wasn't good. She couldn't defend from all sides at once. They were using tactics in combat—bad guys weren't supposed to use actual combat tactics! They were supposed to line up and wait patiently for their turn to attack. Apparently these orcs hadn't gotten the memo. How inconsiderate of them.

An orc charged her from the right. She turned as he raised his warhammer, preparing to bring it down on her head. Tasha saw movement out of the corner of her eye. A second orc was charging from behind, his buster sword drawn. Before Mr. Warhammer could reach her, she stabbed him in the heart with her gunblade. Unfortunately, impaling him in the heart didn't kill him. He still had heart containers left.

Tasha tried to liberate the sword from the orc's chest, but the blade was stuck and wouldn't budge. Tasha jerked forward from a sharp blow to her back as the buster-sword-wielding orc sliced her for three hearts. She screamed and fell to the ground, a puddle of blood forming around her. A bleed debuff appeared on her HUD, informing her that an additional half heart of health would be lost per minute. The impact had knocked the breath from her, and she struggled to draw in uneven breaths.

She forced herself back up to her feet and, unarmed, took stock of her enemies. There was the guy dual-wielding axes who'd damaged her for just under one heart container and the buster-sword guy who'd hit her for three hearts. The remaining orc was standing away from the battle, not approaching.

Mr. Buster Sword swung the weapon at her, but his moves were so slow and easy to read that Tasha was able to step out of its way.

Suddenly, time slowed down to half its normal speed. Tasha could see the buster sword slamming down onto the cobblestone. From the corner of her vision, another axe was flying toward her head, spinning rapidly. Her Bullet Time ability must have been invoked by the projectile, slowing her perception of the passage of time.

It felt like trying to run through a sea of marmalade. Her body was moving but at the same slow speed as everything else. Though her perceptions were faster, her body wasn't. Tasha focused on leaning back and lifting her hand into position before the axe arrived. Catching the axe in midair, she leaped into the air and threw it at the buster-sword orc, opening a shallow cut in his neck and knocking him to the ground, his enormous sword knocked aside.

After landing, she performed a *Dark Souls*-style roll away from the remaining orcs. From the ground, she picked up a piece of cobblestone and threw it at Mr. Dual Axe's head, knocking him unconscious. That orc's health was already low, so that was enough to knock him out.

The orc who had dropped the buster sword went to pick it up, but Tasha moved between him and his sword. Giving up on getting his sword back, the orc shouted, "I'll get help, just hold her off." With that declaration, he ran off.

Mr. Warhammer was still struggling on the ground, her gunblade impaled in his chest. That just left one remaining orc, the latecomer who hadn't joined the fight.

Tasha ran back to her gunblade and set one boot on the dying orc for leverage. She pulled on the sword, yanking it out of his chest. Blood spewed, and he fell to the ground, dead.

Seeing his allies all either killed or unconscious, the final orc pulled out twin cutlasses.

Towering over her, Mr. Cutlass stabbed down with both blades. She rolled out of the way, but not without one of the cutlasses tearing into her left leg. Tasha was able to stand, but it was painful. That one hit brought her down to one heart container. A familiar tone began to play in her head.

Beep beep. Beep beep. Beep beep.

"Yes, I know I'm almost dead. Thanks for the reminder," she mumbled. Blood continued to pour onto the cobblestones from her open wounds.

The orc lowered his weapon and grinned. "You fought well, but it's over. Come quietly, and I won't kill you. You may have the level advantage, but I still have plenty of health, while you are barely alive."

Tasha spit at the ground in front of him. "I'll never surrender to kidnappers like you! Death first!"

"As you wish, human," he said. "Though why you would think us kidnappers is a mystery to me."

He rushed at Tasha with both cutlasses drawn and prepared to strike. She picked up a piece of cobblestone and threw it at his head, but he just tilted his head to one side, dodging the incoming rock. Both cutlasses came down in a vertical strike, and she put up her sword to deflect them. Both swords impacted with her gunblade and sliced right through it, shattering it into multiple pieces. The remains of her gunblade clattered to the ground.

Not having time to mourn her poor lost weapon, she scrambled backward and got to her feet. Blood continued to spill from her wounds, painting the cobblestones red. Her sword was gone... what could she use? The buster sword was lying on the ground next to her. She hadn't been strong enough to wield buster swords before, but she had a higher strength stat now. Maybe she could use it.

Unlike her earlier attempt, this time she was able to actually heft it, though it took a significant amount of effort. Tasha couldn't use it effectively as a weapon since she lacked the raw strength needed to swing it freely. But if she couldn't use it as a sword, maybe she could use it as something else.

Holding its immense weight in both hands, Tasha began to swing it around in a circle. Sparks flew as the sword scraped along the cobblestone ground. She spun it around faster, the centripetal force lifting the enormous blade up off the ground. Eventually it came to shoulder height, its speed increasing with every revolution.

Mr. Cutlass was still holding back, not daring to get too close to the rapidly spinning buster sword of death. The muscles in Tasha's arms were reaching their breaking point, and she was getting dizzy from spinning around so many times in rapid succession, already weak from blood loss. The marketplace was a vague streak in her vision, and her foe was a blur that appeared once every revolution.

When Tasha felt that the sword had accumulated as much kinetic energy as it was going to, she waited until just the right moment to release it. Finally, its tangent was just right, and she released the buster sword's handle.

The blade flew through the air, spinning around its center of gravity toward the onlooking orc. The orc held up his cutlass to block it, but the momentum of the buster sword just knocked it away and continued on its flight to cut through the hapless orc, dealing three hearts of damage and knocking him to the ground.

Tasha was still dizzy but scrambled to pick up one of the cutlasses. She rushed over to the dazed orc and stabbed him in the gut over and over. Each hit did less than a heart of damage, but she hit him repeatedly until finally he died.

Tasha collapsed to the ground in exhaustion and dizziness as the combat log appeared:

Victory! All enemies have been vanquished.

+271 experience gained. (769 to next level)

Level   **up!**

You   **have**   **reached**   **level**   **8.**

You   **have**   **4**   **unassigned**   **stat**   **points.**

Choose either a heart container or a mana container.

Ethereal mist covered her body, and she was instantly healed from her earlier damage. Although it felt like a long drawn out battle, it really couldn't have taken more than three or four minutes. Most of the surviving citizens had cleared out, and a good portion of the plaza had been destroyed. Tasha found herself wondering when the city guard was going to arrive to arrest the kidnappers.

She looked sadly at the shattered remains of her gunblade. Saying a fond farewell to Kermit, Tasha turned back to the heart and mana container that floated in the air.

Thinking carefully, Tasha decided that as much as she would love to have more health, she was relying more and more on magic and needed to be able to cast more spells per battle.

As Tasha reached out to take the mana container, she found her body being lifted into the air. Her hand brushed against the mana container, causing it fall to the cobblestones with a clunk.

A squishy blue tentacle had wrapped itself around her waist and held her aloft. Tasha panicked for a moment as the ground rushed away from her. Looking to the source of the tentacle, she saw an ovaloid blue slime below her.

A moment later, the tentacle flung Tasha at the ground. She crashed against a vegetable stall, shattering it and sending cabbages flying everywhere. The impact cost her one of her heart containers.

"Hey!" she said, getting back to her feet. "What's the big idea? Are you with them?"

A dwarf arrived on the scene and stood next to the blue slime. He looked like many of the other dwarves that she had seen wandering the city. He had red hair and a red beard in an elaborate braid. Unlike many of his kin, he did not have much in the way of ornamentation. In fact, he only wore a single gold ring on his right hand.

The most distinguishing characteristic of this dwarf was the fact that his left arm was missing. In its place was a large metallic six-barrel machine gun. She wondered how the dwarf's minigun arm attachment operated.

Her curiosity was cut short by the dwarf's reply. Like all dwarves since the advent of Tolkien, he spoke with a Scottish accent.

"Of course we're with them. I just arrived, but I still saw enough to know that you killed these people. Now, tell us what you know if you want to live."

"You're with them? These are the kidnappers. I was about to interrogate Mr. Dual Axe over there."

"No, girl," he said. "These orcs aren't kidnappers. They're the city guard. Didn't you notice their badges? They were chasing one of the ninjas, and you helped her escape. Tell me where the princess is or die where you stand."

Whoopsie.

"Listen," she said, "I don't know where the princess is. That's why I'm here. I'm looking for clues."

"I don't believe you. Everyone knows that orcs serve as the bulk of the city's police force. Their badges have the word '*police*' on them. Nobody could be that stupid."

"I wouldn't be too sure about that," Tasha protested as the dwarf's machine-gun arm began to spin up. Tasha had the feeling that their conversation about to take on a more murderous tone.

From somewhere in her head, Tasha could hear boss battle music starting to play. The dwarf and slime appeared in the combat menu. The dwarf was a level 9 machinist and the slime was level 8 paladin.

Though she'd reached level 8 she hadn't had time to allocate her stat points, so she might as well have been a level 7.

As the minigun spun, it emitted a whirring sound. She took that as her cue to start running. Bullets shot out at an incredible rate, reducing the cabbage stand behind her to a mess of splintered wood, ruined vegetables, and shattered dreams.

Tasha continued running, and the line of bullets continued to spray just behind her, penetrating the building where she was standing. The bullet-riddled sign above the building read "Saint Sara's Home for Orphaned Children".

The gunfire had almost caught up to her, so she dove to the ground, and the spray of fire passed over her head, continuing above her and incinerating a bookseller stand. Ripped pages flew everywhere.

Though Tasha had avoided most of the bullets, a few of them hit her and cost another heart container.

Thinking quickly, she leaped into the air toward the dwarf, *Crouching Tiger Hidden Dragon* style. His gunfire tried to follow her, bullets spraying into the orphanage behind her. As Tasha reached the apex of her jump, a tentacle lashed out at her. She double jumped out of the way, just barely avoiding the tentacle.

As Tasha landed, she invoked Sprint and rushed at the dwarf. Tentacles lashed out furiously, but she dodged between them. The dwarf was lowering the minigun, and the spray of bullets was almost pointed at her when she reached him. Tasha dodged behind him and put the cutlass to his throat.

She leaned into him and said, "I have an idea: How about you stop shooting up the marketplace, and I'll stop murdering orc guards, and we can discuss this like civilized people. How does that sound?"

The dwarf nodded, and his minigun vanished from his left hand, revealing a metallic nub where his arm ought to be. The slime retracted its tentacles into its body, returning to its earlier ovaloid shape.

Tasha lowered her cutlass. "I didn't kidnap the princess. I'm trying to find her. I only came here to find you two because the court jester told me you might have information."

"What about the ninja you let escape?" he demanded.

"I didn't know she was a ninja," Tasha said, exasperated. "I thought she was just a cat girl who was being chased by kidnappers. She said the orcs were trying to capture her. When I see cute cat girls being chased by orcs, I need to rescue them, okay? I'm sorry, but that's just how I was raised."

"You can't kidnap a kidnapper," the dwarf said, crossing his arms.

"Why not?"

"You just can't. So you just let the kidnapper go and murdered half a dozen city guard by accident."

Tasha pursed her lips. "Yeah, seems that way."

A moment later, a dozen more orc guards arrived on the scene. Unlike the low-level guards she had fought just a moment ago, these were all level 30-70. She wouldn't stand much of a chance against even a single one of them.

"What happened here?" said the largest of the guards.

"I saw the whole thing," said a small elf who was hiding behind one of the few intact stalls. "This woman helped a fugitive escape justice and killed all of these guards."

"That one's not dead," Tasha said, pointing at Mr. Dual Axe. "Also, one of them ran off."

"Listen, I think there may have been a misunderstanding," said the dwarf.

The elf continued, his face turning red. "And then this guy pulled out some kind of machine gun and started shooting up the place. He destroyed *everything*! The once beautiful marketplace is in shambles. Even the orphanage behind me is now riddled with bullets. I think the two of them were working together."

The orc guard pulled out a pair of metal handcuffs. "Well, I've heard enough. You are both under arrest. Please don't resist. Hasn't the city seen enough death and devastation for one morning? Hand over your weapons and surrender."

Tasha dropped the cutlass and didn't resist as the guards secured her hands behind her back. They were similar to handcuffs but didn't have a locking mechanism. She figured they required some sort of magical key.

"But I don't wanna go to jail," she protested.

As Tasha was led away, she realized that her half hour was probably just about up. She wouldn't be able to meet Ari and Pan after all. She could only hope that they would visit her in prison.

CHAPTER 17

The Slime Who Loved Me

Ninety-two years ago

K ing Iolo Questgiver paced in circles outside of the save point just beyond the inner walls of the capital. Stars dotted the night sky, and only moonlight and the save point's faint glow provided illumination.

"What is taking so long? It's been six hours. How long does this usually take?"

His wife, Queen Kiwano, had come to the end of her three-year-long pregnancy and was in the throes of childbirth. For her safety and the child's, the birthing was being performed at the save point just outside the capital. Generally speaking, elven women could only give birth on save points when complications were expected, but due to the unborn child's importance to both the realm and to the king himself, an exception had been made.

He was confident that the child was going to be a boy. There were spells and technologies that could divine the child's birth, but his wife steadfastly refused to use any such thing. She didn't want to know the child's gender until after the birth, and the king had relented. Even so, Iolo was certain that his child was going to be a boy who would grow into a strong and wise king. A king who would lead the elven people into the future. Fathers had a sense about this sort of thing.

The queen was hidden behind a curtain that offered her some privacy. Elves as a race were not a prudish or modest people, but the queen and midwife had both decided that a modicum of privacy was appropriate.

One of the king's advisors approached him. "Perhaps Your Majesty could return to the castle. There's no way to know how long this might take. It's not unheard of for elven childbirth to go on for days. There is work to be done on integration negotiations. The counter proposals with the hill dwarves and dark elves still need your attention. You know how important this is to our survival as a race."

He was distracted from what the advisor was saying by his wife's cries of pain. "I... believe I will stay with my wife. Bring me the counter offer from the hill dwarves, and I'll review it over here."

The advisor wasn't wrong about the importance of the unification and integration of non-elves into the kingdom. Their war with the humans would inevitably lead to their defeat and ultimate enslavement if nothing was done. During battle, humans from Zhakara captured elves, imprisoning and enslaving them. The elven population decreased every year, and it was but a matter of time until humans won the war through the slow process of attrition. Elven births were rare, celebrated events. Elven women didn't reach childbearing age until well past their five hundredth year. Humans, on the other hand, multiplied their population at a rapid and exponential pace.

Unifying the kingdom with non-elven races and integrating them with their people was the only way for them to survive long term. Perhaps Zhakara would hesitate before attacking a unified kingdom.

Before the advisor returned from his errand, the sounds of childbirth abruptly stopped and were replaced by the cries of a newborn child. Iolo pushed his way through the queen's personal attendants and into the save point, where his wife was waiting. Queen Kiwano held the newborn child, a look that somehow combined extreme exhaustion, satisfaction, and motherly joy all at the same time.

"She's so beautiful," Kiwano said. The baby had a small tuft of green hair, just like her mother's, and emerald eyes.

"Yes, she is," Iolo replied. His earlier hopes about the child being born male were already forgotten. He held out his arms, and the queen let him hold their newborn daughter.

"Does she have a name?" asked the midwife.

The queen turned to her. "Her name is Kiwistafel."

The small elven child raised her right hand. Her eyes began to glow faintly.

"*Fraisha ûl!*"

A ball of fire formed in the air before her and flew toward the training dummy. Before the fireball could reach its target, its intensity diminished, and only a small flickering ember hit the target, bouncing away and falling to the stone floor.

Princess Kiwistafel stomped her foot. "It's not working."

The dark-elven sorcerer looked at her, his disappointed eyes partially obscured by his long white hair. "Drink a mana potion and try it again."

"But it isn't working, Magus!"

"You should be able to incinerate that target even with the meager amount of mana you have at your disposal. When you draw mana, focus on channeling it through your entire body rather than simply from your core."

"That's what I've been doing, but it's not working."

Savik D'hagma was the high magus from the dark-elven city-state of Gothmër. He crossed his arms and scowled. He did not enjoy spending his time teaching this high-elven brat the fundamentals of magic. The child had yet to prove herself worthy of his time. "Then try harder."

"I am trying harder, Magus. I don't see why I can't equip my staff or my robes."

"You refer to the Staff of Fates and Gown of Daybreak passed down through your house? You want to use unrestricted legendary gear to attack a training dummy? Is that what you are saying?"

"It's just... it would make it easier," she mumbled.

He crossed his dark gray arms over his chest. "Yes, and that's the problem. Training isn't supposed to be easy. Just think about it. Your legendary equipment would make a mighty spellcaster out of any talentless fool. With that sort of gear, even a bumbling weakling would be made mighty. Are you a weakling, Princess? Are you nothing without your equipment?"

"No, Magus. I'm not weak," she said and drank the mana potion. Her mana containers returned to full.

She closed her eyes and imagined a glow of energy originating from her core, just above her pelvis. She visualized energy forming at the points of her fingertips and at the ends of her feet. The energy traveled from her feet, through her legs, and into her core, through lines of energy. She continued to pull mana into her core until it was a bastion of pulsating energy.

Having drained her arms and legs of mana, she formed a vein from her core, upward through her solar plexus and into her heart chakra where, like every time she'd attempted this previously, the mana flow slowed and died to little more than a trickle as it reached her throat.

When she opened her eyes, they were glowing a dim white. Her vision was filled with white clouds, though her target was still clear enough for her to make out. She had to cast the spell now or even the meager concentration of mana that she had gathered would be lost. She raised her right hand. "*Fraisha ûl!*"

A ball of flame originated just beyond her hand, flew toward the target, and died before it even got to the halfway point.

The dark elf laughed. "That was even more pathetic than your last attempt. You'll have to do much better than that, unless you're planning on having your enemies laugh themselves to death. Again."

"Maybe if you let me level up," the princess stammered, "I can put more points into intelligence and—"

"No!" the magus cried, his voice dripping with barely repressed disgust. "If you level up even once, you'll never master mana control. You would be building your house upon sand."

"Yes, Magus."

The dark elf watched as the young princess tried and failed to hit the training dummy a third time, and then a fourth. When the dark-elven leadership agreed to teach their mana-channeling technique to the young princess, it had seemed like such a good idea. Their newly unified Questgivrian empire would benefit from having a strong princess and future queen.

But he had been trying to teach her how to channel mana through her chakra points for over a month. Most dark-elven children picked it up right away. Long ago, the dark elves had learned that it was possible to amplify the effect of any magic spell by purifying mana as it left the body. Mana had varying levels of quality, completely independent of stat points.

Stat-point augmentation and magic-boosting equipment amplified a person's natural magical capability, which was why mastering mana control had to be done before leveling.

After the seventh attempt, the princess sat down on the floor and crossed her arms. "This is taking too long. Why am I not getting any better?"

"Stand up, child. You aren't done yet. Impatience is the prerogative of those who age and wither, but you and I will live forever."

The princess slowly got back to her feet. "You could be a bit kinder to me, you know."

The magus just laughed. "Tell me, why do you think your attacks are so weak?"

"It seems okay until the energy moves into my chest, and then it gets stuck there. Only a small amount of mana makes it to my throat and head."

"I thought as much. That isn't an uncommon problem. The blockage is most likely due to unrealized emotion."

"If you thought as much, why didn't you say something?"

"I had hoped you would realize the problem on your own. I won't always be here to solve your problems for you."

"Okay, so what do I do to... clear the emotional blockage?"

The dark-elven sorcerer circled around her. "Rage. Frustration. Jealousy. Hatred. For a dark elf, these are the most powerful and purest of emotions. You must harness the anger in your heart, covet the strength that others have and you do not, and use your hate as a cudgel, a tool to amplify your power. Doing so will clear the mana blockage in your heart chakra."

"But I'm not a dark elf, and I don't hate anyone."

"What about the humans? They capture us one by one and use us as though we aren't superior beings. Don't you hate them?"

"I've never met a human. I'm sure they're not that bad."

"Then what about me? I'm the most powerful elven sorcerer in the whole of the Questgivrian Empire. Aren't you jealous of my power?"

"Not really. Besides, you're trying to help me."

The magus put his hand on his forehead. A headache was coming on. "I'm baffled by how you high elves can survive with so little enmity."

"I'm going to try something." Kiwi again began to focus on her mana, gathering it into her core and then upward through her solar plexus and into her chest. She filled her mind with emotion, but not hate as the magus had suggested. Instead she focused on the love that she held for her father, a wise and strong man. The flow of mana began to increase. She pictured her mother, who had always shown her such love. Again the flow of mana increased as if floodgates within her were being opened.

As the spell activated, her eyes turned a brilliant white, and a fireball appeared, ripped through the intervening distance, and slammed into the dummy.

Kiwistafel hits Training Dummy for 1.25 hearts of damage.

"That's much better," said the magus. "We'll make a mage out of you yet. I'm glad you took my advice. So what emotions were holding you back? Envy? Spite?"

Kiwi was beaming. "No, I don't think I have any of that. I just thought about how much I loved my mom and dad."

The magus shook his head. "Really? You used the emotion of... love? How incredibly bizarre."

"Loving my parents is weird?"

"It is. Dark elves might feel respect for their parents, but that tends to translate to jealousy and anger. Rage pushes us forward and makes us more determined and passionate about our goals. Whatever. As long as it works for you, that's good enough for me."

"I'm going to try again. It still feels weaker than it should be. Like only half my mana is getting through."

She drank another mana potion and once again began to draw mana. This time, when the energy reached her chest, she pictured her friends. Hermes, the dwarf that had been her best friend since childhood. Kaze, the dragon prince who went on adventures with her and once let her ride him. Who else? She thought of Slimon, the funny slime in town who'd played with her when she was younger. She fondly remembered the tickle fights they used to have as children and how he always said the right thing to make her feel happy. The floodgates that had been restraining her mana opened completely. As the spell completed, she opened her eyes.

Critical Hit! Kiwistafel hits Training Dummy for 2.75 hearts of damage.

When she opened her eyes, the training dummy was wreathed in flames. One of its arms had been torn completely off by the force of her blast.

"Nicely done," said the magus. "If you can keep producing mana at this level of power, you may be formidable indeed."

Kiwi was still thinking about Slimon. Was it wishful thinking to hope that he still thought of her? She pushed thoughts of the slime from her mind.

"Can you teach me advanced spell-scripting techniques?" She had always enjoyed spell programming but lacked understanding of the more intricate techniques used by master mages.

The dark elf chuckled. "Of course, Princess. Demonstrate that you can focus this quality of mana reliably, and then we can move on to spell scripting. I'll have the dummy replaced with a fire-resistant one. There didn't seem to be much point in doing so until now."

The child raised her arm toward the charred remains of the training dummy, and her eyes shone a luminescent white.

Several decades passed, which was but the blink of an eye to an elf. If Princess Kiwistafel were human, she would be in her late teens. In only a few more decades, her physical appearance would stop changing altogether.

Two rapid light knocks came at her door. She placed her hairbrush back on the dresser and got to her feet. "Come in."

Her father, King Iolo, stepped into the room, shutting the door behind him. "Daughter, can we speak?"

"Of course, Father, I'm always glad to see you."

"Um... yes. Likewise. Listen, I've just finished speaking with your friend, Sir Slimon."

"Oh, how is he?"

"He's... in good health. When you suggested that I consider him for knighthood, I had my doubts, but he's more than proven himself to be a worthy addition. But that's not what I'm here to speak with you about."

"Okay, then what is it?"

"The thing of it is... Slimon just asked for your hand in marriage."

"It's about time," said the princess. "It certainly took him long enough to speak with you."

"You mean that you knew about this?"

"Of course. It was my idea. We've been talking about marriage for years."

The king paced for a moment as though trying to very carefully consider his words, "Listen, I know that the two of you were dating, and I didn't say anything at the time, but this is different. You can't marry him."

Kiwistafel's smile vanished. "But... why not?" Tears began to form in her eyes. "Is it because he's not elven royalty?"

"No, that's not it," said the king.

"Then is it because he's not an elf?"

"No, that's not it, either. I wouldn't mind if you married someone of a different elvenoid race."

"Then why?" She was barely holding back tears.

He looked uncomfortable as he answered. "Honey, he's a slime."

"You bigot! I don't care about his race. We love each other."

"I'm not bigoted against slimes," he protested.

"You just don't want one of them to marry your daughter."

"Kiwi," he said, trying to reason with her, "the country needs you to produce a legitimate heir. Slimes reproduce through cellular mitosis, which means that he *can't* give you an heir. If you weren't my only child, I might allow it, but producing a successor to continue the bloodline is essential to the survival of the nation."

"But why?" She sniffed. "Couldn't we just adopt?"

"No," he said, "it has to be a legitimate child. I've told you of the contract that we arranged with Snickers. If there isn't a legitimate heir, the throne would fall to him. Though we are immortal, you will feel the call to return to our homeland. When that happens, if there is no heir, the kingdom will fall into ruin."

"There has to be some way..." she said.

"Kiwi, dear, you need to understand, slimes only live long enough to reproduce. When a slime's body splits to create their children, the parent is lost. All slimes eventually die, giving rise to the next generation. One day, when that time comes, you will be alone."

"He said he wasn't going to do that. He said he would stay with me forever."

"Forever is a concept that mortals cannot understand. One day, he will tire of this world, and the love that you have will die. It is the way of mortals. If you love him, you should let him go before that happens."

"No... he wouldn't do that. He wouldn't leave me. Please, you have to let us try."

The king paused. "I'll make you a deal. If you can find some way to bear Slimon's child, I will allow the marriage. There are many things we still don't know about this world. There may be some spell or artifact that would make it possible.

"It is still at least several decades before you are old enough to marry, according to Questgivrian law. If that time arrives, and you still haven't found a way, please let him go and consider taking a different husband."

Princess Kiwi nodded and wiped the newly formed tears from her eyes with a red embroidered handkerchief. Iolo kissed her on the forehead and went to the door, shutting it behind him.

The captured princess sat in a dusty room at the top of the tower, surrounded by a number of bored-looking shinobi, all of whom were clad fully in black. She'd been here for over a day since being captured.

None of the princess's escape attempts thus far had been successful. She'd tried stringing together some bedsheets to form a makeshift rope to climb down with, but they only reached about a quarter of the way to the ground. She'd tried to bribe the shinobi, but none of the ninjas would take her money. What kind of mercenary for hire didn't take bribes?

She considered feigning illness and then taking the ninjas by surprise, but that tactic never worked outside of badly written fiction. Also, it would have required two people, one to play the victim and one to attack the unsuspecting guard.

Nevertheless, she wasn't going to give up. She knew that her friends would come for her. That is, if they could find her.

The princess stood from the chair, and under the watchful gaze of her captors, gracefully walked to the tower's single window. After opening the window, she cleared her throat and began to sing.

Her powerful voice was smooth and clear. It rolled over the valley in sorrowful waves, a haunting melody born of longing and pain. She sang of her hero, a stalwart warrior poet, a man of honor and grace, and of the love that the two of them had shared.

The princess had been born with high charisma, and like most politicians, she had socketed the bulk of her stat points into charisma. Her high charisma served to amplify her naturally brilliant singing talent. Her voice was so good that she could have chosen bard as her primary class, but her natural aptitude for magic and training under the high magus led her to choose a caster class.

As her song ended ten minutes later, one of the taller shinobi kidnappers walked up to her, asking, "This true love, this man among men whom you sing of, who is he?"

She sighed. "He is my true love, a paladin, a warrior poet and a knight of the kingdom. Though he is not of royal birth and also a slime, I hope one day the two of us might wed. Of course, as I'm only ninety-two years old, I'm still too young, but I hope someday..."

"Well, he's a lucky man, Princess Kiwistafel," said the ninja through his black face mask, "So... do you know any other songs?"

"Just call me Kiwi. I know a few other songs you might like. Let me sing some of my favorites for you."

The princess opened the window and began to sing into the surrounding hills. As she reached the third stanza of her second song, a small fairy garbed in black flew into the room and started screeching, "STOP IT! Stop the singing! What the hell is going on?"

"Sorry, boss," the human ninja said. "It's just that she has such a beautiful voice and was pining for her true love. The least we could let her do was let her sing about it."

The small fairy hovered before him at eye level and crossed her arms. "Idiots! I'm surrounded by morons! Let me explain this to you. She's. Trying. To. Escape. Anyone within miles will be able to hear her voice." She turned to Kiwi. "But don't worry, Princess. There's no one nearby who can hear you."

"Who are you?" said Princess Kiwi.

"She's the leader of our village, Trista Twinklebottom," one of the other human ninjas said.

Trista flew up behind the ninja and whacked the back of his head. "Don't give the captive that sort of information."

"Sorry, boss. So did you find a way for us to get the princess out of the kingdom? We don't want to keep the queen waiting."

The fairy facepalmed as she hovered in the air. "The captive is standing right here. She. Can. Hear. You. I literally just said not to give her that kind of information." She groaned with exasperation. "Whatever, I don't actually care. If nobody else wants to be professional and take this kidnapping seriously, then I don't see any reason why I should either.

"Yes, to answer your stupid question, I've put up job postings at the capital city for mercenaries to help you bozos smuggle her out of the kingdom. Once you're up to full force, make a dash for the southern border. I'm going back to the base to set up a diversionary force. We're going to attack the blockade while you idiots sneak past it."

Princess Kiwi nodded with approval. "That seems like a good plan. I can see that you've really thought this through."

Trista Twinklebottom flew up to the princess's eye level. "You're not supposed to be complimenting your kidnappers. Don't you know that's a basic violation of victim-kidnapper etiquette? You're supposed to be screaming and crying and shit." She threw her tiny hands in the air. "Why am I the only one who's taking this affair seriously?

"This is about all I can stand of you morons. I'm off to set up the diversion. Take off as soon as you're ready. Later, losers."

The fairy flew through the window and off into the horizon.

"What a strange woman," Princess Kiwi observed. Half of her kidnappers were nodding their heads in agreement.

They sat in silence for several minutes before one of the ninjas spoke up, "So, do you know any other songs?"

A smile crossed Kiwi's face as she went to the window and started to sing.

CHAPTER 18

Honor Among Thieves

Ari was glaring daggers at Tasha through the jail cell bars. "I leave you alone for half an hour, and you murder five guards and destroy a marketplace."

"I'm sorry. It was all just a misunderstanding. I thought that they were the kidnappers, and they were all ganging up on this girl. Besides, technically I only killed three of them. One of them ran away, and the other was just knocked out."

But then she thought back to when she died and came back to life. Though her memories were intact, she wasn't the same person. Not really. She was wrong to have killed them.

"I do feel badly about it. I guess I just sort of overreacted. It's this new body and mind; it tends to act without thinking."

She wondered if maybe she should send a fruit basket to the victims' families, sort of as a "sorry I changed your orc's personality" gift. She would have to escape first, of course.

Ari, Pan, the dwarf, and the slime were all gathered outside her cell. They had found one another in the aftermath of the incident.

"I... saw it happen," Pan said.

"Then why didn't you stop her?" her father asked.

"Too far. It happened too f-fast."

Ari turned back to Tasha. "Anyway, the constable says that your trial is set for this evening."

Tasha looked at her feet. "Will I get an attorney? What do you think of my chances for acquittal?"

"Not likely. The evidence against you is pretty overwhelming."

"Don't be sad," Pan reassured her. "We'll visit you in prison."

"Your confidence overwhelms me," Tasha said dryly. "In any event, I can't wait that long. We still need to rescue the princess, and the menu clock is still counting down. Besides, this is *boring*! Why aren't the slime and the dwarf in jail? They did more damage than me, after all."

The dwarf, who was standing alongside Aralogos, said, "My friend's name is Sir Slimon, and he's a knight of the realm. My name is Prince Hermes, and I'm the crown prince of Dwarselvania. Slimon didn't do any real property damage, and I was able to claim diplomatic immunity."

"You shot up an orphanage with a machine gun!" she cried. "How does that qualify for diplomatic immunity?"

The dwarf wasn't meeting her eyes. "The orphans will all be fine— this can be a learning experience for them. Besides, it was an accident. I've decided to join up with Ari and Pan since they're also trying to find the princess. Tasha, I was impressed by the way you killed those guards and then overpowered Slimon and myself. If you weren't in jail, I'd ask you to join us as well."

Tasha just shrugged. "I don't plan on being here for long. Do we have any leads?"

"No, I'm afraid the ninja that the guards were trailing escaped. We know that they are hiding the princess within a hundred miles of the castle. Slimon and I were both with the princess when she was kidnapped. We were killed trying to protect her. As soon as we respawned and I told King Questgiver, he set up dragon patrols at key points to keep people from leaving the area unchallenged."

Tasha thought back to the dragon who was flying over the caravan the previous day. The dwarf continued speaking. "When kidnappers take someone, the first thing they do is change which save point the victim is registered to. They will try to find a save point that they can control."

"And have you already checked all of the save points in the area?" Tasha asked.

"Yes, but there could be save points that we aren't aware of. Save points hidden in caves or forgotten dungeons to name a few possibilities."

Suddenly Slimon stuck his tongue out and gave out a loud *"Pfffpt! Pfft pffpt."*

"Uh..." Tasha said apprehensively, "did your slime friend just blow a raspberry at me?"

Ari turned to the slime. "I apologize. I'm afraid our companion isn't familiar with your strange but beautiful language. Tasha, slimes don't have vocal chords and can't produce words humans can understand. This is how they communicate. He can understand spoken English just fine, though."

Tasha threw up her hands in exasperation. "Okay, fine. On the scale of strange things that I've encountered in Etheria, this isn't so bad. So what was he saying?"

"Slimon suggested that we go back to exploring the area she was taken from," said Hermes. "We might get lucky and find something new. Let's meet by the entrance in another hour. Well, not you, Tasha. Obviously you'll still be in jail for the foreseeable future."

So Ari, Pan, Hermes, and Slimon all left her holding cell and disappeared from view. After they left, Tasha started looking for some way to escape. She didn't see any obvious breaks in the stone tiles, and the bars on the windows wouldn't budge. There wasn't anything in her inventory that she could use to break out. They had left her with her armor but had affixed a collar onto her neck that prevented her from casting magical spells.

After ten minutes of looking around fruitlessly, she sat down on the bed and decided to spend her stat points.

After her interaction with the elven guard earlier that morning, Tasha had come to understand the value of charisma. While it may not have any usefulness in combat, it played a major role in convincing the guard to let her into the castle. She doubted that she would have been able to convince him to quit his job on the spot without the aid of a boosted charisma score.

Then she thought about the fight in the marketplace. She was only just barely able to lift the buster sword. Another few points of strength would have made lifting it much easier. An additional stat point would also increase the amount of damage that she could apply to enemies. Ultimately she opted to divide her stats between charisma and strength. She hadn't had a chance to allocate the mana container due to being interrupted by Slimon. Hopefully it was still lying on the ground in the marketplace. She pulled up her stats window:

Tasha Singleton (Level 8 Couch Potato)	
Race	Human (Player)
Subclass	None
Weapon	Unarmed (ATK 0.5)
Armor	Standard Running Shoes (DEF 1)
	Iron Bangle (DEF 1)
	Light Chainmail Armor (DEF +8)
	Collar of Magic Silencing (DEF 0.5)
Heart Containers	7/7
Mana Containers	5/5
Amusement Index	4.1
Strength	9
Intelligence	10
Agility	10
Precision	6
Charisma	6
ATK	9
MAG ATK	16
DEF	16
MAG DEF	8

The moment Tasha spent the stat points and hit the confirm button, her muscles increased in bulk. She looked around for something to lift to test out her new strength, but the cell was mostly empty. She attempted to bend the bars, but they didn't budge. Just how many points of strength would she need to be able bend the bars with her bare hands? It would still be another three hours before she could use Stat Shuffle again, as it was still on cooldown.

She decided that she would focus on agility for the next two levels in order to improve her ability to dodge attacks and move quickly.

Allocating her stats had killed a good five minutes. The mind-numbing boredom began to set in once again.

Escape ideas began to run through her head. Picking the cell's lock wasn't an option because she didn't have a lockpick or any of the requisite abilities. She couldn't force the bars open with her bare hands. If only she wasn't wearing that damn magic-silencing collar, she might be able to spellcast her way out.

Then she had another idea. She had the Sprint ability. Maybe if she slammed her body into the bars, it would be a strong enough force to dislodge them.

She backed away to the far end of the cell, put one leg behind her, and crouched down into a starting position. She invoked Sprint and ran headlong toward the bars.

In the days and weeks that were to come, she never did figure out why she thought this was a good idea. As her body impacted the bars at high speed, they didn't give even a tiny bit. Tasha had hit the bars with her head and neck, losing three heart containers all at once.

Tasha wanted to scream in pain, but it was too intense for her to do anything but lie on the ground. For a good ten minutes, she didn't move, barely conscious, pain throbbing through her body. Blood was pouring out from her head injury, coloring the cell floor. Several of her teeth had been knocked out and were lying on the ground beside her. The sight made her nauseous.

Then something occurred to her. If she did this another two times, it would drain the remainder of her heart containers and kill her. Tasha would be reborn at the save point, and she would be free to resume her adventure.

Still dizzy from the blood loss, she stood up, causing additional throbs of pain to pulse through her head. She slowly hobbled to the back of the cell and got into a starting position once again. She just needed to ignore the pain and hope that she didn't pass out.

Again Tasha invoked Sprint and made a mad dash toward the bars. As she was about to collide with them, she heard someone call out her name from behind her. It was hard to make out who it was. Making a split-second decision, she attempted to stop but had built up too much momentum and slammed into the bars, losing two more heart containers.

"Tasha, what are you *doing*?" a female voice cried out.

"Slamming my head into the bars," Tasha explained. "I thought that was pretty obvious."

Tasha turned around and saw the cat girl that she'd rescued on the other side of the window. Tasha approached the window. There were bars on the window, but she could see outside just fine. The cat girl was crouching just beyond the window.

Tasha's head was pounding from the impact, and her vision was starting to blur. "Hey, I remember you. Why are you here?"

"I came to bust you out. My name's Ally," the cat girl said. "You saved me from being captured, so I owe you a debt. Exactly why were you slamming your head against the bars? I don't think you'll be able to break them that way."

It was hard for Tasha to focus on her words through what was probably a concussion. "If I die I'll respawn, right?"

Ally just frowned at Tasha with disapproval. "If you die from a suicide, you'll lose half your levels. Didn't anyone tell you that? The developers use it to stop people from using death as a travel tool."

"Half my levels?" Tasha said, confused. "Huh?"

She was finding it hard to focus on anything. Her thoughts were progressively more distorted as time went on.

"Here," the cat lady said, "drink this. You probably have a concussion."

Through the bars, Ally handed Tasha a vial with some red liquid in it. Tasha looked at it, uncertain. What was she supposed to do with it? What did people normally do with bottles of liquid?

"Drink it," Ally prompted.

The kitty cat lady was right. Bottles of liquid were for drinking. She popped the cork and put some of it in her mouth, sloshed it around a bit, and swallowed. Her heart containers refilled, and her confusion subsided. "Thanks. I'm okay now. You're right, that was a bad idea. No more trying to murder myself in the most painful way imaginable. Girl scout's honor."

Tasha really needed to start thinking through her actions before putting them into effect. Her acting without thinking was the reason she'd ended up in jail in the first place. She was a genius at coming up with bad ideas.

"I'm glad you understand. Anyway, like I said, you saved me from being captured by the orcs, so I'm going to help you in return."

Ally tapped at the air in front of her, operating her menu. A moment later, a wooden log appeared in her hand. She set it on the ground.

"Uhh," said Tasha, "thanks, but I don't see how that will help me out of my current predicament."

Holding her furry hand in front of her, Ally's hands spelled out a number of signs. Tasha knew from her vast wealth of experience watching Japanese cartoons that the cat girl was weaving a ninja spell of some kind.

A tone signified that the spell had been invoked, and the world around Tasha faded. Vertigo filled her for a moment, and the next thing she knew, Tasha was standing outside of the jail looking in through the window at the cat girl, the wooden log lying beside Tasha at her feet.

Ally weaved the spell again and vanished from the cell in a puff of smoke, appearing next to Tasha. The log was now lying in the cell where the cat girl had been a moment earlier.

"What just happened?" Tasha asked.

She smiled and got to work on removing Tasha's magic inhibiting collar. "It's ninjutsu. The substitution jutsu is one of the commonly used abilities. I can switch places with a person or object standing within an arm's length of me. It's traditional to swap places with wooden logs, but any person or object would do. A cell like this would never be able to hold someone like me, since I'd probably just pick the lock."

"Well, you have my gratitude," Tasha said. "I owe you one. Ninjas are really cool. You have some impressive abilities."

"Thanks! I'm not as good a fighter as you, though. You don't owe me anything. This is me paying you back for helping me. Now that you're a fugitive, you need to keep clear of the law."

She tapped at her menu, and a black cloak appeared in her hands.

"Here, put this on. It's a Cloak of Dusk. We use it in the thieves' guild for all kinds of cool stuff. Well, mostly stealing, if I'm being honest. It's enchanted to help you blend in with the crowd. You won't actually be invisible, but it doesn't drain much mana, and people are less likely to notice you while you are wearing it."

It looked similar to the cloak that Pan had been wearing. She put it on, wearing it over her armor. Tasha pulled up the hood and found that it covered her face. She could see how this could hide her from prying eyes.

"Now, I know that being a fugitive from the law is scary, but I've already taken care of your employment needs," Ally said.

"Really? I'm on a quest to rescue the princess right now, though."

"I didn't even realize that she was missing," she said, then shook her head. "I should really pay more attention to current events. I hope she's okay. As far as I know, the thieves' guild doesn't know anything about that."

"So... you're with the thieves' guild, then?"

She nodded. "We aren't above a bit of light kidnapping, but we didn't have anything to do with taking Princess Kiwi. I don't think any of our members would touch her. We don't need that kind of attention. It's probably someone from outside the guild. Maybe a foreign power."

"Then I don't have any leads," Tasha said.

"In that case, you're free to accept this job. I can't offer you a thieves' guild contract since you're not a member, but there's been word on the street about some mercenaries that need to hire some muscle. They're holed up at an abandoned tower to the south. If you're interested, just head to these coordinates."

She listed off some latitude and longitude coordinates, and Tasha entered them into her map as a waypoint. There was at least a chance that these mercenaries were the same people that she was looking for.

"Thanks, Ally, I might just do that," Tasha said.

"Next time you're in town, let's hang out. I'll find you," the cat girl said, winking at Tasha.

She threw something on the ground and vanished in a puff of smoke.

Tasha decided that the best course of action would be to head for the city gates and hopefully meet up with Ari. But before she did that, she needed to pick up a new weapon. Hopefully she still had enough money left over to get a replacement for her ill-fated gunblade.

Heading toward the city gates, Tasha was careful not to be seen by any guards. She consulted the map on her HUD and retraced her steps to find the entrance. The cloak did seem to pull people's eyes away from her. It was possible it was just her imagination, but she felt more hidden now than she did before.

Coming upon a weapon shop along the side of a city street, she entered the building. The gnome proprietor nodded at her as she entered. This was the first gnome she'd met on Etheria. He was extremely short with gnarled skin covered by a long white bushy beard and a red cone-shaped hat. He looked rather like David the Gnome from her early childhood cartoon-watching days.

"Do you have any gunblades for sale?"

The gnome adjusted his glasses as he took the newcomer in. "We do indeed, miss. I've got three in stock. Let me just scan you real quick... Okay, you're a level 8 couch potato. I've only got one that meets your level and class restrictions."

He disappeared into the back room and returned a few minutes later carrying a large gunblade nearly three times the small man's height. He laid the weapon on the counter, and Tasha picked it up by the handle. The blade itself seemed to be made out of water encased in glass, and the handle looked like it was a splash of water frozen into a solid shape.

"Why is it made out of water? How do you even forge something like this?"

The gnome raised up a single finger and began his explanation. "Well, miss, it adds a water element to your attack when you pull the trigger. It should be super effective against fire-based enemies and might even be able to block some fire-based attacks."

Tasha put her finger to the edge and tested it. It was sharp. The blade was actually *made* out of water that had a cutting edge. She tried pulling the trigger, and a splash of hot steam appeared along the blade.

She examined it more closely, pulling up its stats.

Namaka
ATK: 5
Level Requirement: 7
Cost: 1,200 GP
Adds water element to attack.
Namaka is prebuilt with the following spell:
Tsunami
Class: Enchantment
Increases damage by 50% and adds water element for 0.41 seconds
Casting delay: 1 second
Cost: 0.11 mana

The stats were a major improvement over her ill-fated training gunblade, which only had an attack of 1. The trigger action was more powerful than her beginning gunblade, but would be more difficult to master since there was a one-second delay.

Unfortunately, 1,200 GP was about 1,100 GP more than she currently had. But she needed that weapon, and wasn't sure if she had anything of sufficient value to barter with.

"I only have 100 GP right now. Can I give you the rest in trade?"

"Let's see what you have," the gnome grumbled. Clearly he would have preferred cash.

She pulled up her inventory and started pulling out the various monster drops that she'd received. The dwarf started picking through the items one by one.

The gnome scrunched up his nose as he examined the various bits of detritus that Tasha had deposited on the counter. "Thanks, but I don't need any more toilet paper right now. Let's see what else you have. Some cheeseburgers, slips of raw metal, some ornamental rings of low value, a ball of string, uncooked frog meat, and some spider silk. The spider silk is the most valuable item and might be worth about 800 GP. It's an ingredient in higher-level light armor. You might be able to sell the frog meat to a butcher for a few hundred, but I have no use for it. I'll take the cheeseburgers and rings for another 100 GP."

Tasha decided that she wasn't likely to get a better deal from the gnome. "Deal, but that still leaves me 200 GP short. I need that gunblade. Isn't there anything I can do to make up the difference? What if I promised to pay you a larger amount later on?"

"Hmm, sorry, miss. We don't extend credit, even if it's good. It's store policy, you see. How about that nice cloak of yours? It looks to be enchanted."

The Cloak of Dusk was a necessary part of her plan to get out of the city and past the ever-watchful gaze of the guards. Besides, Ally had given it to her. She never felt right selling gifts right after receiving them.

There was also her phone, but she couldn't bring herself to part with it. It wasn't as though she was pining away for home, but the phone was her only physical link. Besides, she needed it for her character class. What kind of couch potato would she be without Netflix? She wasn't ready to give it up, so it remained stored safely in her inventory.

"I can't sell this. What about my iron bangle? I've also got some books."

She laid the bangle and the books that she'd pilfered from the Temple of the Player upon the counter. The gnome examined the collection.

"Hmm..." he said, "I can give you 70 GP for the bangle and 100 for the spellbook. The other books are common and have barely any resale value. Besides, do I look like a bookseller to you? The fireball is a pretty common spell, so you can't expect to get much more for it." He crossed his arms in front of him. "You still owe me 30 GP for the gunblade."

Tasha kept rummaging through her inventory, tapping at the menu screen, looking for anything she might have missed. "I don't think I have anything else I can sell."

The gnome thought for a moment. "Hmm... well, I want to make this sale, but I can't bring the price down any more than it is. Tell you what... do you know how to sing? I'll pay you the remaining 30 GP for a song."

Tasha gave her best performance of "Bad Romance," proving once and for all that Tasha was correct in her career choice not to be a professional singer. The gnome seemed mildly entertained and handed over the gunblade. Most of the surrounding onlookers were relieved that her singing had come to a merciful conclusion.

She gave Namaka a few practice swings and returned it to her inventory. There was no way of knowing the current time, so Tasha would have to rush to meet her friends, but there was still one thing that she needed to do before leaving town. Something that she needed to retrieve from the scene of the crime.

She made her way back to the fisherman district. It took maybe ten minutes to get there. She climbed up onto the roof of a building, which was relatively easy given her high agility score.

Overlooking the marketplace, she could see guards wandering around the crime scene.

There, in the center of the ruined marketplace, was the mana container that she'd earned when she leveled up after fighting the orcish police officers. Tasha had touched it before Slimon grabbed her, causing it to fall to the ground. The guards either hadn't seen it or couldn't see it. If she didn't take it, she would lose her chance for another mana container. Tasha didn't want to risk waiting for things to cool down. She knew where it was now—that might not be true in the future.

Tasha watched their patterns closely. A few of them were doing a forensic study of the dead guards. Others were patrolling the area, ensuring that nobody disturbed the crime scene. There was no way that

Tasha would be able to enter the crime scene on foot. she would need another way to get the mana container.

She spent a few minutes looking for something that she could use and finally discovered a tool that just might do the trick. It was a discarded fishing pole resting against the side of a crate set against the building. She picked up the fishing pole and examined it. It was heavily worn, which is probably why it had been discarded. It still had a line with a hook at the end and a mechanism to reel the line back in.

She climbed up onto the roof of the building that overlooked the crime scene. Tasha cast the fishing pole in the direction of the mana container. It wasn't even close and landed on the ground amidst the guards. She quickly reeled it back in, ready to try again.

Her aim was much closer this time; the line was thrown past the mana container, but when she reeled it in again, the hook brushed against the mana container but didn't latch onto it.

One of the guards turned to look at the place where the mana container was. Fortunately she'd already pulled up the fishing line.

Tasha waited for him to return to his rounds and gave it one more try. The hook again landed at a place just beyond the mana container. She slowly reeled the line in and gave it a tug when it got close to the mana container, moving the hook into position. She continued reeling it in, and this time it latched on to the mana container's handle.

Quickly reeling it up the rest of the way, she took the mana container in her hands and turned around as though to leave. Unfortunately, her foot slid on a loose tile, and she tumbled down the roof and toward the crime scene. Bits of ceiling tile broke off as she rolled toward the edge.

With one hand, she caught the edge of the roof, but her fingers slid right off of it, and she fell on her back and into the watching gazes of the orcs. She lost three heart containers from the fall. Her mana container had also fallen out of her hands and rolled a few meters away.

A burly orc towered over her, his hand over his weapon. Tasha backed away just a bit, holding up her hands in front of her.

The orc reached out and took her arm, pulling her to her feet.

"Are you hurt, miss?" he said. It appeared that he didn't recognize her as a criminal. Tasha had made a stupid mistake, but dumb luck had saved her.

He pointed his open palm at her and said "Heal!" The pain left her, and her heart containers were fully restored.

"Thank you, sir," she said.

"We aim to serve. Please be more careful in the future, miss."

Tasha quickly scooped up the mana container and made her way toward the city entrance. When she was out of sight, she used the glass mana container, adding one to her mana reserves, bringing it up to six.

Tasha rushed back to the entrance. She saw guards occasionally but tried to keep a good distance from them. The trick was not to *look* like she was keeping her distance.

By the time she arrived at the city gate, Ari was already there with Pan. They must have been waiting for Hermes and Slimon. She waved at them, but they looked right past her, as though they didn't see her. At first Tasha was a bit offended, but then she remembered the Cloak of Dusk. It would probably be wise not to remove it.

As Tasha got closer, Pan finally noticed her and pointed in her direction. Aralogos squinted as though trying to figure out what she was pointing at. Eventually he saw Tasha, and his face registered surprise.

"Hey, Ari, how are ya?"

"Wha... How...? Tasha, how did you get out of jail? You didn't kill yourself to escape, did you?"

"Of course not," she said, laughing nervously. "How dumb would I have to be to do that? So yeah, no, I didn't do that. I sort of broke out of jail, but I have some other good news for you. I think I might know where the princess is being held!"

"That's great," he said. "The princess thing, I mean, not the jailbreak. Your jailbreak could add years to your sentence if they catch you."

"We'll worry about that once we rescue the princess and I get my audience with the king. I prefer to handle my crises one at a time. The girl who broke me out was with the thieves' guild, and she told me about a group of mercenaries who was hiring help. It's not a sure thing, but it's our best bet right now."

"T-the thieves' guild?" Pan said. "C-can I join?"

"I can introduce you later if you want," Tasha said.

Ari shot Tasha a dark look. "I've failed as a father figure. My beloved daughter has fallen in with criminals."

The trio continued waiting for a few minutes until Hermes arrived with Sir Slimon in tow. The look at the dwarf's face when he saw Tasha was priceless.

She held out her hand to him. "Listen, Hermes, no hard feelings from earlier, okay?"

After the dwarf shook it, she realized that she'd been lucky to extend her right hand. It could have been awkward if she'd extended her left, since Hermes's was a machine gun.

"It was a good fight," he said. "Well, except for the collateral and property damage, of course. And all the civilian injuries and deaths. Besides that, it was a good fight. I won't hold a grudge if you won't."

"I feel the same way. Let's be friends."

Tasha extended a hand to Slimon, who produced a tentacle and shook her hand.

"Pffpt," he said boisterously.

"Like I said earlier, I *may*, emphasis on may, know where the princess is being held. There's no time to waste, though. Let's get moving."

"Pffppt!" Slimon said, as eager as she was to rescue the princess.

CHAPTER 19

Princess Rescue

Before leaving town, the party stopped at the rent-a-raptor station. An elven girl wearing a straw hat and work clothes was managing the stables when they approached.

"How can I help you fine gentlemen? Looking to rent a velociraptor?"

"I'm not a gentleman," Pan grumbled quietly to herself.

"How much for four raptors?" Ari asked. "We have a dwarf, a slime, and two humans."

"We have a slime mount available, but I'll need a minute to hook it up. How far do you need to travel?"

"We're exploring the countryside," Tasha said. "No more than ninety miles but as little as thirty."

"That won't be a problem," she said. "It's one GP for every five miles traveled per raptor, plus a base cost of five GP per raptor."

The girl tapped at the air in front of her, operating a menu visible only to her. She was most likely using the calculator in the tools section of the menu to figure the cost.

"It comes to ninety-two GP. I'll need a deposit of 150 just in case you go over. You can claim your refund at any rent-a-raptor station. Remember, once you dismount, the raptor will return to the nearest rent-a-raptor station after about a minute. If you want your raptor to wait for you, make sure you tell him to wait. They're more intelligent than most people think and will understand you."

Prince Hermes gave the woman a number of GP coins of different sizes and colors. Pan, Aralogos, and Hermes all received their raptors, and after a moment the stable girl returned with a mount specially designed for slimes. The saddle seat was taller and had a cup-shaped recess designed to contain slimes and keep them from sliding off the saddle.

"Hold it," Tasha said. "Better make that five mounts instead of four."

"Why?" Ari asked. "You can ride Denver."

"True, but we're setting out to rescue the princess. We'll need another raptor for her to ride on the way back, assuming we find her."

The stable girl tapped her menu screen closed. "No problem. Your rate will be the same, and your current deposit should be enough to cover the cost. Have fun rescuing the princess, if that's what you're doing!"

They led the raptors to the city entrance. After visiting the stable and claiming Denver, they walked through the main gates. The guards gave only a cursory glance, seeming more interested in challenging people who came in rather than people who left.

Having left the walls of the great city, they mounted up. Denver crouched down, allowing Tasha to climb up. She stepped into one of the footholds attached to the saddle and lifted the other leg over him, putting it on the second foothold.

Denver lifted his body back to a standing position. Checking on her companions, she noticed that Pan was having trouble mounting her raptor, and Ari was helping her up. Her velociraptor was much smaller than the others and more suitable for her small frame.

When everyone was finally ready to disembark, Tasha urged Denver forward gently. This was the first time she'd ridden a velociraptor since training with the dwarf several days prior. It felt natural enough.

"Hyaa!" Aralogos yelled, and his raptor broke into a run, passing by her. She urged Denver to go faster to keep up.

Tasha finally came in range of the waypoint after following her compass for several hours. Upon reaching the peak of a large hill, a watchtower became visible in the distance. Dismounting, Ari instructed the rented raptors to wait.

They crept silently to the top of a hill, being sure not to expose herself to the enemy. Pan handed her a pair of binoculars. The structure in the distance was an ancient watchtower that had fallen into disrepair. She focused on one of the windows and saw a beautiful elven girl with green hair. That had to be the princess.

Focusing on the base of the tower, she saw two figures stationed at the base. They were covered from head to toe in black cloth and wore black ninja face masks. Tasha felt warmer just looking at them in such hot weather.

Tasha handed Pan's binoculars to Aralogos, and he looked over the scene. "It seems we found our shinobi," he said. "The princess is on the top floor, and there are at least two ninjas at the base of the tower. We have to assume that there are many more inside. There might be a save point inside. Unfortunately, the save point will give them a major tactical advantage, as they could use it to heal up."

Tasha hit the quick-slot button on her HUD, equipping her chainmail bikini armor. Namaka materialized in her hand.

"I don't think we'll be able to approach them undetected," Ari said, "but we might be able to flank them. Tasha, take Pan and circle around to the east. I'll move southwest of their position. Hermes and Sir Slimon, I'd like you to attack from here. We'll attack at the same time. If we're very lucky, they won't see us until we get close."

"Hmm..." said Hermes. "How can we synchronize our attacks? The menu clock isn't working, so we can't time it."

"Just get into position and watch where I am," said Ari. "Make sure you stay out of sight. I'll start counting to give you the time you need. Once I start moving, that will be your signal."

"Tasha, take Denver into battle with you. If the enemy tries to run, you might need to chase them down if they try to escape with the princess. Rental raptors won't follow us into combat, but Denver will."

Tasha nodded. "Well, look at you. I didn't realize you were such a tactician. I'm on it, boss."

She put a waypoint to the east of the tower. Mounting Denver, she helped Pan get on behind her. Tasha urged Denver to move into position, hugging the sparse hills to keep them between her and the watchtower. It occurred to her that the purpose of a watchtower was to be able to see long distances, so it was unlikely that they could avoid detection if the kidnappers were actively watching.

Tasha briefly wondered if they should have waited for nightfall, but it was too late to think about that now.

After a few minutes, she reached her position. Pan and Tasha dismounted and observed the tower, waiting for Ari's signal. Several long minutes passed, and there was no activity from the tower. They had a better vantage point than before.

After several minutes, she saw Aralogos running toward the tower. That was the signal. She mounted Denver, and Pan hopped on behind her, arms wrapped around her waist, and Denver darted forward. Out of the corner of her eye, Tasha could see Hermes and Slimon approaching the tower from the other direction. It took about a minute for Tasha to reach the base of the hill where the tower was stationed.

As they rushed the tower, the ninjas finally detected their presence. Ten of them emerged from the tower entrance, joining the two who were already there. The two guards remained at the entrance while the ten new arrivals took up a circular defensive formation around the tower.

Four of the ninjas broke away and started running in Tasha's direction. Their arms were trailing limply behind their backs, ninja style. Tasha wondered for a moment why ninjas ran that way. Did they think that it more aerodynamic somehow, or was it just for show?

As she rode toward them, Tasha pointed her gunblade in their direction and pulled the trigger. A ball of compressed steam shot forth from the tip of Namaka. Apparently, the water nature of her gunblade had changed the elemental makeup of her fireball spell.

The ninjas split to either side, avoiding the ball of compressed steam, which passed by them ineffectively. It impacted the ground and exploded outwards, not hitting any of her targets.

At some point, Pan had jumped off Denver. She saw a bolt whiz past her and strike one of the ninjas, who collapsed to the ground. The ninja tore out the small arrow and got to his feet.

Two of the ninjas rushed Tasha at the same time. One of them was tall with a muscular build and the other was a female ninja wearing a pink bodysuit that showed more cleavage than was strictly necessary. Tasha wondered idly how a pink bodysuit would contribute to stealth.

Scantily clad pink female ninjas. Anita Sarkeesian would have a field day with this.

She jumped off Denver and swung Namaka at the closest one. The sword slashed right through him. Unfortunately, the moment it struck the ninja, he vanished into a puff of smoke and was replaced by a wooden log, which hit the ground with a thump.

A substitution jutsu. Hmmm, well played.

She lost track of him, but the remaining male ninja was keeping his distance and throwing a barrage of shuriken at Pan. Tasha couldn't see her but hoped that Pan was avoiding the thrown projectiles successfully.

The pink female ninja weaved some strange hand spell, and two clones of her appeared to either side. Tasha shot a fireball at one of the clones, which vanished into a puff of smoke. The original and the remaining clone each pulled out a pair of nunchucks and started swinging them in a rhythmic pattern. Unfortunately, she lost track of which one was the clone and which was the original.

One of them jumped at Tasha and struck her in the head with her nunchuck. This brought her down to six and a half hearts. Her chainmail bikini armor must be doing its job, because the impact didn't hurt as much as it should have. She thrust Namaka at the attacker and plunged it into her gut. She gasped in pain and looked at the wound. Blood started rushing from where she had been impaled.

Her clone dashed at Tasha, enraged. She withdrew the sword from the ninja's gut and slashed lengthwise, severing the ninja girl's head from her body. The dead ninja's clone vanished, leaving only smoke where it had once been.

Unlike mobs, this body didn't vanish. The ninja wasn't a random spawn; she was a person, like the orc guards. Her headless body remained on the ground, a pool of blood collecting around her. Tasha was slowly becoming accustomed to killing people. Apparently video games really had desensitized her to violence.

This wasn't the time to lose her nerve. People didn't die here—that ninja kidnapper would be reborn, in a manner of speaking.

Pan had killed another of the ninjas, but the one who had been throwing shuriken at Pan was still standing. He turned his attention to Tasha and hit her with multiple throwing stars. Two of them struck her in the leg, and the other fell away, leaving a scratch. She was down to four hearts. Tasha raced at him, but he jumped out of range.

Invoking her Sprint ability, she quickly made up the distance. The world was racing past her at an impossible speed. Before Tasha knew it, she had already run past him. She skidded to a stop and started running at him again, this time slashing as she passed.

His head fell to the ground as it was severed from his body. The difference in her attack power and the ninja's defense was so great that she had been able to finish the ninja off in a single critical hit. Tasha was getting pretty good at cutting people's heads off.

Pan and Tasha had just cornered the last remaining ninja when out of the corner of Tasha's eye, there was a flicker of movement coming from the tower. The two ninjas who were guarding the entrance had mounted raptors, and one of them had the figure of a bound and gagged elven woman with green hair strapped to the mount.

Tasha quickly mounted Denver and cried for Pan to join her. The girl shook her head and pointed, indicating Tasha should go alone. Pan would hold off the remaining ninjas by herself.

Tasha urged Denver to give chase, but they had a significant lead, and it would be difficult to close the distance. On the other hand, their raptor was carrying an extra passenger, which was slowing down their getaway.

Still, after about ten minutes of riding, she realized that she wasn't closing the distance. The ninja's raptor must be at least as fast as Denver. A small dinosaur-shaped mob started to form just ahead, but Tasha raced right past it, avoiding combat.

What would Mario would do in this situation? He would probably throw a red turtle shell at the enemy. Unfortunately, that information did not help her in her current situation.

Tasha equipped Namaka and leveled it at the closer of the two ninjas—the one that didn't have the princess. She focused on the ninja, but it was hard to keep her arm steady while riding a velociraptor at high speed over uneven terrain.

She aimed as best as she could and pulled the trigger. A ball of steam shot from it, just missing the ninja, passing over his shoulder and exploding in a hill in the distance.

The two ninjas were discussing something between each other, and the one that she'd fired at split off at an angle, riding off in a wide arc. He was going to come at her from the side. Tasha still had enough mana for three more spells.

As he came at her, she turned her sword to face him, then lowered it to hit the ground in front of him. She pulled the trigger, and another ball of steam shot from the gunblade and hit the ground. His raptor came to a stop to avoid the explosion.

The raptor ahead of her with the princess was able to keep its distance while the ninja behind her began to close in. Tasha felt a stab of pain in her back and turned to find a kunai lodged in her shoulder. She tried to ignore the pain, but her health had dropped to two and a half hearts.

Using her uninjured arm, Tasha pointed the gunblade at the ninja behind her and pulled the trigger again. A fireball erupted from the sword and successfully hit the ninja, knocking him from the raptor.

The ninja's raptor kept on running without him but eventually veered off.

That should buy at least a few minutes.

Swirls of purple mist were forming around her. As she turned to look forward, she saw a large shadow assembling on the ground around the ninja with the princess. It was as though a cloud was passing overhead, but this shadow started to form into a coherent shape. Tasha looked up and realized that the shadow was from the ethereal mist overhead. It was forming into the largest monster that she'd seen so far.

It wasn't spawning for her but for the ninja she was chasing. The cloud of mist took on the shape of an enormous dinosaur that Tasha recognized straight away.

Ginormasaurus Rex (Level 38)
Would gladly shake your hand, but his comically small arms
can't reach, so he'll just eat you instead!
ATK 68 Mag ATK 0
DEF 64 Mag DEF 30

The giant creature towered above her. It strongly resembled the *Tyrannosaurus rex*, but this creature was quite a bit larger.

Seeing a creature that resembled his natural predator before him, Denver slowed down, but Tasha urged him onward. He kept moving, but the ninja's mount turned and started to run away, right toward Denver. As the ninja passed, Tasha swept her sword at him, cutting him and knocking him from his raptor. The bound and gagged princess fell to the ground, and the kidnapper's raptor ran off into the distance.

Tasha quickly dismounted. Denver looked like he wanted to run but somehow found the courage to stand his ground.

The princess was staring wide-eyed at the monster. She wasn't able to speak, having been gagged by the kidnappers. It seemed like she wanted to say something.

The ninja got to his feet and placed himself between the princess and the dinosaur. He weaved some sort of spell, and three clones appeared beside him, each of them focused on the monster.

The dinosaur lunged forward and scooped up one of the hapless shinobis, but it vanished into smoke when the monster bit down on it.

Tasha wondered what she should do. Who should she attack first? She could probably take the shinobi, but the dinosaur was far too great for her to challenge. According to the battle menu, it was level 38. Tasha was sure that she wouldn't survive a single strike from it, much less a battle.

Instead, she decided to free the princess and make a run for it. She crouched next to the princess and removed her gag.

"Free my hands!" the princess cried. "I can use magic to help us!"

"Magic? That would be helpful." Tasha didn't have any sort of knife, so she started working on her restraints with the gunblade.

Note to self: Get a utility knife. The edge was sharp enough, but a gunblade wasn't exactly a precision instrument.

The *Ginormasaurus rex* snatched up another ninja, but this time it wasn't a clone. Blood sprayed as it crushed the ninja with its massive incisors. The other clones flashed a momentary expression of fear, and then each vanished in a puff of smoke.

Finally, Tasha finished working on freeing the princess's hands just as the dinosaur turned its attention to them. Princess Kiwistafel's eyes glowed a bright white, and she cried "*Tétha Lishkâ!*" Threads of arc lightning emerged from the princess's hands and struck the G-Rex's head, dealing four hearts of damage and staggering it.

"Nice going!" Tasha said. "If you can hold it off for a bit, I can free your legs, and we can make our escape. I'm Tasha, by the way. I'm here to rescue you."

The princess looked fearful. "I'll try to hold it off, Tasha. We can't fight this creature; it's beyond both of us."

There were forty-two heart containers above the scan data. The princess was right; they weren't going to defeat this enormous creature.

Once again Kiwistafel's eyes glowed, and she cried, "*Ashîl a Palúrin!*"

A knot of thick vines rushed out of the ground beneath the monster's feet, holding it in place. The monster tried to bite at the princess, but the vines forced it to stay just outside of biting distance.

The spell didn't last long, though. In a contest of strength between the *Ginormasaurus rex* and a handful of vines, the monster was clearly going to be the victor. One by one the vines snapped under its relentless struggle.

Finally, Tasha cut through the last of the bonds holding Kiwi's legs. She scrambled to her feet and ran toward Denver, the princess following behind. Denver was extremely agitated and running in place. As they approached, he lowered his body to the ground to let the two get on.

Tasha quickly climbed up, and Princess Kiwistafel climbed on behind her.

As she squeezed her legs together and urged the raptor forward, Denver burst into a sprint. She turned his reins so that they were running back the way they came. Tasha and the princess couldn't defeat it by themselves, but maybe they could make it back to Ari and the others. Together they might be able to either bring it down or find some other way to escape it.

The last of the vines tore, and the great dinosaur sprung toward Denver, running at a mad dash. It was gaining quickly.

"Can you cast that vine spell again to slow it down?" Tasha asked.

"I can't," she said. "It has a two-minute cooldown. I need another seventy-eight seconds."

"What about your other spells?"

"I don't think they'll even slow it down. It would just waste mana."

"Seventy-eight seconds?" Tasha said. "He'll catch us long before then."

Their gargantuan pursuer was closing the distance rapidly. The ground shook from the impact of its footfalls.

"I've got an idea," Tasha said.

In the distance was the ninja who Tasha had knocked off his raptor, and he was still chasing after the wayward mount. It seemed his raptor had detected the inbound G-Rex and decided that discretion was the better part of not being eaten by a giant predatory dinosaur.

"I can kill that kidnapper with my magic," offered the princess.

"No!" Tasha said. "We need him alive to distract the G-Rex so we can escape. Hopefully the ninja can buy us some time."

She adjusted the reins so that their bearing took them straight toward the recovering ninja, who had given up on catching his raptor and was now fleeing from the oncoming monster in abject terror. He barely noticed Denver as they ran past him.

Ultimately, she'd overestimated the time that the G-Rex would take to kill and eat the hapless kidnapper. She'd delayed it by precious few seconds, but again it started the chase.

Tasha could see the tower in the distance. At their current speed, they might be able to make it in ten minutes. Denver was burdened by two riders rather than just one, but he was still making good time.

Every time their pursuer almost caught them, the vine spell's cooldown elapsed, allowing Kiwi to cast it and create additional distance. It was a delicate equilibrium, but they were able to use it to close in on the tower.

As Tasha approached the tower, she caught sight of her allies. Shinobi corpses littered the ground surrounding the tower. Pan, Sir Slimon, and Prince Hermes were running toward them with their weapons ready. Ari was waiting at the tower entrance, signaling for Tasha to enter. They reached the tower and both dismounted.

"Get the princess into the tower and keep her safe," said Ari.

"Got it," she said and ran into the watchtower with the princess. The watchtower was in a severe state of disrepair, but a save point occupied the center of the room. Empty crates and time-worn barrels lined the corners of the room.

They both touched the save point and were restored to full health and mana. Tasha returned to the entrance. She wanted to help her friends, but Ari had told her to protect the princess. That was the whole point of this quest, after all.

The two of them watched the battle as it played out. Prince Hermes shouted insults and shot at it ineffectively while Sir Slimon cast recovery spells as fast as he could. Hermes was nearly eaten several times, but he always managed to dodge the dinosaur's attack. Pan fired bolts at it, but most bounced right off its tough skin.

Ari climbed onto its back and began hitting the dinosaur with a barrage of punches. Its health was slowly inching downward, one quarter of a heart at a time.

A small explosion lit up from the G-Rex's side. Hermes had equipped a rocket-propelled grenade launcher in place of his minigun and had hit the G-Rex, but even that only dealt one heart of damage. The party was just too outleveled to deal anywhere near the amount of damage needed to bring the creature down.

Princess Kiwistafel turned to Tasha. "Tasha, I'm a practiced mage. I know I can help. We must go to their aid."

"I know how you feel," Tasha said, sensing what she wanted to do, "but if you get killed, then this will all be for nothing."

"In that case, I'm going to the top of this tower. I can cast my damage spells safely from there."

"Fair enough, Princess. Let's go," Tasha said. She wanted to join the fight as well.

Tasha turned to the stairwell and began climbing. The wooden planks that composed the individual stairs had become weakened through age. The walls vibrated as they heard the sound of the G-Rex's footfalls from outside. One of the planks broke into pieces as the princess put her weight on it, but Tasha caught her and pulled her back up.

They passed a window and could see the fight raging on. The G-Rex still had over thirty hearts of health remaining.

None of her friends had been killed yet, but they were barely doing any damage—still only a quarter at a time. Its weakness was lightning, and the princess was the only one in the party who could deal lightning damage.

They continued their ascent. It was slow going since much of the stairwell had collapsed. Tasha reached the top first, and when she entered the room, was struck in her chest with a katana. Her eyes opened wide in shock, and she staggered backward. One of the ninjas had been waiting. He drew back his sword. The surprise attack cost her two heart containers. Being impaled like that would have been enough to kill a normal person, but fortunately she was in Etheria, and she still had heart containers left.

He struck again, but Tasha deflected this strike with her gunblade. He swung his sword at her and hit Tasha again, bringing her down to the last heart container and sending a surge of pain to her midsection.

Tasha just wasn't used to fighting people who knew what they were doing. At some point she needed to learn how to fight with a sword properly. She circled around the ninja, holding him at bay with her gunblade.

An overpowering roar caused her body to vibrate and the tower to shake. Their friends needed them—now. Tasha couldn't afford to let this fight draw out.

The princess arrived on the tower roof behind the ninja.

"Hey!" Kiwi yelled, causing the ninja to turn around. Tasha took advantage of the distraction and stabbed him in the back, pulling the trigger just in time to deal three hearts of damage. She drew out the weapon and finished the ninja off with another slash.

Kiwi ran up to a large wooden cabinet and tried to open it, but it was locked. "Help me with this! My equipment is inside!"

Digging around in the dead ninja's black bodysuit, Tasha discovered a key. She used it to open the chest, revealing an elaborate green outfit and an oak staff capped with a green orb. The princess took the clothing and the staff, then started tapping the air in front of her. A moment later, her tattered clothing was replaced by a sorceress outfit with long green sleeves, leggings, and a white cape. There were some potions in the chest as well, and Tasha didn't waste any time in downing one, restoring her health to full.

"Thanks for getting me here, Tasha. With my staff magnifying my power, I should be of more help."

She ran to the edge of the outpost and began chanting a spell. A glow surrounded her body.

"It's a magic buff," she said raising her staff. "What you saw before was a mere fraction of my power..." Her eyes glowed a brilliant white. The dinosaur was below and no more than a few dozen meters from the tower.

"*Tétha Lishkâ!*" she cried and a bolt of lightning significantly more intense than the one from earlier emerged from her staff and slammed the dinosaur in the chest. The great mob flinched from the impact, falling to the ground. It scrambled back to its feet and let out an enraged roar. Its health dropped by eight hearts, bringing it down to just over half of its starting health.

At once the great dinosaur ceased its attack on the dwarven prince and turned its attention to the princess. It looked up at the tower, scanning for some way to reach her.

"*Tétha Lishkâ!*" Kiwi shouted again, and a second bolt of lightning struck the creature. This time the dinosaur didn't flinch, though the shot did eight more hearts of damage, bringing it down to thirteen hearts. It turned its massive body and charged the tower.

Tasha leveled her gunblade at the creature and shot a ball of compressed steam at it, dealing only half a heart of damage. Maybe for now she would leave the spell casting to Kiwi.

With a thunderous boom, the dinosaur rammed its massive body against the tower. The entire building began to shake. Kiwi lost her balance and fell on her back. Tasha grasped her hand to help her up. Together they ran to the edge of the building. The G-Rex was leaning against the building, trying to get to them, and the brick wall crumbled as the G-Rex put its weight against it. It could almost reach the princess.

"*Tétha Lishkâ!*" Kiwi casted, firing another bolt of lightning at the monster, dealing another eight damage. It flinched from the hit, stepping back.

It still had three hearts remaining. One more lightning bolt would be enough to finish it off. Unfortunately, the G-Rex wasn't going to give her the opportunity. It rushed at the tower, slamming its body into it. The tower had lost all structural integrity and began tipping away from the creature. After a moment, it stabilized but was angled away from the dinosaur. Tasha grabbed the ledge but watched in horror as the princess began sliding away from her.

Tasha tried to catch her, but Kiwi was already beyond the reach of her arm. The princess caught herself at the ledge on the other side of the tower. Some of the bricks gave way, but she was able to secure herself against one of the tower's windows.

While they were both gripping opposing sides of the partially collapsed and tilting tower, the G-Rex circled around it. Tasha struggled desperately to pull herself up, realizing that the princess was now low enough to be within the dinosaur's gaping maw.

The beast darted straight at her, opening its mouth wide. The princess just stared at it in fear.

"Hit it with another spell!" Tasha said.

Kiwi regained her wits and cast another lightning bolt, but it missed its target, the shot arcing ineffectively to the ground.

As it was snapping at her, Kiwi grabbed the ledge with both hands. She lost her grip on her staff, and it tumbled down the angled tower roof, hit the G-Rex in the face, and fell to the ground. Tasha groaned. Casting any spells would be impossible with her hands holding the ledge. There wasn't any wall left to separate her from the dinosaur, and the G-Rex looked ready to attack.

In desperation, Tasha released her grip from the ledge. She could land on the other ledge that Kiwi was hanging from and help her to her feet. But that didn't happen, because at just that moment, the tower began to tilt laterally. It was collapsing.

As Tasha slid, her angle was adjusted by the tilt of the tower—she was going to miss the princess completely. She looked at Tasha in a panic, but Tasha was unable to do anything to help. She slid past the princess and focused forward. The G-Rex had seen Tasha and opened its giant maw, ready to swallow her whole. With her adjusted angle, Tasha was going to slide directly into its mouth. She could see its giant pearly-white teeth with perfect clarity. How was she supposed to defend herself against that? If they chomped down on her, she was finished.

It was only by pure luck that he didn't bite her as she slid into the dinosaur's mouth. On the other hand, that at least would have been a quick death.

She slid down the dinosaur's throat smoothly and gasped as she was forced down its esophagus. Pressure pushed against her body from all sides. There wasn't any air to breathe, and she was being slowly crushed to death. This was far worse than her earlier experience of being swallowed by a slinker. Worst of all, she saw nothing—she had been plunged into darkness.

Quarter hearts were slowly vanishing on her HUD as Tasha continued to suffocate. As she was forced downward on her journey toward the creature's stomach, Tasha realized that she was still gripping her gunblade. It wasn't much help since she was unable to swing it in such a confined area, but she did still have enough mana for a few more spells.

Tasha willed herself to pull the trigger. As a burst of steam erupted from the edge, she feel the intense heat from the aftermath of the spell. Tasha saw that it had dealt three hearts of damage to the monster. Heat burned her hand, but she willed herself to fire once more.

This time the ball of steam tore a hole through the creature, letting in sunlight. Tasha eagerly drew in a breath, and a moment later saw the world fade in as purple clouds of ethereal mist replaced the dinosaur. She had killed it! The ground became visible, and she realized that without the dinosaur's esophagus to support her, she was about to fall a great distance.

She hurtled through the purple clouds toward the ground. Her hand no longer burned from the steam like it had a moment ago. As she fell, a tentacle shot forth from Sir Slimon, catching her and carefully lowering her gently to the ground. Another tentacle lowered Princess Kiwi to the ground beside her.

At that point she noticed that a window had appeared:

Victory! All enemies have been vanquished.
4660 experience gained. (670 experience to next level)
7200 GP found.
Level Up!
Level Up!
Level Up!
Level Up!

You have reached level 12.

You have 16 unassigned stat points.

Choose either a heart container or mana container.

She'd just gained four levels in one battle and made it halfway to the next. It was an epic fight, and the G-Rex was of a vastly higher level. It was a small miracle that they'd survived.

"Sir Slimon, you came to rescue me," said the princess, who embraced the slime fondly. "Oh, it was so awful, but then you came to save me. I knew you would."

She just continued hugging him for about half a minute. It was actually rather awkward.

Prince Hermes wasn't able to meet the princess's eyes. "We failed to protect you before. Can you ever forgive us?"

"There is nothing to forgive," she said, tearing herself away from the slime. "The important thing is that you came to save me. I'll always rem— Holy crap! I just gained three levels!"

"I just gained two as well," said Aralogos.

"Four," reported Pan.

"Sir Slimon and I just gained two levels apiece," said Hermes.

"Due to our immortality," Kiwi explained to Tasha, "elves have slow experience curves. I wasn't expecting to level up again for at least another decade. How can this be?"

"There she goes again," Hermes grumbled, "mentioning her immortality, lording it over the rest of us mortals."

"Sorry, Hermes, I know the looming specter of death is a touchy issue for ephemerals. It's just that I didn't expect to make level 12 this soon. Now I've gained three levels all at once."

"Our friend Tasha here is a player," Ari explained. "It seems that players and their companions level quickly."

"A player? There hasn't been a player for many hundreds of years. Tasha, you have my thanks. You should meet my father, the king. He would want to meet my saviors, particularly if one of them is a player."

Tasha smiled shyly. "Are you sure you want to be friends with a mortal like me?"

"Oh, don't be that way," she said, giving Tasha a hug. "Hermes and I are just teasing each other. Some of my best friends are ephemerals."

"It's okay," said Tasha, "but I'm a bit confused. If people are reborn at save points when they die, isn't everyone immortal? How are elves any different?"

"Oh, well, elves can't die of old age the same way everyone else does. That's why most elves usually keep their distance from the other races. The loss of a mortal loved one is more keenly felt by someone who can never die and never forget."

"But I saw lots of different races when I was in the capital city," said Tasha.

"Things are different now under my father's rule, more than they ever were. My father invited all races to live together in the nation of Questgivria in the hopes of strengthening the bonds between races."

Sir Slimon hopped up to Kiwi and returned her oaken staff.

"Thank you again, my love," she said.

A loud crack rang out from the tower as it gave way, collapsing to the ground, leaving nothing but a pile of rubble.

Tasha saw a large loot cylinder on the ground. Opening it, she discovered that it was a large case of G-Rex meat. She smiled, wondering if she could sell it. Barring that, they could host the mother of all BBQs. Tasha couldn't lift it, but Ari was able to pick it up and add it to his inventory.

"Let us return to the safety of the castle," said Hermes. "I wouldn't want to be caught out here at night."

"Agreed," Tasha said, scrunching up her face. "I'm completely covered in dinosaur digestive fluids. I'll never be able to get the smell out."

Ari cast a cleansing spell, and the dirt, digestive juices, and sweat fell from her body and onto the ground. Tasha was perfectly clean, and her chainmail bikini armor was as good as new.

"You have *got* to teach me that spell," she said.

"Wait a moment," said Kiwi as she tapped at her menu. A moment later, a suit of high-quality silken clothing appeared in her hand along with a silver dagger with elven letters engraved in the hilt and blade.

"Tasha, I'd like you to have these. I know that these clothes aren't as strong as your armor, but they have a high style bonus. And this dagger was given to me as a gift by my father, the king. It bears the name of Questgiver, so if you show it to the guards, they will allow you entrance to the palace.

"Thanks, Princess."

"Call me Kiwi," she said. "I hope we can be friends."

"Sure, Kiwi. We're already friends." Tasha took the clothes and knife from her.

"Pan didn't get a p-present," Pan mumbled as she went off with Ari to reclaim the raptors.

Tasha took two heart containers and two mana containers from her new level ups.

Reclaiming the raptors took longer than expected. Several of them were keeping their distance from the tower. Denver had kept away from the tower as well, but he came when Tasha called. Once they'd found all the raptors, they started back toward the city.

Following Ari's map, they managed to avoid running into more high-level mobs. Due to the circumspect route, it took over two hours to reach the entrance to the capital city. But the time flew by, as Tasha spent most of the travel time recounting her adventures with Princess Kiwi, Prince Hermes, and Sir Slimon.

Finally the gates to Brightwind were once again in view.

As Princess Kiwi approached the castle gates, one of the elven guards greeted her happily

"Princess!" he said. "We're so relieved to have you back. I'll call an escort for you right away."

"Tasha, when you and your friends are ready, come by the castle. I'll have a feast prepared in your honor."

Tasha liked feasts. "We'll be there."

"I'll see you tonight, then. Guard, please escort me back to the palace."

"At once, Your Highness. Please follow me," said the guardsman.

Kiwi gave Sir Slimon a goodbye kiss and followed the guard back to the palace.

"So," Tasha said to the remaining orc guard, "where can a girl find a bath? Is there a bathhouse nearby?" The Cleanse spell had gotten most of the smell, and she looked clean, but she would feel better after a bath. It was more a psychological thing than an actual need to be clean.

"Yeah, there's a common bathhouse just down this road," he said, pointing.

"Pan, Ari, shall we?" she said.

They were about to set off, but just then another guard appeared. Tasha recognized him by his gray skin, dual cutlasses, and powerful build. It was Mr. Cutlass, the orc guard that she'd accidentally murdered earlier with his friend's buster sword.

"That's the escaped criminal! Get her!" the orc commanded.

Before Tasha could do anything, the city guard grabbed her and secured handcuffs to her wrists.

"Where are you taking her?" demanded Aralogos.

"Down to the courthouse," said the orc. "I don't know how she escaped, but her trial is scheduled within the hour. It's time for her to face justice."

"We're coming with her," Ari said.

"Pfffpt!" agreed Sir Slimon adamantly.

"I don't care if you come. It's an open trial, so feel free to watch from the stands."

Tasha sighed. It seemed her actions had caught up to her. The guard led her away toward the courthouse, her companions in tow.

CHAPTER 20

Turnabout Identity

I t took about fifteen minutes of walking to reach the courthouse, which was an enormous building with artistic columns. From what Tasha had observed, pretty much every elven building was elaborate in some manner or another. This one sported the symbol of a balanced scale above the entrance.

They were led into the courthouse to a small room with a table and chairs. The guard pointed at Tasha. "Just you. Your companions will see you again at the trial."

He pushed Tasha inside the room and closed the door behind her. Another man was in the room. It was a male gnome, similar to the one who had sold Tasha her new sword.

"Hello, human," he said with an irritated voice.

"I have a name," Tasha said. "You don't need to call me human."

"I don't care what your name is," he said, sounding extremely bored. "To me, you're nothing but another burden on my caseload. I'm your state-appointed attorney, you see. I've looked over your file, and they've got a pretty strong case against you. Not really worth defending. You should just plead guilty and beg for mercy. Sometimes that works, and it would save me the bother of having to defend you."

Tasha looked at him with disgust. "You're, like, the worst attorney ever. Aren't you supposed to believe in the innocence of your client?"

"*Are* you innocent?" he asked, doubt evident in his eyes.

"Well... no, but that doesn't mean we should just give up."

The gnome yawned, clearly bored by their conversation. "There's no way you're going to plead anything but guilty. The trial's about to start, and I don't have any strategy to defend you. Trying to get a not-guilty verdict isn't worth my time, and neither are you."

"Fine, then you're fired! I'll defend myself and make you eat those words."

To this he just smiled and laughed. "The funny human thinks it can defend itself? If you can get a not-guilty verdict, I'll not only eat my words, but I'll eat my pointy hat as well."

Without any further words, the grumpy gnome jumped off his chair and left the room. Tasha didn't have the faintest clue how to defend herself in court, so she pulled out her phone and started streaming an episode of Law & Order in the hopes that it would give her some kind of legal knowledge.

Twenty minutes later, a knock came at the door. "The trial is about to start. You and your advocate are requested in the courtroom."

"One moment," Tasha said and turned off her phone.

> **Ability unlocked: Legal Beagle (Level 0)**
> **Type: Passive Scholar ability (unlocks at level 10)**
> **Ensures basic understanding of Questgivrian law and legal strategy.**
> **Would you like to set this as your current ability, replacing Bullet Time? Yes/No**

She tapped "yes" and opened her menu. She had sixteen free stat points to spend. Thinking carefully, Tasha decided to put five points into intelligence and eleven points into charisma. She had intended to spend more points on agility, but right now what she needed most was public speaking and investigative abilities. With luck, a higher charisma score might serve to ameliorate her less-than-stellar public-speaking ability.

In order to exonerate herself, she would need to dish out some triple-A-grade bullshit. Strength and agility wouldn't make her into a bullshit artist, but intelligence and charisma just might do the job.

The moment Tasha confirmed it, she felt a bit taller and more certain of herself. She also had a newfound appreciation for how stupid she had been to attack the guards. Oh well. It was too late to do anything about that now. Her intelligence and charisma were now both at fifteen.

"Human!" said the terrible gnome lawyer. "Did your boobs just get bigger?"

"Get lost, creep!" Tasha said. He wasn't wrong, though. That seemed to be one of the effects of higher charisma. Tasha still had no intention of doing a charisma build, but maybe a few more points wouldn't hurt. The clothing that Kiwi had given her fit much better than they had a moment before.

Following Mr. Cutlass, Tasha left the interview room and headed to the courtroom. It was time to put her new charisma and intelligence to use. She equipped the fine silk clothing that the princess had given her. It had a style rating of thirty, which might improve her chances somewhat. It also seemed to have a scan ability attached to it, which could come in handy as well.

Doguary 2nd, 3205, Third Era, 4:15 p.m.
Brightwind Courthouse, Courtroom 3

The interior of the courtroom was more like a small colosseum. It was open to the outside, and citizens of all races filled the bleachers. In the center of the circular open area were two prominent podiums for the defense and prosecution. The judge was a wizened owl-type person who was perched on a large pedestal atop a row of stairs, which allowed him to look down upon the court. Several rows of seats held the audience, giving them a view of the proceedings.

Tasha took her place at the defendant's corner. Across from her towered a giant green middle-aged orc with a mostly bald head and a rather unconvincing comb-over. He wore a giant warhammer on his back. He would have been intimidating, but the comb-over made it difficult to take the man seriously.

Tasha scanned the audience and spotted her friends. Pan smiled meekly and waved to her. Tasha waved back. Hermes was sitting in the stands eating from a tub of buttery popcorn, sharing some of it with Slimon.

The judge slammed a gavel, calling the court to order. He spoke in a dry voice. "The trial to decide the guilt or innocence of Tasha Singleton is about to begin. The defendant has been charged with three counts of murder and two counts of attempted murder. Is the defense ready?"

Tasha took her place across from the prosecutor and said, "The defense is ready, Your Honor."

"Defendant, where is your attorney?" said the judge.

"I've decided to defend myself," Tasha said.

"You... have the right, but I don't recommend it. Questgivrian law isn't something for amateurs. Is there a reason why you won't use your public defender?"

"Yes, Your Honor, there is. I'm not confident in his ability to defend me."

The judge ruffled his feathers a bit. "Do you have any experience as a lawyer?"

She shook her head. "Oh, I'm not a lawyer, but I've played one in a video game."

"Your Honor," said the prosecutor, "the prosecution is okay with this. The case against the human is airtight. Let the human have its fun before experiencing the bitter taste of defeat."

"I'm not an *it*," Tasha said.

"Very well," the judge said. "The court shall allow Tasha Singleton to defend herself in place of her attorney. Is the prosecution ready?"

"The prosecution was born ready, Your Birdliness. Human! My name is Borgrim Deathhammer! Remember it! My victory over you shall be quick and absolute! Prepare to face a humiliating defeat by the iron hand of District Attorney Borgrim Deathhammer! Huaaargh!" The prosecutor proceeded to brandish a small throwing axe.

Why does this guy have weapons in a courtroom?

"Very well," said the judge. "Prosecutor Borgrim, your opening statement, please."

Borgrim puffed out his chest and began his narration. "Earlier this morning, at around 10:20 a.m., five of the city guards were chasing the infamous Ally Cat, a prominent member of the thieves' guild. The defendant, Tasha Singleton, intervened in the guards' chase and proceeded to murder three of the guards. Only two of them survived her attack. Because of this human's interference, the culprit was able to escape. The defendant caused significant property damage during the attack, and many businesses were destroyed in the carnage. Several citizens lost their lives in the ensuing chaos.

"There were multiple witnesses to the battle, and I have assembled evidence to prove that she was the one who attacked the guards."

The judge looked at Tasha gravely and made a tutting sound. "What a horrible tragedy. I'm shocked that such a massacre could occur in our once peaceful city. Well then, how does the defense plead?"

Tasha held her head up high. "Not guilty, Your Honor. I intend to prove that I didn't kill those poor people."

Borgrim burst into laughter. "You poor, poor, foolish human. If you had pled guilty and thrown yourself at the mercy of the court, they might have shown pity and reduced your sentence. Now I will make sure that shall not happen. Forthwith, I shall destroy you utterly with the warhammer of justice!"

"Yes, yes, very good," said the judge. "Well, you could start by calling your first witness."

Borgrim just chuckled darkly. "Then I call Ripgore Blood Slicer to the stand."

An orc walked into the courtroom and took the witness stand. It was Mr. Cutlass.

"Witness, please state your name and occupation," the judge said.

The witness cracked his neck. "I am Ripgore Blood Slicer, a lieutenant in the city guard. I am also—"

"Yes, yes, Ripgore," Borgrim said, "we don't need to hear your life story. Just tell us what you witnessed earlier this morning."

"I saw the whole thing, because I was there. We had just managed to track down Ally Cat and were giving chase. She led us to the marketplace in question, where a human woman with dark skin and frizzled hair exchanged words with the Ally Cat and interceded in her behalf. She attacked four of my best subordinates with a gunblade.

"She managed to defeat them all, killing two, disarming one, and severely injuring another. Even though I destroyed her gunblade, she picked up one of their buster swords and threw it at me, knocking me to the ground. She killed me moments later. I just respawned half an hour ago and was brought here to give testimony."

"Lieutenant Ripgore," Borgrim said, waving his hands dramatically, "take a good long look at the people in this courtroom and tell us if anyone here is the human woman in question."

Ripgore pointed right at Tasha. "That's her. I remember her face."

The judge turned to the court reporter. "Let the record state that he pointed to the defendant. And what was the name of the human woman in question? Check your battle log. Be precise."

Ripgore started tapping at the air in front of him and a moment later said, "Her name was Tasha Singleton."

The audience started murmuring to each other.

"She's guilty!"

"It must be her!"

"That's what we get for letting *humans* into the city."

Tasha spoke over the crowd loud enough to be heard. "Hold it! I would like to see a copy of your battle log. I ask that a small portion of the attack log be transcribed and submitted as evidence."

Tasha was surprised to hear herself saying such things. It was probably an effect of the Legal Beagle ability. Normally she was a quiet and reserved person. A week ago Tasha had been afraid to leave her apartment after dark and couldn't work up the courage to ask a guy out on a date. Now she was holding her own in a court of law.

The judge nodded. "Very well, you have that right. Bailiff, bring the witness pen and paper. Witness, please dictate a portion the battle log."

It took Ripgore about five minutes to write it out. Tasha took the piece of paper from the bailiff and examined it carefully.

> **Critical Hit! Tasha Singleton (Level 7) attacks Berbellik Axe-Rend (Level 5) for 4 damage.**
>
> **Berbellik Axe-Rend (Level 5) dies.**
>
> **Helbad Bloodrain (Level 5) attacks Tasha Singleton (Level 7) for 1 damage.**

The battle log continued like this for some length.

The judge turned back to Borgrim. "Do you have any further questions for this witness?"

Borgrim shook his head and crossed his arms. "No, I believe this constitutes incontrovertible proof that my witness saw the defendant attack and kill several honorable city guards. Judge, I see no reason to continue this farce of a trial. The defendant is guilty, and she just proved it to everyone here. Let's have a verdict."

"It does seem rather airtight," the judge said. "Very well, I shall now render my verdict." He raised his gavel, preparing to slam it down.

This was not going as planned. There had to be something that Tasha could do. Some piece of evidence had to exist that could prove she wasn't at the scene of the crime... even though she actually was.

"Objection!" Tasha slammed her hands down on her podium.

The judge stopped. "Yes, what is it?"

"I still haven't cross-examined the witness," she said.

"Oh, come *on!*" whined Borgrim. "We all know she's guilty! The guard pointed her out and even transcribed the evidence at her request. She's just trying to waste everyone's time and make us late for dinner."

The judge looked at her with even eyes. "Do you have any evidence at all that you weren't the attacker? If you can present some evidence, I'm willing to let this trial continue. Otherwise I will render my verdict here and now."

Tasha needed to draw this trial out, but did she really possess any evidence that proved her innocence? She ran through her inventory to check for anything that might be relevant. There was nothing. She read again through the transcribed battle log. Why had she thought it was important? Tasha reread the first line:

Critical Hit! Tasha Singleton (Level 7) attacks Berbellik Axe-Rend (Level 5) for 4 damage.

There had to be something... Tasha stared at it for several seconds, and then she saw it. "Your Honor, I'm ready to present evidence that I wasn't at the scene of the crime."

The judge looked at her with keen interest. "Really? Such evidence exists? Why didn't you present it before now?"

Tasha tapped the piece of paper with her hand. "I didn't have it before this. The witness was kind enough to give it to me. Ripgore's battle log contains... a contradiction!"

The audience again began to murmur again.

"Order!" The judge banged his gavel loudly. "I will have order in this courtroom! Defendant, show me what part of the battle log contains the contradiction."

Tasha pointed to some writing on the paper. "The battle log indicates that the guard was attacked by Tasha Singleton. Right next to the name is a level indicator. The Tasha Singleton in the attack had a level of seven. Isn't that right, Ripgore?"

Ripgore again opened his menu and scrolled through the battle log, "Yes, that's correct. I'm looking at it right now. It says level 7."

"I still don't see the contradiction," said the judge.

Suddenly Prosecutor Borgrim staggered backward as though he had been hit. He must have just scanned her. Tasha offered a wicked smile. "I request to be scanned and the results transcribed to the court record. This transcript will prove beyond any doubt that I wasn't at the scene of the crime."

The judge turned to the bailiff. "Bailiff, scan her and write down the results."

"No!" cried Borgrim. "Don't do it! Don't you see? This is just a stalling tactic! She just wants to continue the trial!"

The bailiff handed the paper back to the judge, who looked at it. "And where is the contradiction showing that you weren't at the scene of the crime?"

"Your Honor, please read the level indicator in the scan. What level am I now?"

The judge peered at it through his glasses. "It says here level 12. Oh, I see! Yes, that does seem to be a contradiction. If you are the Tasha Singleton described in the battle log, you would have the same level."

Tasha crossed her arms triumphantly. "For me to be the same person, I would have had to gain four levels since this morning. I submit to the court that it is impossible for any person to gain four levels over the course of only a few hours."

Borgrim physically collapsed to the ground as though he had been struck by a great force. As he pulled himself back to his feet, giant gobs of sweat rolled down his face. His shirt had become ripped at some point during his fall.

"No!" he cried while desperately trying to regain his composure. "This can't be. I can't be defeated here. I won't let it happen. Not here. Not now! Not by this... this... human!" He turned to glare at her.

"You! Human! I demand that you tell me how it is possible for you to not be the same person when you have the same name and even look the same! Tell the court now!"

It was time for Tasha to put her bullshit artistry to work for her. "Why, that's actually quite simple. Haven't you ever heard of identical twins?"

"Identical... twins?" Borgrim sputtered. "Isn't that when siblings are born at the same time and look the same?"

"That's correct," she said. "I have an identical twin. It's really that simple. She's the evil yet attractive woman that you are looking for, not me."

"This is quite alarming," said the judge, his eyes wide in astonishment. He looked at Borgrim sternly. "Prosecutor Borgrim, did you arrest the wrong sister?"

"No... no..." Borgrim managed to say. There may have actually been foam coming out of his mouth. Great gobs of sweat were falling to the ground from his face.

"H-human! If we are to believe that you have an identical evil sister... then why is your name also Tasha Singleton? Answer me!"

Tasha just smiled slightly. "My father and mother were both rather uncreative and stubborn people. Tasha is the only name they could agree on. Also, it isn't pronounced the same. My name is TA-sha, but hers is pronounced ta-SHA. That's how you can tell us apart."

At this point, Borgrim must have slipped on some of his own sweat because he fell to the ground a second time, shattering his chair. When he got back to his feet, blood was pouring down his face from where he had hit his head on the podium.

The judge looked at him pityingly. "There does not seem to be enough evidence to indict the defendant. It appears that she could not have been the same person. Unless you have any other arguments, I'm ready to render my verdict."

Borgrim pointed at her with his left hand and declared, "She... might have leveled up since the battle. In fact, the battle itself might have triggered a level up."

Tasha pointed back at the prosecutor. She had this trial in the bag, and they both knew it. "Who ever heard of anyone leveling up four times in only a few hours? Witness Ripgore, how long did it take you to reach level 8 from level 7?"

He looked around sheepishly. "It took me nearly four months of constant level grinding."

"And do you believe that it is possible for someone to gain four levels in only a few hours?"

He shook his head. "No, that's not possible. As someone who has put hard work into leveling, I can't believe it."

A mischievous grin suddenly appeared on Borgrim's face. His unbridled panic from moments earlier had all but vanished. "Ripgore, I agree completely. It isn't possible to level up that quickly. I believe this contradiction can be easily solved."

"Really? It can?" asked the judge.

"Really? It can?" Tasha asked nervously.

Prosecutor Borgrim nodded. "Yes, I'm quite sure of it. Ripgore, isn't it possible that you misread your battle log? I mean, seven and eleven both sound the same, and it would be easy to mistakenly transcribe the wrong number from your battle log. Now, transcribe it again, and don't mess up this time, or you and your men are all *fired*!"

"Objection!" Tasha said. "He's clearly threatening and leading the witness."

A tear came to Ripgore's eye. "No, he's right. Why do I always mess those two numbers up? I'll fix it right away, sir. Please don't fire me. My wife just had a baby and... well... we need the income, or they'll put us out on the street. We might end up living out of a cardboard box."

Borgrim held his belly as he laughed. "Just make sure it doesn't happen again, foolish underling."

"Very well," said the judge. "Bailiff, make the adjustments to the transcript of the battle record. Tasha Singleton was level 11 at the time she attacked the guards."

"*WHAT?*" Tasha cried, and she fell to the ground in shock from this new development. She stumbled back to her feet and held herself up, holding both sides of the podium.

Borgrim spread his arms out victoriously. "Well, of course she was! That's the only thing that would explain how she so easily defeated my incompetent underlings. Well, judge? I think that's sufficient evidence for an indictment, don't you? You played a good game, defendant, but your time is over. Oh, how I will enjoy watching you suffer in defeat!" He began to laugh heartily.

"And now, Your Birdliness, a verdict ,if you please."

The judge looked at Tasha. "Does the defense have anything to add before I render my verdict?"

She thought desperately. There wasn't anything to show as evidence. She had to prove that she was at level 7 at the time of the attack... but how? If she didn't continue this trial, she was finished, but there was nothing in her inventory that would convince the judge.

"I.... um..."

The judge just shook his head. "I see you have nothing to add. Then without further ado—"

"HOLD IT!"

Tasha looked around to see who spoke. It wasn't her, or the prosecutor, or the judge, or the witness. She looked to the audience and saw a gnome standing upon his chair. The gnome leaped down from the audience seating area and landed on the witness stand, knocking poor Ripgore from his place. The gnome was a nimble little guy.

Then she realized who it was. This was the gnome who had sold her the sword.

"I knew you were trouble from the moment I saw you, human," said the gnome. "This she-human bought a sword from me earlier this morning. I never forget a face."

The judge rolled his eyes. "We don't need your testimony. I've already reached a decision."

"Wait!" Tasha said. "Your Honor, let me cross examine this witness. I believe I can still prove my innocence."

"Very well," said the judge, "but be quick about it. I'll have no more shenanigans in my courtroom."

"Yes, Your Honor." Tasha then addressed the gnome. "Tell me more about the sword that you sold me... I-I mean her. Tell me about that weapon."

He grinned at her. "I remember it perfectly. I take my business very seriously, you see. You asked if I had any gunblades for sale, so I showed you the Namaka, a water-based gunblade."

"And did you have any other gunblades in stock?"

"Yes," he said. "I had two other gunblades for sale."

"I see. And did you show these other two weapons to this woman?"

"No, I didn't," he admitted, shaking his head. "One of them had a level 14 restriction, and the other had a level 9 restriction."

She looked at the gnome thoughtfully. "But that doesn't make any sense. Why didn't you show her the sword with the level 9 restriction?"

"Because she wasn't high enough level. The only weapon that she met the level requirements of was my Namaka."

"Your Honor," Tasha said, "from this man's testimony, it's clear that the person this gnome sold the sword to was lower than level 9. I've never seen this man before in my life. My twin sister must have purchased the Namaka from him. I don't own one myself."

"No!" the gnome said. "It was you! I'm sure of it! You must have the Namaka in your inventory right now!"

The logic of his argument took Tasha by surprise. She almost lost her footing but remained standing. Glancing at her inventory screen, she saw the Namaka sitting there, just like he said.

She needed to think of another lie and think of it quick.

"No, I really don't. I don't fight using gunblades. I don't like them; they're kind of dumb. It's like they can't decide whether they want to be a gun or a sword. Just pick one, right? The design doesn't make any sense. I prefer other sorts of weapons. Besides, do I really look the same as my sister? Aren't I actually a little taller than her?"

"Hmm..." the gnome said, "now that you mention it..."

Borgrim let out a war cry, lifted his hammer, and slammed it onto his podium, smashing it to pieces. "This is *my* weapon, human! Let's see yours. If you really have a twin sister, you should be able to show that you have a different weapon. And don't try to say that you lost it or don't use weapons. You couldn't have reached level 12 without a powerful weapon. Besides, you were caught entering through the city gates. Nobody would travel outside the city without a weapon."

The judge nodded. "Defendant Tasha Singleton, can you present your weapon to this courtroom? If you really don't have the Namaka in your inventory, you should be able to show me another weapon."

"Of course," Tasha said, opening her inventory. She pulled out the silver dagger that Kiwi had given her earlier. She held it for everyone to see. "This weapon is mine! The princess herself gave it to me. Why would I use any other weapon when I have a dagger of such value?"

"Bailiff, bring that dagger to me," said the judge, who then proceeded to inspect the dagger. "This is indeed a weapon belonging to the Questgiver royal house. It seems that this merchant must have sold the weapon to her twin sister after all."

"N-no!" cried Borgrim. "This can't be! It's impossible! I can't lose! I'm undefeatable!"

The gnome looked at her, confused. "So... I really did sell the Namaka to your evil identical twin sister?"

"I'm afraid so," Tasha lied, nodding her head.

"I'm ready to lay down my verdict... Unless there are any *other* last-minute interruptions..."

Tears were running down Borgrim's face. He just stood there amidst the shattered remains of his podium and chair with his hands covering his head. His comb-over had come undone, and he'd torn out his few remaining bits of white hair.

"Very well, then," said the judge. "In the trial to determine the guilt or innocence of Tasha Singleton on the charges of assault and murder, I find her... not guilty!"

There was a popping sound, and she saw what appeared to be swallows flying overhead carrying open bags of confetti that rained down on the open courtroom.

Congratulations! You have reached Level 2 in Bullshit Artist. Your lies will now be 10% more creative and people will have an additional 4% chance of believing them.

Tasha met her friends outside. Ari and Pan were waiting for her. Hermes and Slimon were there as well, still munching on popcorn.

Ari clasped her on the shoulder. "I'm impressed by how well you did in court. It's hard to believe that you're the same woman I met a week ago."

"Thanks," she said.

Looking up at her, Hermes said, "That was some amazing deception you spun out there in that courtroom. I'm shocked that they fell for it."

Tasha motioned at the exit. "Well, let's get going. It's time to finally meet the king. Maybe now I can finally get some answers."

They left the courthouse and started back on the path to the palace. Aralogos had been thoughtful enough to leave Denver at the city stable after returning the rental raptors. Tasha wanted to check on Denver, but she would have to tend to it later.

One mustn't keep royalty waiting, after all.

CHAPTER 21

Brightwind Keep

In this week's Who's Who in Royalty, we go in depth with the exiled Prince Hermes. Hermes was raised by the Questgivrian royal family from a young age. He is a familiar face in the capital city of Brightwind, particularly the drinking establishments, and is known to have a taste for Dwarven Death Whisky. He is a close personal friend of Princess Kiwi and is best friends with Sir Slimon, a paladin and knight of the realm.

His father is Dourmal, son of Thronin and King Under the Laundry Mountain. After ascending to the throne, Dourmal made some unpopular decisions, including the exile of dragons from the mountain. He began to see enemies everywhere and would spend entire weeks in solitude. The paranoia had grown so great that when his son, Hermes, was born, he saw his own newborn son as a potential threat and tried to kill him. He drew his great axe and brought it down on the newborn child before he could be registered at a save point.

Somehow Dourmal missed and only took his son's arm. One of the nurses took him from the room and registered him at a save point, but the damage was already done. The first time a person uses a save point, their physical template is locked, including any deformities or injuries.

The dwarven nurse who rescued Hermes feared for his welfare, so she took him to the elves, who have raised him ever since.

Excerpt from "Who's Who in Royalty" in the **Adventurer's Digest,** *Billbember 3202, 3E edition*

T

he journey through the city to Brightwind Keep took nearly an hour. It was early evening, and the sun was setting.

As they approached the castle entrance for the second time, a different elven guard stood at attention. Fortunately, Tasha had Kiwi's dagger, so she wouldn't have to convince this guard to follow a new career path just to gain entrance.

Tasha looked at the guard, invoking her Scan ability:

Torrin Evenhame
Race: Elf
Level: 64
Characteristics: Loyal to the king, never retreats in battle, cruel to enemies
Relationship: In an unhappy marriage. One child, male.
Likes: Elven cuisine, sword combat, elven brothels
Dislikes: Humans, dwarven singing

Her scan ability was much more useful than she had expected. Tasha held out the dagger. "I'm here to see the king, Lord Iolo Questgiver. Princess Kiwistafel gave me this dagger so that I could gain entrance."

The guard looked at the dagger. "Very well. You are expected inside."

Upon entering the castle, they walked down the great aircraft-hangar-sized hall toward the door on the far side. There were guideposts indicating the correct way forward.

As Tasha was walking, she felt a tingle in the back of her neck and somehow felt that she was being followed. She turned around and saw an elven guardsman in the distance. He was shadowing her, though he wasn't coming too close. It seemed they didn't fully trust a human not to make off with the silverware.

They entered the throne room, and there were three figures, each sitting upon a throne. Princess Kiwistafel sat to the left alongside the king and queen. Hiding in the shadows lurked Snickers the Bumble, a wide, ever-present smile on his face.

As they approached, Ari signaled for them to stop a few paces from the stairway, which held the elevated throne. Tasha looked to her side and saw that Ari, Pan, and Prince Hermes had already assumed a kneeling position. She quickly got to one knee as well. Then she noticed that her companions had all lowered themselves to the other knee, so she quickly changed from one to the other.

The king himself was a tall elven man of moderate age. No elf that she'd seen so far could be described as elderly, but somehow he looked older than most. His features were both powerful and beautiful. He was dressed in black robes and had pitch-black hair.

"Please stand," he said. "I'm to understand that you rescued my beloved daughter. The kingdom is indebted to you, and so am I."

She got to her feet. "Thank you, my lord."

Tasha hoped she'd said that correctly. Would Majesty or Highness have been more appropriate? Proper etiquette around nobility wasn't something that she was overly familiar with. Most of what she knew about addressing kings she'd learned from binge watching *Game of Thrones* and *Merlin*. Maybe she should have let someone else speak first and then followed their lead. Whatever the case, the king took no notice and continued speaking.

"As a small sign of our gratitude, we have prepared a reward for you. The bridge to the north that serves as our main connection to the Slime Federation has been destroyed in a recent storm. I have decided that it shall be rebuilt in your honor."

"A... bridge, my king?" Tasha said in a deadpan voice. "I saved the princess, and you are building a bridge in gratitude? No offense, but that sounds more like a public works project than a proper reward."

He continued as if she hadn't spoken. "She also told me something else about you that I find more challenging to believe. She told me that you are a player."

"I am a player, Your Grace," she said. Dammit, why hadn't she stuck with "my lord"? That one was at least safe!

"You must forgive my curiosity," King Questgiver said. "There hasn't been a player in Etheria for hundreds of years. And now, the clocks throughout the kingdom have all turned into countdowns, and under a week later, a person claiming to be a player appears. What am I to make of this?"

Tasha considered her words. How much should she tell him? Tasha had come here to learn about the countdown and what it represented. She had no reason to hold back information from him.

"I witnessed the same events on my world before I was brought here. Every clock that I could see had changed into a countdown. I was offered a choice by an eidolon to travel to this world, and I accepted. When I arrived, I met Ari and his daughter, who have served as my guides.

"At his advice, I traveled here to seek your counsel. It took us about a week to arrive. When we got here, we discovered that the princess had been kidnapped by ninjas, so we set out to rescue her.

"Tell me, Your Grace, do you know what the countdown signifies? Do you know why I was summoned?"

The king stood from his throne. "We do have some knowledge about that. We will discuss that in greater detail later. For now, we would have you all join us for dinner."

"Pfffpt!" said Slimon.

"I couldn't have said it better, honey," said Kiwi. "Tasha, we'll meet you and your company at the atrium."

The queen turned to a middle-aged human servant woman who stood off to the side. "Alina, escort our guests to somewhere they can clean up, and then bring them to the atrium."

Tasha was escorted to a small room at the bottom of a curved glass tube dotted by holes to allow in air from outside. As she entered, she came to the realization that it was a lift. When Tasha had seen the castle from the outside for the first time this morning, there were circular rings that hugged the castle. She had seen a light moving along one of those rings. At the time, she thought them mere ornamentation, but now she understood that they were actually transport tubes designed to ferry people to different sections of the castle.

The servant who was escorting them shut the door, and a moment later it began to move upward at an angle along the direction of the tube. There wasn't anything supporting the lift floor—it was being elevated through magic. The entrance hall shrank away from her as the lift slid through an exit in the wall.

The lift was now outside the castle, and Tasha gaped in awe at the castle city of Brightwind stretching out before her. The glass tube was now a series of transparent bars, close enough together to prevent anyone from falling out but wide enough to allow air to pass through.

After a few minutes, the lift reached a connection point. The servant reached through an enclave and turned the lever in one direction. The lift began moving laterally and toward another part of the castle. As the lift passed into the room, a large apartment was revealed.

"These are the guest quarters," Alina said. "There's a private bathhouse you can use, and I'll prepare a change of clothes for each of you. Well, except for the slime. I'm sorry, I didn't get your name."

"Ppppt!" he said.

"Oh, so *you're* Sir Slimon. The princess has spoken about you. Incessantly and in great detail, actually. Ahem, as I was saying, please use these rooms as you see fit. I will return to collect you in an hour for supper."

Taking a bath was a rare and wonderful experience. Tasha hadn't properly bathed since arriving in this world. The Cleanse spell was effective in keeping her clean, but it didn't have the relaxing and recuperative properties of an actual bath.

When she was done, there was a set of clothing waiting for her a nearby dresser. It looked similar to the elaborate dresses that elves tended to wear. Maybe it was a touch more elaborate than she was used to, but the keep was a formal setting.

Tasha met up with her colleagues, and their guide used the lifts to carry them to the atrium. The altitude presented a magnificent view of the city below. The sun was just beginning to brush the horizon.

Surrounding Tasha were gardens containing all manner of flowers and artistic statues. A translucent crystal fountain occupied the center of the atrium. Everything in this place seemed elaborate and beautiful.

Another elven servant entered. "Presenting His Majesty, Lord and Protector of the Realm, King Iolo Questgiver, along with his wife, Queen Kiwano, and the Crown Princess Kiwistafel Questgiver."

The three of them entered the room through a doorway at the far end of the atrium. Their guide ushered Tasha to a large table, and she took a seat, putting herself between Ari and Slimon. Slimon's chair was somewhat different from hers in that rather than a regular human seat, it had an insert that would hold him and stop him from sliding off the chair, just like his saddle.

All manner of dishes were laid out on the table, most of which she didn't recognize. The roast chicken seemed safe enough, but Kiwi insisted that Tasha try one of the brontosaurus ribs. Tasha hadn't actually seen any brontosauruses in the wild, but if this world had velociraptors, it wasn't really that outlandish a possibility.

It turned out that brontosaurus tasted nothing at all like chicken. Beef would be a much closer comparison. It was served with a sweet and spicy brontosaurus sauce.

Watching Slimon eat was an interesting experience. Tasha did her best not to stare, but she was curious. When Slimon drank his wine, he formed a thin tentacle that went inside of the glass. The level of the wine in the glass went down and traveled through his slightly transparent tentacle into his main body.

He didn't use utensils. In fact, Tasha had never seen him using weapons or tools, either. Instead he simply absorbed the food into his body.

Tasha tried to start up a conversation with Slimon, but the language barrier made productive communication impossible. She tried to figure out the basics, but he only seemed to communicate by saying "Pfffpt" or something similar. How exactly that translated into a language, she had no idea. Maybe one day Tasha would have the opportunity to find out.

During dinner, there was no discussion of the countdown or other serious topics. Queen Kiwano was sitting across from her and wouldn't stop thanking Tasha for rescuing her daughter.

She listened raptly as Tasha recounted the story of the rescue, wisely leaving out the part where she accidentally murdered the city guard and collaborated with the thieves' guild.

As everyone finished eating, the soft pitter patter of raindrops began to fall. At first Tasha thought they would have to move inside, but Queen Kiwano asked a servant to turn on the atrium shield. The human manservant raised a lever on some sort of machine set in an alcove. As soon as he did this, the rain stopped hitting the floor and instead splashed against an invisible dome. Lines of rainwater ran down the magical shield, falling outside of the atrium.

The food had been cleared away. Ari was reclining against the wall while Pan was showing off Tasha's phone to the dwarven prince and Sir Slimon. That left Tasha alone with the princess, the king, and the queen.

Lord Iolo Questgiver turned to the short figure lurking in the shadows. "Snickers, tell me the truth. Is this woman an incarnation of the player?"

The jester made a mighty leap, vaulting over the royal family and landing on the table right in front of Tasha. His elongated nose was mere millimeters away from hers. Such a jump must have taken either a great deal of precision to pull off or a great deal of luck. Tasha was betting on the former.

He jumped off the table and circled around Tasha, sniffing at her. She watched him nervously as he turned his monstrous ears to listen to her heart. He rapped twice at her head with his fist. It didn't hurt but wasn't comfortable either.

"Snickers," said King Questgiver, sighing, "haven't I asked you not to invade the personal space of others? Tell me what you've found."

Snickers grinned even wider than before.

"The girl is a player, a consumer of games,
you need have no doubt that she is what she claims."

The king nodded gravely. "So it's true. Then the kingdom must turn to you for aid as my family has many times in the past.

"My apologies for his behavior, but I had to be sure. Snickers is my advisor. If he says that you are the player, I believe him. I'll make sure he doesn't trouble you in the future."

"Your advisor? What is he, exactly? I've heard... interesting stories about him."

"Some leaders choose to surround themselves with advisors who tell them what they want to hear and don't provide useful counsel," the king said. "I didn't want a yes-man serving as my chief advisor."

"So you decided to go with evil clown instead?" Tasha asked, her forehead wrinkled in confusion.

"Tasha, please," Ari said. "You are in the presence of the high king. You can't talk to him that way."

Tasha lowered her head. "Forgive me, Your Grace."

"It's quite all right," said the king. "I prefer that you speak plainly. We have much to discuss. I have learned what the countdown signifies. There will be a council meeting tomorrow morning. Let us retire for the evening, and we will continue this discussion on the morrow. Please remain in the castle tonight as our guests."

"Thank you, Your Grace," she said.

As she stood to leave, Queen Kiwano said, "Tasha, don't forget to loot the castle for treasure chests."

"Treasure chests? You mean you've got treasure chests lying around the castle and you're cool with me looting them?"

"Of course," said the queen. "That's what treasure chests are for. Aren't there treasure chests in the world of players?"

"Not really. At least, we don't leave them lying about for anyone to pillage. Can you explain them to me?"

"Of course, Player Tasha. Treasure chests are naturally occurring artifacts that appear in dungeons. Each one contains a random treasure that is different for everyone who opens it. Each person can loot it once and only once. We place the harvested treasure chests in public areas around the realm for the welfare of the people. They expire after about five years of being separated from their dungeon, so we need to continue exploring dungeons to collect new ones. For some reason, they tend to provide better loot when they are hidden or out of the way. That's why we don't keep them all in one place.

"You should open a chest whenever you find one. They are usually placed in areas accessible to the public, but we have some in the castle as well. Look for them in hidden alcoves and out-of-the-way areas."

She indicated a large chest hidden in the corner. "There's one here in the atrium. Please take the contents for yourself."

Tasha approached it and looked at the large wooden box. It was large as far as chests went and came up to about her waist. It wasn't locked, so she opened it. For a moment, light spilled out of it, and an object appeared at the bottom of the chest. It was a small cloth bag of coins totaling 200 GP. She added the money to her inventory.

Tasha, Ari, and Pan spent the remainder of the evening exploring the castle, searching for chests to loot. In the end, Tasha found several thousand GP, a beef-and-bean burrito, and an iron bangle to replace the one that she'd sold.

The guest rooms were decently sized and quite comfortable, certainly a far cry better than camping in the cold and unforgiving outdoors. Hermes and Sir Slimon had their own quarters in the castle.

After Pan fell asleep, Tasha found Ari on the terrace. He was sipping from a glass of alcohol. "Ah, Tasha. Care to have a drink with me?"

She sat next to him. "No, thanks. I don't drink alcohol. What is that you are drinking, anyway?"

"Dwarven Death Whisky. I've never had the chance to try it before now. It's rather famous, but dwarven imports were hard to come by back in Zhakara. Are you sure you don't want to try some? There's some elven wine if you prefer."

Tasha smiled and shook her head. "I've always preferred my mind to be sharp and in a constant state of high alert, especially with my job. That's why I drink coffee and lots of soda."

"That sounds stressful," said Ari.

"Uh, you have no idea. But that was who I used to be. I'm still coming to terms with the fact that I just died last week and am no longer the same person." She picked up a carafe of elven wine from the table, poured herself a glass, and held it up. "To relaxing the mind."

They clinked glasses and sat in silence for several minutes, looking out at the city below the castle. Dim lights could be seen from the streetlamps below.

"What will you do after this?" Tasha asked.

Ari shrugged. "I'd hoped Pan and I could keep traveling with you. I'm glad to have met you."

"Really? Why is that? I'm really not that interesting."

"That's not true. Of the entire city, you are the one person who was able to find the princess."

"That was just dumb luck," she said, waving her hand dismissively.

"Maybe, but the clues were all there—you had the will to follow through. You went after her when most people would have found some excuse not to. You are a woman of action, and that's what I like about you."

Thanks, Ari. Nobody's ever called me a woman of action before. Well, at least they haven't called me that unironically."

"It's true," he said. "You've made my life much more interesting. I'm sure Pan feels the same way."

"Stop complimenting me; it'll go to my head."

She was about to pour herself another drink when she noticed something odd about Ari's hand. At first she thought that it was a trick of the light, but the more she looked, the more she was certain. His left hand was partially transparent. "Uh, Ari, what's wrong with your left hand?"

He looked confused for a moment, then glanced at his left hand. It was see-through, just like Tasha thought.

"I... didn't want you to see this," he said, shoving it in his pocket. "It's a... condition I have. It's nothing you need to worry about."

"A condition? Ari, your hand is literally disappearing! This is serious."

He brought it back out and looked at it casually. "Don't worry. I have things under control. I need you to stay focused on the quest. Don't worry about me."

"Are you sure you're okay?"

"I'm sure. It's something I've grown used to. It doesn't hurt or anything. By morning everything will be back to normal."

"All right, Ari. I'll drop it for now if you want me to. If you're sure it's okay."

They spoke for some time, and Ari seemed completely at ease about the fact that his hand was only partly there.

She considered pouring herself another drink, but instead excused herself and went to bed. She didn't want to be hung over the following day... assuming hangovers were even a thing in Etheria.

The meeting the following morning was held in a vast garden some distance from the great keep. A small stream wound its way through a small pine grove. The rhythmic chirping of songbirds and insects filled the air.

By the time Tasha had arrived with Princess Kiwistafel and Prince Hermes, a number of delegates had already been assembled and were engaged in heated conversation. Ari and Pan had been asked to remain behind in the castle, as Tasha was the only member of the group to be invited. Tasha would have enjoyed the moral support of her friends, but the need for secrecy was entirely reasonable.

Several orc chieftains were in attendance as well as an ogre and a giant spider. Not a humanoid spider, but one that very closely resembled the mob that had very nearly killed Tasha in Webwood Forest.

Tasha turned to Kiwi. "Who are all of these people?"

"These are delegates and ambassadors from the member nations of Questgivria. They have all come here to take part in this meeting. I'm sure they all want to know what's wrong with the menu clock."

Kiwi indicated a gathering of slimes. "That green-colored slime is the slime minister."

"Did you seriously just say 'slime minister'?"

"Oh, yes," she said, "the slime minister is the head figure in charge of the Slime Federation."

Great, more slime puns. "Is the slime kingdom also a part of Questgivria?"

"No," said Kiwi, "but we are close allies with them, and they are our neighbors."

"I don't see any other humans here."

Kiwi shook her head. "And you won't. Most of the humans you encounter in Questgivria will be refugees from Zhakara. There are no human member nations of the Questgivrian empire."

A shadow rushed across the garden, followed by a gust of wind. A great red dragon with immense batlike wings and a scaled underbelly flew overhead. Its sheer enormity was on par with a Boeing 747. The reason why this meeting had to be held outdoors became immediately evident. There wouldn't be enough room to store everyone inside comfortably.

The great red dragon landed some distance away and was joined by a number of its smaller brethren. There was a blue snake-like Chinese-style dragon who remained aloft and formed patterns in the air. A green SUV-sized gas dragon with a large belly stood next to the larger red dragon.

One of the smaller dragons landed close by. It was a smaller greenish-gray dragon only slightly larger than Denver. He approached Princess Kiwi, who patted his head in greeting. Tasha scanned the dragon before approaching.

> **Kaze (Level 19)**
> **A steam dragon. Enjoys fish, elven singing, and taking long naps on piles of treasure.**
> **Hates vegetables, especially spinach.**

As Tasha moved closer to the dragon, and Kaze turned his long neck to look at her. A childlike voice spoke within Tasha's head.

Hello, human.

The words formed themselves in Tasha's mind, but nobody had spoken. The dragon tilted his head. *I said hello. Can you not hear me?*

"Are you... speaking in my mind?" asked Tasha.

Of course I am, silly biped. This is how dragons communicate. Have you never spoken with a dragon before?

"Tasha, this is Kaze," said Kiwi. "We've known each other since we were children. When we were younger, we used to level together."

"Are the dragons part of Questgivria?" asked Tasha.

"No, they have a small settlement at the North Pole called Dragonholm, but most dragons are nomadic these days, ever since being displaced by the mountain dwarves."

Tasha looked around. "I don't see any dwarves here other than Hermes."

"And you won't, either," said Hermes. "My father's mountain kingdom has cut itself off from the affairs of the rest of the world. Besides which, dragons and mountain dwarves hate one another. If the mountain kingdom was in attendance, the dragons would certainly refuse to attend. Even if the hill dwarves from Dwarselvania were here without their presence, the dragons might take it as an affront."

"Why is that? Did something happen between dragons and dwarves?"

Hermes nodded. "Indeed. Long ago, dwarves and dragons lived together under the great Laundry Mountain, deep within Dwarselvania. Dwarves would mine for precious ore and craft great treasures. The dragons, in turn, protected that treasure and the mountain kingdom from invaders. It was a beneficial arrangement for both dragons and dwarves that persisted for centuries."

"I take it something happened?" Tasha said.

"My father, King Dourmal, happened. When he became king, he inherited an artifact known as the Orb of Earth that gave him the power to command the element of Earth. My father wasn't happy with the relationship between the dwarves and dragons. Most of the time, dragons merely slept on piles of gold and consumed huge amounts of food. He felt they provided nothing of immediate monetary value.

"King Dourmal decided that they didn't need the protection of the dragons anymore, so he slaughtered them all in their sleep, reinforced the mountain using the orb, and kept the crystalline dragon eggs as hostages.

"Their home had been taken from them, so the dragons turned to a nomadic lifestyle. The dragons might tolerate my presence here but just barely."

Tasha frowned. "Sounds like the dragons have good reason to hate dwarves. I take it you don't agree with your father?"

Hermes cleared his throat. "Well, considering he tried to kill me at birth... yes, our relationship is less than optimal."

"Your father tried to *kill* you? I thought there was no death in Etheria outside of old age?"

"Aye, once a person has been registered with a save point, they can resurrect upon death. By the time I was born, a madness had already taken root in his heart. He had decided that I represented a future threat and decided to kill me the moment I was born, before I could be registered at a save point. So he took a great mythril axe and tried to cut me down. For some reason, he missed and only succeeded in cutting off my left arm."

Tasha looked at Hermes with horror.

"The nursemaid took me from the chamber and registered me at the save point, but the damage was already done. Whenever I respawn or use the healing power of the save point, everything but my arm is restored."

Tasha pursed her lips. "Well, that explains the machine-gun arm."

"That's right. I've been living with the elves most of my life. I think King Questgiver hopes I will one day claim my father's title of King Under the Laundry Mountain, but I don't think that will ever happen. The dwarves of the Laundry Mountain have been made to hate me. I'm considered an outcast."

Kiwi sighed sadly. "The humans of Zhakara enslave the elves, most of the races fear and hate humans, the dwarves and dragons hate one another, and now a god of chaos is trying to destroy the world. We stand upon the brink of war and total destruction."

A chime rang out in the air from where the delegates had assembled. The meeting was about to start.

King Questgiver spoke. "Fair greetings to you all. I have called you all here to discuss the strange behavior of the menu clock, what it represents, and what can be done about it."

A dark-elven woman wearing a knotted golden crown said, "And what have you learned, high king? What calamity does this foretell?"

"Calamity indeed. I assume that you are all familiar with the contract that our kingdom has with Entropy. For the sake of our human guest, I will describe it briefly."

One of the elven lords scoffed. "What is this human doing amongst us? I do not wish to treat with Zhakaran spies."

"This human is a player," Questgiver said. "She is here by my invitation. Tasha, what do you know about Entropy?"

"Only what I've heard from my friends. Entropy is the god of destruction. From what I've heard, an elven king struck some sort of Faustian deal with him. People living on Etheria would receive immunity to all forms of death save for old age. In exchange, after 3,000 years, he would destroy the planet. Your advisor, Snickers, appeared disguised as one of Entropy's priests and bargained on Entropy's behalf."

"That's correct," said the high king. "The king who struck that bargain was my grandfather, the first high-elven king. After completing the contract, Snickers made a second deal with him.

"It turned out that Snickers was a trickster god in disguise and lusted after the Questgivrian throne for some reason. Eidolons such as he cannot directly interfere in the affairs of mortals without the permission of those mortals. If he simply tried to take the throne, the other of his kind would step in to stop him. Instead, he made a bargain.

"He promised King Lorien two things in exchange for the crown. First, that he would loyally serve him and any of his descendants for as long as the bloodline continued. Second, that he would adjust the terms of the deal that was made with the destroyer god. Entropy would still destroy the world, but there would be a hundred hours of forewarning, and the means of his arrival would be something that we could hinder. When the end came, at least there would be hope.

"King Lorien accepted the deal. Since then, Snickers has been the chief advisor. My daughter, Kiwistafel, is the last of the Questgivrian bloodline."

Tasha nodded.

"Snickers, would you bring out the Deathslayer Scroll?" said King Questgiver.

Snickers the Bumble approached the table and removed something from his jacket. It was a wooden tube, far too large in size and length to fit inside the pocket he had just removed it from. He opened the tube and removed a large scroll, which he unrolled onto the table.

The contract was written in English, using elaborate lettering. At the bottom of the contract were two signatures.

"This is the same contract that Lorien signed with Entropy," King Questgiver said. "It is signed with the blood of a god and is utterly indestructible. It is this contract that ended death and now gives Entropy admittance to destroy Etheria."

A deafening voice filled Tasha's mind. *And are you saying that this contract is the reason for the countdown?* It was the large red dragon, who towered over the assembled races.

"Yes," said the king. "Over the last week, our astronomers have been observing the lesser moon, Entropy. That moon's orbital period has been slowly decreasing in time with the countdown. As the second moon is Entropy himself, we can infer that he's getting closer to Etheria as the clock runs down."

One of the orc chieftains spoke up. "Then what can be done about it? How can we kill a god?"

"Our researchers have been searching for an answer for days, ever since the countdown started. I believe we may have found a solution."

He removed an ancient tome from his inventory and placed it on the table. Carefully turning the pages, he found the one he was looking for. The script was in elvish, and Tasha couldn't read any of the words, but on one page there was a circle with diagram of six points and a building in the center. A second illustration showed what appeared to be a temple surrounded by columns.

"This ancient text describes a ritual that creates a portal to a place known as the Hallowed Chapel. The Hallowed Chapel is a separate realm which exists in Etheria for only minutes at a time and only when invoked. We've only summoned it a handful of times when we needed a place to store dangerous objects."

Tasha looked at him warily. "Like what sort of dangerous objects?"

"It contains dangerous magical objects as well as certain cursed objects that are harmful to elvenkind and can't be easily destroyed. There is the Crown of the Werehuman, the Uncertainty Bomb, and the Mirror of True Reflection, amongst other dangerous artifacts."

"What is this... Crown of the Werehuman?" asked Tasha.

"It transforms any sentient being into a human on the next full moon."

"That doesn't sound so bad," said Tasha.

"No offense," Kiwi said, "but no elf would want to become human, and there is no way to undo its effects."

"Okay, what about the Uncertainty Bomb?"

"We're... not actually certain," said Iolo. "We believe that it divides the universe when used. It may have already done so; there's really no way to tell. It's best to leave these dangerous artifacts where they can't harm anyone. Before you ask, the Mirror of True Reflection reveals your true nature. Through its use, we've learned that most people prefer a slightly less accurate self-image."

The giant spider that Tasha had seen earlier approached the table and spoke in a high, guttural voice. "How does this knowledge help us deal with the matter at hand?"

The king stood in thought for a moment. "If we place the scroll in the Hallowed Chapel, it would cease to exist once the Chapel vanishes. That might nullify the contract. No Etherian could do this because we are all bound by the contract. Only an outsider could carry the Deathslayer Scroll within."

"Wait a minute," Tasha said. "If I'm not bound by that contract, how is it that I respawned after death?"

The king thought for a moment. "I'm not sure. What normally happens to players when they die?"

"It depends on the game. I guess we would usually respawn."

"Then it seems you can respawn on death because of the very nature of players. The rest of us only respawn because of the Deathslayer Scroll. Once the scroll is nullified, the contract with Entropy will end, meaning that death will once again become permanent."

"It doesn't seem like there is any choice," Tasha said. "I'll carry the scroll into this Hallowed Chapel. So where exactly is it?"

"The Hallowed Chapel does not currently exist," King Questgiver said. "It must be summoned. In order to reach it, we must construct a suitable building. Any structure will do so long as it is a place of deep thought and contemplation. A synagogue or temple would suffice.

"Next, the six elemental orbs must be collected and placed around the structure. The elemental orbs form the cornerstones of the world, and placing them around the structure will channel vast amounts of energy from Etheria, allowing the portal to form.

"These will transform the building into a portal that can be used to reach the Hallowed Chapel. The portal will only last for mere minutes in our world—enough time to place an item inside and leave. Just go in, deposit the scroll, and exit.

"I will order the construction of an appropriate structure. As for the orbs, you'll have to collect them. The Zhakaran queen has the Orb of Fire, and"—he looked at Hermes awkwardly—"the dwarven king has the Orb of Earth. As far as I know, it is somewhere within the Laundry Mountain. The Orb of Air is in the possession of the pirate K'her Noálin, whose current whereabouts are unknown. The whereabouts of the Orb of Water is currently unknown, which is part of the reason I called this gathering of nations." He looked around. "You must each search for the orb in your own lands."

There was some general murmuring, but no one protested outright.

"That just leaves the orbs of Life and Death. The six elemental orbs form partnerships and ally themselves with individuals, lending those individuals their power. The Orb of Life was once allied with me and before that it was allied with my father. It resides in a structure known as the Spiral Tower, where it serves to power the healing effects of the save-point network. This one should be the easiest to retrieve."

"So what about the last one?" Tasha said. "The Orb of Death?"

"An age ago, there was a being who possessed the Orb of Death who came to be known as the Lich Queen. She drained the lifespan of others to add to her own. The player who proceeded you, Jak, slew the Lich Queen. All that remained of her was a single eye, which resisted every attempt to destroy it. In the end, the eye had to be stored in the Hallowed Chapel with the other dangerous artifacts."

Tasha's stomach twitched at the name. "I can't be sure, but I think this player named Jak was my father."

The king shook his head. "I'm afraid that's impossible. Humans don't live that long, and these events took place many hundreds of years ago."

"I see," said Tasha, but she wasn't really convinced.

The king continued. "After the Lich Queen was slain, we had the Orb of Death deposited in the moon's core to keep it out of the wrong hands. In those days, the dwarves made excursions to the moon on a regular basis, but that was a different age. Nobody has been to the moon in centuries. Getting you there will be tricky, but not impossible."

Tasha's face brightened. "Are you saying I'm going to get to fly to the moon?"

"Let's not get ahead of ourselves," the king said, holding up a hand. "At the moment we lack the ability to do anything of the sort. We should focus on the other orbs for the time being. The Orb of Life would be a good place to start, since we know where it is.

"Player Tasha, I must ask you to travel to the Spiral Tower to retrieve the Orb of Life for us."

"Must I do this alone?" Tasha said.

The king shook his head. "No, it is doubtful that any single traveler would survive the journey without escort." A grave look came over his face. "In fact, I fear that I must send my own daughter along with you. Long has the Orb of Life served the Questgiver line of kings. For a time it served me, but I haven't felt its presence in my heart for a long time. I believe that it may have changed allegiance to my daughter."

The princess nodded. "Then I will go in your stead."

"Is that wise?" Tasha asked, making a face. "She's being hunted by ninjas."

"There's little choice in the matter," Kiwi said. "Besides, next time they try to take me, I'll be stronger. Tasha, you will escort me to the Spiral Tower."

Tasha nodded. "I'll do my best."

"Count me in as well," Prince Hermes said. "I shall see you safely to the tower."

Slimon hopped up and put a tentacle on the princess's shoulder. "Pfffpt!"

"That makes four of us," Tasha said.

"Six," a small voice said. Pan stood up from behind a nearby shrub and removed the hood from her cloak. "C-count me and Ari in."

"How did you get i—" Tasha started to ask.

"I'm a thief," Pan said by way of explanation. She cast her eyes to the ground. "It's what I'm good at."

"Are you sure you can speak for Ari?"

Pan nodded. "We t-talked about it."

Kaze, the small dragon whom Tasha had spoken with earlier, approached. *Make it seven. I want to come too.*

At this declaration, the large red dragon who had been overlooking the meeting turned his head to face the smaller steam dragon.

No. I forbid you to travel with them. I understand your desire to become stronger, but they will travel far too close to the dwarven realm. We dare not approach the dwarven kingdom, lest we make them angry.

The deeper thought-voice of the older red dragon was replaced by Kaze's own. *I won't go as far as Dwarselvania—only as far as the edge of the slime kingdom.*

NO, the red dragon thought-spoke. *It is far too dangerous. You will return with us to Dragonholm once this meeting is concluded.*

"That's too bad," Tasha said. "We could have used him."

"It is just as well," King Questgiver said. "You should be traveling in secret, and dragons will be a rare sight in the lands to the east."

He turned to the slime minister. "Your Slimeliness, please arrange for appropriate travel passports for these six adventurers into your kingdom."

"Pfffpt. Pfft, ffpt," the slime minister responded sagely.

"Tasha," he said, "you will leave in two days. I will contact the dwarven ambassador and at least try to get King Dourmal to lend us the Orb of Earth. I will also contact Queen Murderjoy about the Orb of Fire, though I doubt anything will come of it."

Tasha's eyebrows shot up. "Her name... is Queen *Murderjoy*?"

"Yes," said the king, as if nothing was amiss. "Two days will give them time to respond to my request and time to arrange your passport. We can't afford to delay longer than that."

Tasha nodded, despite her qualms about going to see a woman named Murderjoy. "Of course, Your Grace. We'll be ready in two days."

A thought struck her. "How far is this... um..."

"Spiral Tower," Kiwi provided helpfully. "It is several months of travel, longer if we have to avoid the main roads."

Tasha gawked at her. "Can we *fly* there? I mean, there are flying dragons, and we're kind of on a time crunch."

We are not beasts of burden, human, thought-spoke the large dragon. *Even if we were willing—which we are not—we cannot approach the tower, as close as it is to dwarven lands.*

Well, there went her thoughts of a giant-eagle solution. "Okay, just thought I'd ask."

Having come to a plan of action, the meeting ended, and the delegates began to leave. King Questgiver had busied himself with contacting the human and dwarven kingdoms, and the dragons had all taken to the air.

Tasha left the garden and returned to the castle to meet up with Ari. They spoke at length and agreed to spend the next few days level grinding. The road ahead promised to be full of challenge, and they would more easily face it armed with greater stat points.

CHAPTER 22

The Queen and the Pirate

Unless you've been living under a rock for the last three hundred years, you've most likely already heard of the Zhakaran Dominion. Given the living situations of our readership, that may not include everyone, so this month we're giving a brief overview of Zhakara.

The continent of Zhakara is situated to the southeast of Questgivria, across Ultros Bay. The only land route to Questgivria skirts the Uncrossable Veldt through the Slime Federation.

In Zhakara, there is only a single law: No human may claim mastery over another. There are no other laws to govern conduct. In Zhakara, you can commit any action that doesn't imply mastery without fear of interference by the government. Violent acts like killing and thievery are not punishable by the government and are, in fact, commonplace. Individuals are expected to take care of themselves.

This has led to a unique form of serfdom. Rich landowners restrict access to their lands for the purpose of level grinding. They wall off NPC quest givers and merchants and charge a portion of any loot found for access. Save points are often camped by the opportunistic for easy experience.

Although humans in Zhakara cannot be enslaved under the law, that same restriction doesn't apply to non-humans. The Zhakaran economy is largely slave-based, and slave raids of elven lands has become commonplace. Slave ownership is also considered a desirable status level within Zhakara.

Amongst the human inhabitants of Zhakara, the divide between rich landowners and the low-level peasantry has led to a large and impoverished lower class. The resulting rampant starvation and homelessness has led to a refugee crisis. Lower-level humans have been pouring into Questgivria by the hundreds, all seeking a chance at a better life than as serfs to the lords.

Zhakara is known as the land of perfect freedom, but does it live up to its name, or is it a libertarian social experiment gone horribly wrong? That depends largely on who you are. If you are a well-off human with flexible moral scruples, Zhakara could expand your personal liberties. If not, you may wish to choose another place for your summer getaway.

—From the *Billbember edition of* Hermit's Digest, 3187 3E

The pirate captain K'her Noálin stood upon the deck of his airship. The dark elf looked down upon his handiwork that was the smoldering remains of the city below. The once great city-state of Adreála was now a shattered remnant of what it had once been. Its Crystal Keep had been leveled to the ground, buildings had been reduced to flaming cinders, and the surviving citizens had been imprisoned. His crew waited by a city save point, capturing elven citizens one by one as they respawned.

He grinned in satisfaction as the captured elves were marched onto his slave transports to be ferried onto his airships. Adreála never stood a chance against his flying armada. Only dragons or other orb bearers could offer any challenge while he was in the air.

K'her regarded the orb affixed to his wrist. Patterns of flowing wind danced within. It had come into his possession centuries ago, when he was nothing more than a seafaring trader. Oh, how far he had come since then. King of the Pirates, they called him. The orb had bonded with him and with it he could control the ebb and flow of the very air around him. This was vital, as it allowed him to control the air pressure below his dirigible fleet, providing lift. It also put the wind to their backs, allowing them to move at great speeds. He could even enchant regular objects with the ability to levitate.

Although both Zhakara and Questgivria had agreed to a cease fire, a proxy war between the two great empires was in full effect. Queen

Murderjoy promised good money for each and every elf that he captured and brought to her. Moreover, she offered a small fortune in GP for any of the elven royalty. That's why he'd chosen to attack the city-state of Adreála—the Crystal Keep was home to Count Sigred Elsander and his family.

At the save point below, there was a flash of light as another elf appeared wearing nothing but the plain sleeveless shirt and short pants that everyone resurrected with. One of his pirates on the ground used a large wooden device to clamp an iron collar around the elf's neck, then pushed him outside the circle. Another one spawned, this time a young elven child. The captain turned away. Slavery was dirty business, but it was against his ethical code to turn down cash.

"Mr. Malarkey," he called, "where 'ave ye gone?"

"Here, sir," a small gnome replied, running up to his captain. He held his hands together nervously.

"'Ave ye done a proper accountin' o' th' plunder?"

"Indeed, sir. Though many of the citizens have yet to respawn, I can confirm that we have captured three members of the nobility. Our lookouts report three lightning dragons to the south, but I don't believe they have noticed us."

"An' how long will it be afore we can be underway?"

"The rate of respawns has already begun to slow. I recommend we wait for another hour before leaving so's we can pick up the stragglers."

"Nay," Captain K'her said. "Hoist th' mainsails 'n prepare t' set out at once. I'd be loathe t' risk a confrontation wit' dragons while weighed down wit' elven cargo."

Though his mastery of the orb allowed him to repel dragons and let his fleet escape into the stratosphere, flying creatures were still dangerous. A single burst of dragonfire would be enough to destroy one of his dirigibles, and that would cut heavily into his profit margins.

"Aye, sir," the gnome said. "Shall I set a course for the Zhakaran capital?"

"Aye, Mr. Malarkey. Let us offload this merchandise as swiftly as possible."

Ten minutes later, the elven slaves and ship's crew were loaded aboard their ships, and the armada was airborne. The captured elves had been crammed into cargo holds, shackled and drugged into a state of unconsciousness to keep their fighters and casters from resisting. An unconscious prisoner was one unlikely to attempt escape.

Captain K'her called upon the power of the Orb of Air to propel his fleet of ships southward along the coast at best speed. The fleet continued on this course for nearly a day before crossing eastward in order to stay well outside Questgivrian borders.

Three days of flight elapsed before the fleet crossed into the continent of Zhakara. During flight, the prisoners were woken from their drug-induced slumber in small groups. They were fed and rehydrated before being put back to sleep.

It wouldn't do for their elven livestock to expire before reaching their final destination.

Deep within the kingdom of Zhakara, in the capital city of Bastion, an evil queen sat upon her throne. She didn't self-identify as evil, but just about everyone viewed her in that regard. Given the fear and respect that the moniker "Murderjoy" implied, she didn't object to its usage.

The queen was receiving supplicants, but so far there hadn't been any. Apparently, word had gotten around that she had incinerated the last group, and nobody wanted to take the risk of being her next victim.

Queen Murderjoy sighed. Being a tyrant wasn't as easy as she made it look. The rabble probably thought it was a walk in the park, and while she did find wanton destruction and recreational murder enjoyable, the day-to-day operations of running a kingdom tended to drag on. While it was true that she could reduce anyone who glanced at her the wrong way to cinders with little more than a thought, the logistics involved in running an evil empire was the very definition of tedium. She left such minor details of governance to her trusted advisors.

Every so often one of her advisors would betray her and attempt to unseat her as queen, but that was a small price to pay to avoid the crippling mountains of paperwork that leadership entails.

Aralynn Murderjoy was a tall, slender human woman with long black hair. Her most noticeable part of her ensemble was a large headpiece comprised of several levels of concentric golden semi-circles with pointed spikes emitting from the center like rays from the sun.

Her advisors tried to tell her that it looked ridiculous, so she'd incinerated them, thus solving the problem. It was the queen's privilege to look as ridiculous as she wanted to, and nobody was going to tell her otherwise.

The real problem with her headpiece came when she had to cross a narrow doorway. Her headpiece gave her a substantial magic boost, so she never took it off. But it was so large that when she came to door, she would either have to duck and edge in sideways or blast a hole in the wall to allow for easy ingress. Eventually her citizens just started making larger doors to accommodate their queen and avoid the property damage.

She had been notified by swallow that Captain K'her had arrived in the country and was bringing a fresh batch of elven captives. It was about time, she had grown bored waiting.

Her focus was on capturing as many members of the elven royal family as possible. If she couldn't destroy them by force of arms, perhaps she could destroy their government and break the Questgivrian spirit.

She sat on her throne, examining the artifact known as the Orb of Fire, which was affixed to her staff. It looked like a small glass orb with a ball of fire in the center, and it warmed her hand as she held it. It was this orb which gave her the power to maintain her position of unquestioned authority over her people and the might to challenge King Questgiver. To most people it would just be a pretty ornament, but to her it was the ultimate destructive weapon. And most importantly, it was hers. The orb answered to her and her alone.

She had managed to reach the exalted level of 107, and she was barely into her midforties. Such a feat should have been impossible—the level curve for humans was such that even the most dedicated level grinders would never achieve level 70 before their bodies gave way to old age.

Finally a supplicant walked into the huge chamber and approached the throne. It was a teenage human girl. She stopped a dozen paces away from the throne and bowed deeply. "If it pleases Your Majesty, I come bearing a message."

The queen looked at the poor girl in much the same way that a bored cat looks at a particularly plump and tasty-looking mouse. "Well? Is it good news or bad news?"

"I cannot say, my lady. I haven't read it. It's addressed to Your Majesty."

"Go on, girl, read it to me, then," Queen Murderjoy commanded.

"Yes, Majesty," she said, producing and opening a scroll. "It's from the Hidden Smog Ninja Village. It reads, 'It is to our shame to report that we failed to capture Princess Kiwistafel. Our shinobi took her as planned, but our agents were unable to escape the kingdom and were ultimately killed by adventurers. The princess was lost to us. We already have a second plan in the works to reclaim her. Our agent in the castle informs us that a human woman who self-identifies as a player is currently visiting the castle and will be escorting Princess Kiwistafel on a level grind. We intend to take the princess at this time.'"

"*What?*" she screamed. "The ninjas failed me? I'll have their village burned to the ground!"

With that utterance, a ball of flame shot from the queen's outstretched hand and engulfed the messenger girl, who collapsed and was reduced to a pile of ash.

Queen Murderjoy looked at the pile of ashes where the girl had stood moments before. That'll teach the girl a lesson for bringing bad news to her queen. Someone would have to clean that up. The cleaning staff would probably take care of it.

On second thought, perhaps she had been hasty. The ninjas were still her best chance to capture the princess. She would allow them this last opportunity.

A familiar voice came from the throne room entrance. "Did I come at a bad time, me queen? I hope I don't find ye in an overly murderous mood this fine evening."

She smiled. "It's never a bad time for you, my captain. Tell me, have you brought the commodities that we discussed?"

"Aye," Captain K'her said. "The prisoners have already been transferred to yer facility. Three of them are from the Elsander royal house. The capital city of Adreála has been destroyed an' the Crystal Keep be no more than rubble."

Captain K'her was one of the few people in Etheria who didn't fear Queen Murderjoy. Though her level and stats were far beyond his, they were both orb bearers, and the raw power that the orbs possessed far exceeded the power of either of them.

The queen walked toward the pirate, stepping carefully around the pile of ash. "It is agreeable to see you again, my love. Will you be staying long?"

"We'll needs be setting sail on the morrow. I must be honest wit' ye. I don't mind killing fer a bit o' filthy lucre, but slavin' be dark business. What need have ye of so many slaves?"

She hesitated before offering a small smile. "Even though you don't approve, you still captured them and sold them to me. Why is that?"

"Why, for the filthy lucre, o' course! Pay me enough GP an' I'll do whate'er needs doin'. Be at ease, me love. If I ever had a conscience, I'd have sold it many years ago."

She looked the dark elf straight in the eyes. "Listen, I'm no more a fan of slavery than you are, but the truth is that I need as many slaves as possible, as quickly as possible."

"But why?" he asked.

"Come with me, my captain. Come with me, and I will show you the secret to my power."

The left the castle and walked through the city streets of Bastion, escorted by her royal guard. People lowered themselves to their knees in submission as she passed. One man was too slow in bowing to the ground, so she incinerated him.

Finally, they arrived at a large building in the heart of Bastion. "This is our slave orientation and reeducation center. There are similar structures throughout my kingdom, but all new acquisitions pass through here before being sent on."

It was a multilevel building with cells along the outer edges. There was a save point situated at the center of the room, enclosed by metal bars. As Captain K'her regarded the save point, there was a flash, and a dark-elven woman appeared wearing a simple white shirt and short pants. The moment she appeared, two elven slaves pushed a bar on the outside of the cage, which forced the newly spawned dark elf through the single opening. She tumbled out, and another slave chained and collared her before she was led to one of the cells.

On one edge of the room was a giant vat of boiling acid. Two elven slaves carried the dead body of an elven child and threw it into the vat.

"What dark place have ye brought me to?" he asked. The building was eerily silent but for the occasional scream of pain or the sound of weeping.

"Follow me. Everything will be made clear," she said. She motioned to a guard, who guided them to a small room on the bottom floor, closing the door behind them as they entered. The room was dimly lit by a magical torch along the wall.

The queen indicated two captives. "Behold, the Elsander royal family."

Two elves were chained to manacles, suspended against the brick wall. They both wore simple white shirts and pants—the same clothing they had worn when they respawned.

The elven man tried to stand, but his feet were too high above the ground for him to be successful. "Are you... Queen Murderjoy?"

"Indeed, I am," she said. "And you are Count Sigred Elsander, leader of the once great city-state of Adreála."

"What do you want with us?" the elven man said. "What have you done with my people?"

She smiled. "Your people will serve us, and so will you. Tell me, where is your son? He wasn't on the manifest."

"The prince is beyond your reach. He was on a level grind when the attack came."

"Oh yes, that's right. You Questgivrians force your children to fight monsters despite their tender age. In Zhakara, we would never be so cruel to our own children."

"Ye mean to say that yer young don't fight mobs to gain experience?" Captain K'her said.

"No," said the queen, "we have found a better way to level them up. A safer way. Come here, my love. Let me show you."

She drew a long dagger with a jagged edge. Taking the captain's hand, they both grasped the handle. She thrust it into Sigred's heart, dealing five hearts of damage. She pulled it out and struck again and again and again as his wife screamed. Finally, the elven count expired, and a combat notification appeared:

Victory! All enemies have been vanquished.

+112 experience gained. (103,067 to next level)

The queen grinned, dismissing the combat notification. "He will return in a few hours, and I'll kill him again and again until I've drained him of all of his levels. Every day, I kill thousands of elven slaves. This is how I've gained a higher level than anyone else in Etheria, through the mass blood sacrifice of my enemies."

The elven queen was weeping quietly, so Aralynn killed her, earning another 99 XP.

"This is diabolical," the captain said. "Your ambition and bloodlust is truly without equal, my lady. I tip my hat to ye."

"Stop it, you're making me blush!" she said. "Don't get the wrong idea. I'm not the only person to benefit from our prisoners in this way. Like I said to the good count here, we don't force our children to fight mobs. Using elven sacrifices, we power level them to level 5. This gives them a major advantage over our enemies. Once the elves are drained of their levels, they are reeducated and sold as laborers or domestic servants. Some of them are forced to level grind so that we can extract additional XP from them."

The captain nodded. "That's why ye have need of elven slaves."

"Elves have the highest level curve, and as such are worth the highest amount of XP when killed. Due to the recent ceasefire, raids such as yours are our only source of new elves."

If the captain was fazed by this revelation, he didn't show it. It was an impressive use of resources, nothing more. This was an opportunity for him to earn GP, and he cared about little else.

A few hours later, the unfortunate messenger, whose name was Paula, came back to life. She had resurrected at the save point in Bastion's town square. An elderly man greeted her and helped her step down from the platform that held the glowing save point.

"How did the queen take the news?" he asked.

"Not well, boss," said Paula. "She was furious. She said she was going to burn the ninja village to the ground. After saying that, she set me on fire and killed me."

"I'm sorry you keep having to go through this," he said.

"It's okay," said Paula. "Dying and coming back to life in a new body is a rush. Becoming someone new over and over again is just about the best thing ever. Besides, being a professional bad-news-giver is a good job and easy money."

"And the painkiller we gave you?" the man said.

"I didn't feel a thing."

The man nodded. "That's good. I have a feeling that we may have need of your services soon. The menu countdown spells troublesome times ahead."

He gave her a sealed yellow envelope. "Here's your payment with a nice bonus. Please stay in the city. I may have more work for you soon."

"I always do."

He looked toward the queen's palace. "Without us to advise her, the queen's madness could consume this realm. She needs us, even if she doesn't realize it."

The man left her, and Paula opened the envelope, adding the 4,500 GP to her inventory. This would be enough money to pay for all of her living expenses for the next three months, allowing her to maintain the lifestyle to which she had grown accustomed.

CHAPTER 23

Level Grind

A foreign human named Tasha Singleton was arrested last Wootsday morning in connection with the Marketplace Massacre. Three of the city's guardsmen were killed in the incident and two were wounded, along with at least fifteen civilian injuries and four fatalities. Property damage from the scuffle was estimated to be in the hundreds of thousands of GP, and at least one orphanage was damaged beyond repair.

The human in question escaped captivity briefly but was arrested again that evening when she was spotted entering through the western city gates. After a brief but intense trial, which involved lots of shouting, the human was found to be not guilty by reason of being a completely different person.

The prosecutor, Borgrim Deathhammer, had this to say when asked about Ms. Singleton's not-guilty verdict: "This is a travesty of justice! Tash-AH Singleton, if you are reading this, I want you to know that Borgrim Deathhammer is coming to bring you to justice!" Borgrim Deathhammer then started laughing maniacally, and it is against this newspaper's policies to transcribe maniacal laughter.

Article from The Brightwind Tribune, *Doguary 4th, 3205 3E*

Tasha was still in dreamland when Pan shook her awake.

"Wha? It's too early," she whined, retreating deeper into the fluffy bedsheets. The bed needed her and refused to let her go.

"Breakfast," Pan said.

Hmm... sleep or breakfast. Breakfast or sleep. That was the eternal conundrum. "Are there pancakes?"

"Mmm hmmm," said Pan.

It was a tough decision, but eventually her desire for syrup-drenched pancakes dripping with butter won out over her natural morning laziness. She pried herself out of bed and put some early-morning clothing on.

Tasha and Pan met Ari, Hermes, and Slimon in the dining hall and shared a light breakfast consisting of fried eggs, sausage, bacon, the pancakes she'd been promised, a blueberry muffin, the elven equivalent of grits, and lots of coffee.

After eating enough pancakes to send a mid-sized elephant into a carbohydrate-induced coma, the gang met up with Princess Kiwi. Together, they left the castle and made their way through the city streets. Kiwi was riding her own mount, a smaller grayish velociraptor. The rest of the party visited the rent-a-raptor station. It wasn't cheap, but moving quickly was the best way to face the highest number of random encounters. They wanted to level quickly, after all.

Aralogos indicated a lightly used path which wound its way through the hilly grassland. This path was not protected against random encounters. "If nobody has any objections, I've already consulted the map and found some good hunting areas to the southwest. We'll mostly be facing level 14 through 20 mobs. Once we all reach level 15, we can move on to higher-level opponents."

"Sounds good to me," Tasha said. "Stronger enemies means we can level up faster."

"Just remember," said Hermes, "don't put too much stock in an opponent's level. With the application of care and strategy, a level 1 warrior can defeat a level 100 mob."

"Is that really true?" Tasha asked. "From what I've experienced, my attacks barely did any damage to the Ginormosaurus Rex, and it was only level 38."

"It is," he said. "While it is true that low-level attacks will barely do any damage to high-level monsters, they will still take damage from natural effects like fire, drowning, or a fall from a great height. The greatest advantage we have over them is that we are capable of complex thought and they are not.

"If a level 1 warrior can trick a monster into running off a cliff, that monster will still die, and the warrior will receive all of the experience points. Until you came along, it still wouldn't be enough to gain a whole level, but now it just might. Mr. Aralogos, I say we go farm the Ginormosaurus Rex rather than spending time fighting weaker enemies. I've gained multiple levels from killing it once. If we can set a pit trap for it, we might be able to finish it off easily."

"He's right," said Kiwi. "We only have two days before we must set out. This might be the only chance we have to actively farm monsters."

"Tasha, what do you think?" asked Ari. "In the past, Pan and I have always worked within our capabilities, erring on the side of caution. On the other hand, Hermes's plan could gain us levels much more quickly."

Tasha thought for a moment. "Do we even have any shovels? I mean, digging a hole big enough to contain the G-Rex could take days."

Hermes laughed at this. "Ha! I'm a dwarf. We were born to mine and dig into the earth. I could have a pit of sufficient size dug in a few hours at most. Besides," he said with an evil grin, "if the pit doesn't work, we can just throw Tasha into his mouth, and she can finish him off from the inside. Now that we know its weakness, defeating it should be easy."

"Don't worry Tasha," the princess said, "he's just joking. Probably. Hermes has a dark sense of humor."

"Thank you, Kiwi," Tasha said. "I knew you would be on my side." She turned to the slime. "What do you think, Slimon?"

"Pppft!" Slimon suggested.

Ari nodded. "Slimon is right—there is little to be gained without risk. Besides, the worst that could happen is that we all die horrible, agonizing deaths and respawn to try again."

So, armed with a plan, the party headed back to the fallen watchtower. It took an hour of riding before reaching G-Rex territory.

They were attacked by several groups of plant-based mobs called tulicoptors. They had propellers allowing them to fly, and they fired seeds. Kiwi and Tasha belted them with fire-based projectile attacks, making short work of them. After each battle, Sir Slimon used healing magic on any injured party members. It was nice to have a healer in the group.

Finally, they arrived at the plateau overlooking the now destroyed watchtower. Pan used her binoculars to scan the area and found a spot not too far off that formed a natural pass and was surrounded on either side by low cliff walls. If the G-Rex gave chase, they could lead him through the narrow canyon. Assuming Hermes could make good on his claim to dig a pit in two hours, that would make the perfect point for a trap.

Fortunately, there were no new monster encounters as they approached the small canyon. It would still be difficult to defeat the G-Rex in a conventional fight.

Tasha spent the next two hours watching Hermes dig a hole. She didn't really think he could do it but quickly developed a newfound respect for the dwarf's hole-digging capabilities. His hole-digging technique was unconventional to say the least. He casted a spell that separated large parts of the ground into cube-shaped blocks of dirt. He then put his right hand on the segmented ground and simply added it to his inventory. It was not unlike watching someone play *Minecraft* in real life.

After about an hour of this, they had a hole that looked like it would be big enough to contain a G-Rex. They carefully covered the pit with sticks, leaves, and dirt in order to conceal it from their prey. It didn't really look natural, but hopefully it would trick the mob.

"Don't f-forget where the pit is," Pan said.

"And what kind of idiot would be foolish enough to forget where they dug their pit trap?" Hermes said.

Dozens of *Pokémon* episodes ran through Tasha's mind where Team Rocket dug a trap but covered it up so well that they forgot where it was and ended up falling in themselves.

Tasha smirked and snorted out a laugh. "Good point. Yeah, who would do that? So, which of us will pull the G-Rex and bring him here?"

Kiwi patted Denver on the neck. "I think that will be you, me, and Denver."

"She's right," said Ari. "Other than Pan, you two weigh the least among us, and Denver will need to move fast to keep ahead of the G-Rex. Also, most of our mounts are rentals. They won't follow us into combat like Denver would."

Kiwi equipped her staff. "And you need me to cast the vine spell to slow it down."

Tasha steeled her nerves. "Okay, let's do this."

She mounted Denver ,and Kiwi got on behind her, holding on to her for balance. She spent the better part of the next hour riding in circles, but most of the mobs were lower level. It turned out that the G-Rex was a somewhat rare spawn.

Finally, a large amount of mist began to form all around and coalesced into the form of the mighty Ginormosaurus Rex.

"Hit it!" she yelled, and Kiwi raised her staff with her free hand and shot a bolt of lightning directly at its face, dealing six hearts of damage.

Not wasting any more time, she pulled the reins to one side, turning Denver about and leading him back the way they had come. The chase was easier this time, but there were still some close calls. Every two minutes, Kiwi cast the vine spell, which added some distance from the G-Rex. They took care not to allow too much distance to form, as that could prompt the mob to despawn.

When they finally reached the cavern, they led the G-Rex right into it. Tasha circled around the area where she knew the pit was, careful not to travel over it. As the monster stomped over the pit, the sticks and leaves that concealed the hole snapped apart, causing the G-Rex to lose its footing and tumble inside.

Though the G-Rex filled the hole, the hole was only covered part way. They were gambling on the G-Rex's inability to pull itself out of the hole on its own. It began to struggle, trying to climb out, but it wasn't making any headway. Its tiny arms were ill-suited to climbing.

"Okay, everyone," said Aralogos, "hit it with everything you've got!"

Slimon cast some sort of debuff on the monster while Hermes opened fire with his machine-gun arm, and Tasha shot it with a Kamehameha blast. Aralogos had jumped on its back and was punching it on the neck repeatedly, pulverizing it. Pan shot it with her crossbow over and over again.

After less than a minute, the G-Rex let out one final cry and vanished into the mist.

> **Victory! All enemies have been vanquished.**
> **1840 experience gained. (1,365 to next level)**
> **1200 GP found.**
> **Level Up!**
> **Level Up!**
> **You have reached level 14.**
> **You have 8 unassigned stat points.**
> **Choose either a heart container or mana container.**

Tasha put everything into agility and took two heart containers. She now had 18 agility and ten hearts.

She jumped up as high as she could and was shocked to find the ground racing away from her. She wondered if she could pull off ninja-style moves like jumping from one tree to another. Of course, what goes up must come down, and her landing was far less graceful than she would have liked. Her landings were something that she would need to work on.

"We did it!" said Kiwi, who was hugging Slimon happily. The last time she'd defeated the G-Rex, she was lucky to have survived. This time they attacked it head-on and won using strategy and wit.

Once everyone settled down from celebrating the victory, they collectively decided to call a lunch break. Kiwi removed some folding chairs and a collapsing picnic table from her inventory and set it up. Lunch was a light affair consisting of sandwiches, potato chips, and cheesecake for dessert, making it about a quarter the size of their breakfast.

As the luncheon wound down, Tasha was still engaged in conversation with the princess. They had been discussing the differences between this world and the world of players.

Kiwi looked at Tasha in shock over a bite of cheesecake. "So what you're telling me is that when someone from your world eats food, they get fatter and lose agility?"

Tasha nodded. "More or less. We have to physically train our bodies to gain strength and agility, and if we eat too much of the wrong things, our bodies become out of shape and gain weight."

"But... that's utterly horrible! What manner of nightmarish universe do you come from?"

"Oh, it gets worse—gaining strength and agility isn't enough. If you don't physically exercise every day, those attributes diminish over time."

"Oh, you poor thing!" she said, embracing Tasha in a deep hug. "I had no idea the world of players was such a horrible place."

Tasha found herself wondering how food actually worked in Etheria. "Just to be sure, I can eat as much as I want and not gain weight, right?"

Kiwi swallowed a piece of cheesecake and answered, "Yes, that's mostly correct. Excess calories from food restores health and mana. So long as you expend mana or lose health before eating, any extra calories from the food will be used to recover. I believe one mana point is about equal to a chocolate bar, which is why mages eat so much. I suppose if you kept eating but never expended any mana, you could gain weight, but that's easy enough to avoid. Just cast some spells before eating."

"In that case, I think I'll have another piece of cheesecake. By the way, Kiwi, you and Slimon make a cute couple. How did you meet?"

Kiwi explained to Tasha how they had been friends since she was little and had grown closer throughout her long childhood. She told Tasha about how the two of them wanted to get married, but how her father wouldn't allow it due to their "issues of fundamental reproductive incompatibility."

"So you're telling me you can't marry Slimon because he reproduces through mitosis?" Tasha asked.

"That's right. We're searching for a way to have children together. The two of us have searched throughout all of Questgivria for a solution, but to no avail."

"I know how you can do it," Tasha said.

Kiwi's face lit up. "Really? How?"

"Remember back at the council of nations yesterday? Your father was listing the contents of the Hallowed Chapel."

"I remember, what of it?"

"Well, one of the items stored inside was the Crown of the Werehuman. It turns anyone into a human being during the full moon."

"Yeah, I remember studying about. A truly horrific artifact. I shudder to even think about such a thing. What does that have to do with anything?"

"It's simple. Once we make it to the Hallowed Chapel, Slimon can put on the crown."

Kiwi looked confused. "That... would make him turn into a human once every month or so. How would that help?"

"Well, elves and humans are sexually compatible, right?"

"I suppose technically that's true. Sorry, Tasha, but I don't see where you're going with this."

Do I really need to spell this out for her? Tasha took a deep breath. "Once a month, when Slimon turns into a human, you can... *copulate* with him. That way you'll be able to have children."

It took a moment for Kiwi to fully process what Tasha had said. The idea of copulating with a human had simply never occurred to her. "So... you're saying when Slimon turns into a human, we would..."

"...have sex," Pan piped in helpfully. Ari shot her a dark look.

Princess Kiwi retched involuntarily. "S-sorry, I think I just threw up in my mouth a little."

"Oh, come on, we humans aren't that disgusting, are we?"

"No! No, of course not. I've just never thought about... humans that way. No, you're right. This could be the answer to all our problems. I... I'll do it. For love! Thank you, Tasha. You might have just saved our future marriage."

"Pffpt," Slimon said.

"It's no big deal," Tasha said. She finished off her cheesecake and got to her feet. There wasn't much time left, and they had monsters to kill.

CHAPTER 24

Twinklebottom's Fury

Most of that afternoon and early evening was spent repeatedly trapping the G-Rex and killing it. They had successfully killed seven G-Rexes in total, and as a result Tasha had gained another two levels. The amount of level growth had gone down significantly, but it was still progress. She put four points into strength and another four into agility and claimed a heart container and a mana container.

Unfortunately, Tasha's lucky streak wasn't to continue for much longer. It was getting dark, and they decided to kill one more G-Rex before returning to the castle for the evening. At first things went the same as they had the last half dozen times they killed it, but this time Tasha made a mistake. Maybe it was because of the darkening sky, but she couldn't see the boundaries of the pit.

After leading the G-Rex to the pit, Kiwi and Tasha dismounted from Denver, and Tasha ran up to the edge of the pit trap. Unfortunately, Tasha had lost sight of its edge and ran straight into it, snapping a branch under her foot and falling into the pit. The fall cost four heart containers and hurt like hell, but it wasn't enough to kill her. She looked up and saw a faint sliver of light shining through the branches above.

"Oh shit!" Panicking, she jumped upward toward the edge of the pit. She could *almost* reach the top.

Ability Unlocked: Wall Climb (Level 0)

Type: Active ability
Improves your ability to climb vertical walls. You are 5% more likely to discover usable handholds.

She scrambled and scraped against the dirt wall but wasn't able to get a grip on the edge. Instead she grabbed a fistful of dirt and fell back into the pit. Ari called out Tasha's name in a panic.

A moment later, there was a large snapping noise, and an angry G-Rex tumbled into the hole, falling right toward her.

There wasn't any pain from the impact—her death was instantaneous.

It was the second time that she had died, and like before, she found herself in a place devoid of sensation. For an uncertain amount of time, her body was formless and weightless. There was no air to breathe or lungs to process oxygen. After the initial panic attacks brought on by the inability to breathe, Tasha actually began to find the formlessness peaceful. Her perception of time was affected, and one moment blended with the next.

She didn't know how much time had passed, but finally, she heard a soundless voice calling her name. It was her own voice, but different than she remembered it. She could make out the naked body of the woman before her. The apparition spoke the word "Tasha" a second time. Tasha looked into the woman's eyes, and together they spoke her name one final time.

Then she regained consciousness. Tasha was wearing the familiar white loose-fitting shirt and a pair of short pants. Her armor was gone, and so was her gunblade. She felt different, like something about her had changed.

A hand reached out to take hers. Ari helped her off the save point.

"How do you feel, Tasha?" he asked, taking his hand back.

She shook her head, trying to clear it. "I feel... different than before. Guess I screwed up with the trap."

"Don't feel bad about that, Tasha. It could have happened to anyone," Ari said, trying to console her.

"Next time," Hermes added, "just be sure to remember where you put the trap."

"Shut up, Hermes," she said. "Ari, Thanks for being here when I came back to life. It means a lot."

"Of course, Tasha."

"Anyway, thanks, Ari. How did you get here? So... what happened after I died?"

"Well, we finished it off quickly once it fell, but it was too late. You were completely flattened. We all came here as fast as possible. I thought you use a friendly face once you respawned. Here." He handed Tasha her gunblade.

Pan walked up to Tasha and gave her a quick hug before backing away.

"Thanks, Pan, but really, I'm okay. What about my armor?"

"Gone," Pan said. "S-sorry."

"It's fine. I needed to buy some new armor anyway."

Tasha rejoined the others and they started back toward the castle. That night they shared a dinner consisting of spaghetti noodles served with brontosaurus meatballs and tomato sauce. Tasha had always thought that elves were vegetarians but quickly abandoned that assumption.

Kiwi had already reached level 18, and Tasha was level 16. They were ahead of schedule, but given that the same mobs yielded less experience for higher-level adventurers, it was anyone's guess whether they could really make level 20 in one day by fighting the G-Rex.

The next morning, they set out early. Tasha had no problem waking up. She looked at her bedsheets in utter confusion. Why would she want to stay in bed when there were so many exciting things to do, monsters to kill, and foodstuffs to be eaten? Not even the lazy sleeper aspect of her personality had survived her resurrection. She wondered again about this stranger she had become. Waking up early? This wasn't who she was at all.

She shook her head and joined her friends for a light breakfast before heading out into the city. Pan offered to join her for some armor shopping. Ari was off purchasing some restoratives and picking up the raptors.

One of the shops had a sign above it that read "Charlotte's Armor." It occurred to Tasha that a female armor maker might design armor that offered a more reasonable amount of body coverage. She didn't really buy into the last armor seller's explanation about minimizing coverage to preserve the armor's durability.

Tasha entered the armor shop, and there before her was a woman with the body of a spider. Tasha froze in instinctive terror for an instant, but the moment subsided. The woman before her had the upper body of a human and the lower body of an arachnid. Her hair was long and silky white, and she was wearing a tank top.

"Is the human unwell?" asked the spider lady, concerned. She spoke with a heavy accent.

"I'm okay. S-sorry about that." Her voice was shaking. She could deal with this. This spider wasn't a threat; she just wanted to sell armor to her. Since when was Tasha arachnophobic? Another aspect of her new personality? She hoped that wasn't the case.

"C-c-can I see some armor, please?" Her voice sounded broken, and she was stammering. Tasha needed to get control of herself.

"Okay," said the proprietor. "Charlotte hopes her appearance isn't upsetting to the human. Charlotte knows. Some humans fear our kind, but do not fear Charlotte. She will not harm the human, no."

"I was just taken by surprise," Tasha said still trembling. "I'm okay now. Sorry."

"Good, good. Will the human kindly step into the parlor?"

Her parlor. Yeah. Why not? What could possibly go wrong?

So Tasha stepped into the spider's parlor. It actually turned out to be quite cozy. Charlotte served some tea and biscuits to Tasha and Pan before getting down to business. Tasha was sitting in a cozy armchair, and Pan was in one next to her, gobbling up the snickerdoodles while playing a Japanese RPG on Tasha's phone. Tasha's hands were still shaking, but at least Pan seemed at ease. Pan was a native to Etheria and was probably used to seeing spider women all the time.

"What kind of armor would human prefer?," she asked.

"Light armor. Something that improves my maneuverability. My stats are optimized for agility. If you have something that isn't too revealing that would be better as well."

"Charlotte has just the thing.," she said and returned a moment later with a suit of spider silk armor.

"Charlotte made this one herself," the spider woman said. Tasha wasn't entirely sure whether that meant she produced the source material herself or just assembled it into armor. She focused on the stats:

Light Spidersilk Armor
Defense +25
Movement Speed +36
Style +40
Cost: 4800 GP

The stats were much nicer than her old chainmail bikini. It would boost her movement speed by a large amount and improve her defense as well.

"Can I try it on?"

"Yes, yes, try it on, human. If it doesn't fit, Charlotte can adjust."

She took the armor and opened her equipment menu. As she equipped the item, the clothing that she was wearing vanished to be replaced by a bodice and skirt. Both seemed to be made out of strands of silk webbing. The webbing wasn't sticky, but was cordlike and molded itself to her body, accentuating her curves. The skirt was knee length and open on one side.

"I'll take it," she said. "I think it looks good, and I like the stats. I do have a question. There's very little exposed area above the legs. The last armorer I visited said that they made armor that had as little coverage as possible in order to stop it from being damaged. This armor seems to have very little uncovered areas."

The spider woman looked at her quizzically. "The proprietor of that armor shop, was he male?"

She remembered the elf who sold her the chainmail bikini. "Yes, he was."

She laughed. "Well, that explains it. He's not entirely wrong about the durability problem, and Charlotte can't promise that it won't get damaged, but spidersilk armor can be easily repaired. If it is damaged, bring it back to Charlotte, yes?"

She paid the spider lady her 4800 GP for the armor and another 300 GP for a good pair of shoes to replace the ones that had been flattened.

Pan and Tasha headed to the stables at the city entrance. Tasha collected Denver and met her friends by the city gates.

Ari walked up to her. "You look... amazing."

"Th-thanks, Ari. Do you really think I'm pretty?"

"Uh, yeah," Ari said, looking away. "Anyway, we should head out."

The party returned to the place where they were the day before. To the place where she had died. There was no sign of her corpse, for which she was grateful. Kiwi had incinerated her corpse after everything of value was removed from it. In Etheria, it was generally good practice not to allow your own corpses to remain for too long.

That morning they continued hunting G-Rexes. After killing two more, it became clear that they no longer needed the trap. The Ginormasaurus Rex was no longer the insurmountable challenge that it had been just days before. They started hunting the spawns together as a group.

They killed six more G-Rexes before returning, and Tasha had gained another two levels, bringing her up to level 18. The rate of level gain had gone down considerably because the amount of experience gained from each kill was reduced as she leveled up. XP gain was a function of the person's level compared to the mob's.

Tasha evenly divided her stat points between strength and precision. So far she had barely put anything into precision, and many of her fireballs ended up missing the target entirely. She took one additional heart and one mana container. She opened up her stat page:

Tasha Singleton (Level 18 Couch Potato)	
Race	Human (Player)
Subclass	None
Weapon	Namaka (ATK 5)
Armor	Light Spidersilk Armor (DEF 25 Mag DEF 5) Sturdy Travel Shoes (DEF 2)
Heart Containers	11/11
Mana Containers	12/12
Amusement Index	8.6
Strength	17
Intelligence	15
Agility	22
Precision	10
Charisma	15
ATK	20
MAG ATK	14
DEF	40
MAG DEF	16

Tasha considered looking for stronger enemies, but the sun was already starting to set, and it was time to return to the castle. Unfortunately, fate had other plans in store for them.

As the party traveled toward the castle astride their velociraptor mounts, they were ambushed by a small army of ninjas. There were over a hundred shinobi, each astride a raptor. They surrounded the party in a circle, cutting off any escape.

"I was afraid of this," said Kiwi. The idea that her assailants would give up their target was far too optimistic.

The combat menu had appeared on the corner of Tasha's vision. She read the opponents' data, scrolling through the list of enemies.

"It says we have a hundred and five enemy ninjas. Most are between level 5 and level 8, and the highest of them are level 31."

Pan looked anxious. Tasha didn't blame her.

Hermes equipped his machine-gun arm, saying, "It's time for some payback! Let's kill them all."

A small winged fairy woman dressed in a ninja outfit flew up to Princess Kiwi. "Hello again, princess. You may have escaped my idiot subordinates before, but you won't find me as easy an opponent. Your days of freedom are ov— Wait a minute, is that slime thing over there your true love? *He's* the guy you were singing love songs about back at the tower? Holy crap, that's really weird."

"It's not weird!" Kiwi protested angrily. "We love each other and are going to get married."

"Pfffpt," rebutted Slimon.

"Whatever, weirdo." The fairy turned to Ari. "You look like a reasonable guy. If you give us the princess and walk away, we'll let the rest of you go free. I'll even pay you for your trouble. See how much sense that makes? You can't defeat this many of us, so why not just give up and make a profit from it?"

Ari was about to say something, but just then there was a spray of gunfire that shot toward the fairy. Trista Twinklebottom dodged the attacks.

"So that's your answer? How predictable and boring. Underlings! Capture the princess and kill everyone else. I'll be over by that tree taking a nap."

The circle off ninjas began to close in. Suddenly, rather than there being 104 enemy ninjas, there were thousands of clones. For a moment Tasha was overwhelmed, but then she remembered that the clones she'd fought earlier were incredibly weak. They could be easily defeated with just a light attack.

She turned to Kiwi. "Do you have any large area-of-effect spells?"

"Everyone, gather around me," Kiwi said. They moved as close to her as possible. Her eyes glowed a brilliant white, and her green air began to lift in defiance of gravity. She performed a quick dance and recited the spell. "*Mâhlâi pendurshi kaluhür!*"

The wind began to rage, forming a cyclone centered around her. Tasha could feel the strong wind blowing even from within the storm's eye. The ninjas who had been charging her a moment before were now being lifted into the air and flung in all directions. Tasha's battle log read that ninjas were falling, one after another.

At one point it read 430 ninjas, most of them clones had no more than a quarter heart of health. All of the clones were killed instantly by the attack, bringing the number to 96. Then 95. Then 88. Then 81. After the wind subsided and the dust started to settle Tasha's battle log read that there were only 46 ninjas remaining.

"That was amazing," Tasha said. "I didn't know you had a spell like that! You know you're hogging all the bad guys, right?"

"Thanks. It didn't really make sense to use it against the G-Rex, and it uses a large amount of my mana. Now that I'm level 19, I can afford to cast it one more time."

"Don't you dare!" said Hermes. "Slimon and I want some payback too."

Hermes opened fire on the surrounding line of ninjas, destroying clones as soon as they were formed and killing the originals once they could be identified. Slimon shot tentacles at the shinobi, lifting them into the air and slamming them against the ground.

Most of the remaining opponents were between level 8 and 14. Kiwi's initial Tempest area-of-effect spell had neutralized most of the low-level enemies and damaged those still standing. Tasha was currently fighting five ninjas who had her surrounded. She dispatched one quickly and sliced at another, but he turned into a log and vanished, evading the attack.

Her Bullet Time ability kicked in, and at that moment, she became aware of a kunai flying at her from behind. Tasha dove to the ground, and the knife flew right overhead. From a prone position, Tasha put her knees close to her face, placed her hands on the ground next to her head, and pushed away, jumping to her feet. She'd seen martial artists and anime characters do this and decided that it looked cool, so she wanted to try it out.

Once again, Bullet Time was activated, and time slowed down, but Tasha didn't see anything. Then from above her, the fairy darted into her field of view and stabbed Tasha in the eye with a long, needlelike sword. Tasha screamed as her hand instinctively flew to her now useless eye. The fairy followed up by stabbing Tasha in the neck. Blood was filling Tasha's lungs, and she was having difficulty drawing in breath. She swung the sword uselessly but had no idea where the enemy was. The fairy was too small and fast for her to catch.

Then the fairy struck Tasha in the heart. She collapsed to her knees, her life force draining away.

The fairy spoke. "All you big people assume that I'm weak just because I'm small. Being a ninja isn't about strength—it's about stealth, the element of surprise, and speed. Nobody takes the adorable purple-haired fairy seriously because she's bite sized. Hey, why aren't you dead yet?"

While the fairy was blathering on, Tasha had chugged a health potion, restoring her broken eyes and healing her wounds. If Trista Twinklebottom hadn't stopped to gloat, the fairy would have won for certain.

Tasha jumped back and put some distance between her and the fairy. She had to think quickly. Swinging the gunblade at the fairy would be a futile effort. Just imagine trying to kill a mosquito with a cutlass. Using projectile attacks would be similarly useless.

If only Tasha had an area-of-effect attack.

"Oh, that's just lovely," the fairy said. "You healed herself up so I can pluck out your eyes a second time!"

Tasha needed a way to defeat her. There was no way that she could match Twinklebottom's speed... Or was there? Actually, there was a way she could do that. Invoking Stat Shuffle, Tasha put everything into agility. Her agility went up to 74 while her strength fell to 2.

Twinklebottom flew at Tasha, holding out her sword, darting directly for her still aching right eye. The Bullet Time ability went off, and Trista was suddenly moving in slow motion. Tasha moved her hand to catch her and found that moving while in Bullet Time was no longer like wading through marmalade. Before the fairy could reach Tasha, she snatched her up and slammed her to the ground. After a several seconds of tugging, Tasha tore off the fairy's left wing. She picked up a stone from the ground and began smashing it against Trista's body over and over.

"Die!" she screamed as she continued slamming the rock against the small fairy. Each hit took off a quarter of a heart container, but over time it added up. Eventually, Trista managed to wrestle free of Tasha's grasp. Her health was down to only two heart containers. She began crawling away from Tasha, desperate to escape. The fairy tried to take off into the air, but with only one wing, she flopped back to the ground.

Tasha held up the stone, ready to bash the fairy's skull in again.

Tasha's companions had gathered around her. The remainder of the shinobi had all been killed by her allies.

"Aren't you going to finish her?" asked Hermes.

"Don't do it," Ari said. "She's defenseless. There's no honor in killing a defenseless opponent."

Tasha willed herself to bring the stone down on her, but she couldn't bring herself to do it. She'd already beaten the fairy ninja into submission. The fairy's wings were torn, and her allies had all been vanquished.

"Do it!" spat the fairy.

Tasha dropped the stone to the ground.

"No. I can only take pity on you. It's over, and you've lost completely. Never trouble me or my friends again."

There was fear and hate reflected in Twinklebottom's eyes. Tasha mounted Denver, and the party went off to retrieve the raptors and return to the castle. She left the corpse-ridden battlefield behind her.

"I don't understand why you didn't finish her off," Hermes said. "I don't think she will be grateful that you spared her."

Tasha shook her head. "No. She'll probably want revenge. It doesn't matter. I can't kill someone in cold blood. I still don't know who I am in this new body, but that's not the kind of person that I want to be."

"You did the right thing, Tasha," Ari said. "Just as I knew you would."

The sun had almost set, but they still had time to return to the castle. Their level grind had come to an end, and the long road remained ahead of them.

CHAPTER 25

Attack of the Flying Monkeys

Tasha and Aralogos were in the castle's library, looking over a large map. They had been in heated argument over which course they should take.

Ari pointed to a gnomish city to the north. "If we traveled north to the city-state of Gnome's Rule, we could hire an airship captain to take us directly to the tower, bypassing the Uncrossable Veldt and sailing right over the Bog of Most Likely Death."

Tasha shook her head, objecting to this plan of action. "No, we would be heading in the wrong direction. It would take us months to reach Gnome's Rule on foot. We could travel straight to the tower in the same amount of time."

Ari stood his ground. "Yes, it would take the same amount of time, but with my route we never have to leave the safety of Questgivria."

Tasha put her hands on her hips and shifted to one side. "While in Questgivria, I've been eaten by a giant dinosaur, had another dinosaur crush me to death, been nearly killed by ninjas—twice—and very nearly become a tasty snack for an oversized spider. What definition of 'safety' were you using just now?"

Ari held up his hands. "Fair enough, but even given what we've faced so far, the direct route has even greater danger. Going north is the safest plan."

"And what if the gnomes can't or won't take us to our destination?" Tasha said. "We would have to turn right back around, and a two-month journey would stretch out to half a year. Winter is coming, man. I'm just saying."

It was a moment before Ari responded. "You're right, I admit it. Traveling north is too much of a gamble. We have no choice but to go east."

He drew a path across the bridge to the east and into the Slime Federation. "This is the bridge that the king is building in your honor. From there, we should travel eastward cross country. Once we leave the borders of Questgivria, we should avoid the main roads. I think we can assume that Queen Murderjoy is hunting the princess, and it won't be long before she learns of our quest, if she hasn't already. Moving across open country is slower, and we will need to avoid higher-level zones.

"The Uncrossable Veldt serves as the natural border of the Slime Federation. As the name suggests, we won't be able to cross on foot, but there is a dwarven locomotive that runs across it. The final leg of the journey is the Bog of Most Likely Death. Most travelers simply go around it, but we'll have no choice but to travel through it to reach the tower. I have no idea what dangers lurk therein, but based on the name, I doubt we will be able to pass through it without incident."

"Listen Ari," Tasha said, "I'm very happy to have both you and Pan along, but you don't owe me anything. You don't need to come if you don't want to."

"We both want to come with you. We've already decided this."

"But why? When we first met at the Temple of the Player, Pan said you were searching for a cure. Is it a cure for her autism?"

Ari looked away. "I can't talk about that. I'm sorry, but even between friends, some things must remain secret. Her secrets aren't mine to tell."

He put both hands on her shoulders. "Tasha, we're here for you because we're your friends. Our other quest is of secondary importance."

"Thanks, Ari, but whatever you and Pan are dealing with, you don't need to face it alone."

"It's kind of you to worry about us, but your concern is unnecessary. We'll be fine."

He removed his hands from her shoulders. "Now that we have a plan of action, we should meet up with the others. The journey ahead of us is a long one, and time is not our ally."

The two of them left the library and made their way to the castle entrance to meet up with the rest of the party.

The six companions left the castle for what would be the last time in the foreseeable future.

The princess was dressed in simple traveler's clothes rather than her usual frilly and princessy ensemble. She explained that it would be easier to travel in and help hide her identity. She would switch into her mage's robes right before any random encounters. The convenience of being able to change clothing by tapping at a menu screen couldn't be overstated.

The princess selected five of the swiftest raptors from the royal stables to carry them on their journey. Tasha, of course, would be riding Denver.

The six adventurers rode side by side through the city streets. A couch potato, a thief, a slime paladin, a human monk, a dwarven machinist, and an elven sorceress.

They stopped just outside a small stand in the marketplace by the eastern gate. A man in nondescript work clothes and a funny hat was standing under a store awning. The words "Class Change NPC" were floating over his head. Tasha had meant to change her character class, but she'd not had the opportunity to interact with an NPC before.

The Couch Potato class was certainly powerful, but it wasn't without its drawbacks. She was always losing stat points and needed to take a TV break every six hours to restore her stats to prevent herself from getting hit by a pretty devastating debuff. The ability to learn any skill by watching the right program was useful, but she didn't get to keep any of those abilities without constant training.

Something like a fighter or mage would be a much simpler class to play.

She dismounted from Denver, and the man spoke as she approached. "Greetings, traveler! How may I be of service?"

"Hi," said Tasha, "I'm interested in changing my job."

The man repeated the same phrase. "Greetings, traveler! How may I be of service?"

"Um... job change activate?"

"Greetings, traveler! How may I be of service?" the man repeated. It turned out that NPCs were not especially engaging conversationalists.

"Just face the NPC and approach," Kiwi said. "A menu should appear."

"Greetings, traveler! How may I be of service?" he repeated in response to Kiwi.

"Oh, be quiet!" said Tasha.

"Greetings, traveler! How may I be of service?"

Not saying anything that might trigger a conversation flag, Tasha approached the NPC. Just as Kiwi had said, a menu appeared. There were options for changing her main class and setting subclasses. There was also a grayed-out option for unlocking new classes.

"You can unlock classes?" asked Tasha.

"Greetings, traveler! How may I be of service?"

Kiwi hit the NPC's mute button. "Yes. Some classes can be unlocked. If you see a class in the job change menu that's grayed out, you can unlock it once you reach a high enough level in the required classes."

Tasha tapped on the "Change Main Class" button. A large scrollable list of classes appeared. Her current job "Couch Potato" was highlighted. It was certainly a powerful class to have, but she wanted something more combat oriented. Maybe a spellsword-style class.

She passed over Thief, Pugilist, Paladin, Ninja, Pirate, Alchemist, and stopped at Mage. She would love to be able to spellcast like Kiwi. As a computer programmer, she had a natural advantage. She would probably make a good mage, but that would mean giving up her gunblade. She paused her search at the fighter class. There were major attack buffs, but her magic would suffer. It was tempting, though.

She scrolled through the different classes. There must have been hundreds. There was Merchant, Chemist, Ranger, Grenadier, Scout, Gunner, Machinist, Priest, Healer, Acrobat, Scanmaster...

What the hell is a scanmaster? Never mind. She started to scroll into classes that were grayed out.

"These grayed-out classes. I suppose I need to unlock them by playing as other classes first?"

"That's right," Kiwi said. "Most of them have low-level limits so that they can be unlocked in a single lifetime. I was hoping to unlock the sage class one day. I'll need to reach level 20 in both healer and mage before that happens."

Tasha stopped at one option. It was grayed out but didn't list the parent classes to unlock it. "What about this one? It says Summoner. The description says I would be able to invoke summoning creatures known as figments."

Pan looked away. "Sorry. You c-can't be a summoner."

"Why not?"

"Summoners are a special class," Kiwi said. "They are incredibly powerful. The summoner can invoke figments into the world that are much stronger than the summoner herself. These are mighty beings who fight and serve on behalf of the caster. A figment's special move can turn the tide of even the most hopeless battle."

"Well, that sounds amazing," said Tasha. "That just makes me want to choose summoner even more."

"Weren't you listening?" Kiwi said. "Pan just told you that you can't be a summoner."

"But why not?"

"For one thing, you need to be born into it. It's not something you can unlock."

"You mean I have to be a chosen one?" Tasha said. "I'm already a player and the only person who can defeat Entropy, how much more chosen could I get?"

Kiwi took a deep breath and continued. "Even if you were a natural summoner, there's still another special requirement that you don't have."

Tasha frowned. "What special requirement?"

"You have to be a child. The ability to summon figments relies on a child's imagination. Think of it like having an imaginary friend that can actually fight for you. When a child grows up, they stop believing in imaginary beings. An adult just doesn't have the necessary imagination and faith. Because of this, only children can fill the role of summoner. In fact, once a summoner reaches adulthood, the class is lost and all experience in that class must be distributed to other classes.

"There's a summoner working in the king's employ. He aids the king by summoning powerful fighters and knowledgeable tacticians."

Tasha slumped. "Well, that's disappointing. Sounds like summoner's off the table. What about this one? It says Saint. It has high physical and magical attacks, bonuses to ability growth, and several powerful class specific abilities. This is an overpowered class if I've ever seen one. What's the catch?"

"It's a third-generation job class," Kiwi said. "The only way to reach it is to combine the mage and couch potato classes to form the savant class, and then combine savant with fighter."

"Then that's what I'm going to do. I'm already level 19 in couch potato. What level do I need in couch potato and mage?"

Kiwi checked. "It says level 30 in couch potato and level 20 in mage."

"Then I'll just keep leveling couch potato until I reach 30 before switching to mage. It's decided. I'm going to unlock the saint class."

Kiwi looked at her with surprise. "Nobody's ever done that to my knowledge. It shouldn't be reachable given the human lifespan, but maybe with your rapid leveling ability... it might not be impossible. If you're done, let me use the NPC. I'm going to switch to healer and set mage as my subclass."

After the princess finished changing her class, her body underwent a transformation. She was still beautiful, but not to the extent that she had been. Her face was less perfect, with minor flaws and imperfections. She even had a small amount of belly fat. It made her seem more real somehow.

"Back to level 1," Kiwi said, "That means I've lost my stat points from mage, but I'll get half of them back as I level up Healer."

"Pffpt," said Slimon.

"Thanks, Slimon, that's sweet of you to say. Don't worry, Tasha. I'll try not to slow you down. Even without your leveling ability, the first handful of levels can be gained fairly quickly."

"It's nothing to worry about," said Tasha. "I'll help level you back to 20, and then you can get your sage class. Let's get going, while we still have sunlight."

The six travelers rode through the city gates toward adventure. As they began their journey, none of them noticed the small figure that was little more than a dot in the skies behind them. In the cloudless sky, the steam dragon named Kaze watched them. He made sure to keep his distance but kept them in sight at all times as they traveled away from the city.

The next few days of travel passed easily. Since they were still within the Questgivrian borders, they traveled along the road, which was protected against random encounters with mobs. On the third day, they reached the bridge. A significant amount of work had already been done, considering that construction had only started a few days ago. A team of dwarves wearing hard hats were hard at work building the foundation of what appeared to be a suspension bridge. It was nowhere near finished, though, so they ended up hiring a ferryman to carry them to the far side.

They had finally crossed beyond the borders of Questgivria and into the Slime Federation. Having abandoned the open road, the company of six was riding in a northeastward direction across hilly terrain. There wasn't much opportunity for level growth. Half of the time their route took them across an area of low-level monsters, which provided minimal XP. Whenever this happened, they simply avoided combat so as not to lose travel time.

Other times the party encountered regions of higher-level monsters, which they were forced to circumvent. As a result, their actual route ended up being a sort of zigzagging pattern. At the outset, Tasha had assumed that moving over the open country would be fast, but nothing could be further from the truth. She quickly grew to miss the monsterless roads.

They simply couldn't risk one of them dying. If someone died, they would have to backtrack to the beginning of their journey, where they had most recently saved.

On rare occasions, their route took them across similarly leveled monsters, which provided a reasonable amount of experience, but typically that resolved to only three or four profitable random encounters per day. Those few encounters were enough for Kiwi to reach level 3 in the healer class, however.

The nature of the random encounters varied greatly from day to day and seemed to change based on the region. Some of the mobs were simple animal-based constructs like wild boars, giant killer squirrels, and mountain lions, and others were boblins, orcs, and ogres. There were also more outlandish ones, ones that didn't seem to have any analogue in the animal kingdom or typical fantasy monsters.

One example of this was a monster in the form of a floating thundercloud. Physical attacks were ineffective against it, and Kiwi's low-level fireballs just went straight through it. Tasha scanned it and determined that it was weak against earth-based elemental attacks but strong against all other elements. Though Kiwi had some earth spells, those were higher-level mage spells that she didn't have access to in her subclass. She would eventually be able to use most of her subclass's spells but only once her healer class was high enough.

Since nobody had any earth-based weapons, Slimon and Ari ended up throwing rocks and clumps of dirt at it. The damage was very minimal, but eventually they were able to bring it down through the sheer force of tenacity.

After the fifth day, Pan finally reached level 21, though Tasha was still only halfway to level 20.

In the evenings, when they made camp, they would watch Earth movies together. Tasha continued to employ the illusion spell that she had concocted to make her phone appear big-screen TV sized. Ari and Pan generally enjoyed action movies with lots of fiery gas explosions and car chases, while Kiwi preferred drama and romance. Slimon enjoyed shonen anime.

Hermes grumbled constantly about the lack of dwarven representation in film. In response to this, Tasha did her part to placate him with *The Hobbit*, *Snow White*, and *Time Bandits*.

On the tenth day, they reached a ravine. High cliff faces separated the east and western edges. A river ran through the canyon deep below and flowed southward to feed the ocean.

"This could be a problem," Tasha said. "I don't see any way across."

Ari was looking over the folded map. "Let's follow the ravine. There should be a bridge further upstream."

For the next day, they traveled northeast along the edge of the ravine. Along the way, Pan spotted a swarm of flying creatures in the distance above the ravine, moving southward.

Ari looked through Pan's spyglass at the approaching flock. "Everyone, hide! Those aren't birds—it's a murder of flying monkeys."

They moved the raptors to an outcropping on the terrain that would hopefully serve to conceal their presence. Several minutes later, the sky was darkened by a cloud of flying monkeys. There were hundreds of them, hooting and gibbering in the skies above. It took a minute for them to pass overhead and fly out of sight.

"Flying Monkeys are agents of Queen Murderjoy," Princess Kiwi said. "She must be searching for me. They seem to be patrolling the ravine."

Tasha pointed at a bridge in the distance from where the monkeys had approached. "There! We can get across. Let's hurry before they come back."

They rode at high speed toward the bridge. It was a rickety rope bridge with wooden planks. "I'm not sure this is safe," Tasha said. "We should go one at a time."

The group looked at the bridge apprehensively.

"I'll go," Tasha said. She put one foot on the first plank and shifted her weight onto it. The plank immediately snapped in two and collapsed. One of the pieces fell into the canyon far below. Tasha's foot fell forward, and she nearly fell in, but Ari grabbed her by the waist and pulled her back.

"Ari... Th-thanks for saving me again."

"It's no trouble, Tasha."

"That must not have been one of the good planks. I guess I shouldn't have had that burrito for lunch."

"Are you sure about this?" he asked.

She put her foot on the second plank, and though it curved downward under her weight, it held. She took firm grip of the handholds and continued onward. When she looked back, she saw that Ari was watching her, concerned.

After five minutes of moving carefully across the bridge, she finally reached the far side. None of the other planks had broken. Maybe it was because Tasha had kept part of her weight on the rope handholds.

Pan led Denver across bridge next, and they were both able to make it across. Then came Ari. Though he weighed more than she did, none of the wooden rungs gave out.

That left the dwarf, the elven princess, the slime, and the rest of the raptors.

It occurred to Tasha that the dwarf would most likely destroy the bridge if he attempted to cross. Despite his small frame, he had to be at least twice her weight. On the far bank, it seemed as though they were discussing something, though it was impossible to pick up any of the conversation given the distance.

Kiwi and Slimon were exchanging words with Hermes, who suddenly seemed agitated. Hermes began backing away from the slime and elf, shaking his head, and put his hands in front of his body as if to ward off an attack. Without warning, Slimon fired a tentacle at Hermes, wrapping it around his body and lifting him into the air. It swung him around in a wide arc twice and then released him. The dwarf flew in an arc across the canyon, over Tasha's head, and into some bushes a dozen meters away.

Ari and Tasha both ran to where he landed. He had lost fourteen of his heart containers but still had six left. She fished out a health potion and offered it to him. Ari gave him a hand, helping him to his feet.

Hermes took the health potion and downed it in a single gulp. "Next time I see Slimon, I'm going to kill him! Toss a dwarf, will he?"

Tasha grinned. "Well, you were pretty aerodynamic."

"Hrmf," was the dwarf's reply.

"You do realize it was the only way to get you across. The bridge couldn't have held up under your weight."

"Are you saying I'm fat?" he demanded.

"Um... n-no... of course not..." Tasha stammered. "Oh hey! It looks like Princess Kiwi is about to cross."

Kiwi stepped onto the bridge, her leather shoes pressing against the wooden planks. With each step she took, the wooden planks bent but did not break. She made it about halfway across when a flurry of rapidly shifting shadows moved across the bridge. Tasha turned her head to look upward and squinted. There were a large number of shadowy objects suspended in the air against the sun. They looked like birds.

Tasha pointed at them. "The flying monkeys are back! Kiwi, hurry!"

Then Tasha turned back to the rope bridge and started running across it.

"Tasha, no!" Ari yelled. "It's too dangerous. You'll fall!"

One of the planks gave out under her weight but she recovered and kept going. Kiwi looked at Tasha, confused. She must not have sensed their presence. Tasha pointed above her. "Monkeys!"

It was too late. Two of the flying monkeys grabbed the princess and slowly lifted her off her feet. She swung her hands, trying to knock the monkeys away, but a third one grabbed her hands, restraining her.

Tasha quickly equipped her sword and jumped the remaining distance, driving the gunblade into the neck of one of the flying monkeys holding her friend. It died, falling into the ravine below.

Another one took its place, grabbing Kiwi and lifting her into the air. Slimon was jumping through the air across the bridge. He shot out tentacles, grabbing the edges of the bridge for support and wrapped another one around Kiwi, pulling her back onto the bridge.

Kiwi screamed in pain as her body was torn in different directions. A flurry of gunfire ripped across the bridge, some of the bullets hitting flying monkeys. Most of them missed. One of the bullets struck Tasha's leg, dealing half a heart of damage.

"Not helping!" Tasha yelled at the dwarf.

She aimed her gunblade at one of the flying monkeys holding Princess Kiwi. Pulling the trigger produced a ball of compressed steam that took the monkey out but also dealt a small amount of splash damage to the princess. The monkey let go and fell into the canyon below. Slimon was being surrounded by dozens of flying monkeys, and Tasha tried to go to his aid, but there were just too many of them.

Several of them grabbed Tasha and tried to pull her over the edge of the rapidly collapsing bridge. From the periphery of her vision, she could see Ari, Pan, and Hermes fighting against their own monkeys on the other side.

Kiwi wasn't able to do much with her recent class change. Unable to defend herself, she watched helplessly as everyone else was overrun by more flying monkeys than they could deal with.

While all of this was happening, above them and far to the south, a dragon flew. Kaze had been trailing the group for over a week from as far a distance as he could manage. His plan was to approach them and offer to join their group. They had an elf, a dwarf, a slime, and even a few humans, but they didn't have any dragons. Kaze didn't entirely understand this Entropy business, but it was clear that this was an important quest, and the dragons were being left out.

It was hard to tell at this distance, but it seemed like they were being attacked by a large number of small flying creatures. Curious, he gradually reduced his altitude and moved in.

Several minutes later, he was finally near enough to properly make out the princess's attackers. It was rare to see flying monkeys this far to the north. Flying monkeys were a semi-sentient species native to

Zhakara. Well, whatever brought them here, they were obviously causing trouble for the princess.

Maybe this would be his big chance to prove his value to her as a traveling companion. He would swoop in, fight the monkeys off, and once all was said and done, they would be so grateful that they beg him to join their group.

Of course, that plan was problematic. Despite being a mighty steam dragon, he was still only level 19. Against so many enemies, how much help would be really be?

He glided toward the bridge—if it could even be called a bridge. It was more like a few bits of rope connecting the two ends of the ravine. A battle HUD popped up in his field of view as he glided toward the battle. He twisted his neck downward to read through the enemy list. He couldn't manipulate the menu while airborne since his arms couldn't reach, but simply reading the battle HUD was no trouble.

There were several hundred flying monkeys, ranging in level from 12 to 23 with an average level of 14. Their strength lay in their vastly overwhelming numbers.

Several of the flying monkeys were trying to drag the princess off the bridge and into the air. He picked his targets and dove, unleashing his breath, sending jets of super-hot steam into his enemies. The heat from the steam quickly transferred to the monkeys' bodies, killing one and draining the health of the others. They released their grip on the princess, who was struggling to stay on the bridge.

The dark-skinned human, the one they described as a player, was helping the princess back onto the bridge. They were trying to make it to the far end, but the flying monkeys were swarming the pair. Kaze banked and prepared to make another pass. None of the monkeys were attacking him, as they seemed focused on attacking the princess. He would have to do something about that.

If he couldn't deal enough damage to reduce their number by a significant margin, maybe he could draw them away.

Steam dragons dealt less damage than fire dragons, but they had far more versatility. While dragonfire could melt stone, such attacks only lasted for a few dozen seconds before the dragon completely ran out of fuel. Fire dragons needed to conserve their attacks for critical moments in battle. The same was not true of steam dragons, however. While his breath attacks lacked the raw power of fire, he could continue using it for hours before needing to refuel.

As he made his next pass, he targeted clusters of flying monkeys and hit them with wide blasts of steam, dealing only small amounts of damage. Though these enemies weren't bound to the same laws of aggro as mobs, many of them broke off and started chasing him. He turned around and fired a narrow stream of steam, damaging several of them.

He made another pass, targeting additional groups. This was working—nearly half the monkeys were now focused on Kaze rather than the princess. The player and the princess had nearly reached the far end of the bridge.

The rope bridge was swaying from side to side in response to the constant movement. There was a snap as one of the ropes that secured the bridge gave out. The rungs swung in one direction, having lost their lateral support. The bridge was collapsing—the stress from the combat had been too much.

Given enough time, she probably could have made it. Unfortunately, the ropes snapped off at the western end, removing all support from the bridge. It gave way, causing the princess and player to tumble unsupported into the cavern below.

Kaze dove toward the princess in an attempt to catch her, but she was falling too quickly, and she slammed into the water below along with the player. A moment later, the two of them emerged on the surface of the water. The river carried the princess and the human for a time until it wound into an underwater cavern.

The dragon followed them into the cavern, and thankfully most of the monkeys who had been following him kept their distance. A notification appeared:

> **Now generating dungeon: The Bunny Grotto**
> **Recommended levels 23–27, party of 3 to 8**
> **Stand by... Dungeon will be ready in 3 minutes.**

He could still see the remaining monkeys gathered at the cave entrance, seemingly wary of entering. He didn't know how long the monkeys would remain there but suspected that he would not be able to leave the same way that he had entered. He pulled the unconscious pair from the water and onto the bank.

Swirls of purple mist began to form into torches on the wall next to a doorway that materialized in the rock wall. A few minutes later, the dungeon's generation counter ran down, and door opened on its own, revealing a detailed artificial stone corridor lined with torches. A grinding noise came from its direction—the sound of the rest of the dungeon being generated from the raw material of the cavern.

Kaze had heard of dynamically spawning dungeons like this but had never encountered one. It was a rare form of random encounter—an entire dungeon would form from solid rock. These sorts of dungeons were short-lived and would despawn once cleared.

Thanks to the flying monkeys, going back wasn't an option. They would have to progress inside and hope that another exit presented itself.

CHAPTER 26

Golden Axe

"Tasha, wake up!"

Gradually, Tasha came awake and found that she was lying prone upon a rocky floor. Atmospheric instrumental music was playing, which thankfully meant that she was no longer in combat. She pushed herself to her feet and opened her eyes. She awoke to find herself face to face with Princess Kiwi and a small dragon.

She blinked her eyes in confusion. "What happened? I remember falling, and then..."

Memories of the fall came back to her. She had been dragged underwater by the currents and had lost consciousness. Somehow she was still alive.

"I remember you," she said to the dragon. "You're Kaze, right? What are you doing here?"

"Apparently he's been following us," Kiwi said. "He said he wants to join our quest."

Tasha nodded. "I don't see why not. He did help us out with the monkeys."

Kiwi pursed her lips. "I told him I'd think about it. I've not decided yet. For one thing, traveling with a dragon would make us much more conspicuous. Also, if he is seen close to the dwarven kingdom, it might make trouble for his people."

The dragon's voice appeared in her thoughts. *I'm aware of that. I would only stay with you until we reached the borders of Dwarselvania.*

"What happened to the others?" Tasha asked. "Did everyone else escape?"

"I don't know," said Kiwi, "but I'm pretty sure the flying monkeys were trying to get me. I'm worried about Slimon and the others. We should hurry and find a way out."

Tasha hoped her friends were okay. She took in her surroundings. They were in corridor lit by wall torches. The shackled skeletal remains of some poor adventurer adorned the wall. The floor and walls were a combination of natural and carved stone. A large red wooden door lay open at the far end. The sound of rushing water trickled through. "What is this place?"

We escaped the flying monkeys by entering a dungeon. They won't follow us in.

"But it's only a matter of time until Queen Murderjoy learns of our location," Kiwi said. "We should proceed further in."

She got to her feet and began to move inward. The corridor opened up into a large chamber filled with stalactites and stalagmites. There were several exits from the room, and the layout of the dungeon began to fill in Tasha's mini map. Half a dozen level 16 vorpal rabbits hopped around the room in repeating patterns.

Vorpal Rabbit (Level 16)
He can leap about... he's got huge, sharp... Just look at the bones!
ATK 20 Mag ATK 16
DEF 12   Mag DEF 16

Tasha turned to the dragon. "Kaze, can you pull those mobs over here one at a time?"

The dragon's voice resonated in her mind. *I think so.*

"Okay. Kiwi, stay behind us. Since you're only level 3, the mobs will most likely target you—particularly if you start casting. Kaze and I will try to take them out one by one. I want you to injure them right before we finish them off so you can get a more even share of the XP."

Kiwi nodded and moved to the back of the chamber. Kaze stepped forward and shot a narrow jet of steam that expanded the farther out it went. Due to the distance involved, it only dealt one-quarter heart of damage to one of the isolated mobs. The horned rabbit turned and hopped angrily in Kaze's direction. When it got close enough, it turned to attack Kiwi instead, its targeting algorithm having decided that her low level made her a preferred target.

Tasha intercepted the bunny as it hopped past and sliced at it with her gunblade over and over, each hit drawing blood and dealing between one and one and a half hearts of damage. It changed its target to her, but Kaze was already hitting it with a close-range steam attack. The battle lasted less than ten seconds and hadn't caused Tasha to lose any health.

They repeated this process six more times and cleared the room of monsters. When the enemies were defeated and experience was finally awarded, Kiwi gained two levels, bringing her to level 5. Due to the high density of monsters in the dungeon, her level gain came at an accelerated rate.

They continued to explore the dungeon. The grotto was a complex natural labyrinth. The layout continued to draw itself out in Tasha's map as they explored. Most of the mobs were high level yet manageable. The monsters all seemed to be rabbit themed. Horned rabbits were common, there were also red-eyed demon rabbits, anthropomorphic rabbits, stuffed rabbits, and large stone bunny golems. It seemed that whichever designer built this dungeon had a thing for rabbits.

After about three hours of exploration, Kiwi brought their party to a halt. Kiwi had reached level 9.

The princess looked around cautiously. "I think we're about to reach the first boss battle."

Tasha looked around. "How can you tell?"

"Listen."

Tasha tried to listen but could only hear the in-game music. "I can't hear anything."

"It's the background music. Notice how it's quieter and full of suspense? That's usually the prelude to a boss monster or event. Let me cast some buffs before we continue."

The princess had put most of her stats into intelligence—Etheria's stat system didn't have a separate stat for wisdom. Unlike intelligence, wisdom was subjective and did not lend itself to numerical quantification.

Kiwi cast defense and strength buffs on Tasha and Kaze but decided to hold off before doing any additional casting. There was no way to know what kind of enemy they would fight and what kind of attacks they would make. The only thing she knew with relative certainty was that the boss monster would most likely be something rabbit themed.

That prediction turned out to be correct. After they moved into the next room, the door behind them slammed shut as high-intensity Asian music began to play. From the shadows, a white anthropomorphic rabbit garbed in a samurai outfit emerged.

Yojimbo (Level 20)
Dual-blade-wielding ronin rabbit.
ATK 30 Mag ATK 0
DEF 28   Mag DEF 22

The midboss drew its katana and leaped directly at Kaze, cutting into him for three hearts of damage. He jumped away and repeated his attack. The dragon managed to dodge but was unable to counterattack due to the samurai rabbit's uncanny speed. It seemed as though the samurai rabbit left an after-image.

"I'll cast a haste buff," said Kiwi, whose eyes began to glow white as she chanted. Unfortunately, the mob cut her for five hearts of damage before she could finish the spell. Changing plans, she cast a recovery spell on herself.

This foe's main advantage over the party was speed. It was a risk, but Tasha decided to invoke Stat Shuffle and divided her stats between agility and strength—that would allow her to counter the rabbit's speed.

Using this ability reduced her overall stat point count by 15% and came with a twelve-hour cooldown. She just hoped that she wouldn't need it again anytime soon. Her extra agility gave her the speed she needed to damage him. The samurai wasn't especially difficult to defeat once she was able to hit him. It was just a matter of outlasting his attacks.

Five minutes later, the midboss had been defeated, and a treasure chest appeared in the center of the room. Tasha had finally leveled up as a result of the boss battle, reaching level 20. She took the heart container and allocated two stat points into strength and the other two into intelligence.

Tasha had grown to really like treasure chests. They always contained something good, whether it be GP, some new piece of armor, food, or some other knickknack that she didn't even know had been missing from her life.

This one contained a glowing golden carrot. When she scanned it, the description read:

Golden Carrot

Dungeon key item 1/3

When she attempted to put the thing in her inventory, she found herself unable to do so. A message popped up, informing her that she couldn't store key items in her inventory. Instead she stuffed it into her back pocket and they continued onward.

They spelunked through the dungeon for several hours before coming to another large chamber. The in-game music stopped, but it wasn't in anticipation of a boss battle.

The large brick room was surrounded by glowing neon lights. Against one wall was a machine that Tasha instantly recognized as a video game cabinet. Along the lighted bezel were the words "Rabbit Punch." A large red rabbit and a green rabbit stood on either side of the cabinet.

"I love this game! I used to play this as a kid. They had one at the pizza restaurant. My dad would play it with me every weekend."

Kiwi approached the machine. "I've never seen anything like it. You said it's a game?"

"Yes, it is. You control your character on the screen using these joysticks. Look at the wall: It's numbered one through twelve. I'll bet the way forward will appear when we clear all twelve levels."

Tasha fished out two 5 GP coins and inserted them into the coin slot. "It's a two-player game, so I'm going to need your help."

Tasha taught Kiwi the fundamentals of how to play. It was an early side-scrolling bullet hell arcade game. Both players piloted their respective bunny robots while punching and shooting down enemies in an attempt to save the royal family of Bunnyland. There were carrot-themed powerups to collect and bosses to fight. When she was a kid, she'd never made it past level 7, but that was only because she kept running out of quarters. She had more than enough GP to clear the entire game.

Tasha chose the red rabbit so that Kiwi would be able to choose green, which she assumed to be her favorite color. It only took Kiwi a few tries to get the hang of the controls, and before long the two of them became a well-oiled *Rabbit Punch*-playing machine. Together, they'd overcome this challenge in no time.

The bridge finally gave way under the intense stress of the tempest. Pan wrapped her hand around the railing and held on tight as the bridge collapsed and smashed into the side of the mountain. Aralogos was hanging on to the remains of the bridge above her.

"Behind you!" he cried.

She turned and saw half a dozen flying monkeys flying toward them. She swung her knife using her free hand, yelling, "G-get away!"

Multiple tracers impacted the flying monkeys from above. Hermes had opened fire and was shooting them down with much more accuracy than before. The monkeys that came too close were riddled with gunfire and fell out of the sky.

"Hurry up and climb!" he shouted.

Aralogos climbed to the top and helped Pan the rest of the way as Hermes continued to hold them off with his machine gun. The three of them stood together as the flying monkeys approached, then turned away, retreating into the ravine. It seemed that they had suddenly lost interest in the battle.

"Hermes, did you see what happened to Tasha and the Kiwi?" Ari asked.

"Aye, I did. They both fell into the water, and Kaze, that dragon who came out of nowhere, followed them. They might still be alive."

"Follow the river downstream," Pan said. "Tasha might be there."

Hermes nodded. "Let's get moving."

The followed the path of the stream as it rode inside the ravine. After some time, Pan saw what they were looking for. She removed her glasses and peered through her binoculars into the ravine below.

"C-cave, there."

"There are hundreds of monkeys just outside," Ari said. "We can't fight that many as we are."

"Have you two forgotten that I'm a dwarf?" Hermes said. "Digging is kinda my thing. If they are trapped in the cave, I can create a second entrance. We'll need to get close, though."

It took them nearly an hour to reach the bottom of the ravine. There was a ledge that led downward, but it wasn't exactly a safe way to climb down. Slimon was able to help them make the descent by lowering them down with his tentacles. Unfortunately, they were forced to leave Denver at the top of the ravine since there was no way for him to climb down the rock face. They would have to return for him later.

By the time they reached the base, the sun was already setting. There was only a small amount of dry land along the side of the cliff face, but it was enough for Hermes to do his thing.

The flying monkeys were still congregating by the cave entrance. Hermes got to work right away and starting tearing large cubelike blocks out of the cliff face. Pan was concerned that the monkeys might hear Hermes's efforts, but they were making such a racket of their own that it wasn't a problem.

Hermes would remove a large chunk of the cave and deposit it in his inventory. They kept digging inward for fifteen minutes and then turned in a right angle toward the cave. The light from the outside was no longer reaching them, so Aralogos cast a light spell.

Hermes continued digging for several more hours until finally they connected with the adjoining caverns. A prompt appeared:

Now entering dungeon: The Bunny Grotto
Recommended levels 23–27, party of 3 to 8.

They were in an opening that connected to a downward sloping corridor.

"Which way should we check first?" Aralogos wondered aloud.

Pan checked her map. She had set a waypoint at the spot where she thought the flying monkeys were at and compared that direction to where the corridor led.

"There." She pointed to where she thought the entrance was.

Hermes just shrugged, not preferring one way over the other. They descended together. It wasn't long at all before they were attacked by mobs. They were all rabbit themed but didn't pose any real threat to the three seasoned adventurers.

They seemed to be getting closer but kept hitting dead ends and having to backtrack. The cave system was a twisting, convoluted labyrinth.

One room they came to seemed to be leading the right way, but as they entered they came upon a great fountain of water set in the middle of the otherwise empty chamber.

"What is it?" Pan asked.

Aralogos cautiously approached the fountain. "I think it's an abnormal spawn. Maybe a puzzle."

Hermes grunted. "These sorts of spawns are usually high risk, high reward. If this is a puzzle, it might be worth trying to solve it."

Aralogos, as usual, wanted to play it safe. "We can't afford to die right now. Maybe we should ignore it."

"Screw that, I want the treasure!"

Hermes marched up to the pool, and as he approached, a figure rose out of the water. It was a stunningly beautiful fairy about two feet tall with glistening blue wings and bunny ears. She wore an elegant dress made out of flowing water.

"Greetings, kind woodsman," said the fairy.

Hermes looked down at his heavy armor. "And just what part of my attire makes you think I'm a woodsman?"

The fairy continued as though Hermes hadn't spoken. "Oh, did you drop something in my pool?"

"Um... maybe?"

From somewhere in her watery dress, the fairy pulled out two large axes that were each easily twice her height. She batted her eyelashes and said, "Well, then, did you drop a silver axe or a golden axe?"

Hermes squinted at them closely. "Which of them has the higher resale value?"

"Please choose which one is yours. The silver axe or the golden axe."

Aralogos put a cautionary hand on Hermes's shoulder. "This is obviously a test of honesty. We should tell her that we didn't drop anything. Otherwise she might become angry and murder us all!"

"But if we tell her the truth, she might go away without giving us any axes."

Ari put his hand on his forehead. "None of us are axe users. We don't actually need any axes."

Hermes groaned. "Fine, have it your way! Well, there goes my dreams of riches. Eh... Great fairy of the pool, we didn't drop either axe in the water. So, now that we've been so honest, what kind of reward can you give us for our honesty?"

"Well," the fairy said, "if you didn't drop the silver axe and you didn't drop a golden axe, then you must have dropped this!"

She held forth a bottle of carrot juice. It seemed to be a key item. The description read:

Carrot Juice

Dungeon key item 3/3

"Oh ho ho ho ho!" laughed the fairy as she vanished back into her pool which then dissolved into purple mist.

Hermes took the dungeon key. "Carrot juice? Seriously? We shoulda taken the golden axe. Ah, well. Let's not waste any more time goofing off around here."

The four of them left the room, continuing their search. They spent the next six hours mapping out the dungeon, trying to find Tasha and Kiwi. Eventually they reached an area where there were no mobs. Since monsters didn't respawn in dungeons like this one, it was an indication that Tasha had come this way.

Now they just needed to follow the trail of no monsters to catch up.

Tasha *hated* this game. *Rabbit Punch* sucked. No, that wasn't true. She just sucked at playing it, was all. Why did she ever think she was good at this? She'd been playing it for two hours and couldn't get past level eleven. The game let you continue, but only from level nine. That meant every time they died, they had to continue from that point and replay levels nine, ten, and eleven. Whose idea was it to design a game where you had to fight difficult bosses without being able to continue?

They couldn't stop—arcade cabinets had no pause button, and if they stopped, they would have to start over from the beginning. Besides, she was in the zone. They could do this.

Kaze had grown bored watching Tasha suck at video games, and he lacked the opposable thumbs to take over for one of them. Instead he curled up in the corner to take a nap.

Finally, after the third hour of the damn game, the two of them made it to level twelve and defeated the boss. The actual boss, not the fake immortal boss that the game teased her with. At the end of the day, she had spent over a hundred GP on this dumb game, but it was worth it for the sense of satisfaction gained by defeating it.

A compartment at the bottom of the arcade machine opened up, and Tasha retrieved a small object from within. It was a slice of cake.

Carrot Cake
Dungeon key item 2/3

A door on the far wall opened. There were three carrots icons inscribed in the doorframe.

After taking a short taco break to satisfy her growling stomach and refill her MP, they continued into the next room.

This seemed to be the boss room, though it looked more like a dance floor than anything else. The entrance was set on an elevated platform, with a view of the dance floor below. There were no other exits from the chamber. An electric force field filled the door frame and blocked progress. They both stepped onto the dance floor.

The floor was composed of tiles that changed color in rhythm with the music. The in-game music had stopped, and dubstep music filled the air in its place. Tasha felt the rhythmic vibration of the music reverberating through her body.

Dubstep. Tasha hated dubstep, but that was mostly because she couldn't dance. And how was this kind of music appropriate for a swords-and-sorcery-themed adventure? As a game developer, the lack of thematic consistency bothered her more than anything else.

Before she could vocalize her displeasure, the boss dropped from above and onto the dance floor. It was a stainless-steel robotic bunny exo-suit. The moment it landed, the boss started dancing to the music.

Retro Robot Rabbit Rebecca (Level 25)
Her power armor makes her an indestructible dubstep-dancing dealer of devastation. Only the sweet, sweet smell of carrot-themed sweets can distract her.
ATK 33   Mag ATK N/A
DEF N/A   Mag DEF N/A

Tasha's battle HUD appeared and the enemy's info filled the combat log. Retro Robot Rabbit Rebecca had thirty heart containers.

Enough was enough. Tasha charged at it and hit the robot with her gunblade. A big fat zero appeared at the impact point. She hit it several more times with a similar lack of success. Then the breakdancing robot performed a spin kick, knocking her clear to the other side of the dance floor.

That's right. Tasha remembered now. It was impossible to damage boss monsters unless you targeted their weak points. She examined the exo-suit, searching for some telltale glowing surface but found nothing.

From out of nowhere, the robot grabbed a bunch of bombs with lit fuses and threw them into the air. They each landed on different squares on the dance floor. When they exploded, they did so in horizontal and vertical directions *Bomberman* style, each bomb reaching two squares in either direction.

Tasha and Kiwi watched the floor where the bombs landed and made sure not to stand adjacent to any. Kaze, who was much too large to participate in this boss fight effectively, remained at the top of the stairs watching the battle play out.

Strangely enough, standing diagonally to the bombs only one square away was perfectly safe. It made sense from a video-game logic point of view, but not in a real-world physics sense. The bombs had to be very carefully designed and precisely thrown to operate in such a fashion.

As the attacks continued, a perfectly visible and opaque thought bubble appeared above the robot, the image of a slice of carrot cake floating in the middle.

After the fifth round of bombs, the bunny robot mixed in a glass plate with the bombs, throwing it on the center dance tile. Tasha looked at it in confusion, but the robot destroyed the plate with the next set of bombs.

Kiwi grabbed Tasha by the arm and said, "I think you need to put the carrot cake on the plate!" Tasha nodded in agreement.

She nodded and continued to dodge the bombs, wave after wave, until once again, Retro Robot Rabbit Rebecca mixed in a dinner plate along with the bombs. Not wasting any time, Tasha took out the carrot cake and placed it on the dinner plate.

"Yum yum!" came a squeaky female voice from the robot. The exo-suit opened, and a short anthropomorphic rabbit girl hopped out and ran to the carrot cake.

"Get her!" cried Tasha. Kiwi blasted the rabbit with lighting attacks while Tasha wailed on her with the gunblade.

"Ow! Ow! Ow!" the rabbit cried as she wolfed down the carrot cake. Once she was down to twenty heart containers, she was able to dodge every attack and quickly ran back to her exo-suit. "Why you!"

The attack patterns began again, this time at a faster pace. Retro Robot Rabbit Rebecca was now firing twice as many bombs, making them much harder to dodge. Kiwi was repeatedly casting recovery spells on the two of them as they were hit.

Between attacks, Rebecca said, "Is that a carrot in your pocket or are you just glad to see me?"

If Tasha had had more time, she'd have facepalmed. Who wrote that line of dialogue and why? Was it supposed to be a clue? Did the developers think they were being funny? What was *wrong* with these game developers?

At the end of the bomb cycle, the robot fired her fist at Tasha. The robotic fist had rockets attached to it, allowing her to rabbit-punch Tasha from a distance. The robot's rocket-fist attack cost her seven hearts of damage. It rushed forward and lifted her fist before firing again.

Finally, she started throwing bombs again, and once that was finished, fired another dinner plate into the air. It landed in the center. Tasha knew what to do. She removed the golden carrot from her other pocket and dropped it on the plate.

"Yum yum!" said Retro Robot Rabbit Rebecca as she once again left her exo-suit and ran to the plate. She started gobbling up the carrot as Tasha and Kiwi attacked her, bringing her down to ten hearts. She finished off her carrot and said, "You realize... this means war!" before rushing back to her exo-suit.

The attacks began again, but this time the robot was firing missiles from her shoulder pads. When the bombs were flying, she also had a spinning laser attack that Tasha and Kiwi had to jump over or duck under.

"I'm running out of mana," said Kiwi, who had been healing almost nonstop. "Just keep dodging!"

"Golly, I'm parched," Rebecca said. "Yessir, could sure go for some carrot juice right about now."

Kiwi gasped. "Tasha, did you find any carrot juice?"

Tasha dodged a spinning laser beam and stepped out of the way of a bomb. "No. I think we have a problem!"

They continued to dodge the attacks for another two minutes, Kiwi's mana reserves falling dangerously low. Then, to Tasha's utter shock, Pan ran into the room, followed by Ari, Hermes, and Slimon.

Pan ran onto the dance floor, easily dodging the bombs and lasers. When she reached the plate, she set the carrot juice on it.

"Yum yum!" said Rebecca, who exited her exo-suit and started chugging carrot juice.

Tasha, Kiwi, and Pan started beating the crap out of Retro Robot Rabbit Rebecca, and before long she was down to one heart. The dance floor began to crack and opened up to a cavern below. Before plummeting into the hole, Rebecca cursed, "Suffering succotash!"

Tasha, who was having none of this shit, walked over to the exo-suit and lifted it up, her augmented strength stat giving her the boost she needed. Time to end this. She carried it to the hole in the dance floor.

"Hey, Rebecca! You forgot something!"

She threw the exo-suit into the hole, and it landed on Rebecca, creating an explosion that shook the room.

> **Congratulations! You have cleared the dungeon: The Bunny Grotto**
>
> **1200 experience gained. (2091 Experience to next level)**
>
> **Level up!**
>
> **Level up!**
>
> **You have reached level 22.**
>
> **You have 8 unassigned stat points.**

"Ari, Pan! How did you guys find us?" she asked.

"We discovered the dungeon and then just followed the sound of dubstep," Hermes said.

"Well, thanks, Hermes. We couldn't have beaten them without your help."

"Let's catch up later," Ari said. "There's a good chance the flying monkeys will lead Queen Murderjoy right to us. Is there another way out of this place?"

"I think so," Hermes said. "We should be close to the surface. Give me an hour, and I can dig us out."

While Hermes was hard at work digging a tunnel to the surface, the rest of the group went through the loot that Retro Robot Rabbit Rebecca had dropped. There was 14,000 GP that they divided amongst themselves. Pan got a new invisibility cloak to replace her tattered Cloak of Dusk.

Tasha added one mana container and one heart container and assigned two points into precision, two into strength, and four into agility.

Half an hour later, Hermes had tunneled his way to the surface, and they found themselves a good distance from the ravine, though it was still in sight.

"We should get as far away from here as possible," Ari said. "This place will be crawling with monkeys by morning."

"Where's Denver?" Tasha asked.

Hermes shook his head. "Don't know. We left him at the ravine when we climbed down after you. He might still be there, but that place must be swarming with baddies. It's too dangerous to go back for him."

"I can go," Pan said, patting her new cloak. "They won't see me."

Kiwi nodded and indicated a nearby cluster of trees. "We'll move into the tree line and stay out of sight until you return."

"Be careful," Ari added.

Without another word, Pan left the group and slipped on her cloak, vanishing from sight, her body blending into the surrounding landscape.

CHAPTER 27

Secrets and Revelations

Silently, Pan made her way back to the ravine, her cloak concealing her from sight, removing her scent and silencing her footsteps. Invisibility cloaks were immensely useful, though they were a continual mana drain. She was able to offset its cost by eating a candy bar every ten minutes. The extra calories would convert to mana, allowing her to remain invisible for longer periods of time.

Unfortunately the only kind of candy bar she had available was nougat. Pan hated nougat. She much preferred peanut butter and chocolate candy bars, but she'd long since exhausted her supply of those since leaving Questgivria.

It took her about twenty minutes to arrive back at the ravine. Denver wasn't there and was nowhere in sight. There was somebody else of note, however. Standing upon the ledge, surrounded by a legion of flying monkeys, was Queen Murderjoy with several of her human servants.

Pan had never seen the queen in person, but every Zhakaran-born human knew who she was and would recognize her on sight. Faint red light emanated from an orb at the end of her staff. Pan was in reach of the Orb of Fire. She hated to pass up such a prime opportunity for burglary, but there was no obvious way to get the orb away from her. If Pan used Steal, she would either fail and be captured and killed or she would succeed and then be captured and killed. The Orb of Fire would serve no master but the queen—it would be useless in her hands.

But if the queen were to set it down and walk away from it, she might stand a shot at taking it, but such an occurrence wasn't likely to happen.

She began to inch closer, staying hidden in the shadows as much as possible. Her invisibility cloak should shroud her from sight, but there was no point in taking unnecessary chances. The invisibility cloak was slowly draining her mana; she couldn't delay indefinitely.

An elderly balding man walked straight past where Pan was hiding and approached the queen.

Queen Murderjoy turned to face him. "Ah, Gelkorus... my most trusted lieutenant. What do you have to report?"

"The dungeon just despawned about ten minutes ago," Gelkorus said. "It pushed all of our explorers outside. It is possible that the princess and her companions died within. That would explain why she wasn't seen leaving the dungeon. We did find a second entrance along the cliff face, but nobody has emerged from there either."

The queen stood in thought. "Or perhaps they cleared the dungeon and either found or made another exit. If it is true that they died, then we will learn about it soon enough when the princess respawns at the castle."

"What are your orders, my queen?" Gelkorus asked.

"Continue patrols along the ravine and search the surrounding area. I believe they are heading eastward toward Slimewater. Set patrols along the roads and passes."

"Yes, my queen."

Pan decided that it was time for her to leave. She turned around and moved away as slowly and quietly as she could, heading back to where Ari was waiting. She was disappointed at not being able to steal anything, but a good burglar knew when to cut her losses. It took her and Ari three hours to reach the waypoint.

She removed her hood and approached Tasha. "Sorry. D-Denver wasn't there."

"It's fine," said Tasha, who pointed happily at Denver napping on the grass. "He actually found us a few minutes after you left. It was too late to stop you."

Ari sighed with relief. "That's good. Listen, Queen Murderjoy was there. She's planning on having her servants patrol the roads to the east. We'll have to stick to the wilderness."

They spent the remainder of that night traveling at high speed away from the ravine and further into the wilderness. There were powerful enemy spawns, but fortunately everyone was able to flee from the mobs without incident.

Everyone agreed to allow Kaze to join the group, at least for as long as they were in the slime kingdom. Even a young dragon would be a valuable asset, and they were in no position to refuse his aid.

Kaze scouted for the enemy by air, but it appeared that they we not being pursued. After several days of uneventful travel, it became evident that they had escaped from the queen's pursuit.

As they continued their journey, the shadows of mountains became visible to the north. They crossed great fields of purple wildflowers that decorated the valleys and hills.

Having Kaze in the party made combat much easier. He took over Hermes's role as a tank. Since he could taunt the enemy and then fly out of their attack range, that enabled the others to deal damage without being on the receiving end.

It wasn't a perfect strategy, however. If Kaze flew too far away, the mobs would consider him an invalid target and switch to the grounded party members. It was a matter of striking the right balance of being hard to hit from the air while not actually being out of range.

An entire month passed in this manner. They would wake up and spend the day traveling cross country, trudging in their zigzagging pattern to avoid areas of high spawns. At night they would rest and watch movies on Tasha's phone. The tensions of their close encounter with the queen had become a distant memory.

But at night, Ari would still turn transparent and begin to fade away. Whenever Tasha asked about it, Ari played it off as if it wasn't a big deal. Tasha never really became comfortable with it, but she stopped asking to respect his wishes.

As the days passed, Tasha continued to keep track of what abilities could be unlocked by different TV shows, songs, and novels. Some of them looked useful while others had no combat application. She jotted the newly discovered abilities in her notebook.

Moby-Dick – Hell's Heart
Wayfinder ability, unlocks at level 19
Adds bonus damage when attacking aquatic enemies with a harpoon.

The Sound of Music – Spontaneous Dancing
Bard ability, unlocks at level 40
Chance to cause a crowd of people to spontaneously break into song and choreographed dancing. Chance of success depends on the aggregate personality of the crowd.

Naruto – Shadow Clone
Ninja ability, unlocked at level 5
Ability to make a duplicate of yourself at a temporary cost of one heart container. Any damage to the clone will cause it to despawn.
Cost: 1 heart container lost per clone, 1 mana point per 10 minutes per clone

She experimented with Shadow Clone but quickly discovered that her clone was not especially good company. Quite the opposite, in fact. When they tried to fight monsters together, they kept getting in each other's way and more often than not ended up fighting each other. She wondered whether this was a natural part of meeting one's self or if it just the way she was.

Big Trouble in Little China – Chinese Language
Classfree ability, unlocks at level 6
Grants user ability to speak and read fluid Cantonese and
passable Mandarin.

This one caught her attention. Although the ability to speak Chinese offered no practical benefit in Etheria, it was just too cool to pass up. She would be able to watch Bruce Lee movies without needing to focus on the subtitles. In order to learn it, she spent nearly an entire day speaking nothing but Cantonese, much to the annoyance of her travel companions. Once she received the ability level-up notification, she switched back to English.

War Aeternus – Create Bacon
Classfree ability, unlocks at level 8
Exchange mana for uncooked bacon at a rate of one-eighth
pound of bacon per mana spent.
Cost: variable
Cooldown: 10 minutes

Create Bacon was a useful ability. It was good to have an emergency food source. Though it consumed most of her mana, she would be able to get it all back within an hour just by eating some of the bacon. After unlocking this ability, bacon became a common side dish during their travels.

There was another ability that caught her interest, though it was out of her reach for the moment. She'd discovered it while watching the even-numbered *Star Trek movies* with Ari and Pan. After the first movie, the following notification appeared:

Ability Unlocked: Warp
Time mage ability, unlocks at level 40
Fast travel to any settlement that you have previously visited.
Anyone in physical contact with you will make the journey as
well, though at a higher mana cost.
Cast time: 45 seconds
Travel time: 60 seconds
Cost: 3 mana plus 1 mana per additional traveler
Cooldown: 20 minutes

You will not be able to use this ability since you do not meet the level requirements.

She was currently nowhere near level 40, but it might be worth holding on to the class if only to unlock such a convenient ability. In video games, fast travel was something the player usually unlocked early in the game. Fast travel was a way game developers allowed players to travel around the game quickly without forcing them to spend hours manually trudging the distance.

When playing games, Tasha hardly ever used fast travel because it made it too easy to miss interesting or useful diversions or side quests. Fast travel also discouraged combat, ultimately leading to underleveled characters. As a game developer, she understood that even though fast travel was often convenient, it was the enemy of fun.

In her situation, however, there could be practical advantages in being able to quickly warp between cities and dungeons. This was a world where traveling time between distant points was measured in months. She was working against the clock, so the ability to fast travel could mean the difference between success and failure. Level 40 was still a long way off, particularly given the higher experience curve. It was ten levels higher than she had intended to go in the class, but that fast travel ability was just too useful to pass up.

Though they had traveled for several months, there was still a good distance left to travel. They had been avoiding the roads and had to travel in a far less direct path over the open terrain. Their stores of consumables had grown thin, and soon they would have to rely on Kiwi's magic for healing. They did eventually find relief in the form of an NPC village.

NPC villages were abnormal spawns that provided a place to rest, buy supplies and equipment, and earn some extra experience by performing procedurally generated fetch quests.

This NPC village had an item shop, a weapon shop, a clothier, and a pub. There was also the mayor's house. Tasha counted, and the entire village had thirty-one men, women, and children who wandered around randomly spouting the same scripted lines over and over again.

Pan pulled on Tasha's sleeve. She was pointing to the weapon shop.

Tasha nodded. "Sure, let's go. I need a replacement for Namaka anyway."

They passed by a bunny girl NPC who wore a sexy leotard. The bunny girl spoke to them as they passed. "Would you care for a puff-puff massage?"

Pan just shook her head. "I'm just a kid, so I don't understand."

The pair of them entered the shop. A bearded dwarf was standing at the counter. "Buy something, will ya?" he demanded.

"Good sales pitch, that," Tasha muttered under her breath.

Tasha and Pan both opened up shopping windows and examined what the dwarven NPC had for sale.

"Let's see," Tasha said, "how about this one? It's called 'Grasscutter' and deals wind damage. Plus 31 attack. That's way better than my Namaka's +5."

She looked at the item details. Its trigger action, Air Slicer, added a 75% boost to attacks and applied air elemental damage, but the effect would only last for 0.25 seconds with a 1-second delay. That meant she'd need to work on timing her strikes. It made sense that a more powerful weapon would be more difficult to use.

The Grasscutter certainly didn't come cheap. The cost in GP would consume most of her savings to that point, but she'd put off upgrading her weapon for far too long. She made the purchase.

While traveling over the past month, she'd gained an additional two levels, bringing her to level 24. She'd divided her stat points between charisma and intelligence. Her strength stat, combined with the attack bonus from her new weapon, brought her attack from 24 to 50, which would be a major help in combat. If she used Air Slicer, her attack would rise to 88, if only for a quarter of a second. The new weapon cost her nearly everything she had, but it was worth it.

Normally in an RPG she would have purchased new weapons regularly as she leveled, but since they had been avoiding towns, the upgraded weapons attack rate was many times higher than the weapon she'd used previously.

Pan tapped at an option on her shopping interface. It was a dwarven-made handgun with a +20 attack damage rating. Pan was sad to part with her trusty crossbow, Josephine, but she'd outgrown it many years ago. She had long wanted to use a firearm rather than a crossbow, but this was the first time she'd saved up enough to afford the higher cost. After purchasing the weapon and naming it Winona, she ran off to practice.

Having already interrogated the entire population of the NPC village and looted the houses for treasure chests, Tasha headed to the pub. She saw Pan and Hermes out of the corner of her eye. Hermes was teaching the young girl how to hold a firearm. Kaze was watching from where he was perched on top of the mayor's house.

She shoved open the saloon-style door and stepped inside, allowing them to swing shut behind her. In the corner of the room, Ari was drinking some ale and relaxing in a chair. He got up as she approached and set the book he was reading on the table.

"Hey, Ari," Tasha said. She purchased a pint of ale from the NPC bartender and joined him. "What are you reading?"

"It's a romance novel. An old friend of mine wrote it, and I'm just now getting around to reading it. It's painfully bad. There are so many interlocking love triangles. I had to diagram them to keep everything straight in my head. It seems just like the kind of thing she would have written."

"If it's that bad, why do you keep reading it?"

"Well... I have come this far already. Now I'm emotionally invested, and I need to find out how it ends."

"I prefer science fiction," Tasha said. "Or maybe fantasy. Or sometimes video game strategy guides. Anyway, I wanted to ask you, what are our plans from here?"

"Why are you asking me? I'm not the leader," Ari said.

"Yes, you are, you're totally the leader. You planned our route and usually make decisions about which enemies to fight and where to train."

He shook his head. "I'm the last person who should be in charge. We have an actual princess here. She should be the leader. If not her, then maybe you."

"I'll pass," Tasha said. "Leading is boring. Just give me a thing to do, and I'll go do that thing. I'm not someone who tells people to do things. I'm a thing doer."

"If you say so. I actually do have a plan of action for us. There's a farming village to the south of here called Slime's Row. If we can hire a covered wagon from there, we might be able to take the main road, right under Murderjoy's nose. From above, it will look like any other raptor-led carriage. We should be able to make better time that way."

"See, I told you that you were the leader," Tasha said. "I wouldn't have thought of that. I probably would have just blundered toward our destination in a straight line like an idiot."

"But you would have found a way to make it work."

"Enough of the mutual admiration society already," said Hermes, who had been standing in the doorway for who knew how long. "I take it we have a plan?"

"Yeah," said Tasha. "We're headed south. Let's get some rest. The village will probably despawn in the morning. That's how these things work, right? I don't know about the rest of you, but I want to rest on an actual bed for once."

Hermes nodded slightly. "Say, Tasha, before that, how about some more of that historical documentary that we've been watching? I've been finding the history of your people strangely compelling. In fact, I'm eager to learn more about the downfall of this tyrant king we've been learning about. What was his name again?"

"His name's Lord Frieza, and like I keep telling you, *Dragonball Z* isn't a historical documentary. It's an anime."

"But, anime is real, right? Anime is real! Right?"

Tasha didn't have the heart to destroy his happy worldview, so they spent the evening watching several episodes of the Ginyu saga. Although Tasha enjoyed *Dragonball Z*, her main purpose in watching it was to unlock a couch potato ability called Zenkai Boost.

Dragonball Z – Zenkai Boost
Classfree ability, unlocks at level 6
When lowered to one heart, gain triple experience when the fight ends. Usable once per calendar day.

While she didn't want to be in a situation where she was less than a heart container away from dying, the benefit of triple experience was hard to pass up.

When she awoke the next morning, Tasha considered her situation. She was on an adventure, precisely like she'd wanted. She had become the strong person who she had always wanted to be. She was surrounded by a fellowship of companions who she viewed as friends.

Everything in her world was perfect. That's how the day started, at any rate, but good things were never made to last.

The NPC village didn't actually despawn until after they left. Slime's Row was still several days of travel to the south. Or it would be if they could just manage to travel in a straight line. Unfortunately, as was often the case, they were frustrated by a large zone of high-level spawns that prevented them from traveling in the direction they wanted. They spent the entire day trying to circumvent it, but the arbitrarily shaped zone just seemed to go on forever.

Finally, Ari had Kaze scout the high-level zone from overhead to find the shortest path through it. Upon the dragon's return, he reported that there was a narrow four-mile strip of land which would take them straight through to a lower-level zone.

Their plan was to cut straight across it. Once they were through they would have nothing but manageable monster spawns for the rest of the trip to Slime's Row. It was a risk but a reasonable one—or so everyone thought.

It turned out that Murphy's Law was in full effect, and after they reached the halfway point, a mob spawned—one of a much higher level than they had anticipated. There was only a single enemy:

Jabberwock (Level 47)
Bringer of death and devourer of the weak. Flee now, lest you

become part of the Jabberwock's balanced breakfast.

ATK 71   Mag ATK 51

DEF 36   Mag DEF 30

Weaknesses: none

Resistances: Fire, Lightning, Earth, Poison

Special ability 1: Rage

Special ability 2: Drain Mana

Special ability 3: Dismiss Summon

Special ability 4: Gravity

It was an enormous beast with forty heart containers. It had a huge catlike body with great batlike wings and six tentacles that each originated from its side and waved about in a threatening manner.

The usual strategy involved Ari, Slimon, and Tasha engaging it directly while Kiwi hit it with debuffs. Kaze would try to pull aggro from above, leaving Pan and Hermes to flank it with gunfire.

This wasn't the first time Tasha had faced enemies that employed a rage ability. Rage buffed a fighter's damage output but made any actions other than direct physical attacks impossible. It was devastating to magic users but mostly ineffective against frontline fighters since fighting was what they probably would have done anyway. Sometimes the mobs would even cast rage on themselves to increase their own damage.

Drain Mana was troubling, and it changed their strategy somewhat. This ability reduced a target's mana pool. Rather than conserving MP to use later in the fight, Kiwi would need to spend as much as possible on buffs and debuffs, holding back only enough to not receive aggro.

The Dismiss Summon ability looked like it was used to dismiss conjured beings. She remembered Kiwi telling her about the summoner class back at Brightwind. Summoners were children who invoked conjured beings known as figments to fight for them. She assumed Dismiss Summon wouldn't be any threat since none in the group were summoners.

The Jabberwock started by invoking its Gravity ability on the group. Gravity magnified a person's personal gravity field, making them heavier and slowing their movements. It also had the effect of bringing

Kaze to the ground, holding him down. Running from this battle was now impossible given their inability to move faster than the mob.

The monster cast Drain Mana on Pan, draining all of the girl's mana. She wasn't a magic user, so that didn't concern Tasha overmuch. They were lucky that the Jabberwock hadn't used the ability on Kiwi.

"Pan, Hermes," Ari said, "take sniping positions along the side. Kaze, protect Kiwi and draw aggro. Tasha, Slimon, you're with me!"

For a time, the strategy worked. Kiwi buffed everyone and focused on recovery spells. The creature performed AOE fire breath attacks, but since the group was mostly spread out, damage was concentrated on only one or two people, and Kiwi was able to patch them up with heals. They steadily chipped into its health, bringing it down a quarter heart at a time.

The Jabberwock was now down to half health. Just over twenty heart containers remained when the horns on the creature began to glow. The battle log read:

Jabberwock (Level 47) is charging for Firestorm.

"Everyone spread out!" Ari yelled. The mob must be getting prepped for some kind of high-yield area-of-effect attack.

The sun disappeared from the sky, cloaking the land in a crimson red. Hundreds of fireballs were forming in the skies above them.

The Jabberwock screeched, and a rain of fireballs fell from the sky, each impacting the ground at a different place. Spreading out was not the right strategy against this kind of attack. Half of the team was hit—Hermes and Kaze, who had been clustered together, were hit the hardest. They were both down to critical health.

Hermes pulled out a potion and ran to the dragon. "Drink this quickly, dragon!"

The dragon snapped the glass bottle from his hand, shattering the vial and drinking the recuperative liquid, which brought him back to full health. Hermes turned around and pulled out a second health potion, but before he could bring the bottle to his lips, an ice lance shot forth from dragon and impaled him. The potion fell from his hands and rolled onto the rocky ground, useless. The dwarf's heart containers had run out, and he collapsed to the earth. The life left his eyes, and he died on the battlefield.

"Hermes!" cried Kiwi, but the Jabberwock was already stomping toward her.

"There'll be time to mourn later," Ari said. "We need to finish this."

"O-okay Ari."

The Jabberwock reared back on its hind legs and dashed across the battlefield. Pan was sniping it with her handgun over and over from the sidelines, dealing a quarter of damage at a time. Slimon was hitting it repeatedly with his tentacles but was dealing even less damage than Pan.

Kiwi backed away. "I'm out of mana!"

The Jabberwock still had nine hearts left. Tasha sliced at it again and again but dealt only nominal damage. It swiped at her with its foreclaws, knocking her away and costing her five hearts. Her defense buffs had already worn off. She quickly drank a health potion before returning to the battle, but the creature had changed targets. Pan had been shooting at it nonstop throughout the battle and had earned much of its hate.

"Pan, stop shooting! Wait for me to gain aggro."

The Jabberwock leapt into the air and landed right in front of Pan, towering over the small girl. Ari appeared in front of her and struck a martial-arts pose, ready to defend his daughter. Tasha and Slimon kept attacking from behind the creature, but there were still five heart containers left to go, and each one cost precious seconds.

Instead of attacking, the Jabberwock began to invoke an ability. The combat log read:

Jabberwock (Level 47) invokes Dismiss Summon.

For a moment Tasha wondered what would cause the mob to use Dismiss Summon at a time like this. There weren't any summoners here. That's when she saw Ari's eyes. They were open wide with panic and realization. Tendrils of blue energy circled his form and motes of lights flew away from his body. He looked directly at Tasha and mouthed the words, "Tasha... I..." before vanishing into mist.

Tasha collapsed to her knees in shock and confusion. Why had Ari turned into mist as though he were a mob? Before she could react, the Jabberwock unleashed a fire attack, shrouding Pan in flames. Operating on instinct, Tasha ran forward and drove the sword into the Jabberwock's mouth and pulled the trigger, dealing critical water damage to the creature's brain, killing it. The Jabberwock faded away into ethereal mist.

Tasha just stared at the place where Ari had been standing, confusion evident on her face.

Kiwi was the first to recover. She got to work handing out health potions and retrieving Hermes's items for safe storage.

Kaze approached and thought-spoke to her. *The dwarf gave his life to save my own. He gave me the potion rather than use it to save himself.*

"I've known Hermes since he was young," Kiwi said. "I know he can be greedy, stubborn, and quick to turn to violence, but deep down he's fiercely loyal to his friends. I suppose we won't see him again until we return home."

As Kiwi and Kaze were speaking, Tasha approached Pan. The girl was curled up on the ground, shaking and holding her legs in a fetal position.

"Pan, what happened? Why did Ari vanish?" Tasha asked. She already knew the reason but didn't want to believe it. There had to be some other explanation. Pan looked up, but it was clear that she was barely holding her emotions in check. She was on the verge of a meltdown.

"I'm... so sorry," Pan said.

"Why are you sorry? What did you do?"

"I lied to you. I d-d-didn't tell you."

Anger filled Tasha's voice. "Tell me what? That you're a summoner? That Ari was a figment of your imagination? It's true, isn't it? The 'thief' class is just for show."

Pan nodded. "I wanted to tell you..."

Tasha's anger continued to grow hotter. "But you *didn't* tell me, did you? Instead you kept it a secret."

"I know." Fresh tears were running down her cheeks. "I can explain."

"You can explain? You can *explain* how the man I've known for months was nothing more than a figment of your imagination?"

Tasha was consumed by a rush of rage and bitterness. "I don't want you to explain. I don't want to hear anything you have to say."

"Tasha," Pan said, "you're... you're my only friend. I love you."

"I'm not your friend. Friends don't lie to each other."

Congratulations! You have reached ability Level 1 in:
Pretentious Jerk
People whom you belittle are now 8% more likely to question their self-worth.

Tasha instantly regretted the words as she spoke them but was too angry to apologize. She pushed the notification away. She was too angry to trust her words and didn't want to say something else that she would regret. "I'm going to bed."

Pan continued rocking back and forth with her arms around her knees. After Tasha set the campground and pitched the tent, she looked at Pan one last time before turning away.

Pan's mind was a cage of guilt and self-hatred. Why had she hurt her one and only friend? She'd finally met someone who actually liked her for who she was. No, that wasn't really true. She had kept her true nature hidden from Tasha, just like she had with everybody else. Tasha would be better off without her. The world would be better off without her. She berated herself, wishing she could disappear.

The hours passed, and she sank deeper and deeper into depression. The world around her was dark, and her mood darkened with it. And why shouldn't she hate herself? She was certain that Tasha hated her. Tasha had even said she wasn't her friend anymore. If only Tasha would forgive her, tell her that it was okay. But that would never happen.

Almost without knowing what she was doing, she stood up and equipped her cloak of invisibility from her inventory. She couldn't face Tasha or the others. Not now. Not ever. She had to disappear. She picked a direction and started walking.

By the time the sun came up, she was miles away.

CHAPTER 28

Mad Marina and the Child of Phantoms

There once was a peasant woman who lived alone, deep within the human nation of Zhakara. She wasn't wealthy by any means and made her living as a level serf. She had an arrangement with a local lord to fight mist monsters on their land in exchange for 80% of the GP that she earned. In exchange, she was given a small room to sleep in and two meals per day.

It wasn't a fair arrangement, and the woman knew this. She despised the lord, and yet she didn't blame him. It was more accurate to say that she envied the power he had over others. She would have done the same in his place. As a peasant, she could never hope to be rich or powerful. She would spend her days in service to those more affluent and wealthy, until old age finally took her.

She did have an achievable ambition, however. She wanted to be a mother more than anything else in life. She saw how motherhood brought joy to the women around her and wanted that for herself.

She wasn't a great beauty and didn't hope to attract a desirable husband. That suited her just fine; marriage held little interest for her. She had no interest in sharing her child with another person. To her, the only purpose men served was to provide her with said child.

Learning that she was pregnant was the happiest moment of her life. She did not know who the father was, nor did she care. For the next nine months, she lived off her meager savings, taking crafting jobs when they became available.

She used the last of her GP to pay off a lord to allow her access to the save point for the birthing. She didn't want to risk losing the child after everything.

The long-anticipated day finally arrived. Despite planning for the worst, the birth went off without a hitch.

The doctor handed her child to her, and she looked at it for the first time. Her expression of joy quickly turned to one of confusion and then disgust as the scan results appeared in a floating window. The child looked just fine, but her stats were pathetic, not to mention the permanent debuffs.

> **??? Branford (Level 1 Summoner)**
> **Race: Human**
> **Class: Summoner**
> **Subclass: None**
> **Conditions:**
>> **Autism (permanent debuff)**
>> **Hereditary Anemia (permanent debuff)**
>> **Congenital Muscular Dystrophy (permanent debuff)**
>> **Nearsightedness (permanent debuff)**
> **Hearts: 3/3 Mana: 2/2**
> **Strength: 1 Intelligence: 4**
> **Agility: 2 Precision: 3 Charisma: 2**

She almost dropped the child in surprise. The woman had wasted so much time and money on this.... this defective child?

The newborn baby didn't have a single stat with more than 5 points. She had a strength of 1, and she'd probably need to be carried around or use a wheelchair until she was old enough to be power leveled. If it was only that, the mother might have been able to work with it, but the permanent debuffs would make the child a constant and unacceptable burden. The nearsightedness was easily corrected, and even anemia and muscular dystrophy could be mitigated by stat assignment, but the autism was a deal breaker. If the child wouldn't even be able to speak for itself properly, what use was it?

She didn't have any of these traits, so they must have come from the father, whoever that was. Damn him for giving her such feeble offspring.

Why should she accept such a failure? Someone who would be nothing but an unwelcome burden to her? She'd wanted a child who could take care of her when she grew old. The feelings of motherly affection that she had been led to expect were simply not there.

It still wasn't too late. She could try again, and next time it would be a proper child with no disabilities. But that couldn't happen if she had to support such dead weight. She would make sure to choose more suitable mates in the future.

A prompt appeared: "Enter name." She had to give it a name, or the prompt wouldn't go away. She would pick something random; a throwaway name would be fine. She typed "Panella" into the prompt, tapped on the confirm button, and the prompt vanished. Panella had been her sister's name. She despised her sister and figured that if she gave the child that name, it would be easier to hate as well.

She had to rid herself of the disgusting thing as quickly as possible. It was a deformed creature and merited nothing but death. What kind of life could such a person lead? It would be a life of constant pain and struggle. The child would never be able to compete with people who didn't have her weaknesses. It would be merciful to kill her now and keep her inferior genetic material from entering the genepool.

Regrettably, she couldn't kill it as she meant to. The baby had already been registered at a save point. It would just respawn, and then her neighbors would associate it with her. If it became common knowledge that this was her child, she would be stuck with it. Other people would look down on her if she didn't take care of it. If only she hadn't insisted on using a save point for the birthing. Perhaps there was another way to get rid of the thing.

She placed the child in its basket. Following a heavily worn path, she traveled to the next town over. There were no protected paths in Zhakara, and citizens who were too weak to fight mist monsters received the deaths that they deserved.

She didn't want the child to be linked to her in any way. She couldn't do anything about the girl's last name, but Branford was a common enough surname, so at least she had plausible deniability. If anyone asked, she would say that her child died in childbirth. People would feel sorry for her, and she might be able to capitalize on that.

Why wouldn't the damn thing stop wailing? Did it do nothing but cry? Well, she certainly wasn't going to feed it. It wasn't her problem.

Several hours later, she arrived at the next town. As an outsider, she had to pay for the use of the save point, but it a necessary cost. She was careful not to touch the city's save point herself, but touched baby Panella to it, ensuring that when the baby died it would respawn there without her. That way they wouldn't be able to trace it to her, and the child would become someone else's problem.

After registering the child at the save point, she set out into the wilderness. For the rest of that day, she walked through the jungle until she was so far in that no living being would be able to hear her child's crying. She hardened her heart and removed the naked newborn from the basket, putting the basket as well as the blanket into her inventory. She set the naked newborn upon a small clearing of wildgrass.

She looked at the infant girl one last time, and just for a moment reconsidered what she was about to do. The baby wasn't so awful when it was wasn't crying. She could almost forget about its debilitating weaknesses.

Everything she had been raised to believe told her to leave it. The child was weak. It would be nothing but a parasite that would suck her dry and leave her a destitute, bitter woman. She would be caring for it for the rest of her life and receive nothing in return but toil and sorrow.

She resolved to abandon the child now, before she had another chance to reconsider. Gathering her determination, she held her head up high and walked back the way she came. The woman would never see her child again, and the sounds of her daughter crying was the last thing that she heard as she disappeared into the wilderness.

His first memories were of being summoned. The figment known as Aralogos the Pugilist had never been summoned before. He had a basic knowledge of how these things worked and had a vague recollection of other figments that shared the pugilist archetype.

He looked around, trying to locate his master. The first and most important law of any figment was to protect his summoner.

"Master, where are you?" he called out, but there was no answer. His summoner had to be somewhere close by.

He was standing in a small clearing surrounded by trees and dense vegetation. The air was thick with mist. There were disturbed branches as well as a set of footprints leading away from the clearing. Could that be from his master? He didn't think so. When a figment was summoned, it appeared right next to the summoner, and nobody was here.

"Where are you? Why have you summoned me?"

Finally he saw the naked baby lying on the ground and knew instinctively that it was the baby who had summoned him. It wasn't unheard of for babies to use their level one class abilities instinctively before they knew any better. A newborn thief would sometimes "steal" items without understanding what he was doing. Children with the healer class would sometimes heal people randomly. So having a summoner invoke a figment wasn't strange in and of itself.

He made to approach the small child, but as he started to move, the mist rushed together to form four creatures.

4 Boblins appear! Combat started.
Boblin A fingers his sword menacingly.
Boblin B attacks Panella.
Boblin C attacks Panella.
Boblin D attacks Panella.

Aralogos the Pugilist didn't hesitate. If there was one thing he understood, it was combat. He was a level 4 pugilist, meaning that he was highly skilled at unarmed martial arts. He was created with a built-in expert-level knowledge of how to fight.

Typically, a summoned creature would obey his summoner's instructions rather than fight independently. It was the summoner's job to plan combat tactics and direct her figments accordingly, but since his summoner was an extremely young child, she couldn't be counted on to give orders. He would just have to make his own combat decisions.

He quickly interposed himself between his master and the attacking boblins. One of them tried to dodge past him, but he grabbed it by the arm, put it into a hold, and threw it at another attacking boblin, knocking them both to the ground. The third attacking boblin changed its target to him and cut him with its sword, dealing half a heart of damage.

Aralogos laughed at their feeble attacks. He kicked one of the prone boblins, killing it before taking another hit by the fourth boblin's blade. He hit that boblin with five rapid punches, finishing it off. The remaining two injured boblins didn't last more than a minute against his onslaught of kicks and punches.

He was justifiably proud of the fight. He'd killed all four of the mobs and only lost a single heart container during the battle. They hadn't even touched his summoner. He collected the GP and experience and opened the loot capsule.

The loot capsule contained a single beef-and-bean burrito wrapped in aluminum foil and a small cola. Babies couldn't eat burritos, could they? Well, it might be somewhat difficult, given his master's lack of teeth. What did babies eat? He was *so* in over his head. The burrito vanished as he added it to his inventory. As an imaginary person, he didn't need to eat, although the food would restore his HP over time, so it was worth keeping just in case. If nothing else, he could sell it to a merchant NPC.

The battle was over, the loot was collected, and Aralogos was at a bit of a loss as to what to do next. Normally the summoner would dismiss her figment once combat was finished, unless there was other business to discuss. Figments were transient beings, entirely at ease with the idea that they would only exist for brief periods of time. Thus, he was not accustomed to the idea of long-term existence.

He approached Panella and picked her up. As he did so, the child stopped crying. It was clear that the child wasn't going to dismiss her summon. He could only assume that she'd somehow realized she was in danger and summoned him on pure instinct.

"Master, where are your parents? Are you alone?"

He didn't expect her to answer. As a combat-type figment, he was ill-suited for this sort of interaction. There were still three hours on the summon timer. Once the timer ran out, he would be dismissed automatically. In the meantime, he needed to try to find her parents, or at least someone who would take care of her. Surely she must be hungry. She didn't have any clothing, so he wrapped her up in his vest. It would have to do until he could manage something better.

He moved to examine the footprints that he had found earlier and began to follow them. He didn't have the skills of a tracker, but following the tracks wasn't challenging. Whoever had left them clearly did not expect to be followed. The trail of human footprints and broken vegetation was clear. He wondered what sort of person had left them.

One of the footprint trails led back the way he had come. He didn't have the expertise to determine whether they were the same person, but it was a safe guess. This meant that whoever had made the tracks most likely carried Panella to this place and left her. Even if he found the person who had left the tracks, there was no guarantee that they would take care of her. But at the very least, they might be able to provide some information about her.

While traveling, there were several subsequent mist attacks, but fortunately he was in a low-level area, and he didn't take any additional damage. The amount of GP from those battles was not substantial, but he collected it anyway. Normally the summoner would receive the spoils from combat, but until he found someone to take care of his charge, he would hold on to the loot.

The baby started crying again, but Aralogos didn't know what to do about it. He didn't have any food to give her. He had to find someone who could help.

As a combat-style figment, he knew little about life outside of battle. He knew how to fight and how to follow orders, but that was about it. He knew that GP was used to purchase goods and services from merchants. If he could find one, maybe he could purchase some milk or whatever it was that babies ate.

Finally, the tracks ended at a worn path. There was no way to know which way to go from there. He picked a direction and just started walking, carrying the child, who had cried herself to sleep.

The summon timer had run out. Aralogos instinctively knew that he only had a handful of seconds remaining in this world. He placed Panella on the ground beside the path, making sure that she was wrapped in his vest.

He crouched down next to her and looked at her sleeping form. "I'm sorry I couldn't find your guardians, little one. May you find a way home." Moments later, he dissolved into a cloud of mist.

Some time passed before Aralogos was once again summoned. It was early evening, and it wouldn't be long before the sun set. His master was crying on the ground. He reached down and picked her up. As he lifted Panella into his arms, the child stopped crying.

"Little one, there are no monsters for me to fight. Why did you summon me? I don't know what to do. I'm not your guardian. I'm just a figment. I know how to fight for you, but that's about it."

She babbled a response.

"Okay, okay. I'll follow this road with you until we come to a town. Don't worry, I won't leave you by yourself. I'll stay with you until my time runs out."

Aralogos continued to walk the heavily worn path. Every time his timer was about to run out, he placed the infant on the ground and disappeared, only to be summoned again some time later.

Night had fallen, and the mist monsters were now many levels above him. Fortunately, he was able to escape from each battle without taking too much damage. He kept Panella safe, until finally they came to a crossroads. During the night, he despawned twice but each time was resummoned minutes later.

A sign indicated that the town of Wilmarth was only a few miles to the east. When he arrived at the town, it was early morning. As a figment, the passage of time didn't bother him. Real people needed sleep, but Aralogos didn't have that particular burden. He wasn't entirely sure sleep was even possible for a being like him.

He passed through the town gates and was challenged by a guard, who charged him a 10 GP entry fee.

Aralogos wasn't actually sure what he was looking for. If he could find the child's guardians, that would be best. If nothing else, he could get some supplies to take care of her. Maybe some baby food, blankets, disposable diapers, and whatever else he could think of. He only had 80 GP left and was unsure whether that would be enough.

Just a few blocks inside the town gate, he found what he was looking for. A plump redhaired human woman stood outside a wooden building. The words "NPC Merchant" hovered prominently above the woman's head. Three strong-looking men and one woman were playing cards at a table right next to the NPC merchant.

Aralogos approached the NPC, but one of the men placed himself between it and Aralogos. "What do you think you're doing?"

"I think I'm using the NPC merchant."

"If you want to use the NPC, first you need to pay the fee," he said, unjustifiably proud of his rhyme. "This NPC is the property of Lord Hempledon of Wilmarth."

"Who?"

"You're not from here, are you? Look, all you need to know is that if you want to use the NPC, you need to give me 30 GP."

"Why should I have to pay you to use an NPC? NPCs are created by the aire for everyone to use. A human can't own one."

One of the card players turned to the other. "Will ya listen to this tree-hugging socialist drivel? Nobody can own an NPC... right. Lord Hempledon controls access to it and keeps it guarded. How is that not ownership? Look, are you going to pay the fee or not?"

Aralogos thought for a minute. "I just need to use this NPC to buy some food and supplies for this baby."

The woman at the card table said, "I don't see how that's our problem. Either cough up the money or stop bothering us."

"Can I check the price of baby formula, diapers, and some clothing?"

The man crossed his arms. "Money first. And don't get it into your head that you can fight all four of us and live. I'm a level 12 swordsman, and my buddies are all level 7 to 8. We're more than a match for a level 4... whatever you are."

Aralogos thought for a minute. "I'm not sure there will be enough left over to buy the supplies if I pay the fee. Can you check the prices for me?"

"Why would we do that?" one of the card players asked.

"Because I'm carrying a starving baby," Aralogos said. "Isn't that reason enough?"

At this, the entire group started laughing. The laughter didn't let up for about a minute. Finally the swordsman said, "I'll tell you what, funny man, I'll check for you, but it'll cost you 10 GP."

"Fine." Resigned, Aralogos handed over a 10 GP coin. The man took it and went to join his friends at the card game, throwing the coin into the pot in the center of the table. "I'm in for 10 GP next round."

"Hold on a second!" said Aralogos. "You said you'd check the prices for me."

"I did say that, didn't I?" mused the swordsman. "There's no need. This NPC merchant only buys and sells weapons and armor. It won't sell groceries or clothing. Try the one in the city square... if you can still afford the fee, that is."

"If you knew I wanted baby supplies, why didn't you tell me that this NPC couldn't help me?"

"I was hoping you'd be dumb enough to give us some GP for nothing. Turns out I was right."

For a moment, Aralogos considered attacking the four of them, level difference and numbers be damned. But his only priority was taking care of his master, so he let the matter drop and started walking toward the city square.

"Have a nice day, and thank you for your business," the man called to him while his friends laughed.

He might have had enough before, but after losing 10 GP, there was no way he would have enough left over for supplies. Maybe he could find a human-run item shop or grocery store. Hopefully he wouldn't have to pay a fee to Lord Whatever-His-Name-Was.

An elven man dressed in simple clothing was walking past. Aralogos put his hand on the man's shoulder. "Hello. Can you help me?"

The elf turned to look at him, and for the first time Aralogos noticed the iron collar around the elf's neck. Instead of answering, he cast his eyes to the ground and started walking faster.

Another elf was walking past, this one a white-haired elven girl. She wore the same iron collar around her neck. Aralogos approached her cautiously. "Excuse me, miss?"

She cast her eyes to the ground and whispered, "Please, please don't talk to me. I'm sorry, master." She cast her eyes to the ground and sped away.

"Don't waste your breath, kid. They won't answer you, no matter how times you ask," said an elderly human woman from outside one of the wooden houses.

Aralogos approached the old woman. "Old mother, why won't they speak to me? And why are they wearing those metal collars?"

"Don't call me old, sonny! I'm barely seventy years young. Don't you know it's rude to ask a lady's age?"

"But... I didn't ask about your age."

"Good thing, too. I'm already tempted to give you a piece of my mind for calling me old."

Aralogos looked at her, confused. "But I already have a piece of someone else's mind, why would I need a piece of yours?"

The old woman was used to confusing other people and putting them on the defensive. With his perplexing statement, she had been unexpectedly thrust outside of her comfort zone. "What do you mean you already have a piece of someone else's mind?"

"I'm a figment, and this little child is my summoner. That means I'm using an unused portion of the girl's mind to think for myself."

The old crone looked thoughtful. "I see. I've heard talk of summoners but ne'er met one in my long eighty years of life."

"I thought you said you were seventy?"

"Are you asking about my age again, kid?" The woman was now back in her element.

"Only tangentially," Aralogos said, blundering right into the old woman's trap. "I was trying to ask about those elves. You said they wouldn't talk to me no matter how many times I asked. Also, I wanted to know about why they were wearing collars."

A look of understanding and sadness appeared on her face. "They're wearing those iron collars because they're slaves. If they are caught speaking to strangers, their human owners might punish them in order to reassert dominance. You aren't doing them any favors by trying to talk to them."

"So this country has slavery," he muttered.

"Of course it does," she said, "Where are you from that you don't know that?"

"I'm a figment. I just told you that a minute ago. This little girl summoned me."

The old woman looked around, confused. "What little girl?"

"The one I'm carrying in my arms."

The old woman cackled. "Ah, that little girl. So she's a summoner. I've heard of summoners, but I've never met one in my entire eight-five years of life."

"But you said..." Aralogos started, but then he stopped, deciding it best not to press the issue about her age. That wasn't progressing what was already a circular conversation, and he suspected that the old woman was just toying with him.

"Yeah, I might have guessed that you weren't from around here, judging by your crazy antics and the way you go around asking random girls for their age. Well, then. May I be the first to welcome you to Zhakara, the country of perfect freedom." She spoke the words with clear contempt. "That's what the people in charge like to call it, anyway."

"Perfect freedom? Why is it called that?"

"Here in Zhakara, there is only a single law: that no human may claim mastery over another. Other than that one rule, humans are free to do whatever they like without interference from the government."

"What about those elves from a moment ago?" Aralogos asked. "They were slaves, what's so free about that?"

"Nothing," the old woman said, "I used to think that the right to own slaves made us more free to pursue our own goals, but I was just young and naive. Now that I'm young and arguably wiser, I know that slavery is a terrible thing. Thinking about other people as objects is the foundation of all evil acts. Read that in a book once.

"The elves you passed by earlier are the property of Lord Hempledon, who controls this city and the surrounding land. Under the law, he can't actually force you to do what he wants, but people won't get far in life without being able to level or use NPCs, and he controls access to those things. If you want to get anywhere in life, you should avoid getting on his unhappy side."

She looked at the baby in Aralogos's arms. "Is that your daughter?"

"No," Aralogos said with what he considered to be unlimited patience, "as I said earlier, she's my summoner, and I'm her figment."

"Well, you should be keeping that kind of information to yourself. The people who live here are simple folk, meaning that they fear anything new and different and tend to react violently to things they don't understand. From now on, she's your daughter. Where did you get her, by the way?"

"Actually, I found her abandoned in the wilderness. She summoned me to fight a bunch of monsters but then kept on summoning me. I'm looking for her parents. Why would anyone abandon their child?"

"I literally just told you not to say out loud that you're her figment. If people think you are different, they'll probably kill you, and the girl for good measure. Criminy, some people never listen."

She took the girl before Aralogos had a chance to protest. "Well, that's just typical. Just look at her scan data. It says that she has several disabilities. Autism, anemia, nearsightedness, muscular dystrophy... Tsk tsk. In Zhakara, people who can't take care of themselves are often discarded. Her mother probably saw her stats and debuffs and left her in the woods so she could forget about her. It happens more often than you might think. You might be able to track the mother down, but it's not really worth the effort."

She inspected the child more closely. "She doesn't look well. What have you been feeding her?"

"Nothing at all. I have no food fit for a baby and those... People here won't let me use the merchant NPC to buy food. I'm a fighter, not a nanny. I know nothing about raising children. She hasn't eaten anything in at least a day. The only food I have is a burrito from a loot drop."

"Are you stupid? Newborn babies can't eat burritos. They might get indigestion." The ancient woman seemed to come to a decision. "Well, better bring her inside, then. I'll get her something to eat. If you need a place to stay tonight, you can have the couch. And don't think of getting frisky just because I'm a young unmarried woman in her prime living all by herself."

"Yes, ma'am. Thank you."

"Don't ma'am me, sonny. I never married, so miss is the appropriate moniker. And just so you know, I'm a high-level lightning mage and aspiring romance novelist, so just in case I'm wrong about you being good people, don't go thinking that you're at some sort of advantage."

"I would never take advantage of a beautiful young woman like you," Aralogos said, catching on to the old woman's game. "I do have a question, though. Why are you helping us, miss? Nobody else I've met seemed inclined to help us."

"What kind of a fool question is that?" she said as they entered her home. "Why am I helping a starving child and a clueless traveler? We can't all be self-interested ne'er-do-wells who abandon their children in the woods. Zhakara will try to break you, to turn you into a bitter person with no moral restraint. I'm made of sterner stuff than that. My name's Marina, by the way. They call me Mad Marina, though I have no idea why." She extended her hand.

"Aralogos," he said, taking her offered hand and kissing it. "I'm pleased to make your acquaintance."

The years passed quickly. Aralogos raised his charge as best he could. He rented one of the rooms in Marina's house and opened a martial-arts school to make money. The only thing he really understood was fighting, and opening a dojo seemed like the best way to utilize his talent. Marina suggested he open a casino, but Aralogos wouldn't have known where to even start with that sort of business.

When he wasn't teaching, he fought against mist monsters in the wilderness to gain experience for himself and Pan. Marina told him that he was even madder than her to bring a child into the wilderness, but Aralogos wanted to raise her level as quickly as possible so that when the girl was old enough, she could assign some stat points to strength in order to counteract her anemia. Marina would tag along for support and to keep the girl safe while her father/figment was fighting. She would occasionally cast a lightning bolt or two when things became dicey, but mostly she held back, allowing Pan to get as much of the experience as possible.

Lord Hempledon of Wilmarth took eighty percent of the GP that Aralogos earned from fighting mist monsters, but he got to keep the loot drops, and more importantly, the experience points. Aralogos had been warned that failure to pay his dues would lead to a bounty being put out on both him and his family.

He was always careful to hide the fact that he was a figment. Aralogos didn't really understand people, and so he took Marina's warning very seriously, not wanting to risk angering the simple folk of Wilmarth.

Whenever his summon timer was almost up, he went off somewhere private to despawn, only to be resummoned seconds later. Panella had learned to spawn him every time he disappeared. She had needed a parent, so she summoned one.

Panella's first word was "Ari." Marina had taken to calling him Ari from that moment on. Her vocabulary slowly increased, though by her second year she still only spoke a handful of words.

When she was five, she could still barely speak more than one word at a time, although her vocabulary had grown. She understood complex concepts like language but couldn't articulate her thoughts into sentences. She had learned to read and write and often communicated by writing what she wanted to say into her notebook.

When it came time to assign stat points, she followed her father's instructions and put most of her stats into strength and a few into agility. Because of this, she was able to stand up and move around without needing to be carried.

One day, a royal delegation arrived in town. The queen had sent a large contingent of elven slaves. The procession of slaves was led to the city save point in the center of the town and placed in cages on high platforms surrounding the save point, and a cage was assembled around the save point itself. A large gathering of citizens had congregated.

The elven slaves looked somewhat different than the ones that Ari had seen in the city. For one thing, many of them were high level. One of the grown elven men was a level 42 archer. It was more than that, though. The elven slaves who lived in the city had given up. The eyes of these elves still shone with defiance and hope. Their will hadn't been broken yet.

Once the cages had been fully assembled, a herald stood upon the platform. His voice had been magically amplified so that everyone in the square could hear him speak.

"Good people of Wilmarth, by order of Her Majesty the queen, you are to be given a gift. Bring forth any children in the town of at least two years of age who have not yet reached level 5. Your children will be quickly raised to level 5 and then will be returned to you. This is the queen's order."

The queen's men were moving through the crowd, examining one child after the next. One woman approached the herald, dragging her two boys behind her. "My children are both below level 5."

"Mine too!" said a different woman, who passed up a three-year-old girl.

Marina turned to Ari. "We need to leave, now. Don't let them see your daughter."

"Why not? Level 5 would give her enough stat points to counteract her physical disabilities. She needs this. The man said it was a gift from the queen. If it's a gift, that means it's free, doesn't it?"

The ancient woman grabbed his arm. "Trust me, those 5 levels come at a cost. Think about it. How do you think they would raise her level?"

"I don't know. I..." Then he saw the high-level elves held in cages around the save point. Comprehension dawned on him. "You're right. Let's go."

Ari picked up Pan and turned to leave, but one of the queen's men had already seen her. He approached and took the girl from Ari's arms before he could react. Pan tried to resist, but her meager strength was nothing compared to the man who was carrying her. She was dropped right before the platform with several other children. The entire city had gathered. More children were being brought in every minute until there were nearly a hundred children alongside her.

Pan watched the crowd, seeing her father's eyes upon her, looking confused.

The children were arranged by the queen's men into a line. An elven woman was bound and tied to a post in full view of the crowd below. The elven woman's brown eyes blazed with defiance. She struggled against her bonds, but that just made the crowd laugh and cheer.

One of the little boys was brought to the platform with the elven woman. He looked at the crowd and then back at the queen's man, who was handing the boy a dagger. He took it. The dagger was emerald green and shone with its own light. The guard said something to him and pointed at the bound elven woman.

For a moment, he looked uncertain. He looked to the crowd for support. The queen's men were moving through the crowd, starting a chant. Before long, the entire crowd was chanting, "Kill the elf! Kill the elf! Kill the elf!"

The boy looked at his parents, who had joined in the chant. He nodded and approached the bound elven woman. The elf shook her head, but the boy thrust the knife into her chest. It cut through her like a hot knife through butter. He pulled it out and stabbed her in the belly and then in the face. Each time, the knife ran straight through her with no resistance. Despite her high level, she died after only three imprecise stabs from the small child.

The boy looked at his bloodstained hands in horror, but then his eyes were brought upward, and his expression changed. "I leveled up!" he declared.

The crowd cheered his new achievement, and he held the glowing green dagger above his head in victory.

Several more children were led to the platform, where each of them killed an elf. The victims' cries for mercy were met with laughter and jeers from the crowd. Whenever a child killed one, they were met with cheers and adulation.

The line continued to grow shorter, until Panella stood at its front. One of the men took Panella's hand. "You're next, girl. Come with me."

Panella's entire body was shaking. She didn't like this. The man led her up some makeshift stairs to the platform. The elven woman's body from earlier had already been removed and thrown into a wagon. In her place, a dark-elven man with white hair and red eyes was being tied to the post.

She was offered a glowing green dagger.

God Slayer
Class: Weapon (dagger)
Artifact-tier item
A dagger forged of the holy metal orihalcum.
Damage: 90
Durability: 672/900
Active effects: Temporarily ignores level restrictions.
Time remaining: 42 minutes

Hands trembling, she took the weapon and turned back to the man. Did they expect her to kill him?

"It's easy," said the queen's man. "That weapon will make you strong. Just push it into the elf's chest."

She looked at the shining green weapon and then back up at the elf. His defiance from before was gone, and his eyes shone with fear and hate.

Panella looked at the crowd. A chant had started again. "Kill the elf! Kill the elf! Kill the elf!"

She didn't want to kill anyone, but all those people wanted her to. If she did what they said, she would make them happy. She remembered the boy who had stabbed the woman with the pointed ears. After he did it, the woman stopped moving. The people in the crowd were happy about it and loved him. Would they love her too? An adult was telling her to put the knife into the elf's body. Wasn't she supposed to do what adults told her?

She looked at the dark elf who returned her gaze with hate filled eyes but remained silent.

His scan information appeared. The elf was a level 36 healer named Naclorien.

She looked back to the crowd. Everyone was cheering her on. Well, not everyone. She found her father in the crowd. Why wasn't her father cheering her on? She wasn't the best at reading people's emotions, but she could tell that he wasn't happy with her. He said something to her, but she couldn't hear what it was from so far away.

She touched the edge of the blade with her finger. It cut straight through her skin without any resistance at all. A small trickle of blood poured out of the cut. She could feel power radiating from the knife. It would be easy. Just one push of the blade into his chest would be enough.

The queen's man knelt down next to her. "You have to kill him. It's easier than you think. All of those people out there want you to do it. Don't you want them to love you?"

She looked at her dad who mouthed the word "No." Panella dropped the knife to the ground. Its blade sank into the wood-paneled floor up to its hilt. The cheers of the crowd turned into boos and angry sounds.

"Pick it up," said the guard. "If you don't kill him, someone else will. Remember that he's just an elf. He isn't like us. He doesn't feel pain the same way we do. His kind are lesser. It is the prerogative of the weak to be dominated by the strong. That's just how the world was designed."

Pan didn't understand, but knew she didn't want to be here. She wanted to go home. She started toward the stairs, but the man grabbed her arm, stopping her from leaving.

"You can't go until you do what I've told you. The people out there came to see blood. If it isn't his, it'll have to be yours. If these people think you're an elf lover, you'll never make any friends. The other kids are doing it, and soon they'll be stronger. You don't want to be left behind, do you?"

She shook her head. Why was she so weak? She didn't know what to do. She collapsed to the ground in a fetal position with her hands over her head. Her entire body was shaking.

One of the queen's men stood her up and another punched her in the stomach three times, and then twice in the face. The strikes were painful but not especially strong. After their assault, she still had three and a quarter heart containers. The blows were meant to hurt, not to kill. The man holding her threw her into the assembled crowd, who moved aside as she tumbled to the ground.

She tried to get up, but adults were kicking her and pushing her back to the ground. One of them was her neighbor's father. Why was he hitting her? She coughed up blood. It hurt. It hurt so much. She tried to laugh it off, but that just made the adults angrier for some reason.

She should have done what the man said. Why did she have to be so weak?

By the time Ari pushed his way to Panella, she was down to half a heart container. Ari stood between her and the mob. Most of them backed away, their courage having evaporated. The situation had empowered the mob to attack a low-level unarmed girl, but not one of them wanted to risk fighting a grown man to get to her.

Ari picked up the girl and put a health potion to her mouth. One of the queen's men approached him. "You're this girl's father?"

"Yes, I am," Ari said.

"She disappointed us today, but that's all right. Our benevolent queen is generous with her gifts. If your daughter can find her courage before we leave, we'll still honor the queen's promise to bring her to level 5. I suggest you speak with her before returning. It will take over a month to drain the elves of their levels, so be sure to return before then."

As Panella swallowed the red liquid from the health potion, mist poured over her body, fixing the damaged areas, and her cuts and bruises disappeared.

The crowd had already forgotten about her as they cheered the next child, who had taken her place on the platform. A girl even younger than her held the shining green dagger in the air in victory. Someone unbound the limp figure from the post and threw him into the cart atop a pile of elven bodies. It was the dark-elven man that she'd spared. His lifeless, unseeing red eyes stared in her direction.

"Let's go home," Ari said as he placed her on the ground and led her away from the mob.

"Sorry," she whispered.

"Don't be. You did the right thing. There is no honor in killing an unarmed and bound opponent. It might take us a few more years, and you'll have to train harder, but we'll get you there, and unlike those who took the queen's gift, you will have earned it."

From that point on, Pan began to take a more active role in combat against mist monsters, despite her young age. Ari purchased a lightweight crossbow for her to use.

At first, she had terrible aim, but she trained every day, and bit by bit, her aim improved. Her hands were always trembling, but when she held her breath and focused, she could steady them, even if only for a few critical seconds. She wanted to put points into precision to be a better shot, but Ari insisted that she focus on strength and agility to compensate for her physical deficiencies.

When she was seven, her vocabulary had improved to the point where she could speak in short sentences, though her enunciation and body language didn't always match her words. It was much easier for her to write what she wanted to say rather than try to communicate verbally. She would often become frustrated by her inability to speak like everyone else, and her severe physical disabilities were a constant source of stress. Autistic meltdowns were routine, but she learned that she could reduce their frequency and intensity by spending time in cold, quiet, dark places, such as Mad Marina's broom closet. Silent meditation helped her avoid sensory overload to a small degree.

One day in her eighth year, she wanted to learn more about her class. So while Ari was speaking with Pan and Marina, she asked him about it. She knew how to summon Ari and understood that she would be able to summon other figments at higher levels, but other than that, she really didn't know much.

Ari explained that summoners invoked beings known as figments who shared a portion of the summoner's mind. Pan already knew that, but then he explained that when the summoner grew to sixteen years of age, the summoner would lose the ability to summon, and the class would be lost. Upon hearing this, she grew visibly panicked. She scribbled something on her notebook and handed it to him.

The question was: "What will happen to you when I turn sixteen?"

"I'll disappear forever," he said. "I'm a figment, just a projection of your mind. Without your imagination to bring me to life, I won't exist."

"Wh-why?" she asked. "Why d-d-d..." Tears formed in her eyes, and she wiped them away.

Marina frowned. "You didn't tell her before now?"

She shook her head.

"Because you were too young to understand," said Ari. "Because there's nothing I can do to change it. Maybe because it was too hard to say. You don't need to worry about me, Pan. I'm not afraid or anything. Figments are transient beings who normally only exist for minutes at a time. I've lived longer than any imaginary person has a right to."

For a long time she didn't say anything, but finally she scribbled a response into her notebook and handed it to him. "I don't want you to disappear. There has to be a way for you to remain."

Ari handed the notebook back. "I'll admit that I've become attached to the idea of living, but there's nothing to be done. I've read quite a lot on the topic, and if there is a way to keep me alive, nobody has found it."

She wrote her response. "If no mortal has found a way, then we need to ask a god."

"You're being silly. Even if we knew where an eidolon was, most of them take the forms of animals, weather patterns, satellites, or abstract concepts. Only a small handful of eidolons deign to speak with mortals."

"What about Libra?" asked Marina. "He might be able to help."

Pan looked at the ancient woman. "M-Marina... who is L-Libra?"

Marina looked at her. "Call me Mad Marina. I feel like I've earned that moniker, and I won't have people not showing me due respect by leaving it off. Either that, or call me Gran."

"Was that a triple negative?" Ari muttered at the old woman's antics.

"G-Gr-Gran," Pan offered.

Ari decided to push the issue. "Why do you insist on calling yourself mad? Your wacky antics aside, you happen to be one of the clearest thinkers I know."

"The majority of any society must be sane by definition," Marina said. "Frankly, I want nothing to do with those self-interested bastards. Now then, Libra is the eidolon of prophecy. He's always moving from place to place, disappearing here and appearing there. Nobody knows where he'll be at any given time, but if you can find him, just offer him a coin, and he'll tell you something... interesting. Whether he tells you how to save Ari is anyone's guess."

"Okay," said Ari. "So how do we find this Libra?"

"I just told you that nobody knows where he'll be at any given time. Weren't you listening? I've always suspected that there was some pattern to his movement and the timing of his appearances. So throughout the years I've been keeping detailed logs of where and when he's been sighted."

Ari frowned. "Really? You just happen to have this critical piece of information. Why? Why have you been doing this? What is Libra to you?"

"Why, he asks," Marina said. "Why? It's because I'm mad, obviously! Haven't you been paying attention all these years? "

"You want to ask Libra a question of your own, don't you?" asked Ari.

Marina turned away. "Maybe I did. I doubt I'll have the chance now."

"What is your question, Mad Marina?"

"It really doesn't matter now. Panella's question is much more important."

"Pan. Don't l-like P-Panella," said Pan.

"You shouldn't be so particular about your name, young lady," Marina said. "Just look at me. I don't care what people call me, do I?"

"No... No, Mad M-Marina."

"So, anyway, I'll show you my notes, and maybe we can work out some pattern to its movements, assuming a pattern actually exists."

"What does this eidolon look like?" Ari said. "If we're going to be looking for him, it might help to know what he looks like."

Marina went to a bookshelf and took down an old tome. She opened it to a page somewhere in the two hundreds and showed a drawing of the eidolon to Ari and Pan.

"Libra doesn't look human," she said. "He is a puppet inside an unmoving glass and wooden box. There is a coin slot in the front. Querents are expected to put a 1 GP coin inside the slot while asking the puppet a question. After it does a funny song and dance, it spits out a piece of paper with some interesting piece of information relevant to the querent."

Over the next three years, the three of them tried different predictive models to calculate Libra's historical appearances. Pan began learning some advanced mathematics and needed to allocate some stat points into intelligence, despite her father's insistence that she focus on strength and agility.

At first there seemed to be no pattern to where Libra would appear. Sometimes he would appear in the middle of a field with nothing for hundreds of miles, and other times he would appear in someone's bedroom with no warning. Once, a merchant ship had found the eidolon floating on the surface of the ocean. They were assuming that most of the time, his positions were not recorded, and they were working with limited data. If they had more information, working out a pattern would be easier.

Pan created a list of its locations given what they knew about the latitude and longitude of its appearances. She used pieces of yarn to connect its appearances in chronological order on the interior of a large glass globe, hoping some visual pattern would become evident. In the end, it just looked like a glass globe with bits of string connecting dots.

Marina suggested that they try to connect the points in a different order than chronological. In at least some of the records, the nature of the question had been included. She tried to connect the different points geographically on the globe by matching similar themes together. Oddly, there did seem to be a pattern—no similarly themed question was asked in the same geographical area.

In fact, the distance between similarly themed questions seemed to be the same. Similarly themed questions were always asked exactly 333 miles away from one another. Lines between those questions always formed equilateral triangles.

They started looking for a question that would be similar in theme to "How would you allow a figment to exist without a summoner?" There were only two questions that were even close in theme to that one. One question asked whether a person could continue to exist in Etheria in some manner after physical death. The other question was about how to imbue golems with sentience. Both questions had to do with the nature of life and how to give it to something that had none. Most questions were less of an existential nature and more of a get-rich-quick nature.

Pan connected the points on the globe with uniquely colored pieces of yarn. She drew two circles on the outside, representing a 333-mile radius around each point, showing the possible locations of Libra's next appearance. That was assuming, of course, that Libra kept to the positional pattern and hadn't already appeared at one of those locations sometime in the past.

The circles intersected at two points. One of them was in the middle of Ultros Bay, right in the middle of the water. The other was in Zhakara, not even thirty miles from the village of Wilmarth, where the three of them lived. That seemed too great of a coincidence to be mere happenstance. Now they knew where Libra would appear; what they didn't know was when he would make his appearance. He could appear at that spot tomorrow or in a thousand years for all they knew.

For a while, they were unable to solve this. Pan wanted to go there immediately and wait for it to appear, but both Ari and Marina couldn't agree to that plan. Without a city's monster-repelling field, there was nothing to stop mobs from attacking every few hours. Setting up shop there without enough GP to build a portable monster-repellent field was foolhardy at best.

It was Pan who finally solved the conundrum. She suggested looking for patterns on a four-dimensional hyper-sphere rather than a simple three-dimensional sphere. The difficulty with this was that they couldn't model it using a globe and pieces of yarn. Four-dimensional space wasn't something easily comprehensible by humans. One of the more cerebral races might be able to help them, but in Zhakara anyone who wasn't human was a slave and had long since had their independence and free-thinking natures beaten out of them.

They ended up saving up some of their GP and "renting" one of Lord Hempledon's arachnid slaves. An elf *might* have been able to work out the calculations, and the owlfolk were the wisest, but the spider women were the most advanced at higher mathematics.

The spider woman's name was Spindra. The upper part of her body was vaguely elven in appearance with pointy ears angled backward. Her lower half was that of a spider. She wore a tattered white shirt and a slave color that shone with a dim light.

Ari extended his hand to shake hers. The spider woman took it hesitantly. Her eyes darted to the charts and numbers as well as the large globe in the middle of Mad Marina's study.

"Hello, Spindra," he said. "My name is Aralogos. This is my daughter, Pan, and this lady is Mad Marina. We were hoping you could help us solve a puzzle."

Spindra took her hand back and shot a look at her handler, who stood in the entrance. He was never out of sight. The other slaves might have been broken, but her mind was still as sharp as it was when she was captured many years ago. "Aralogos. Pan. Mad Marina. Spindra greets you and thanks you for letting her leave her cage, even if only for a moment."

"They keep you in a cage?" Mad Marina asked.

The spider woman nodded her head. "When they don't use Spindra to do their pointless budget calculations, they keep her in a cage and show her off as a prize."

Her eyes shot back to her human handler nervously. She moved closer to Mad Marina and spoke in a low voice. "Spindra knows what you want from her. Those charts. Those dates and numbers you have written down on the chalkboard. That globe. You are trying to predict an event that will occur thirty miles from here, and you want Spindra to look for patterns from a higher dimensional perspective."

"You were able to figure all that out just by looking at our notes?" Ari said.

"Spindra already knows the answer," she said. "There's nothing in four dimensions, but in six, the answer is obvious. Spindra knows exactly when this event will occur."

"When?" asked Pan. "P-please help."

Spindra glanced again at her human handler nervously. She then leaned over to Marina, "Spindra will tell you, but first you must free her and kill that guard. Can you remove Spindra's collar? It stops her from weaving spells."

"I want to help," Ari said, "but if we let you go, they'll kill us. We can't fight every guard between here and the city gates."

"If they kill you, you will respawn, yes?" Spindra said. "You are human... Your Zhakaran law will protect you, yes? Spindra can escape on her own, trust her. She will tell you what you want to know, and if they kill you, you will come back and be free! Help Spindra?"

"I for one, like this plan," Mad Marina said.

"You would like this plan," said Ari.

Mad Marina removed an ancient dusty staff from the wall. "Well, no time like the present." She raised her staff and sent a bolt of lightning through the guard's chest, taking off half of his health.

Ari rushed at the guard and lifted him up, suplexing his head against the hardwood floor. Pan drew a dagger and plunged it into the guard's heart, finishing him off.

As Mad Marina got to work on Spindra's collar, Ari said, "Next time warn us before you do something like that."

"I did warn you. Now, Spindra dear, this might hurt a bit." She extended one hand and held apart her thumb and index finger. A line of electricity shot from her thumb to her extended finger. "Hold still."

She moved the arc of electricity so it intersected with the collar. After a few seconds, the iron melted, and she got to work on the other side. Blackened skin appeared on Spindra's neck where the iron had been melted. The spider woman screamed but did not move.

Ari handed her a healing potion. "Drink this, quick."

After Spindra drank the potion, she spoke. "Humans have freed Spindra! Event will happen in two years and forty-one days and two hours. Event will last for eleven minutes."

"That's two years from now," Ari said. "There's still time." He looked at Pan. "You'll only be fourteen when that happens."

"Spindra's debt has been repaid. May they find what they seek." Upon saying those words, a dark cloud appeared, and Spindra vanished.

Ari turned to Marina. "Did you know she could do that?"

Marina shrugged. "She's a time mage. They have a short-range teleportation ability, so it's not that surprising. She said her collar was inhibiting her magic. It's time to leave this town behind us."

"Okay, I have a plan," Ari said. "We'll just leave here quietly and casually head through the town gates before the guards realize what we've done. If we are quiet and careful, we'll be able to... Marina, what are you doing?"

Mad Marina had removed an object from her inventory and placed it on the ground. It was a black ball with a fuse on the end. "I've been waiting for years to use this."

"That's a bomb! You're going to blow up your house?"

"Why not? I'm not coming back here, and I don't want Lord Hempledon getting his smelly little hands on my research. Besides, it's my house. Who are you to tell me whether I can or can't blow it up?"

She created a magical spark that lit the fuse.

Ari gaped at her incredulously. "How long until that explodes?"

Marina shrugged. "I dunno."

The bomb's fuse was getting shorter and shorter by the second. One panicked dash up the stairs and out the exit later and they were running for their dear lives.

There were three guards waiting outside of their house: two women and one man. One of the women said, "Hey, what the hell are you doing out—"

Before she could finish her sentence, the house exploded behind them. As planks of wood and other debris flew in all directions, Mad Marina shot the female guard in the heart with blast of chain lightning that arced to the other two guards. Ari attacked the female guard with a flurry of punches. The remaining two guards who had been damaged by the chain lighting ran off.

"Don't let them escape!" cried Ari as he snapped the female guard's neck. "They'll bring more guards."

Marina shot another bolt of lightning through the male guard's chest. The bolt continued through to the other side, striking the side of someone's house and starting a small fire. The guard collapsed to the ground, dead.

Pan loaded a bolt into her crossbow and fired it at the retreating female guard. Her shot missed entirely and instead hit an innocent civilian in the knee. "Sorry!"

Ari pointed at the city gates, which were just in view from the remains of Marina's house. "We need to be gone *now*. Let's go."

They raced toward the gates. There were two guards, and they were both far higher level. "I'll draw them away," Ari said. "Pan, once you are outside, dismiss and resummon me."

Without waiting for their response, Ari ran up and punched one of the guards in the face. "Hey!" complained the poor guard, but the pugilist who had sucker-punched him was already running off, and the guard chased after him. Mad Marina led Pan by the hand toward the remaining guard. As the old woman approached, the guard pointed his spear at the woman. "What do you want? Stay back, witch!"

Mad Marina raised her staff into the air and began to recite a spell in a language that Pan did not recognize. "*Ba ken ba shri na ba n'kron ba alstulba!*"

Dark clouds manifested in the skies just above the gate. The remaining guard looked about nervously. As the clouds gathered, dancing arcs of lightning conjoined and formed a single blast that shot straight into the gate, blasting it to pieces along with the wall and the remaining guard. All that was left of the gate was scattered rubble.

Mad Marina grasped her heart in obvious distress and retched in pain.

Pan took her hand. "Gran, we h-h-have t-to go." Together they limped through the open gate and into the wilderness beyond.

When they were a sufficient distance from Wilmarth, Pan dismissed Ari and summoned him to her. He appeared in a cloud of mist.

Marina had fallen to the ground and was still clutching her chest.

"Marina," Ari cried. "Marina, what's wrong?"

"It's Mad... Marina," the woman corrected between scattered breaths.

"What's wrong with your heart?" he asked, handing her a health potion, but she pushed it away.

"No," she said, "I can't go with you any further. I'm sorry, Aralogos, my friend, but I'm afraid... I'm afraid that I haven't been entirely honest with you."

"What do you mean?" asked Ari. "What haven't you been honest about?"

"I told you... that I was... a young woman. The truth is... that I'm actually quite old. It's my heart. Too much lightning magic at once. I think I'm dying."

"You can't die," Ari said. "We need you."

"You'll c-come back... right? Right?" Pan asked.

"No," said Marina. "I'm actually 107 years old. Entropy won't bring me back again. There'll be no resurrection for me."

"No," said Ari. "You can pull through this. Just drink the damn health potion."

"No, I refuse. Ari, Pan, my time is over, and I welcome the darkness that awaits me. You need to get away before they find you."

Pan took Marina's hand in her own. "Mad Mar-rina... I love you."

"Mad Marina," Ari said, "tell me just one thing. What was your question for Libra? I'll ask him for you."

"It doesn't matter anymore," said Mad Marina. "The two of you have already given me the answer."

Marina's hand went limp and fell to the ground. The life left her eyes, and she looked sightlessly into the sky. Ari closed her eyes. Marina's inventory emptied onto the ground, putting to rest any uncertainty about her final death. The sound of their pursuers were getting closer.

Ari grabbed Marina's staff, some coins, and a few other items and stuffed them into his inventory. When Pan wouldn't move from Marina's side, Ari picked her up and ran off into the woods, leaving the town of Wilmarth behind them forever.

Two years and forty-one days later, Pan the Thief stood at the top of a hill. She had changed her primary character class to thief partly to avoid being found by Lord Hempledon and partly so she could become more useful in combat. Thief gave natural bonuses to agility and precision, which she had always been in dire need of.

She smiled as she regarded the spyglass that Ari had given her a week earlier as a birthday gift. It was etched with her name in golden stylized lettering. She used it to scan the hills and plains around her for any sight of their objective. Assuming the arachnid Spindra had been honest with them, this was the exact place and the time for Libra to appear.

There was a brief shimmer of light, and out of nowhere, a glass box with a wooden frame appeared. An elfin puppet appeared in the box. With Ari in tow, she ran toward the eidolon.

Ari took out a 1 GP coin and handed it to Pan. She accepted the coin and slid it into the coin slot. She spoke as clearly as she could, focusing on each syllable. "How c-can Aralogos... remain once I lose the ability to summon?"

The puppet performed a small whimsical dance, and a sheet of parchment was printed from a second slot in the front of the box. Pan removed the piece of paper and read it.

"To find a cure, travel to longitude 33.285947 latitude -96.572767 by sundown on Catuary 29th."

"That's less than two months from now!" Ari said. "There isn't enough time."

He pulled out a map and examined it carefully. "Actually, it might just be possible, but only barely. The queen has declared a ceasefire with Questgivria, so we can cross through what used to be the warzone. If we circle the Ultros Bay to the east and take the train, we might be able to make it on time.

"We'll have to leave now, right now. I don't need to sleep, so I'll carry you at night. We'll sell everything we have and use the money to hire caravans. I don't think we have enough GP to purchase our own raptor, so we'll have to rent them as we go."

"Okay," said Pan. "L–let's do it."

Pan turned to leave, but Ari lingered for a moment. He removed another 1 GP piece from his inventory and inserted it into Libra's slot. "Libra," he said, "when a person lets out their final breath and dies, does anything of that person survive?"

Instead of answering, the eidolon simply faded away and disappeared from sight, continuing on his journey.

CHAPTER 29

A Sky Full of Pirates

Pan wandered aimlessly for days through the wilderness in a trancelike state, her eyes cast downward at the ground. She kept running over the events of the past few days. She had finally made some true friends, but she had hurt them, which was the last thing that she had wanted to do. Worst of all, she'd hurt Tasha.

Growing up in Zhakara, friendship was seen as a weakness and was hard to come by. Even after she emigrated to Questgivria, she had great difficulty interacting with other people. But through it wall, she had always had Ari.

She didn't understand why this had happened. Tasha said that Pan had lied to her, but she had never lied. She might have withheld certain truths, but that wasn't the same as a lie. But because she had withheld the fact that Ari wasn't a real person, she had hurt her one and only real friend.

She had learned from past experience that people became uncomfortable when they learned that her father wasn't a real person and was merely a projection of her mind. Was she wrong to keep this a secret?

For days she continued to wander, eyes downcast, without any real destination or purpose. She didn't summon Ari again after the incident. She didn't know what she could say to him, scared of how disappointed he would be. It was easier to not face him.

On the fifth day, a shadow darkened the grass upon which she walked. When she looked up, the sky was filled with a multitude of flying ships. One of the dirigibles was descending upon her position. She stepped back apprehensively, but it was already too late to escape. Too late to become invisible. The only fleet of airships of this grandeur could be that of the pirate group of K'her Noálin.

A port along the side of the main ship opened, and from it descended a small runabout boat carrying a band of four sailors. Two of them were human, along with a gnome and a dark elf. It descended onto the grass not twenty feet from where she was standing.

Without realizing it, Pan took another step back but then stopped herself. She wouldn't be able to escape the armada by running from it. She was in an open field, and there was nowhere to go and nowhere to hide.

She took a tentative step toward the dark elf, who seemed to be the one in charge.

"Fair morning to ye, wee lass. Might I be askin' what brings a child such as yerself t' this faraway place? What be yer name, lass?"

What should she say? She looked up at him for a moment before averting her gaze and looking at the ground. The dark elf had an orb affixed to his wristband that contained swirling patterns of wind.

"A-are y-y-you the p-pirate captain K'her?" she asked.

"Now, that not be fair at all. I do believe that I asked ye for yer name before ye asked fer mine."

What should she say? Should she lie and make up some other name? No, that was a terrible idea. She was amazingly terrible at lying. Despite what Tasha said, Pan wasn't capable of telling a deliberate lie. Ari could always tell when she wasn't telling the truth. She would have to tell the truth, but that didn't mean she needed to tell the entire truth.

"M-my name is P-Pan. M-my mother abandoned me. I am alone and have n-nowhere to go."

"Arr... ye seem to be telling the truth," he said.

"You c-can t tell?" Pan asked.

"I be a high-level thief with an ability fer detectin' untruths. If ye were lyin' ta me, I'd be savvy to it."

"That's really c-cool," she said honestly. She knew about this ability but had never witnessed its use.

"Yes, it is indeed. So, with ye bein' wise t' me truth-discernin' capability, I hope ye will answer me honestly. We be searchin' fer an elven woman who answers to Kiwistafel. Have ye seen her? Can ye tell me where she be now?"

How should she answer? It would have to be the truth, yet not lead the pirates to her. Pan might no longer be part of the group, but she wouldn't betray them.

"Y-y..." she said, trying to get the words out.

"Take yer time, lassie. There be no rush."

It took her a minute, but she was finally able to get everything out.

"Y-yes, I s-saw her just under a w-week ago. She w-was t-traveling with a slime, a monk, a g-gunblade user, a d-d-dragon, and a thief. They didn't want me with them, so I left."

"And do ye know where they be now?"

"No, I don't."

"Well, I be taken aback. It seems that ye do indeed be tellin' me a true tale. I apologize fer troubling ye like this. We'll be on our way, then."

Captain K'her tossed the girl a 100 GP coin. "Fer yer trouble."

He turned back toward the runabout and began to walk away. Panic was rising up within Pan. This could be her last opportunity to help her friend. It was clear that these people meant to capture the princess and they would likely take Tasha as well.

"Wait!" she said.

"Why do ye delay me from me business?"

"Please! Let me join your c-crew! I'm... a high-level thief. I just made level 23, so I'm s-sure I can be useful. I'll do whatever you want. I can swab the d-decks or scrub the toilets or whatever you need. I... have nowhere else to go."

"It won't be an easy life, but if ye be interested, ye can join us. T'ain't every child who can attain the exalted level of 23."

"Thank you so much, C-Captain," Pan said, bowing slightly. She tried to exude confidence, but inside she wanted to curl up into a little ball and hide somewhere dark.

"Ye'll have ta learn ta speak like a proper pirate ta be one o' us, savvy?"

Pan thought for a moment. "Yo ho ho?"

"It needs work, but not bad fer a first attempt. Mr. Malarkey! Find a position fer our most recent acquirement to our crew."

The diminutive little man sighed. "As you wish, Captain. Come with me, girl."

Pan followed Mr. Malarkey onto the runabout, which ascended into the sky. The ground flew away as the boat rose into the sky. It occurred to Pan that this might not be the most opportune moment to reveal her debilitating fear of high places.

What had she gotten herself into?

When Hermes respawned, he found himself standing on the save point by the capital city outside Brightwind Keep. He hadn't died since being killed in the ninja attack many months ago, and it wasn't an experience he enjoyed. With his good hand, he opened his inventory and removed his spare arm attachment and equipped it, covering up the stub of his broken arm.

He equipped some clothing and waited for about half an hour by the save point, hoping against hope that no more of his friends would respawn. Fortunately, he seemed to be the only casualty of that battle. If someone else had died, they would have respawned at approximately the same time.

Hermes headed into the city and made his way to Brightwind Keep. He should report what had happened to the King. At this point, there was little hope that he would be able to catch up with the others. He had to at least try, though.

The guards recognized the dwarven prince and let him through unchallenged. He had grown up in the castle, raised by elves. Though he had nobody who he regarded as father or mother, he had grown close to both Princess Kiwistafel and Slimon. Kiwi was like a little sister to him. A tall, pointy-eared, strangely beardless sister. And if Hermes had a best friend, it could only be Slimon.

Upon entering the throne room, he found King Questgiver standing in front of his throne. Before him was Penryth, an elder red dragon who occupied most of the room. They seemed to be in discussion, but the dragon focused on him when he entered. The dragon's voice came unbidden into his mind.

Dwarven princeling! What are you doing here? Where is Kaze?

"Hello, Penryth." He turned to King Questgiver. "Your Majesty, I'm afraid I died while in the princess's company. We hadn't had the chance to bind to another save point, so I just respawned here moments ago."

"I'm sorry to hear that," the king said. "What news can you offer me?"

"Well, other than my dying, things are doing well. I believe that I was the only one to fall against the Jabberwock. They are in the Slime Federation but have been moving through the wilderness. We now know for certain that Queen Murderjoy has been hunting them."

Was the steam dragon Kaze with you?

"Aye. He joined our group about a week after we crossed the border into the Slime Federation. He played a part in rescuing the princess and offered to join us."

You allowed him to be placed in danger? Tell me where he is at once, dwarf.

"Hold on, we didn't *place* him in danger, he offered to help us of his own volition. He's been a great help to the quest. You should be proud of him."

TELL ME WHERE HE IS NOW, DWARF!

Hermes paced around for a moment. "If I tell you," he said, "what will you do with that information?"

THERE IS NO IF. YOU WILL TELL ME WHERE HE IS, HERMES. The longer you delay, the more danger he will be in.

"And what will you do then?"

I will fly to there and bring him home.

"An enormous fire dragon flying through the slime kingdom might draw undue attention. Did you miss the part about my friends being hunted? You could draw Queen Murderjoy herself right to them."

That is not my concern, dwarf. Great elven king, kindly make this obstinate dwarf give me the information I require.

King Questgiver sat in thought for a moment before turning to Hermes. "Maybe you should tell him what he needs to know. I'm sure he will make every effort not to draw any unwarranted attention."

Hermes shook his head. "Penryth, listen to me. I'm positive Kaze will come home on his own once they reach the borders of the Slime Federation. Just give it a few more weeks."

The dragon crossed the distance to the dwarf and bared his teeth at Hermes.

Dwarf, you are no different from the rest of your treacherous kin. Your kind stole not only our home from us, but also our children. Know that if I ever see you outside the protection of this castle, I will kill you for this. Unless you reconsider now.

Hermes fell onto his back and regarded the dragon in fear. He shook his head before getting to his feet and leaving the throne room. Apparently he wouldn't be trying to catch up to the party or doing much of anything outside the city. Dragons always kept their word, and a threat from a dragon wasn't something to be taken idly.

CHAPTER 30

Chicken Chaser

The GP is the only form of fiat currency backed by the godlike beings known as aire. There have been attempts by various governments over the millennia to mint different forms of currency with varying degrees of success, but the GP remains the primary form of monetary exchange throughout Etheria.

The GP is backed by the aire in several ways, including trade with NPC merchants for goods, consumption of GP during crafting, and upkeep for the magical fields that repel monsters. The actual cost of these services varies based on the amount of GP in circulation at any particular moment.

New GP is created through various means, including the slaying of mobs, the opening of treasure chests, and various NPC quests.

Although GP is an endlessly farmable currency, its value has remained static, changing only as the population increases. This is a result of the self-adjusting cost of crafting, NPC purchased goods, and the upkeep cost of mob repellers, which are necessary for the survival of any society on Etheria.

The only society to reject the use of GP as a common medium of trade is the Zhakaran Dominion. Since Zhakaran serfs and peasantry are denied the use of NPC merchants and are often not allowed to fight against mobs without a lord's permission, other forms of fiat currency have arisen, and the direct barter of goods between serfs is commonplace.

An excerpt from *A Treatise on a GP Based Currency* by Erwin Silcross

T

asha didn't sleep the entire night. The memory of what had happened during the battle replayed itself over and over. Ari was a summoned creature, and Pan was his summoner. Ari wasn't a real person, just a product of Pan's imagination. He was her imaginary friend.

As the hours passed and the night wore on, her anger began to diminish. Tasha had second thoughts—she wasn't being rational. This wasn't like her at all. She wasn't the sort of person who would allow herself to be controlled by her emotions. The original Tasha had been logical, patient, and cautious. That person wouldn't have abandoned a friend just because they had kept a secret from her. Pan was just a kid; she shouldn't have said that they weren't friends.

Deciding to apologize to Pan, she got out of the bedroll and stood up. Being careful not to awaken the others, she opened the tent flap and stepped outside. The sky was dark, but the ground was illuminated by the circular pattern of the campsite, providing a modest amount of light. After the fight, she'd left Pan on her own. The girl hadn't come into the tent, so Tasha had assumed that she would still be outside, but she wasn't anywhere to be seen.

Tasha checked the perimeter of the campsite. There wasn't much ground to search, and Pan wasn't there. Kaze was snoring soundly on the ground beside one of the scorch marks from the conflict with the Jabberwock. Tasha walked up to the dragon and tried to shake him awake.

Leave me alone, Player. Has no one told you not to wake sleeping dragons?

"Kaze, Pan's missing."

She probably just had to answer a call of nature.

That actually might explain things, but in her heart Tasha knew it wasn't true. "No, we had a fight last night. I think she's run off. We need to find her."

What do you expect me to do about it?

"Can you circle around and try to find her from above?"

It's night, and it's a new moon. I wouldn't see much of anything from the air. I'll look in the morning.

The dragon curled back up and went back to sleep.

The hours passed, until finally the sun peeked out over the horizon. Having gotten a full night's rest, Kaze was in a much less grumpy mood and started a search right away. The dragon spent several hours circling the area in an expanding spiral, but there was no sign of the thief girl from the air.

Tasha knew what probably happened. "It's not your fault that you couldn't see her. I'll bet she's wearing her invisibility cloak. We haven't found any clues as to where she went. Maybe we should just pick a direction and start looking."

Kiwi shook her head. "No, we have a mission, and that needs to take priority. I want to find Pan as much as you, but I'm not sure that's possible. We can't afford to waste any more time. Queen Murderjoy is still out there, and the longer we wait, the greater the chance that her minions will find us. Pan knows that we're headed to Slime's Row, so if we're lucky, we might meet her there."

It was early afternoon the following day when they finally reached the thick wooden town gates. There was a save point in the town center, so the three travelers touched it, registering themselves and healing their wounds.

Kiwi, Slimon, and Tasha wandered around the town. The town center was a small gathering of buildings. There was a traditional item shop and a tavern, as well as several other small businesses. Tasha didn't see an inn but figured that they might have some rooms at the tavern. There was no sign of Pan, however.

The town square was filled with slimes of all shapes, sizes, and colors, all merrily hopping their way across town. Although many of the buildings had smaller slime-sized doorways, there were plenty of buildings that looked to be built for people of human or elven stature. In fact, a small number of human townsfolk could be seen walking the street alongside the slimes.

Tasha turned to Kiwi. "I thought that we were in a slime nation. Why are there so many humans?"

"This is the Slime Federation," Kiwi said, "but despite their many fine qualities, slimes lack the ability to manipulate tools. They outsource most of the agricultural work to humans."

The princess directed her gaze toward a human-sized building. "Let's stop at the item shop and pick up some new clothing."

Kaze waited outside with Denver while Slimon, Kiwi, and Tasha entered the building. A bell above the door chimed as they entered. There were items of various types on display as well as some farming implements, a modest collection of swords, bows, and axes, and an assortment of human-sized clothing.

The slime proprietor hopped in from the back room a moment after the customers entered. This slime was slightly smaller than Slimon and had a red tint.

"Pfffpt," the proprietor offered helpfully.

"Pfffpt," Sir Slimon respond politely.

It went back and forth like this for awhile, until finally they reached some sort of agreement. The slime proprietor removed two suits of clothing from the back and placed them on the counter.

Tasha picked one up and equipped it, her spidersilk armor instantly being replaced by a suit of blue-and-brown overalls.

Kiwi nearly refused to wear it on principle, since it detracted from her natural beauty, but reason prevailed. She tied up her hair into pigtails and wore a conical sun hat, which would hopefully disguise her elven nature from casual observers.

Tasha purchased one of the bamboo cone sun hats for herself as well. She did this partly to hide her identity, partly to keep cool in the harsh sun, but mostly because she thought it made her look like Raiden from *Mortal Kombat*. Now she just needed to program herself some lightning magic.

Kiwi asked the slime, "Master Slime, are any caravans leaving town soon bound eastward toward the Uncrossable Veldt?"

"Pfffpt," the slime responded knowingly.

"I see. Well, in that case, is there somewhere we can rest and purchase an additional raptor for my boyfriend?"

"Pfffpt... pfft."

"Thank you kindly."

They left the shop, and Tasha took Kiwi aside, "What did he say?"

"It's not a he. Slimes are non-gendered and most don't have any gender identity. The proper way to address a non-gendered slime is 'it.'"

Tasha adjusted her sun hat. "Okay, so what did it say?"

"It said that nobody in town has any raptors to sell, and there aren't any caravans leaving toward the Uncrossable Veldt for several months. He did say that there is a human farmer nearby who might have what we need."

"Did you get directions? What is the farm called?"

Kiwi pointed toward the southern outskirts of town. "The slime said that the farm is called Belly Acres. It's about a ten-minute walk from here."

They made their way to the Belly Acres farm and were greeted by a fat farmer and his wife. Tasha hadn't even realized that people in Etheria could get fat, since stats appeared to improve fitness and excess calories recovered mana and health. Perhaps there was an ability somewhere that unlocked rotundness.

Tasha extended her hand. "Hello. Are you the owner of the Belly Acres farmstead?"

The man spit into his palm before shaking her hand. Tasha wiped the spittle off on her overalls. "Yes, ma'am. My name's Ernest Belly, and this here's my wife Sally Belly.

"I fear that you find us in a pitiful state. Woe and misfortune have befallen us, for you see, all of our beloved chickens have wandered away from the chicken coop. If only some heroic adventurer would search around the town of Slime's Row and collect them, I would be ever so grateful."

Tasha smirked. "Yeah, I hope that happens for you. In the meantime, would you happen to have any raptors for sale?"

"I'm so sorry," said the man's wife, "but I'm afraid my husband is too distraught and filled with sorrow to answer your question intelligently. But if some kind person would gather our chickens and return them to their pen, we would certainly reward such a person."

Tasha squinted her eyes in suspicion. "What kind of reward?"

"Uh... it would be a generous reward," Ernest said.

"That's rather vague."

"A *very* generous reward."

"That's actually no less vague. You know what, fine. I'll do your little side quest. We'll go out and find your chickens for you. How many did you lose?"

> **Quest: No Harm, No Fowl**
> **Farmer Ernest Belly has misplaced his chickens and doesn't know where to find them.**
> **Conditions for success: Recover Ernest's 8 lost chickens and return them to their coop at the Belly Acres farm.**
> **Conditions for failure: Don't do that.**
> **Reward: Allegedly something very nice**

"Okay, everyone. Let's split up and find this man's chickens. I don't think he'll help us until we do."

It turned out that looking for lost chickens in a town even as small as this one was a massive undertaking. Tasha found the first one squawking about on the roof of somebody's house. Climbing up the side of the building and onto the roof, Tasha slowly inched toward the chicken and picked her up before the little clucker could run away.

Holding the chicken over her head, Tasha jumped off the roof and immediately plummeted downward, slamming into the ground, breaking one of her legs. She somehow thought that holding a chicken over her head would slow her descent, but it didn't reduce her downward velocity in the slightest.

You lied to me, video games. You lied to me.

Tasha chugged a health potion to heal her broken leg. She picked up the chicken and carried her to the coop, tossing her inside. The quest counter updated:

Chickens returned: 1/8

Returning to the search, she passed Slimon, who was carrying a large chicken over his head.

There was another one clucking around in the rafters of the tavern. She had no idea how he got there, but she climbed up over the confused bar patrons and returned him to the coop. Sir Slimon found another hanging around some slime younglings in the playground, and Kiwi found one hiding in an outhouse.

Chickens returned: 5/8

Kaze was just napping in the farmer's chicken coop. "Why aren't you helping?"

Because I don't have any hands. What would I even do if I did find a chicken?

As Kaze went back to sleep, Tasha realized that the dragon had a point and resumed her search.

The next one she found on a ledge overlooking the village. After collecting the chicken, she resisted what she considered the totally natural instinct to jump off the ledge while using the chicken to slow her descent. There was another one balancing along the top of the wooden town walls, and Kiwi found one lounging on the save point.

Chickens returned: 8/8
Quest complete: No Harm, No Fowl
Return to Farmer Ernest to receive reward.
100 XP awarded.

Tasha threw the last of the chickens into the coop.

"We got your chickens. So what's the reward?"

"Oh!" Sally said. "I'm so overjoyed to have our beloved chickens back at home, safe and sound. As a reward for your service, I would like you to have this glass jar. You can store liquids in it and even catch bugs."

"A glass jar? Seriously? Don't they sell this at the general store for like 5 GP? I don't think we need a jar."

Sally put away the jar and brought out another item. "Well, then, how about my old bug catching net? You can use it to catch as many bugs as you like. Collect them all. Impress your friends, confuse your enemies, annoy perfect strangers!"

What was wrong with these people? "Um... no. What we do need is to purchase some raptors. We lost most of our raptors on the way here, and we need to purchase some new ones."

"Nope," Ernest said, "I don't have anything like that. This here's a chicken farm. I could sell you some chickens if you like."

"You mean the chickens that we just recovered for you?" She'd pretty much given up on the idea of getting a reward.

"Oh no. Not *those* chickens. Obviously not those chickens. Don't be silly. I'm talking about some completely different chickens."

"I don't think we need any chickens," Tasha said.

"Well, you won't know for sure until you've seen them. Right this way, missy."

Shrugging, Tasha followed the large man to a large wooden building with a curved roof. It looked like the kind of building she would expect to see in a farm.

The farmer's wife, Sally, led the company through the wire-mesh doorway, and they went inside. The chicken coop was completely different from what she had expected. It was more like a stable. There were several large raptor-sized chickens in their own compartments. One of them was wearing a riding harness.

"Right now we have three riding chickens," Sally said. "We also have an old carriage if you are in the market."

"Ba-kah!" said one of the riding chickens, surprising Tasha and causing her to fall on her butt.

Kiwi ran up to one and started stroking its feathers. "Oh, it's adorable! We'll take all three, plus the carriage. How much will that be?"

An idea occurred to Tasha. "Wait a minute! How about instead of the glass jar, you just let us keep the carriage for free?"

"Okay," said Sally, "but are you sure wouldn't rather have a glass jar?"

Hubert tapped at the air in front of him, clearly operating the calculator in his menu interface. After a moment he said, "14,300 GP for the three chickens. These are strong, trained riding chickens so they're worth every GP. I'll even throw in a month's worth of feed free of charge."

Tasha took the princess aside and said, "The crown will pay for this, right?"

"Of course," she whispered. "But then I would need to tell him that I'm the princess, and that would mean I wore this horrible outfit for nothing."

"*That's* what you're worried about? Never mind. Do we have enough? I have 2,400 GP right now. I just spent most of my money a few days ago on my new gunblade."

They pooled their money and found that they could just barely afford it with what the party had on hand.

"Thank you for your business, miss," Ernest said. "Is there anything else you need?"

"Yes," said Kiwi, "we need a place to stay for tonight. Is there any chance we could rent a room?"

"This ain't no hotel. We don't have any rooms available to rent. Try the tavern in town. They might have something."

"They're already at full occupancy," Kiwi said.

Ernest considered this for a moment. "You can stay in the barn with the chickens if you wanna. I'm still mighty grateful that you brought our beloved chickens back to their home. Oh, and please join us at supper. It's the least I could do."

"Yeah, that sounds great," Tasha said.

The farmer had two young boys and one girl. They each looked like they would have been in kindergarten if they had been on Earth.

"This here's my son Billy," Ernest said. "My other son Bubba, and my sweet little daughter, Bobbi."

"Hi, Billy, Bubba, and Bobbi. I'm Tasha, this is Slimon, and the lady is Kiwi."

"You mean like Princess Kiwistafel?" Billy said. "Is she an elf? Is that the princess?"

Tasha mentally facepalmed. "Well, crap. Why didn't we pick out nicknames beforehand? That would have made so much sense."

"Princess," Billy said, "will you marry me when you become the queen? When we're married, can we live in the castle?"

His sister Bobbi piped up excitedly. "Yesterday I killed two centipedes, three spiders, and two boblins. Pa says I'm going to reach level 3 in a few more weeks."

Bubba butted in too. "Are you the guys who found all of our chickens? Last time I spent five hours tracking them all down. I'm going to take over the farm one day! I'll have more chickens than everybody! I'll breed an army of giant warrior chickens who follow my every command!"

Were warrior chickens really a thing on Etheria? It seemed plausible enough.

Bobbi flexed her muscles. "I want to choose barbarian as my primary class... that way I can kill monsters up close and personal."

The farmer shut his kids up. "Okay, enough with yer jabbin'! Give our guests some breathing room."

The princess turned to each child in turn. "Bobbi, barbarian is a fine class choice. Bubba, I wish you the best of luck with your... future career as a chicken farmer. And Billy, I fear my heart belongs to another."

That evening, Sally served up fried chicken with baked potatoes. By the time everyone finished eating, the sun had already set. Tasha had just said goodnight and was about to go to the chicken coop to get some sleep, but Ernest stopped her.

"Uh, just wait for a minute. Before you go to sleep, I need to slaughter all the chickens. It'll only take me a few minutes."

A horrified look came over Tasha's face, and her eyes went wide.

"Wait, what are you talking about? You mean those chickens we spent all afternoon collecting? The ones you called your 'beloved chickens'?"

"Yep, those are the ones! We slaughter them about once a week. Then we have to go round them up every time they respawn at the save point. What, did you think fried chicken grew on fried chicken trees or something? Bah, youngins these days. And doncha' worry yer bleeding heart. I'll be humane about it."

Muttering to himself, he left the house fingering his hatchet.

Ignoring the sounds of the chickens being slaughtered, she was about to challenge Billy to another round of cards when Bobbi came up to her. "Can you read us a bedtime story?"

"Sure," Tasha said. "what kind of story would you like?"

"One I haven't heard before," said Bobbi.

That night, she told them the story of Rumpelstiltskin and the girl who spun straw into gold and had to guess the man's name to save her firstborn. They all listened attentively. Even Kiwi and Slimon listened in, for this was a story that they had never heard before.

After the story was done, Farmer Ernest came in and declared, "Chickens're dead! You can go to bed now. Just avoid the puddles of blood. Don't wanna get yer fancy new clothing all stained."

"Good night, Ernest," Tasha said.

The company went to the chicken coop and tried to go to sleep. The only chickens remaining were the three riding chickens that they had purchased earlier that day. At some point through the night, a few of the now revived chickens wandered in and went to their compartments.

Back at the tavern, one of the human patrons set his martini down on the counter and drunkenly hobbled to the bulletin board. There was a wanted poster that caught his eye. It was an elven woman with green hair. He squinted in the hopes that doing so would cure his inebriated state for long enough to confirm his suspicions. It didn't work.

He tore the wanted poster off the wall and drunkenly zigzagged toward the save point. The save point would cure his inebriation, which would suck, but he had a strong suspicion that he'd seen this girl running around town messing with some chickens.

He stepped on the save point and was immediately cured of his inebriation. Justin hated sobriety more than anything else, but he had to look at the wanted poster with clear eyes to be sure. It read "Wanted: information leading to the capture of Kiwistafel Questgiver. If sighted, do not engage. Send a messenger swallow with the information to Captain K'her Noálin. Payment will be made if the information leads to her capture. Captain K'her always pays his debts."

It was her, the man was sure. He went to the post office, and a sleepy man handed him a tiny capsule, and he inserted a quickly scribbled message before handing it back.

The post officer read the label. "This is going to... Captain K'her Noálin. We'll have to use one of our higher-level birds since it's a person rather than an address. That'll be 140 GP."

That much GP would have been enough to keep him drunk for a week, but Justin grudgingly handed the money over. It would be worth the cost if the captain caught her and made good on the bounty.

The man at the counter cleared his throat as Justin turned to leave. "Just so you know, smarter customers recognize this as a tipping situation. Just so you know."

Justin ignored him. Having sent the message, he made his way back to the tavern to find a cure for his unhappy state of sobriety.

CHAPTER 31

Knight of Ghosts and Shadows

Early the next morning, Tasha set out with her companions. Their hopes that Pan would show up on her own had not come to fruition. Tasha hooked Denver and the chickens up to the carriage and took the driver's seat. Since they now rode in a covered wagon, they no longer avoided the main road.

Denver didn't seem to have any problem getting along with the riding chickens, despite what was most likely a predator-prey relationship. The covered wagon wasn't in the best condition, which explained why Mr. Belly was willing to give it up for free.

They didn't encounter any flying monkeys, but if there had been any, all that could have been seen from the air would have been a covered wagon being driven by a human peasant.

The following few days were largely uneventful as they settled into the routine of daily travel. They would wake up, have breakfast, ride, and go to sleep. Kiwi and Tasha took turns driving the carriage. Monsters weren't a problem on the road, as every few hundred meters there would be a lamp post enchanted to repel the mist. Kaze followed them overhead and from a distance so as to avoid drawing attention to the group.

Since Pan still had Tasha's smartphone, Tasha spent most of her time reading through the books that she'd borrowed from the library. She had made it halfway through a paperback book titled *An Idiot's*

Guide to Crafting when Slimon got everyone's attention with an abrupt warning of "Pfffpt!"

Using a tentacle, he pointed toward to the horizon on the right. In the distance were a number of dots set against the blue sky. Tasha and Kiwi stood outside the carriage. Tasha turned to her friend. "Princess, what do your elf eyes see?"

The princess looked confused. "Tasha, elves don't have long distance vision."

Tasha smiled awkwardly. "Yeah, okay, sorry. It's just a meme."

Kiwi shook her head. "I don't think it was mean, but I can't see any further than you."

"No, not mean, I— Never mind."

"Now if you'd asked what my elf ears hear, that would make sense. Elves have amazing ears."

If Pan were here, she could have used her spyglass, but Tasha didn't have anything like that. Eventually the dots came into focus, and she could make out their shapes.

"I see zeppelins. An entire fleet of airships, and they're coming this way."

Kiwi backed away in trepidation. "It's the pirate king, K'her Noálin! He must be here for us. We need to hide."

Unfortunately there were no obvious places to conceal themselves. The terrain was flat as far as the eye could see. There was a forest in the distance, but it would be hours before they were anywhere near it. The fleet of airships was closing in at an unnatural speed, despite sailing against the wind.

"Pffpt," said Slimon sadly.

"Slimon's right. There's nowhere for us to hide."

"Then can we fight?" Tasha said.

Kiwi shook her head. "Not against his entire fleet. K'her Noálin himself is an orb bearer which makes such a contest all but unwinnable."

Tasha ran to the harness that bound Denver and the riding chickens to the carriage and rapidly set them loose. "Denver, you have to go now. Go back the way we came, to that farming village. Kaze, go with him. If we're captured, we'll be counting on you to rescue us."

The steam dragon was nowhere in sight, but usually he could pick up on thoughts directed at him. He was probably somewhere circling overhead. Still, she was uncertain whether the dragon had heard her. The chickens ran off, and after hesitating, Denver joined them.

Minutes later, the fleet of airships had encircled the sky above the wagon. A small hovering boat descended and landed on the ground before them. The dark elf K'her Noálin stepped out of the boat along with a team of humans.

The dark elf tipped his pirate hat. "Greetings, Yer Highness. The queen sends her regards." He turned to his minions. "Take her into custody."

The pirate minions were all level 30 and above. They took the three heroes captive without any trouble.

"If it's an issue of money," the princess said, "the kingdom will double whatever offer Queen Murderjoy has made."

"I'm afraid not, Yer Highness. As tempting an offer that be, I shan't be crossing the queen this day."

He walked to Tasha. "So, ye are the player o' legend. Somehow I expected ye ta be more impressive."

"What about the slime?" one of the minions asked.

"Kill it. There be no market fer slimes in Zhakara. T'would be a liability and naught else."

"Pffpt!" cried Slimon as one of the pirates jabbed his lance through his membrane and into his glowing core, killing him instantly.

"No!" Kiwi fell to her knees, tears running from her eyes.

The captain frowned. "Show some dignity, Yer Highness. I don't envy what the queen will do to ye. Ye should consider it a kindness that I spared the slime lover o' yers of that same unhappy fate."

Tasha and Kiwi were moved to the runabout and ferried onto the captain's ship. It had a wide wooden base held aloft by a large balloon.

"Welcome aboard me vessel, princess. This be the *Rhiannon*, flagship of the Noálin pirate group. I hope the accommodations be to yer liking."

Tasha was brought into a small room where she was strapped to a chair by several human pirates. They were raggedy-looking men, each of whom boasted a scruffy, unkempt beard.

Her head and torso were strapped against the chair tightly, so she couldn't move. She resisted and called them all manner of unsavory things while they restrained her until one of them stuffed a gag into her mouth.

The smaller pirate squinted at her. "We're gonna take everything in yer inventory. This'll go much smoother if ye don' resist."

Attached to the chair in the right side was a metal arm with several movable joints that held a glass panel etched with markings. One of the pirates swung the arm so that it was just in front of her. Some of the etchings just about matched up with her HUD icons.

The larger of the two pirates moved her hand so that it touched one of the etchings and swiped upward, opening her menu. From there, he forced her to tap at various points, selecting and dropping every object from her inventory. It took them half an hour to go through everything she had.

"This loot was barely worth the effort," complained the small pirate examining her two gunblades, Namaka and Grasscutter, as well as her spidersilk armor. "Thanks for your contribution, meager as it was."

They unbound her from the chair and brought her to the brig, where Captain K'her was waiting for her. It was a jail cell with thick iron bars. Kiwi was brought in a few minutes later, and they were both tied to the wall with their hands bound behind them.

"Don' even think about escape. For the duration o' the flight, ye will both have yer hands bound so ye can't operate yer menu or be castin' any spells. Someone will be in ta spoon feed ya in a few hours. Enjoy the trip."

Tasha was left alone with Kiwi in the cell. For a long time, Kiwi sobbed silently. Tasha wanted to comfort her friend but didn't know what to say.

Every so often a pirate would come in and check on the prisoners, but for the bulk of the time, they were left alone.

The position she was in wasn't comfortable, but neither was it torturous. She had little freedom of movement and no access to her hands.

"I'm sorry about Slimon," Tasha said. "I know he means a great deal to you."

Kiwi blinked the tears from her eyes. "No, it's okay. Slimon has probably already respawned at the save point. At least I know that he's safe."

Tasha struggled against the restraints. "There's got to be a way out of this cell."

For the next few hours, she tried to touch the "Open Menu" icon with her nose, but it wasn't even close. If her feet were free, she might have used her toes, but she couldn't move more than a few inches from the bench. Tasha screamed as she struggled against the iron manacles, but she was unable to escape.

Defeated, she collapsed back into the bench. "It's hopeless. I can't move a bit. You?"

Kiwi's eyes began to glow white but then dimmed. "No. I can't cast my spells without the use of my hands."

Then Tasha had another idea, but it wasn't a good one. "Maybe I could dislocate my thumb. I once saw this online video of a guy who escaped from handcuffs by doing that."

It turned out that intentionally dislocating her thumb was more difficult than she had hoped. She struggled with this for some time before Kiwi interrupted her efforts.

"Um... Tasha, did that box just move?"

Tasha stopped and looked toward the wooden crate that the princess was referring to. "No, princess, the box didn't move. And do you know why the box didn't move? Because it's a friggin' box. Wooden crates aren't capable of self-agency."

Tasha slumped back into the bench. "I'm sorry, Kiwi... I tend to get a bit edgy when attempting to break my own thumb."

She thought back to the events of the past month. The new friends she'd made. She thought about Ari... He had become one of her best friends, but now she didn't know what to think. Was he nothing more than a product of Pan's imagination? And if he was no more than a fictional person, how much did that really matter? He certainly seemed to be real in every way that was important.

"I shouldn't have been so hard on Pan before."

"Don't worry," Kiwi said. "We'll escape from this prison, and you can tell her. I don't know how we'll get out, but you'll come up with something. I have faith in you."

"Why would anyone have faith in me? I never have a plan. I don't think things through. Not what I do. Not what I say. I shouldn't have been so cruel to Pan."

"It's okay," said the box.

"No, it's not okay. I never think through the consequences of my actions. I hate the person who I've become. My original self was never like this."

"Um... Tasha," Kiwi said, "I think that box might be talking to you."

"Don't be stupid, Kiwi, boxes don't ta—" She cut herself off mid-sentence in realization. "Pan?"

The wooden box lifted off the ground, and Pan stood up, setting the box aside. The small girl was dressed in pirate garb. She stepped toward the cage, eyes cast at the floor. "I'll g–get you out."

"Pan!" Tasha said. "How did you get here? I'm so sorry for what I said before. I was... just surprised and hurt."

Pan had already picked the lock to the bars and was working on Tasha's cuffs. "I'm sorry too."

Tasha's handcuffs came free. "Yeah, I'm still not sure I totally understand. Where's Ari? Is he with you?"

Pan nodded. "He's always with me."

Tasha's legs were now free of their bindings. Pan got to work on Kiwi's cuffs.

"Thanks for coming back for us. But what are you doing here?"

"I'm a p–pirate now."

She pointed at her name tag. It read "Assistant Director of Latrine Sanitation."

"So... you took a job cleaning toilets... just in case we got captured?"

Pan nodded. "I b–brought your weapons and armor."

Tasha didn't notice before, but there were tears streaming down Pan's face. "Pan, I still need you. Will you come with us?"

Pan's face scrunched up, and she stopped holding back her tears. Tasha put her arm around her friend, comforting her. They stayed like that for several minutes before Kiwi cut in. "Not to make this all about me, but could you finish untying my hands before we get discovered?"

It was nearly five minutes before Pan was able to get control of her emotions. She used some kind of lockpicking ability, and Kiwi's cuffs fell to the ground.

"We need to get out of here," said Kiwi. "We're probably already bound for Zhakara."

Pan nodded, wiping the last of her tears away.

Tasha just shook her head. "No. You told me that the pirate captain was an orb bearer. The Orb of Air is on board this ship. This might be the best opportunity we'll ever have to retrieve it."

Kiwi shook her head vehemently. "With just the three of us? That's not possible. Captain K'her Noálin is an orb bearer, plus he's a higher level than any of us. With the orb, he could probably hold off a small army."

"Level 47," Pan confirmed.

Tasha turned to Pan. "Then we don't fight him. We just need to get the orb away from him and escape. Pan, can you use your steal ability against him?"

"Yes," Pan said. "I can t-try. He always wears it on an armband."

Tasha thought for a few minutes. "Okay, I've got a plan. Here's what I'm going to need everyone to do."

A pirate walked into the room. He was clothed in all manner of piratey attire, including a striped bandana with matching shirt. He unlocked the door and entered the cell.

"Hello, ladies," said the pirate. "It be dinner time. Nothin' but the finest gruel for our honored guests."

Tasha and the princess were both cuffed to the wall. Tasha looked at the grayish beige sludge. "That sounds wonderful, really, but there's something I'd like to discuss with the captain."

"And why would the captain be interested in anythin' ye have to say?"

"Because I know a secret that will make him rich."

"Oh ho! Well, in that case, ye can tell me the secret, and I'll pass it on to him."

"I can't tell you because it's a secret. I'm sure your captain will be grateful to you for telling him once he finds out what it is."

"Fine, I'll pass on yer message. First thin's first, though. Open your mouth and say 'ah!'"

After being spoon fed some of the worst and only gruel she'd ever had in her life, the pirate locked the cell back up and left the room.

"Do you think he'll get the captain?" Kiwi asked.

"I hope so," Tasha said. "I'd hate to have eaten that gruel for nothing." Her menu was still open in front of her, but she did her best to pretend it wasn't there.

Twenty minutes later, Captain K'her Noálin entered the brig accompanied by two of his minions.

"Good evening, ladies. I hear tell that ye've got some profitable information to impart. It be me personal ethical policy not to turn away from the possibility o' profit. Now, what have ye ta tell me?"

"Can you ask your men to wait outside?" Tasha said. "This secret isn't something you would want known by everyone."

"Normally I'd suspect ye of some deceivery, but I checked those cuffs meself. Aye. Bruno, Jackie, wait fer me outside. I'll deal with the prisoner meself."

The two pirates obediently left the room and shut the door behind them.

"Now," he said, "what be this secret? If this be a trick, I promise retribution. I can tell if ye be lying to me."

"It's a skill specific to players," Tasha said. "I have the ability to rapidly level people. If you let me go, I can help you become the highest leveled person on the planet in a matter of months."

"Arr... that be a mighty boon, indeed. If ye will do this, I might consider not turnin' ye over to the queen o' Zhakara. As fer the princess... her fate be sealed. She be bound fer Murdcrjoy's castle."

Tasha nodded. "I... I understand. It's enough that you let me go. Sorry, princess, it's nothing personal."

"No!" cried Kiwi. "How could you... You betrayer! I cared about you, and you've turned on me in my hour of need. Oh, why has this sad fate befallen me? Now I am surely doomed."

Tasha clenched her teeth. The princess was overplaying her part.

"Arr, yer heart be as black as me own. We have an accord, that is, if ye can deliver. What do ye be needing me to do? I assume ye want me to undo yer cuffs."

"In a moment," Tasha said. "Just come a bit closer and sit on the floor in front of me."

The pirate captain looked at Tasha with suspicion in his eyes but did as she said. He sat cross-legged on the floor.

"Now hold out your right arm," Tasha said.

The captain held out his right arm. As he did so, a man who hadn't been there a moment earlier grabbed his wrist, holding it in place. Kiwi removed her hands from the cuffs effortlessly and cast her grasping vines on the captain, locking him into place.

In one fluid motion, Tasha invoked her Stat Shuffle ability, put everything into strength, and tapped the confirm button. With the level difference between her and the pirate captain, she would barely be able to do any damage at all, but by boosting her strength as far as she could, she would nullify the difference between her strength and his defense.

Quickly invoking her "To the Pain" skill, she sliced downward, cutting into the dark elf's arm. Her second hit cut it off entirely. As the arm fell to the ground, the light from the orb diminished until it was nothing but a dim point. Tasha slashed sideways at the man's head, but as her dexterity was back to a sad two points, she missed entirely and hit him in the shoulder. Still, each strike cut into his heart containers.

"How?" the captain said, panicked. "How did ye get free?"

The captain reached for the orb with his other hand, and it started to inch toward him as though he had the powers of a force master.

"Steal!" cried Pan, and the man's arm flew through the air and into Pan's grasp.

Finally, Tasha swung the sword, and it connected with his neck, dealing critical damage, taking the remainder of his heart containers. The captain died instantly. Captain K'her's body fell limp to the floor as his decapitated head rolled into the corner.

> **Victory! All enemies have been vanquished.**
> **3975 experience gained. (1440 to next level)**
> **Level up!**
> **Level up!**
> **You have reached level 26.**
> **You have 8 unassigned stat points.**

She'd hit level 26, gaining two levels due to the massive level difference between her and the pirate. She took both heart containers and threw everything into agility, bringing it up to 38. At the moment, she was still under the effects of Stat Shuffle.

"That worked better than expected," said Ari, who had been holding the captain.

Whatever deity governs Murphy's Law must have been paying attention, because the room began to shake. The door opened, and the two pirate guards who had been waiting outside came in. "Captain! The ship! It be going down!"

Kiwi cast a lightning bolt that arced between the two pirates, knocking them back. The ship began to tilt forward, and the door flew open. The two pirates fell through the open door and down the hall. The ship was angling back and forth. Finally, the party made their way onto the deck and saw that the ship was rapidly falling toward the forest below.

Tasha looked up and saw Kaze attacking the balloon that held the ship aloft in the air. He circled around it, blasting it in multiple places with directed jets of high-pressure steam. The dirigible was leaking from multiple points and was losing altitude at a fast rate.

"Everyone, use your parachutes!" Tasha yelled. She hadn't planned on using them until after they'd snuck off the ship, but that no longer seemed to be an option. Pan had given everyone some parachutes that she'd liberated from the ship's supply.

Tasha equipped her parachute via the menu and jumped over the Taffrail on the side of the ship. She pulled on the ripcord as soon as she was clear. When she did this, her descent abruptly slowed. The out-of-control airship continued to lose altitude and less than a minute later, crashed into the forest below. Kaze was already attacking another of the ships, and the rest of the pirate armada had broken off and was in retreat.

Kiwi and Pan were both descending slowly to the ground in the distance. Pan seemed to be extremely agitated, but Tasha felt fine. If she ever returned to Earth, she resolved to take up skydiving.

When she finally hit the ground, she unequipped the backpack and discovered that she'd gained another two levels. According to her stat log, she'd earned experience points for everyone who died in the handful of ships that Kaze had destroyed.

So indirect actions can lead to XP gain as well as direct actions. Good to know.

She quickly located Kiwi and Pan. Pan had curled up and was holding her legs in her hands, rocking back and forth. "The sky is scary... the sky is scary..."

Tasha took the Orb of Air from Pan's pack, and the moment she touched it, the wind bit into her hand, leaving a bloody gash. She dropped it with a yelp, and it fell to the ground, rolling to a stop.

Light swirled in a circle, and Ari materialized in front of her.

"Ari! I don't understand. Where did you come from?"

He opened Pan's clenched fist, revealing bloody cuts similar to the one that Tasha received from touching the orb. He gave her a potion, but she kept on muttering, "The sky is scary..."

"Pan summoned me by instinct. She's been doing that since she was a newborn infant. Her mother was a cruel woman who abandoned her deep in the forest. Pan had no caretaker, so she summoned one. She's been summoning me repeatedly ever since."

Then he told her the story about how Pan had summoned him and how he became her adoptive parent. About growing up in Zhakara, their quest to find Libra, and the events which led them both to the Temple of the Player.

Tasha listened carefully until Ari was finished with his tale. Tasha crossed her arms, "Why the deception? Why not just tell everyone? Why not tell *me*? I might have understood."

"Habit, I suppose. She was born in Zhakara, where humans are taught never to show weakness. The one time she told someone, an entire village attacked and killed her. Maybe they were afraid, maybe they were jealous, maybe they just wanted an excuse to kill someone. Zhakara has no laws to prevent that sort of behavior.

"She changed her main class to thief and set caster to her subclass. I've been posing as her father since she was young."

"Ari..." Tasha said, "I'm sorry to ask, but... are you real or just a figment?"

"That depends on what you mean by real," Ari said. "I'm self-aware. I can think."

"But you have no existence outside of Pan's imagination."

"No, I don't. Listen, I've been dealing with this existential crisis for a long time. I'm the dream whose substance depends on the dreamer. As far as I'm concerned, I'm real person. At least I will be for the next year."

"Why, what happens next year?"

"Pan will become an adult and lose the ability to summon. When that happens, I will disappear for the last time."

Tasha thought back to when they first met. "Your quest. The cure that you are seeking. It was never for Pan. This entire time it was for you. I had assumed she wanted to cure her autism, but that wasn't it at all."

Pan slowly got to her feet. "No. I d-don't want to cure it. I need it. It's who I am. Without it, I wouldn't be me."

"So you want to find a way to make him real so he doesn't disappear."

Ari nodded. "I've been in existence for most of her life, and I would prefer to keep living. Pan feels the same way."

"I still say you should have told me before. I would have understood."

"Maybe so. That's the thing about lies—the longer you keep telling them, the harder it is to admit."

Tasha thought back to the Webwood Forest those many months ago. "Back in the Webwood Forest when you rescued me from the Spider Queen, you died, didn't you?"

"Yes, that's true. The mob killed me while Pan and Denver carried you to the inn. Dying is never pleasant, but I'd rather die than see someone I care about suffer that fate."

"What about your arm? Those times at night when you begin to fade away. Like back at the castle before the council of nations when your hand became transparent."

Ari looked down at the ground. "When Pan is asleep, sometimes it's hard for me to remain summoned. You need to understand that on one level, Pan and I share different partitions of the same mind. When she is asleep, her mind relaxes. You saw the results—my body begins to fade away. Tasha... you and I, are we okay?"

"Yeah," said Tasha, "we're okay. But no more secrets from now on."

"I promise," said Ari.

Another ten minutes passed before Kaze returned and landed beside them. *I was able to sink another three ships! Most of them got away, though.*

Tasha hadn't gotten any additional experience, probably because he was out of range. She helped Pan to her feet. "Well done, Kaze. We should get away from here in case the rest of the pirates change their minds about running away."

Kiwi tapped at her menu interface. "According to my menu, we're about a hundred miles to the southeast of Slime's Row. We should head there and meet up with Slimon."

It took just over a week of travel across the open terrain for the company to make their way back to Slime's Row. When they finally arrived, they were overjoyed to find that Slimon was waiting there with Denver and the chickens. He had even secured them a new covered wagon. The fellowship of friends had been nearly restored, all but for Hermes.

CHAPTER 32

Scheming Schemers and the Schemes They Scheme

The queen's personal guard dragged K'her Noálin, a man once known as the pirate king, into the queen's chamber. Fire and disappointment were reflected in her eyes.

"What is this? What has become of my captain?"

K'her tried to stand up, but one of the guards jabbed him in the back of the knee, forcing him back down onto the marble floor.

"Me queen. The orb was pilfered from me by the player. I beg of ye... help me get it back."

Queen Murderjoy looked at him with barely restrained disgust. "You beg of me? Where is your strength? Your dignity? Without the Orb of Air, is this all you are?"

"Please, help me. I thought ye were me friend."

"Friend?" Murderjoy shrilled. "Did you just say friend? Friendship is the ultimate form of weakness and servitude. There are no friends in my country. There are only people who use others and people who are used by others. Until now, your power was equivalent to mine, and you were useful to me, but that is no longer the case."

The pirate continued to plead his case. "If ye help me recover it, I'll have me power back and will be profitable to ye once more."

The queen spat at his feet. "I am disgusted by the weak person you have become. Begone from my sight. If you set foot in my country again, I'll have you drained of levels and made into a slave."

He was dragged from the throne room and a moment later disappeared from sight. Had she been too harsh? No. In truth, she'd been too merciful by letting him go. She meant to install a morality of self-interest in her people, and she could only do that by example.

A messenger arrived in the throne room. It was a teenage girl with brown pigtails. She looked vaguely familiar, but Aralynn couldn't decide from where. The girl approached and knelt before her.

"Your Majesty, I have a message for you. It arrived by swallow just minutes ago."

"Well?" demanded the queen. "Is it good news or bad news?"

"I don't know. I haven't read it."

"Then read it to me now. I don't have all day."

She opened the message. "It's from the town of Slime's Row in the Slime Federation. The letter is from a human farmer named Justin. It reads 'Player Tasha and Princess Kiwistafel are both in the town of Slime's Row. They were staying at the Belly Acres farm. Please send GP as payment for this information.'"

"A human demands payment of me? How dare he!" exclaimed the queen angrily.

The messenger girl winced, expecting a quick death, but nothing happened. She just stood there for several awkward moments. The queen was off script today. "Um... Your Majesty? Aren't you going to incinerate me for bringing you news that made you angry?"

"What's the point?" said Queen Murderjoy sadly, slumping back into her throne. K'her's fall from grace had affected her more than she would have liked to admit.

The girl was having none of that. As a professional bad-news-giver and a resurrection addict to boot, she couldn't accept this turn of events. This encounter was not meeting her expectations. "Your Majesty, fire magic is your thing. It's your personal trademark. Your fans have come to expect it."

"Oh, I'm not so sure anymore," said the queen despondently. "I mean, what's the point of it all? Don't you think people are becoming desensitized to it?"

"Maybe you just need to try something new. Like killing the messenger in unique and interesting ways."

"Okay, I'll try it," said the queen, though it looked as though her heart wasn't in it. "Thanks for trying to cheer me up, anyway. Um... Guard! You, there with the nose. Have this girl defenestrated at once!"

A panicked look came over the girl's face. "Defene-what? What does that mean? *What does that mean?*"

The guard grabbed the girl by the arm and took her to the far end of the room. Lifting her up, he threw her out the window, sending shattered glass with her into the courtyard far below. And that's how Paula learned the meaning behind the word "defenestrated."

The queen turned to the large-nosed guard. "Well done, Stanly, but in the future be sure to open the window before throwing people out of it."

He looked sheepish. "Sorry, my queen. I just thought—"

"You thought what?"

"Well, it's just that if I opened the window first, that might have ruined the excitement of the moment. Defenestration should be visibly exciting."

"Very well then, you have a point. Run off and summon my advisors. We have something to discuss."

The guard left her to fetch them, and the queen sat on her throne and stewed in her thoughts. Finally, several old men entered her throne room. The queen focused on the eldest of them.

"Ah, Gelkorus. I've just received word that Princess Kiwistafel was seen in a farm just outside of Slime's Row. Have it burned to the ground at once. Send our most powerful death knights to capture the princess and kill her insignificant friends."

"As you command."

"No, wait! I've just changed my mind."

"My queen?"

"All right, Gelkorus, I've come up with a new plan. Here's what I want you to do. Send out waves of mercenaries to kill her and her friends. Begin with weak assassins to start, but then send incrementally higher level waves of fighters."

"Okay... may I be permitted to ask the logic behind this action?"

"You may."

"What is the logic behind this action?"

"I'm going to level up Princess Kiwi and her friends. The best way to do that is by sending waves of disposable soldiers."

"I... see," said Gelkorus, who in reality didn't see at all.

"Let me spell this out for you. Our intel suggests that the princess might be the bearer for the Orb of Life. That means that she is the only one who can remove it from where it rests atop the Spiral Tower. Trust me, I've tried to remove it from the tower myself, but it resists my efforts. She's going to get it for us, which means we need to level her up so she can survive the tower. That way, I'll capture her and the orb at the same time. Oh ho ho ho!"

Gelkorus never really knew exactly how to act when the queen was laughing maniacally. Sometimes she asked him to join in, and other times she incinerated people who laughed without being asked, so he just stood there looking uncomfortable until she finished. Unlike the bad-news-giver he had sent ahead of him, Gelkorus had no interest in dying.

"I'll just go see about sending out those assassins then, shall I?"

"Yes, you go do that," said Queen Murderjoy. "Just make sure not to make them strong enough to actually kill the princess but not too weak either."

"One question, my queen. Why do you want the Orb of Life? You wouldn't be able to use it."

"Two reasons," Murderjoy said. "For one thing, sometimes victory means denying power to your enemy. I may not be able to use it now, but if it is in my possession, then the elves won't be able to use it either."

"I see. And the other reason?"

"I plan to kidnap Princess Kiwistafel. Once she is in my control and properly motivated, I'll be able to use the orb by using her as a proxy. Now, go and see about those assassins."

That would be a difficult challenge, since Gelkorus had no idea what level the princess was currently at. Maybe he would start by sending underpowered troops and have them report on her level.

He bowed and left the throne room. K'her's pitiful display still left a bad taste in Queen Murderjoy's mouth. She needed to unwind. She could do with a vacation. Maybe when this countdown business was over she would go on a cruise.

Getting up from her throne, the queen decided to pay a visit to the New Arrival Orientation and Reeducation Center to murder some elves for their XP. That always cheered her up. Hopefully it would help put the sad memory of K'her's fall behind her.

The fairy ninja Trista Twinklebottom reclined in her glass of vodka martini. The nice thing about being as small as she was that she was an unbelievably cheap drunk. She could spend the entire afternoon relaxing in a single glass of alcohol. Today, however, not even a martini bath could calm her nerves.

She leaned over the edge of the glass, hugging the olive like it was a teddy bear. "Why ish that prinsesh so late? She has to come here to get to the Shpiral Tower, right? Right?"

One of the ninjas held up a beer to his face mask as though ready to take a drink, but he set it back on the bar's counter instead. "Yeah, boss, we checked the maps. They'll have to come through here. The steam train is the only way through the Uncrossable Veldt."

"It's not fair," the fairy lamented as she gulped down another handful of vodka martini. She let out a loud burp. "We go to all tha trouble of shetting up an ambush, and she can't do us the courtesy of showing up.

"And that human lady getsh me so... mad! She humiliated me. When I get me handsh on her, I'm gonna murder her to death."

The ninja she was speaking to set his now empty beer bottle back on the counter. He signaled to the dwarven bartender for another.

"Boss!" said a voice from outside the bar. It was a female ninja garbed in pink. "A swallow has just arrived from Queen Murderjoy."

"Yeah?" said Twinklebottom. "Jusht tell that queeny woman to keep her panties on. We're working as fasht as we can. Ashashins like us can't rush things. We need to wait until they get here."

"No, boss, the queen is canceling the contract. She no longer wants us to capture the princess."

"What? She can't do that! Can she do that? She can't! A deal is a deal. If we cansheled the contract, I wouldn't get to murder that shtupid human."

"So... we just keep waiting here then?" the ninja lady asked.

"They'll get here shoon. I'll teach'em fer making me wait."

The fairy put the olive behind her head like a pillow and shut her eyes. As long as she was waiting she might as well enjoy it.

CHAPTER 33

Slimewater

Princess Kiwistafel was in the midst of a heated argument with the bored post office employee. His half-finished novel sat open and facedown on the table. Tasha hated when people treated books like that. Earmarking a book was fine, but leaving it open like that would damage the cover, and the pages would never be the same.

"Listen, Princess, I've told you over and over that our swallows can't carry large objects. It would weigh the bird down. A five-ounce bird cannot carry a one-pound orb."

The princess slammed her hands down on the counter, shocking the post office worker and thereby attaining his full attention. "Listen, the fate of the world may depend on your ability to send this package. I'm the princess, and I order you to find a way to get it to my father at Brightwind Keep."

"Yeah, the princess of Questgivria. Guess what, princess, we're not in Questgivria. You don't have any actual authority here, now do you?"

Tasha looked away from the poor mistreated book and offered a suggestion. "Well, what if several swallows carried the orb at once? They could hold it on a line."

The bored man scratched his chin. He wanted these annoying adventurers and princesses to leave so he could get back to his book. "That might work, actually, but it's still against policy, and I'm not risking my job just because some random princess says the world is in danger."

After several more minutes of arguing with the man, they left the post office. Princess Kiwi turned to the steam dragon. "Well, Kaze, it seems that our only remaining choice is to send you. I'm sorry, but this is where we part company. Will you carry the Orb of Air to my father at Brightwind Keep?"

The dragon thought-spoke to her. His words were projected into her subconscious as well as the minds of everyone in earshot. *I will, you have my word. Thank you for letting me be a part of your adventure, even if only for a little while.*

"Say hi to Hermes when you see him."

I will, Princess.

Kiwi secured the bag that held the Orb of Air to a cord around the dragon's neck. Kaze flapped his wings, lifting off into the air, and he began his trip toward the castle. His travel time would be measured in days rather than the months that it would have taken on foot.

The remainder of the group mounted up and left town through the eastern gate in the covered wagon that Slimon had acquired for them. They rode at a steady pace for about eight or nine hours each day. The road allowed the party to make better time, but they weren't leveling up. This was why they spent a few hours each day fighting mobs off the main road. That and it helped break up the monotony.

Movie nights had resumed. They were slowly making their way through Tasha's Netflix library. As a couch potato, this offered Tasha no small amount of comfort. There were few joys as simple and enjoyable as rewatching the campiest science fiction she could find surrounded by good friends.

Everything was going smoothly until one fateful day, when there was an incident between Slimon and the princess.

It all started when Slimon said, "Pfffpt."

Well, naturally Kiwi was aghast at his words. "How could you say such a thing?"

Slimon, however, held his ground. "Pfffpt."

Kiwi looked away, tears forming in her eyes. "It's as though I don't even know you anymore."

"What did he say?" Tasha asked.

"I'm not saying it out loud," said Kiwi. "Pan, will you tell Slimon that I'm not speaking to him?"

"Slimon," Pan said, "K-Kiwi says she's not speaking to you."

"Pfffpt."

Pan turned to the princess and said, "Kiwi, Slimon said…"

"I heard him just fine!" The princess crossed her arms and made a point of not looking at him.

It occurred to Tasha that maybe she should finally learn to speak Slimish. She'd been traveling with the guy for months and still couldn't understand a single thing that the slime said.

"Hey, Slimon, will you help teach me your language? We seem to have the free time, and being able to communicate without an interpreter would be helpful."

"Pfffpt!"

"Is that a yes or a no?"

"We'd be glad to teach you," Ari said. "We'll start right away, if that's okay with you."

"Sure! Fair warning, though, I've never had much luck learning other languages."

Ari grinned at her naiveite. "Slimon isn't speaking another language. He's speaking English."

"Really? It doesn't sound like English. I can only make out a few distinct sounds."

"Well, they do have their own language, but when in the presence of other races, they switch to English. When elves and humans form words, they string together syllables by making different sounds. Slimes do the same thing, but rather than making different sounds, they move their gelatinous bodies in time with the sounds. The Slime dialect consists of 207 unique phonemes that can combine to form nearly any English word. Once you learn them, understanding slime speech is easy."

Tasha frowned. "So this entire time Slimon has been speaking using body language."

"That's right. The sound they make is just a timing mechanism to separate words and draw emphasis. Let's start with something easy. Slimon, say 'Tasha.'"

"Phhhpt!" said Slimon. This time Tasha was watching him and noticed that his oval body shifted when he spoke. His upper body formed a small cone pointed toward the left for just a moment, and then his body bobbed while a small downward pointed ridge formed along his midsection.

"Now say the first syllable 'Ta,'" Ari said.

The cone formed for a moment and then vanished. She wouldn't have noticed it if she hadn't been watching.

"Now 'sha.'"

His body bobbed, forming the ridge she had seen earlier.

"We'll start with the major phonemes, and we'll get you to the point where you can understand some common phrases. Slimon, while she's learning, I'd like you to speak slower so she can recognize the different phonemes."

Slimon wiggled his body and formed several points saying, "Pffpt... Pfft."

They spent most of that day going through each of the phonemes, and then Ari had her memorize certain phrases. By the end of the first day she was able to recognize a handful of phrases like, "Hello," "Goodbye," "How much for that bag?," and "Which way is the Porta-Potty?" They trained her comprehension of Slimon's method of speech by playing games of Slimon Says. As the days wore on she continued to memorize each of the phonemes and began to recognize certain words and phrases when Slimon was speaking.

By the time Kiwi and Slimon had finally made up from their lover's quarrel, Tasha still had no idea what they had been arguing about in the first place. It was good to see them getting along again.

The journey across the slime nation took just over six weeks of travel. She had made it to level 29 through their intermittent level grinds. Her studies of the Slime dialect had improved considerably. She could now understand Slimon when he was speaking at a regular pace.

By the time she considered herself fluent in the Slimish dialect of English, the group had arrived at the gates of Slimewater.

As they crossed through the city gates, Kiwi said, "We've reached the edge of the Slime nation. The Uncrossable Veldt lies between us and the Bog of Most Likely Death, wherein lies our destination, the Spiral Tower. From here Dwarselvania lies to the north and the continent of Zhakara to the southeast."

"So... do we try to cross the veldt, then?" asked Tasha.

"Are you mad?" Ari said. "One does not simply walk through the Uncrossable Veldt! That's why they call it uncrossable. How is that not obvious? Crossing it on foot has never been done."

"Why not? Why can't it be crossed?"

"The Uncrossable Veldt has scaling mobs," he said. "No matter how high level someone gets, the mobs will always have at least twice that level. I've heard that it contains vast treasures, but nobody survives long enough to explore it. The only mob repellents that work are temporary ones like portable campgrounds, and there are no roads."

"So if we can't cross it on foot, how do we get to the other side?"

"We'll take the Belcross Express, of course," Kiwi said. "It is a railway of dwarven design and manufacture. The train tracks run from one side of the veldt to the other. It travels so fast that by the time mobs spawn, it has already moved far out of range. Laying the tracks was expensive and took decades, but it allows easy travel and trade between Dwarselvania and the Slime Federation."

"Let's do that, then. I've never actually ridden on a train before."

They sold the carriage and made their way to the train station. An elderly gnome with large spectacles was manning the ticket booth.

"Good day," Ari said. "When is the express train leaving?"

"The next train leaves tonight at sundown," the gnome said. "Will that be three adults and one child?"

"Yes, plus one raptor and three riding chickens."

Princess Kiwi pulled out an amulet bearing the royal insignia. She'd been roughing it since leaving home and had decided that enough was enough. "I am Princess Kiwistafel Questgiver, daughter of Iolo

Questgiver. Make them first-class tickets. The crown will be paying for this."

"What happened to going incognito?" Tasha whispered to her. "I thought we were trying to keep our identities secret."

"By this time tomorrow, we'll be a thousand miles away on the other side of the Uncrossable Veldt. I don't know about you, but I could use a break from roughing it."

"I hope you're right about that."

The gnome sighed. "Your animals will have to ride in the livestock cars. That will be... 14,200 GP for all of you. I'll send the bill to the kingdom then, Your Highness."

Pan pointed at a row of shops. "Shopping?"

Ari nodded. "We're running critically short on food and health potions as well."

"Of course," said Kiwi. "We still have a few hours before the train arrives. Let's go get what we need."

They left the station together. Unnoticed by the group, a small fairy peeked over the edge of the fruit cocktail she had been napping in. An evil grin crossed her face. Her long wait had finally come to fruition.

CHAPTER 34

The Undocumented
Perils of Dwarven
Death Whisky

After taking care to ensure that Denver and the riding chickens were safely stowed in the livestock car, Tasha and company were ushered into the train. She'd never ridden first class before, even when traveling by airplane back on Earth. She had always considered it to be a waste of money. It didn't seem worth doubling or even tripling the price of the ticket in exchange for a few hours of slightly less discomfort.

A human stewardess welcomed them onboard and led them to their suites. Ari, Pan, and Tasha shared one suite while Slimon and the princess occupied the next room. There were three couches that folded out into beds as well as a fully stocked wet bar, which Ari and Tasha took full advantage of.

Pan was examining the new weapon she had bought in town. It was a dwarven-made fully automatic machine gun. She had so taken to the handgun she'd bought from the NPC those many weeks back that she wanted to complement it with a second firearm. Since Slimewater was so close to the edges of dwarven territory, she was able to get the weapon at a reasonable price.

The weapon was more elaborate and decorated than strictly necessary. There seemed to be a friendly competition between the dwarves and the elves when it came to decorating their implements of death.

At first Tasha had reservations about the wisdom of allowing a child to hold a machine gun, pointing out the myriad of things that could easily go wrong with that combination. She was surprised that Ari, who was normally the most level-headed member of the group, had no problem with it. Etherians learned to handle weapons at an early age and quickly learned the dangers of their misuse.

Unfortunately, there wasn't time for Pan to learn how to actually use the weapon prior to the trip. She would have to make time for it once the train reached its destination the next day.

Rummaging through the different bottles of alcohol, Tasha picked out a green-tinted one with some dwarven writing on it. She couldn't actually read the letters but had been in Etheria long enough to know that the rune script was dwarven. She performed a scan on it and found that it was called Dwarven Death Whisky. This was the same drink that Ari had told her about before back at the castle. She hadn't indulged at the time, but she was a different person then. Maybe she would try it now. Just a sip. What was the worst that could happen?

She poured herself a small shot glass and downed it in one gulp. The liquid was like fire that burned a path through her throat and into her belly, causing her to shudder involuntarily. Tasha was a bit of a lightweight on Earth, and that seemed to have carried through into her stat-augmented body.

She poured another cup of death whisky and offered it to Ari.

Pan sat up from the bed, pointed her hand at Tasha, and called out "Steal!" The drink flew from Tasha's hand and into her own, the liquid never spilling out. As soon as the girl had it, she put the glass to her lips and swallowed it. For a moment the girl's face showed no reaction. That moment passed, and then her eyes grew large as she collapsed backward onto her couch, clearly in distress.

"You could have just asked," Tasha said, grinning.

"She's too young to drink," Ari said, rebuking her.

Pan sat back up and crossed her arms. Apparently it was okay for her to fight monsters, handle machine guns, oppose evil queens, hobnob with pirates, eidolons, players, and kings, not to mention defy the great destroyer god Entropy himself, but alcohol was where the adults drew the line because alcohol was dangerous.

Tasha poured another glass for Ari, and this time he took it from her successfully. They spent the next hour drinking and making small talk. At some point Pan fell back into her chair and passed out completely. Ari carried her to the cot.

Tasha remembered having several more drinks with Ari, but that was ultimately the extent of her memory from the evening.

She awoke the next morning, and to her great distress, a mariachi band was performing in her head while being pursued by a herd of rampaging elephants. At least that's what her hangover felt like. Tasha realized that she was lying facedown on something prickly. This wasn't her bed. She thought she heard some strange animal noises but couldn't make them out over the sound of the mariachi band.

Gathering all of her courage and determination, she bravely tried to roll onto her back. Halfway through the motion, she fell several feet, landing on a hard wooden floor. Pain swept through the back of her head from the impact, momentarily distracting her from the hangover.

Opening one eye, she could see a big brown spot that gradually resolved into the ceiling of a train car. Why was the train spinning? It felt as though it were moving around her in circles. Shouldn't it be moving forward in a single direction?

Her vision was still blurry, but she could start to make out vague shapes and details. She wasn't quite emotionally prepared to make as bold an adventure as sitting up, but some overly curious part of her mind was wondering where she was.

After several minutes of lying supine, a figure made its way into her field of view. It was an animal, a cow to be precise. It featured a long white nose with a black patch over one eye. She looked at Tasha curiously and let out a dismissive "moo" before moving out of her field of view.

Tasha wondered just what she had been up to last night? Gathering all of her grit and determination, she raised her body to a sitting position and looked around. She was rewarded by an additional wave of pain that superimposed itself over the existing headache. She needed to do something about this hangover, post haste.

Maybe she could ask Slimon to cast a recovery spell on her. Unfortunately, that would involve standing up and walking around, which was far beyond her meager capabilities. Screw it, she was going to use one of her status recovery potions. They weren't cheap, but desperate times called for desperate measures.

First, she had to open her menu. She swiped vaguely upward with one finger, and the menu interface opened. So far so good. Carefully she tapped on "items." Success again! She was on a roll. Nothing could stop her now. The inventory screen opened up before her. The item labeled "cure potion" was close to the top of the inventory list, accompanied by a pixelated image of a flask.

She jabbed at it with her finger, but in her partially drunken state accidentally tapped the item next to it, and a glob of grogre mucus appeared in her hand instead.

Dammit, why did she even have one of these in her inventory? As a gamer, her instinct was to pick up everything that she might conceivably be able to use or sell, but it was hard to imagine anyone paying for this. The item description said it was used in crafting, but she couldn't see how. Little bits of grogre mucus dripped from the glob in her hand and onto the wooden floorboards.

She quickly put it back in her inventory and successfully retrieved the cure potion. Popping the cork off the vial of purple liquid, she quaffed it in a single gulp. It tasted like cough syrup, but as it went down her headache receded, and she was overcome with a feeling of relief. The mariachi band had gone on strike, and the herd of elephants had moved on to greener pastures.

Now that her senses had returned to her, she took in her surroundings properly. This must be one of the livestock cars. She could feel movement beneath her so it was clear that the train was still in motion. Several cows and sheep surrounded her. She'd been sleeping on a small rectangular bale of hay.

She then realized that she wasn't wearing her own clothing. Instead, Tasha was wearing a stewardess's outfit that fit just a bit too snugly. She tried desperately to put the pieces together but couldn't remember what would have possessed her to dress like this and sleep among the cows and sheep rather than in her expensive first-class suite.

She opened her menu in order to equip some more reasonable clothing, but before she could open the inventory screen, she saw the GP indicator in the corner which indicated that she was at 0 GP. Why was she broke? Did she lose all of her money during her blackout?

As she was trying to figure out what had happened, someone came in. An elderly gnome man entered the car and took one look at her. "Hey, were you sleeping? Get back to work, Pollyanna, or I'll report you for sleeping on the job."

"What did you call me?"

He pointed at her chest, saying, "Poll-y-anna. It's your name. It's written right there on your name tag. Did you forget your own name? Or maybe you prefer Paula? I don't actually care, just get the hell out of my cattle car. I've got work to do. These animals aren't going to feed themselves."

"Okay, I'm going." She got to her feet, brushed some rogue pieces of straw off of her uniform, and made her way to the exit. Who was Pollyanna, and why was she wearing that woman's uniform?

Taking the other exit, she moved through several baggage cars and made her way to the passenger section. Rows of seated passengers lined either side of the car. More than half of the passengers were human, although there were quite a few dwarves and slimes.

Not sure what else to do, she decided to make her way to the first-class lounge, which was at the front of the train. She proceeded from one car to the next.

After reaching the third passenger car, a middle-aged human passenger with a shaggy beard turned to her. "Hey, miss. Can you bring me another bottle of Dwarven Death Whisky?"

Tasha backed away, saying, "Yeah, I'll get right on that."

As she opened the door to the next car, Tasha met the eyes of another stewardess. She was tall and blonde, and her name tag said "Susan." She took one look at Tasha and said, "Good morning, Pollyanna."

Tasha wondered how it was that the woman didn't recognize that she wasn't her colleague. Since the stewardess outfit Tasha was wearing was too small for her, she doubted that she looked like this Pollyanna person. Choosing not to question her good luck, she let the stewardess past and left the car.

It occurred to her that she probably shouldn't continue wearing Pollyanna's uniform. She was desperately curious as to how she'd come by it, but she would have to explore that in greater detail at a later time. Moving into the space between the train cars where nobody could see her, she opened her menu and equipped one of the fancy brown dresses that she'd purchased in Slimewater.

She was able to traverse the next dozen or so passenger cars without incident. Finally she made it to the observation cars situated at the midsection of the train. Large windows framed the walls on either side, showing grassy wilderness as it rushed by. Halfway through the first observation car, she spotted a familiar face. Pan was sipping a milkshake at the bar.

"Pan, you've gotta help me!" Tasha said, pulling up a chair.

"Hi. What's wrong?"

Tasha proceeded to explain the events of the preceding night and how she woke up in the cattle car, hungover and wearing a stewardess outfit as well as how all of her GP had vanished. She also mentioned her encounter with the other stewardess, who somehow thought that she was her colleague.

After listening to the story patiently, Pan said, "Your left hand. I think it's a c-clue."

Peering at her left hand, Tasha noticed something that hadn't been there before. Sitting snugly on her finger was a golden ring engraved with a red jewel. It wasn't a particularly elaborate ring, but there was a beauty about its simplicity.

Tasha got to her feet, knocking over the barstool. "Wait, are you saying that I got engaged last night?"

"No, you didn't get engaged," said Pan.

Tasha puffed out a breath. "That's a relief."

"You got m-married."

Tasha scanned the ring, and the description read "Wedding Ring."

Tasha's screams of horror drew the attention of everyone in the observation car.

"It's okay," said Pan. "Maybe you will be happy married."

Tasha took a drink of some kind of booze that someone left on the counter and collected herself. "But... who did I get married to? I don't remember meeting anyone last night. I was drinking with you and Ari, and then nothing."

Pan got to her feet, leaving the empty milkshake glass on the counter. "M-maybe Dad knows."

"Good idea. Let's find him and ask. Couldn't you just... I dunno, summon him?"

Pan shook her head. "Everyone would see."

Tasha sighed. "Okay, let's get back to our room."

They were about to leave the observation car when a stewardess carrying a broadsword entered the car. "Your attention, please."

Everyone in the car turned to look at her. "I have some bad news. There have been several murders on board this train. We've found the bodies of multiple staff members. For the time being, we're asking that all travelers return to their assigned seats for the remainder of the trip."

"That's terrible," said a human man in his late twenties. "I know some of the staff. Who was it?"

"So far we've found five bodies, including Brenda, Susan, Alice, Pollyanna, and Millie. We found their bodies hidden in the luggage compartment, and their clothing had been removed."

Tasha's name tag had said "Pollyanna," and the stewardess that she'd just passed had a name tag that said "Susan." She was about to mention this, but Pan spoke first.

"Tasha, did you k-kill them?"

"No, of course not! At least, I don't think I did. That doesn't seem like the kind of thing I would do. Why would I? I'm a nice person, I don't go around murdering stewardesses. Stewardi? What's the plural of stewardess?"

"Stewardesses?" Pan said.

"Let's get back to our lounge and find Ari. Hopefully he'll have some answers for us."

Looking at her ring, Tasha said, "I'm more concerned about this. Pan, I'm just not ready to get married."

"Excuse me," Pan said to the broadsword-wielding stewardess, "was there a w-wedding last night?"

The stewardess smiled. "I did hear about something like that. Last night a dark-skinned human girl married a pervy samurai named Henimaru the Toad. We'd been getting complaints that he'd been asking every female human that he could find to marry him. I guess someone finally agreed. I can't see what that poor girl sees in him."

"Henimaru?" said Pan, her eyes wide.

"The Toad?" Tasha finished, her mouth open.

"Yeah," said the stewardess. "He's a toad-person. You'll find him a few cars down."

The two looked at each other, Tasha's own horror and concern reflected in Pan's eyes.

With trepidation in her heart, Tasha put one foot after another, walking past the stewardess toward the next car. They proceeded through several more cars before they found any passengers who would qualify as toadlike.

Finally, they found him in the third car. His skin was a yellowish-green tint dotted with red and black patches of discoloration. He had a large mouth and jaw. Perfectly black eyes framed his face on either side. His attire consisted of a plate helm that curved upward along either side, individual sleeve shields, and layers of plate body armor that covered a thick leather vest.

It appeared that Henimaru was eating breakfast. He opened the lid of a small bowl, and a fly darted out. Before it could escape, Henimaru's tongue shot out from his mouth, capturing the fly and drawing it back into his waiting maw.

Pan and Tasha exchanged looks for a moment. Shrugging, the girl walked over to the toad-samurai-person, pulling Tasha along by the hand.

"Hi," Pan said. "Are you Henimaru?"

It was then that Henimaru noticed Tasha and verified her fears. He let loose a loud croaking sound which emanated from his throat and gurbled aloud until finally sputtering out.

"Aha, there thou art," he said, wiping a bit of fly off of his mouth. "Tasha, my own sweet wife! I had wondered as to where thou wast since the ceremony. Yesterday was truly the most joyful day of my life. T'was as though Lord Storyboard Designer himself tooketh note of my desperate need and sent unto one me one of his angels."

"Pan," Tasha said as she took a single step backward, "I think I might be in need of some more of that Death Whisky."

Pan just smiled. "I'm P-Pan, and I'm so very h-happy for my friend Tasha. It's about time she found a n-nice husband. C-c-can you tell me how this happened?"

"Verily, friend Pan," Henimaru said, croaking loudly. "Sorry, yes. Tasha, why don't you tell thy friend about it."

"That's okay," Tasha said. "I'm sure you could tell it much better than me."

"Art thou sure?" he asked.

"Oh yeah. I'm sure."

"Well, this is what happened. It all began several weeks ago. I was taking my tadpoles out for some level grinding when suddenly we were accosted by a band of Zhakaran slavers. I'm ashamed to say that they attacked whilst my back was turned. I was collecting food for them, but by the time I had returned, the Zhakaran swine had already taken my young."

"That's terrible!" Tasha said.

"Verily, that's what you said yesterday when I told you, only you used more artful language, and your words did all slureth together. As I was saying, I tracked them down and discovered that they were to be sold at a slave auction in Zhakara. I doth headeth there now hoping to attempt a rescue, but in Zhakara my kind are considered no more than slaves. Indeed, it is likely that I would be captured and enslaved myself before I could even get close to my goal."

"But you are going anyway?" Tasha asked.

"I must!" Henimaru responded in his typical butchering of Shakespearian speech. " Still, I have little hope of setting them free traveling as I am. Then it did occurreth to me that if I were married to a human woman, that might give me the cover I need to maketh mine approach. I've heard that non-humans who art married to humans are considered the property of their spouses, so most people would just leaveth them alone rather than risk angering their spouse."

Tasha nodded in understanding. "So that's why you've been asking all the human women on this train to marry you."

"Thou understandeth!" he cried with another loud croak. "Oh dear, I seem to have a frog in my throat. As I was saying, thou understandeth perfectly. When I explaineth the situation yesterday, thou offered to marry me in order to aid me in mine attempts to extract my offspring from the vile clutches of the Zhakarans."

A weak smile grew upon Tasha's face. "Now that I understand your situation, I guess I have no problem with this. But since this is just a marriage of convenience, you don't care if I see other people, right?"

"Of course I don't mind. This marriage is only temporary so I can get my children back. Like we agreed yesterday, I shalt file for divorce as soon as I returneth to the Slime Federation," Henimaru said.

"Okay, and just because we're married, you don't expect us to have... relations, do you?"

"Whatever dost thou meaneth by 'relations'?

"Sex," Pan added helpfully. "She means sex."

Henimaru turned to Tasha. "Dear lady, I do not believe that thou art capable of having sex with me. Toad-people mate using a process called amplexus. Unless thou art able to lay a large number of eggs on demand, I would not expect relations between us to be possible. Laying eggs isn't something humans can do, is it? Sorry, I fear that I'm not well versed in human reproductive anatomy."

"Um... no," Tasha said, somewhat relieved, "not as such. I guess that explains the ring."

Pan patted Tasha on the back. "Anything else?"

Tasha paused for a moment in thought. "All of my GP is gone from my inventory. I'd been trying to save up, but it's all gone now. Also, I would like to know why I had Pollyanna's uniform and why I was sleeping in the cattle car with the animals."

Henimaru slurped up another fly and said, "I can help thee with that. Allow me to accompany thee and help retraceth thy steps."

"Thanks, Henimaru," Tasha said.

"My pleasure, wife," he said as he flagged down a stewardess and indicated his bowl of flies. "Miss, can I get this to go?"

After collecting the remainder of his breakfast, Henimaru the Toad led Tasha and Pan toward the front of the car. Finally, they reached the chapel. It was a small compartment where people of various denominations could come and pray. A dark-elf priestess sat at a nearby bench. She was reading some variety of holy book.

"Fair morning, Lorcana," Henimaru said.

"Hello, Henimaru," said the dark elf. "How are the two of you enjoying the bliss of matrimony?"

"It's like nothing I'd ever imagined," Tasha said dryly.

"May the light of the developers be upon you both."

Tasha turned to Henimaru. "Where did we go after we got hitched?"

"Well, I walked thee back toward thine room, but before we could get there, thou stopped and purchased something from a traveling merchant. Thou said that thou sawest someone that thou recognized but did not elaborate."

"Show me," she said.

He led Tasha and Pan through several more train cars toward the front of the train, passing row upon row of passengers. Henimaru indicated a man dressed in loud, ostentatious clothing. He wore a striped top hat of many colors which was as tall as he was. The words "NPC Merchant" floated above his head.

The man smiled at Tasha. "Hello, traveler. Would you like to browse my wares?" Several buttons appeared in front of him including "Buy" and "Sell."

"Last night," Henimaru said, "this NPC sold thee an unbreakable glass jar and a bug catching net in exchange for all of thine GP. I tried to talk thee out of it, but thou said it was important."

The merchant continued to look at Tasha with vacant NPC eyes.

"Great," Tasha said. "A bug catching net. Just what I've always wanted. So what did I do once I wasted my money on this?"

"That be'eth the odd bit. Thou said that thee had spied someone thou recognized. I followed thee toward the back of the car. When I asked thou what thou wert doing, thou said to me, and I quoteth, 'Be vawy vawy quiet, I'm hunting faiwies.' After that, thou did runneth off. I tried to catch up with thee, but had an unexpectedly urgent call of nature and needed to use the latrine. When I was done I could find neither hide nor hair of thee."

"Fairies?" Tasha wondered aloud. "The only fairy I know is that ninja who attacked us. You said I moved toward the back of the car, in the direction of the cattle car? I must have passed out before I caught up with whoever I was chasing. That still doesn't explain why I was wearing the stewardess uniform."

"We could retrace thy steps," Henimaru said. "Mayhaps we can findeth another clue."

"Hold on a moment," Tasha realized. "I'll check my combat log. If there were any entries from last night, they might be a clue."

Opening her menu, she selected "Tools," then "Combat Log." The combat log revealed her entire history of combat since her arrival in Etheria, but she was only concerned with the most recent entries.

>**Combat initiated.**
>**Unknown Ninja deals 1 heart damage to Tasha Singleton (Level 29).**
>**Tasha Singleton (Level 29) deals 5 1/4 heart damage to Unknown Ninja.**

Unknown Ninja deals 1 heart damage to Tasha Singleton (Level 29).
Tasha Singleton (Level 29) deals 5 3/4 heart damage to Unknown Ninja.
Tasha Singleton (Level 29) has killed Unknown Ninja.
Victory! 220 experience gained, 0 GP gained.

"My combat log says that I killed a ninja last night. Perhaps she was disguised as a stewardess, so that explains why I took her clothes. Let's meet up with the others. If there are still ninjas on this train, we are all in danger."

"Then I shalt aid thee," said Henimaru. "If mine wife be in peril, 't'would be cowardice to turneth a blind eye."

And so Tasha joined Pan and her new husband as they made their way to her luxury suite, where she hoped to find her companions.

CHAPTER 35

Rumble on the Belcross Express

"What do you mean you got married?" Aralogos said, a look of distress on his face.

"It's not a real, actual marriage," Tasha explained. "I'm just helping him out so he can get into Zhakara. You're not jealous, are you?"

"Dad's totally jealous," Pan said helpfully.

Ari glared at her. "I am not!"

They were all gathered together in Tasha's suite. Though it was a bit cramped, it allowed the group to meet together with at least some modicum of privacy. She had spent the last fifteen minutes recounting her adventures with Ari, Pan, and Sir Slimon.

"So what's our next move?" asked Ari. "I'm concerned about the princess. If there are ninjas on board, she would be their target. Have any of you seen her?"

Tasha shook her head. "What if they already have her? Could they have left the train?"

"Not likely. They wouldn't leave while we are still in the Uncrossable Veldt. It's a death sentence out there. If they have her, they won't act until after the train has made it all the way through."

"Then we have to find her. If the train's staff has been replaced by ninjas, let's just kill them like we always do. We can take control of the train ourselves."

"Do you know how to drive a train?" Ari asked.

Tasha just shrugged. "Well, no, but how hard could it be, really?"

"So this is it," Ari muttered. "We're all going to die."

"Okay, so here's the plan. We'll head toward the front of the train. If she's not there, we'll double back. We have to assume that the entire train staff has been compromised. Anyone who you encounter could be disguised ninjas."

They left the suite and began making their way from one car to the next in the direction of the engine. They didn't make it more than two cars before the attack came. One moment Tasha was weaving between tables in the dining car, the next moment there was a shuriken flying at her face. She was saved only by her Bullet Time ability and was able to dodge out of the way.

The attacker was one of the waiters, or at least that's how he had disguised himself. Tasha instinctively equipped her gunblade and shot a fireball at him. As the fireball traveled through the air toward him, it brushed against a table, setting the tablecloth on fire. It did, however, hit the ninja dead on, incinerating him.

"How about we hold off on casting fireballs while on a train?" Ari said.

"Yeah, got it."

One of the waitresses jumped into the air and rebounded off the ceiling, leaping directly at Tasha. Before she could react, Pan pulled out her machine gun and fired a stream of bullets into the ninja, killing her before she reached her target. The shots continued through her flesh and into the wall. Rays of light shone through the bullet holes from outside.

Ari yelled in a voice filled with exasperation and no small amount of parental stress, "Pan, you're worse than Tasha. Try not to destroy the train cars while we are *riding* in them."

The passengers were screaming, flailing their arms around, and panicking as only innocent bystanders could do. Tasha pushed them to the side as she continued toward the front of the train. The next car contained no less than seven ninjas. Ari either killed or knocked out one ninja after the next. The party's levels had progressed far beyond the point where these low-level ninjas would pose any serious threat.

They continued in this manner for the next fifteen minutes. Though the party tended to out-level the ninjas, they still took damage. Slimon provided healing support while Henimaru, Ari, and Tasha did most of the damage. Pan had come to the realization that using firearms while inside a train wasn't the wisest course of action, so she mostly stayed back and used Steal to disarm and rob the ninjas.

After they finished clearing one of the cars, a notification appeared.

Now leaving zone Uncrossable Veldt (scaling enemy levels) and entering zone Riverwood Forest (levels 14–18).

The train had cleared the veldt, which meant that the enemy could try to jump the train at any time. "We need to hurry," Ari said. "There's no more time."

Finally, they made it to the power car that fed the engine. Scanning the room, five ninjas clad in black stood between Tasha and Princess Kiwi. The princess was sound asleep, tied tightly to a support post, seemingly unaware of the present danger. Behind her, Tasha made out a small fairy buzzing around. She had drawn her needlelike sword and had it to the princess's neck.

Tasha put her hands on her hips. "Trista Twinklebottom. So we meet again. It's all over for you. There's nowhere left for you to run. If you let her go, we won't have to kill you too."

"If you take one more step," Trista said, "I'll slice your princess's throat."

"No, you won't," Ari said as he approached the nearest ninja. "You're supposed to kidnap her, not kill her. You won't be able to fulfill your contract if the princess is dead. What will the queen do when she discovers you've let her escape?"

Invoking Sprint, Tasha dashed at one of the ninjas and impaled him just as he was starting to weave a ninja hand spell. Ari slammed his fist into one of the remaining ninjas as Henimaru sliced his way through another. After Ari finished beating the crap out of his opponent, Trista was the only one left.

"Grah!" she cursed. "You defeated us... again! What the hell? I'm out of here. So long, jerks!"

"Stop her!" Tasha shouted. She opened her menu interface and removed her bug catching net, but Trista was moving too quickly.

Before the fairy could reach the window, she was captured by Henimaru's tongue. He snatched her up and swallowed her whole.

For a moment nothing happened, but after a few seconds passed, a serious case of indigestion seemed to overcome Henimaru because he coughed her back up and onto the hard wooden floor. The fairy crashed against the floorboards. She tried to take off, but her wings were weighed down, drenched by Henimaru's saliva and digestive fluids.

Before Trista could escape, Tasha brought the bug catching net down and captured her. Grabbing her by her tiny legs through the net, she shoved her into the glass jar and closed the lid tight.

"You asshole!" Twinklebottom shouted. "Let me outta here! You can't keep me bottled up in this jar forever! I'll get out, and when I do, I'll beat the crap out of you!"

Tasha shook the bottle for a moment, and the fairy collapsed to the bottom of the jar, dizzy and beaten.

Ari wasn't wasting any time. Using a short knife, he cut Kiwi's bonds. The sounds of battle had awakened her from her slumber.

She yawned sleepily. "What happened?"

"Oh, nothing much," Tasha said. "You just got kidnapped by ninjas again. I've captured their leader in this jar. We'll just carry her with us so she doesn't cause any more trouble."

"Really? I've always wanted a fairy," Kiwi said.

Tasha opened her inventory and tried to deposit the jar.

Unable to add item "Glass Jar" to inventory because it contains non-storable object.

It was worth a try.

"I think we should move to the engine car," Ari said. "All of the staff seem to have been killed and replaced by ninjas. That means nobody's driving this thing."

Tasha slid open the door that led to the engine car. There was no engineer or operator. The forest was visible through the glass window as it sped past the train at a blinding rate.

Before her was a thoroughly unintuitive control board. Knobs, buttons, levers, and unmarked flashing lights littered the console. Tasha was generally pretty quick to pick up on strange control systems in video games, but this layout seemed to have no rhyme or reason involved in its design. Tasha spent the next five minutes trying to make sense of it when she received a new notification.

Now leaving zone Riverwood Forest (levels 14–18) and entering zone Valley of Happiness (levels 1–3).

As the last of the trees flew past, the landscape opened up into a wide valley. Endless plains filled with multicolored wildflowers extended in every direction before her. In the distance was a walled city. The train tracks disappeared into the walls.

"What's that?" asked Pan.

"End of the line," Ari said ominously.

Concern overtook Tasha as she realized her situation. "Um... we're not slowing down. In a few minutes, we're going to crash into the city! How do we stop this thing?"

"I knoweth not, dear wife," said Henimaru.

Not knowing what else to do, Tasha started pushing buttons and pulling knobs randomly. Suddenly she was pushed against the back wall of the engineering compartment. Something she'd done had caused the train to accelerate.

"That's not helping!" yelled Ari.

"I'll save us," Pan said as she raised her machine gun and pointed it at the control panel.

"No, don't!" Tasha cried out, but it was already too late. The sound of her machine gun filled the air, and lines of tracer fire sprayed between her gun and the control panel. The control panel's fine mahogany finish was destroyed as buttons, springs, and wires flew out in each direction and the panel was destroyed. Finally Pan's gun spun down, out of ammo. The control panel had been completely destroyed.

"We do not appear to be slowing down," said Henimaru. "I don't thinketh thy plan worked."

Trista Twinklebottom was banging against the side of the glass jar. "That's because you morons just blew up the control panel. I could have told you what to do, but nooo, you just had to destroy everything like you idiot humans always do. Let me out of this jar before you get me killed!"

Tasha shook the jar again, and that caused the fairy to stop complaining.

"So, what now?" asked Ari. He was completely out of ideas and hoped that Tasha would have some crazy notion about how to get them out of this situation.

The city was approaching the train at a rather alarming rate. They probably had less than five minutes before crashing into the city. How did one stop a runaway train? She thought back to the various movies and games trying to find an answer. Finally, the beginnings of an idea began to take root in her mind.

"I have a plan," Tasha said. "Pan, Kiwi, and Henimaru, I need the three of you to decouple the cars behind this one, and be quick about it."

"But won't that make the engine move even faster?" Kiwi said.

"Yes, it will make the engine car move much faster since it won't be pulling as much. But it will save the lives of the passengers. Besides, I have another idea about how to stop the train. Trust me."

"Okay," said Pan.

"What do you need me to do?" asked Ari.

Tasha put her hand on his shoulder. "Your part of this is the most important of all. We won't be able to stop the train without your help."

He nodded. "All right. I don't know what you are planning, but I'll do my best."

"That's all anyone can ask. Once the train is decoupled, I'm going to pick you up and use my Sprint ability to move you in front of the train."

"I don't think any of my attacks will be enough to destroy the train engine," he said.

"You're wrong about that, Ari. One of your attacks will do the job perfectly. I'm going to need you to suplex the train!"

He looked at her, aghast, and put his hands on her shoulders. "Are you mad, woman? Nobody can suplex a train! It's impossible. I'm not even sure I can slow it down, much less lift it."

"You can", She said trying to put on an air of certainty, "I know this is possible because I've seen it done before, in a different game. You are much stronger than you were when we met. I know you can do this. I believe in you."

"How can you believe in me?" Ari said. "I'm not real!"

Without warning, the train accelerated forward and the two were thrown against the back of the engineering compartment wall. Pan and Henimaru must have found a way to decouple the train cars.

"You're real enough to me," she said. "It's time. Are you ready?"

"Yes. I can do this. Let's... suplex the train."

The city before her now filled a large part of the view. She kicked open the door on the side of the engineering compartment. The door had lots of knobs and levers and a pull rope, and she really didn't have time to deal with that shit. Her kick caused the door to fly off its hinges, and it disappeared behind the rampaging train.

Picking up Ari, she invoked Sprint and ran as fast as she could ahead of the train. Though she was outpacing the train, it wasn't by much. When the Sprint ability ran down, she was just outside the city gates. The rails ran right past them and into a train entrance into the city.

They both turned to face the oncoming train. It was moving toward her at a blistering speed and would collide within seconds. Tasha began to second-guess her plan but didn't say anything. She needed Ari to know that she believed in him. If he was going to succeed at this, there couldn't be any self-doubt.

"Do it!" she cried as the train was about to hit him.

Ari invoked his God Strength ability and put both hands out to the side. The train slammed right into him and pushed him along the train tracks toward the city. Sparks flew from his feet as the train pushed against him.

Ari's eyes grew a brilliant red, and flames seemed to engulf him. His muscles expanded as he was enveloped in a flaming cloak of power. At that moment, he didn't even look human. For a moment she thought she saw horns on his head, but it might have just been a trick of the light.

A raw, guttural scream escaped him as he planted his legs into the ground and pushed upward into the air, carrying the train car with him. He fell to the ground, all evidence of his momentary transformation vanished. The train flew off into the distance toward the city gates. It slammed onto its side on a road that wound toward the city. The train tumbled over and over until finally coming to a rest little more than a dozen meters before it would have crashed into the city gates.

She turned back around and saw the rest of the train drifting slowly toward the city along the tracks. It came to a full stop before it reached the two of them.

Checking her battle menu, she saw that Ari had critically low hit points. She was about to fish out a potion for him, but before she had the opportunity to do so, a level-up prompt appeared:

> **Victory! Belcross Express Train has been vanquished.**
> **9,200 experience gained. (2,640 to next level)**
> **5,400 GP found.**
> **Item found: Super Elixir x2**
> **Level up!**
> **You have reached level 30. You have 4 unassigned stat points.**
> **Choose either a heart container or mana container.**

Ari's HP had been fully restored, and he stood in the train tracks, covered in blood and motor oil. His martial-arts uniform was ripped and torn, but he was victorious.

At the end of it all, they had saved the princess, killed a shit-ton of ninjas, experienced a crazy drunken adventure, and suplexed a train. Sure, maybe Tasha had accidentally gotten married to a pervy samurai toad, but on balance it had been a good day.

CHAPTER 36

They Call Me Player

Last Tacoday evening, Dourmal, King Under the Laundry Mountain, was kind enough to allow our own Aranrhod Kefling to interview him on location deep within the Laundry Mountain. Little is known about King Dourmal as the mountain is closed off to most outsiders, so this is a rare opportunity for us to learn about those who dwell beneath the mountain.

Aranrhod: Thank you for agreeing to sit down with me today, King Dourmal.

King Dourmal: Don't mention it, lass.

Aranrhod: King Dourmal, I'll get right to it, then. How would you like to comment on the advent of the menu countdown and rumors of Entropy's return?

King Dourmal: Rumors don't interest me. Aye, I've heard talk of Entropy from visitors to the mountain, but the troubles of abovegrounders such as yourselves don't concern us.

Aranrhod: So, you don't believe that Lord Entropy is actually returning?

King Dourmal: Well, I can't say either way. Of course, I wouldn't put it past those pointy-eared bastards to destroy the world for their own personal gains. Eh... no offense, lass.

Aranrhod: Of course not, please go on.

King Dourmal: What I mean to say is that even if what they say about Entropy is true, we dwarves are safe enough underground. We kicked the layabout dragons out of our mountain, after all. No overgrown snake can stand against the might of the mountain kingdom.

Aranrhod: Dourmal, are referring to the power of the Orb of Earth?

King Dourmal: It's King Dourmal, missy.

Aranrhod: My apologies, King Dourmal... So... the Orb of Earth?

King Dourmal: Yes, what about it?

Aranrhod: How do you respond to the rumors that have been circulating among the hill dwarves outside the mountain regarding the orb? Many of them believe that the orb is no longer allied with you.

King Dourmal: Pfft. Ridiculous. I don't respond to such baseless rumors.

Aranrhod: Then, if it wouldn't be an imposition, would you mind demonstrating its use to me? That would go a long way toward quelling those rumors.

King Dourmal: We're done here.

Article from the Sunwell Gazette, *Puff 20th 3205 3E*

The dwarven city of Belcross was abuzz with activity. While some of the townsfolk were understandably concerned about the sudden and unexplained appearance of a dislodged train car just beyond their front gates, most of the revelers were there for an entirely different reason.

The streets were filled with dwarves in celebration. There was live music and expertly choreographed dwarves dancing in the streets.

Tasha looked to Ari for an explanation, but he simply shrugged.

After a moment, she drew a breath and approached one of the revelers. He was a short dwarven man with a white beard tied in an elaborate circular braid.

"Hello there, dwarf."

"Lalli-ho, human," he answered in reply.

"Yeah. Listen, what is everyone celebrating?"

"You don't know?" he said. "Open your menu and see for yourself."

Swiping her menu open, she examined it for a moment, trying to find what he meant. After a moment she saw the menu's clock. It read 80:00:59. Though the menu wasn't moving, it was very nearly at the eighty-hour mark.

"The clock?"

"Exactly. We're celebrating the countdown reaching the eighty-hour mark. We dwarves are loathe to turn away an excuse to celebrate. We just celebrated the eighty-five-hour mark a few weeks ago. I tell ya, lassie, this countdown has been a boon for partygoers like myself. I hope this explains things, lass."

"Thank you," she said and then remembered that there was a proper way to address dwarves. "Um... may your beard grow ever more elaborate."

"And yours as well," he said politely.

"Er... thanks." She turned to her friends. "Let's pay a visit to the save point." There were wooden street signs with floppy disk logos indicating the proper direction.

She made her way through the main street toward the city square, which contained the town's save point. She stopped for a moment at a street vendor and ordered a fried something-or-other on a stick. It was not dissimilar to chicken, whatever it was.

Ten minutes later, they'd reached the city square. Wondering how much time was left before it hit the big eight-oh, Tasha opened her menu. The clock read 80:00:53.

"Hold on," said Ari, "let's stock up on restoratives at this item shop." He was indicating a building with a potion icon on the door. Nodding, she followed him inside and spent the next ten minutes filling up on potions, antidotes, and campsites. Since she'd spent all of her money on a bug catching net, she ended up bumming some money from Ari to cover the party's expenses.

When she left the item shop, she heard the revelers cry a word out in unison. "Ten!"

She opened her menu and looked at it. The moment she did, the word "Nine!" filled the air. The clock read 80:00:09. She tapped the menu closed.

The party waited for a few minutes, but nothing happened. The game clock wasn't going to change. Something was causing it to advance at different speeds at different times.

"I give up," Ari said. "What's the deal with the menu clocks? Sometimes it seems to stay at the same for hours at a time, and other times it decreases by several minutes in a single instant. There must be a reason behind this."

"Maybe there's a pattern," Tasha suggested. "Like what if there's something different when the countdown changes than when it stays still."

"I've not seen any pattern," said Kiwi.

Pan just shook her head.

"Okay," Tasha decided, "I'm going to watch the timer like a hawk and wait for the exact moment it changes."

"Good luck," said Ari. "I've tried that quite a few times with no success."

She swiped open the menu and at that moment the word "Eight!" sounded out from the crowd. The clock read 80:00:08. That was just a coincidence, right?

She closed the menu and opened it again. "Seven!"

After closing it and reopening it one more time, the word "Five!" rang out. This time it had skipped over six entirely.

"Ari," Tasha said hesitantly, "I think I'm doing this. I'm causing the countdown to change. I don't understand how, but every time I open the menu the clock changes by about a second."

"That can't be right," he said, "it must be a coincidence. Try it now."

She swiped the menu open and heard the word "Four!" being recited by an increasingly excited crowd. This time she didn't close the menu. The blue screen floated there in the air just in front of her.

"It's no coincidence," she said.

"No, it can't be caused by you opening the menu.," he said. "I've seen it counting down as we traveled together. I would have seen if you were playing in the menu."

"Maybe there are other things that cause it to change."

"Try removing an item from your inventory," Kiwi said.

Nodding, she opened the item screen and searched through it for a handful of seconds. Highlighting the line:

Chocolate Chip Cookie x 94

She touched it with one finger and clicked on the take button. A single cookie appeared in her hands. The moment it did, a chorus of "One!" filled the air.

She looked at the cookie that she had removed from her inventory, but Pan had already stolen it and was munching on it happily.

She thought out loud, "Opening my menu reduces everyone's clock by one second. Removing a cookie reduced it by three seconds. Ari, try opening your menu."

Ari swiped at the air in front of him. From Tasha's point of view, there was no change, but she knew that he was looking at his menu interface, which would be visible to him alone. There was no change in the timer. The easily amused celebrating dwarves remained more or less silent.

"So we know that I'm causing this. It's only my actions that affect the clock. But why? How does my opening a menu reduce the timer?"

Nobody had an answer. There was something to this, she was certain of it.

Her thoughts turned to the day that she arrived in Etheria. She'd been standing in her apartment staring at the wall clock. The second hand had been slowly ticking in a counterclockwise motion. It had been moving at a normal speed, each second that elapsed causing the clock to move backward by one second.

The speed of the clocks was normal on Earth, but operated at a slower pace here and at irregular intervals. The moment that the flow of time became slow and inconsistent was when she passed from her world to this one.

But how had she done that? How had she actually traveled to Etheria while sitting on her couch? As she had this thought, everything clicked.

"Holy crap! I think I just figured it out."

"Figured what out?" asked Pan.

"I know why the clocks are behaving the way they are. I understand how I arrived at Etheria. Ari, I don't think I'm actually here."

"Of course you're here. I can see you. I can touch you."

"I'm not actually here," she insisted. "Right now, I'm in my apartment, sitting on my couch, and holding a controller in my hand.

There's a TV in front of me. I'm pressing buttons to open the menu and move around."

"What you're saying doesn't make sense," Kiwi said.

"There's a sympathetic link between the menu clocks here and the clocks on Earth. It's been close to twenty hours since I started playing. What's happening to my body? There's gotta be some way out of here."

"You said that you are sitting on a couch with a controller," Ari said. "What's a controller?"

"It's something that players use to make things happen in games. It looks like that thing that appears under the menu."

"No, Tasha," Ari said. "There's nothing like that in my menu."

Kiwi shook her head. "I've never heard of anyone having a 'controller' under the menu."

She examined the floating controller that appeared under her menu. She had assumed that everyone else had one too, but now she was forced to reconsider that assumption.

"So, it's just something that I have," she said. She picked up the floating controller. When she had first arrived, she'd briefly experimented with using it but found the touchscreen interface to be more useful. Now she wondered whether the controller had a different function.

Was there some way that she could escape this world? How did players normally stop playing? Well, of course, they paused the game by pressing the start button.

"I'm sorry, friends," she said, "but I have to stop the world for awhile."

Looking at the controller in her hand, she hit the start button. The long rectangular rubber button pressed in... and then everything changed.

Tasha was no longer in Etheria. She was sitting on her couch with a controller in her hand and her finger over the start button. She released it and put down the controller. On her plasma TV was a pixelated tile-based representation of the city of Belcross. A 16-bit sprite avatar of herself stood in the center of the screen, surrounded by sprite versions of Kiwi, Ari, Slimon, and Pan. The word "PAUSED" blinked on and off in the center of the screen. Light shone in through the window, causing a sliver of light to appear over the screen.

Then the pain hit her. Her eyes felt like they were on fire. Her head pounded rhythmically, more painful than the worst hangover she'd ever experienced. Her throat burned and had none of its usual moisture.

She looked down at her body. Still dressed in her bathrobe, the weight that she had lost in-game had returned. Before she could continue to take in the situation, she was consumed by a desperately urgent call of nature.

One bathroom visit later, she realized that she was exhausted, starving, and in dire need of water. She fished out a frozen lasagna from the freezer and threw it into the microwave. Needing a side dish, she opened a packet of strawberry Pop-Tarts and put them in the toaster. While she waited, she downed half a gallon of water.

There were stories about people who had died of thirst because they became so engrossed in video games that they forgot to take care of their bodies. If she hadn't realized her situation and found a way out of Etheria, would that have happened to her as well?

Shoveling bits of lasagna into her mouth, she pulled out her smartphone. The time said 79:44:51 and was counting downward steadily, one second at a time. The battery had run down to 22%. This whole adventure started on Friday night. She had left work at 6:40 and should have gotten home around 7:30 p.m. If she had been playing the game for twenty hours, that would mean the current time would be about 3:30 p.m. on Saturday. That meant she'd actually been awake for nearly thirty-four hours.

She was late for work! A moment of panic and fear began to rise within her, but she pushed it back down. Why did she care? Neither of her resurrected selves wouldn't have cared, but she had returned to her original body, and the thought of losing her job terrified her. Ultimately the question was moot. Even if she did want to go in, she couldn't work in her condition. Tasha was so exhausted she could barely keep her eyes open.

After wolfing down the Pop-Tarts, she made her way to the bedroom. The bed was covered in piles of laundry that she had never gotten around to folding and putting away. Her eyes began to close on their own. Her head continued to throb in rhythmic pain brought on by the combination of hunger, thirst, sleep deprivation, and exhaustion.

She shoved the clean, unfolded laundry to one side of the bed. Her bathrobe fell to the floor as she sandwiched herself between the mattress and quilt. The moment Tasha's head hit her pillow, she was already asleep.

She awoke to find herself lying facedown on her own bed. A small puddle of drool had appeared on her pillow, so she turned it over and made a half-hearted attempt to go back to sleep. How long had she slept? It must have been a long time. Turning on to her side, she saw the wind blowing against the curtain, causing it to sway back and forth. Sunlight shone through the open window.

Slowly and with great reluctance, she forced herself to push away the covers and get out of bed. Quickly finishing the bottle of water that she'd left by the side of her bed several days earlier, she stood up and made her way to the bathroom. As she walked through the hallway, she made out the TV screen in the living room—an ominous presence with the word "PAUSE" still blinking on and off over and over. Some part of her still waking-up brain told her that it was important, but a more rational part of her mind remained focused on getting a shower. Pretending that she didn't see the TV, she opened the door to the bathroom and went inside.

She turned the knob, and cold water poured from the shower, falling on her skin. It took a moment for the hot water to travel through the pipes and reach the shower, and soon the bathroom filled with steam, fogging the glass. As the warm water washed over her body, the morning confusion and disorientation drifted away.

Ah, yes. She remembered now. She had been sucked into a video game and had only just escaped last night. How much time had passed? Instinctively, she tried to bring up the menu. Of course, nothing happened, and she realized the futility of that action right away. This was the real world, after all.

After showering, she threw on some clean clothing and went to the kitchen. Though she'd managed to escape from Etheria, the idea of not returning never crossed her mind. She was more concerned with how much time had passed since she had fallen asleep. Last night the clock showed less than eighty hours remaining.

The microwave's LED display showed 64 hours, 35 minutes, and 55 seconds. 54... 53... 52... She must have slept for something like fifteen hours last night. Time was counting down in its steady progression, and that was more than a little problematic.

A part of her wanted to pick up the controller and unpause the game right away, but a low rumble emerged from the stomach. She imagined herself eating a big fluffy stack of pancakes covered in maple syrup. And whipped cream. And powdered sugar. And maybe sprinkles. And some sausages. Before she could return to Etheria, she would have to bring this wish to fruition. She was a woman of action now, and pancakes were well within her capabilities.

She went through her cupboards and finally found some pancake mix. Adding some water, oil, and the last of the eggs in the refrigerator, she mixed them together in a wooden bowl along with some blueberries and poured the concoction onto the preheated skillet next to the already sizzling sausage patties.

Ten minutes later, she was drizzling syrup over the stack of pancakes, which was already dripping with butter. Upon applying the whipped cream, powdered sugar, and multicolored sprinkles, her creation was complete. A few rogue splotches of syrup had escaped and covered the sausage. Sausage covered with maple syrup was the best. When she'd finally finished, her belly was full, and she felt satisfied.

This would normally be the time when she'd take a short post-pancake nap, but there wasn't time for that.

She was about to return to the game and attempt to reenter Etheria when her phone started vibrating, moving slightly on the table where she had placed it. Tasha picked it up and looked at the caller ID. It was her horrible boss. Of course it was.

Tasha briefly considered ignoring the call, but an unexpected rush of fear came over her. She could lose her job if she didn't answer. She tapped on the "answer" button reflexively.

"H-hello?"

"Tasha—you incompetent layabout! You blistering nincompoop! You were expected to be at work yesterday. I hope you have a damn good explanation for this."

"Sorry, Hubert. I... was sick. Erm... I came down with..." *Quick, think of some believable illness.* "The bubonic plague."

Crap!

The gruff voice on the other end of the line sounded annoyed. "Like I haven't heard that excuse a thousand times. Look, Tasha—because I'm such a nice guy, I'm going to give you one last chance. But if this ever happens again, I'll have you out on the street! You'll be fired for skipping work, so don't expect to be collecting any unemployment, you parasite! You'll be begging for scraps and living in a cardboard box, which is better than you deserve."

Tasha scrunched up her nose. "A cardboard box?" *Why did it have to be a cardboard box?*

"Tasha, all I need to hear from you is that you'll be at work on time today."

"What time is it now?" Tasha's phone still showed the countdown and wouldn't tell her the time. She could tell that it was early morning from the light shining through the open window, but that was it.

"It's 7:15. I'll expect you in at eight a.m., and since you missed work yesterday, I'm going to need you to stay until eight p.m. tonight."

Tasha sighed. "You do know it's Sunday, right?"

"What, do you expect me to believe that you have church? Just get to work, or you can consider yourself unemployed."

Everything was a power game to her boss. She knew that she'd never win any kind of argument with him, regardless of how bizarre or unfair his argument was. Tasha glanced at the front of her cell phone. 64:05. She didn't want to lose that much time in Etheria, but she really didn't want to be fired.

She opened a ride-sharing app on her phone and called for a car to take her to work. She didn't know the bus's schedule and couldn't afford to show up late.

Rushing to her room, she threw on some clean-adjacent work clothes and rushed downstairs just in time to meet the driver as he pulled up. While riding in the back seat of the SUV, Tasha checked her messages. They were all from her boss, dated yesterday. She didn't have any friends outside of work—Hubert kept her so busy with work that there just wasn't enough time for her to foster lasting friendships. The friendships that she'd built up in Etheria were the only ones that felt real to her. The time that she would be able to spend with them ticked away as the timer diminished, one second after the next. Every second that ticked away was precious to her.

Fifteen minutes later, the driver let her out at her workplace. It was one of countless office buildings that lined the downtown area. She stepped inside and waved to the bored-looking security guy, who didn't even bother to look up as she passed. She pressed the button that summoned the elevator. After waiting for about a minute or so, the door slid open, revealing its cramped interior. A short elevator ride later, and she reached the twentieth floor.

She walked through a maze of corridors that led to her cramped workspace. The company couldn't afford much in the way of niceties or space. She'd often fantasized about working at a game company that was less stingy with their capital when it came to creature comforts, such as reliable air-conditioning and chairs that didn't induce lower back trauma.

Finally, she reached the glass doors that led to a small open area with about a dozen desks all crammed together. The company's name and logo was plastered on the glass entrance. Even though it was the weekend, the office was abuzz with activity. Her employer was not a strong believer in weekends for his underlings.

The lead artist, a squirrely Chinese man named Lee, motioned to her as she entered. "Hi, Tasha. Hubert wants to see you about something."

"Thanks, Lee," she said and dodged between the crowded desks to reach Hubert's office.

Hubert was a short bald man with a stubby nose and an unsettlingly pale complexion. Not as unsettlingly pale as the king's court mage, Snickers, but unsettling nonetheless.

He sat alone in his office, pretending that he hadn't noticed Tasha coming in. He was the only person in the company who actually had an office. Everyone else was relegated to the open studio. His desk was made of the finest mahogany, his chair easily twice the size of everyone else's despite his posterior taking only half the amount of space, making his butt-to-chair ratio the most uneven in the company.

Tasha knocked on the door and opened it. "Hi, boss." Her voice lacked the assertiveness of Tasha #2 or the passion of Tasha #3. She was just plain old Tasha, her normal meek and non-confrontational self. She was not looking forward to this.

Hubert put up one finger to silence her and went back to filing his nails. He was actually filing his nails, it wasn't some sort of act. Tasha didn't even think that she owned a nail file. She waited patiently for him to finish grooming himself. After what Hubert probably calculated to be a sufficient period of time, he turned his attention to her. "Please, have a seat, Tasha."

The only other seat in the room was covered in a stack of paper documents. A copy of *The Fountainhead* was at the top of the pile. Tasha set everything aside and pulled the chair toward the desk.

Her boss didn't even bother to look up from filing his nails. Over the years, Tasha had come to realize that her boss had a pathological need to make others feel inferior in his presence.

For a long time, he didn't speak. Finally Tasha said, "Boss, I—"

But of course, Hubert was just waiting for her to be the first one to speak so he could cut her off. "Tasha, your not coming in to work yesterday was unacceptable. That, coupled with your recent insubordinate attitude, has led me to reconsider your employment here."

"Really?" Tasha asked. "But you just told me that both of my colleagues quit. How are you going to run a game company without any programmers?"

Her boss finally deigned to looked up at her. "You're lucky that's the case. When I said that I would reconsider your employment, I merely meant I would reconsider your rate of pay. For now, I'm cutting your annual salary by $10,000."

She was already being paid way below the industry average. With that kind of pay cut, she wasn't even sure she would be able to cover the rent.

"But..." she started before Hubert interrupted her.

"In six months, if the quality of your work has improved and you've lost that insubordinate attitude, I might consider reinstating your original salary. I'm glad we had this talk. You may go."

"Now, just a minute..." she started, but again she was interrupted.

Hubert went back to filing his nails. "That's all I have to say to you. Now get to work. I want to deliver the next contract to our client by the end of the month."

She inadvertently took a step back toward the door. She was starting to tear up, and she hated it. "Boss, you can't expect me to work for so little. I'm already being underpaid for the work that I do."

Hubert slammed his nail file onto his desk, which wasn't as dramatic as it sounded. "Don't you tell your betters what they can and can't do. I'm sick of you damn millennials always blaming others for your problems and expecting everything to be handed to you on a silver platter. If you can't afford the rent, why don't you move in with your parents? That's what you people do, isn't it?"

She turned toward the door.

"Don't turn your back on me, you over-privileged thief! You are lucky to have a job in the game industry. Do you know how many people would give anything to be in your position?"

"But... I need that money to pay my rent. Won't you reconsider?"

Hubert just laughed. "If you weren't so damn ugly we might be able to work something out. Would it really kill you to skip a meal? I'm doing you a favor by giving you less money for junk food. Now get the hell out of my office."

She didn't move. Her hands were shaking.

"Didn't you hear me? Get out! You have work to do."

She looked up and met his eyes, something that was frowned on in the studio. "No. I quit."

Her boss stood up from his chair. "What did you just say?"

She opened her mouth, but no words came out.

"That's what I thought," he said. "I'll just pretend I didn't hear anything."

Something in her snapped.

"I quit! I hate working for you. I hate this company! 你是一个剥削鬼，我非常讨厌你，厌恶为你工作。你是一个吸血鬼老板，每天让我无偿加班，节假日也没有休息。我们天天工作像机器人，我们都恨你，现在我不要这份工作了，我把你给开了。见鬼去吧。"

She didn't realize it right away, but halfway into her rage-quit, she'd slipped into Mandarin.

The eyes of everyone in the company were on her. The glass partitions around the boss's office were not designed to filter sound.

"Wait!" said her boss. "I didn't mean it! I'll reinstate your original salary."

"他妈的！"

"Look, I didn't mean it. I'll give you a $4,000 salary increase if you stay."

That much money would bring her up to the industry average, but it would mean staying here, at this company that she hated. It would mean working for Hubert. The path of least resistance demanded that she stay, which was why she had to leave.

"No. I'm leaving. Goodbye, Hubert," Tasha said as she headed for the door.

"You can't quit! You're fired!"

"It doesn't work that way."

If Hubert offered any response, Tasha couldn't hear it. She returned to her desk and started gathering up her meager possessions.

The lead artist approached her. "Tasha, I had no idea you could speak Chinese. That was rather unexpected. Where did you learn that?"

"From kung fu movies, I guess," she answered. "I mean, if you can't say something nice, say it in Mandarin."

"So... I could give you a letter of reference if you want."

"Yeah, thanks, Lee. I'll be in touch."

She grabbed the remainder of her possessions from her desk, and five minutes later was in a rideshare car on her way back to her apartment. It finally began to hit her that she'd just rage-quit her job. She expected to feel panicked, but instead she felt a strange sense of peace. If her luck held out, she might be able to find a new job in the industry without too much effort. She wouldn't be relegated to life in a cardboard box... hopefully.

But during her rage-quit, she had started speaking Mandarin. That was a Couch Potato ability that she had unlocked while playing. If her ability to speak Chinese carried over from Etheria back to Earth, what other abilities might she have?

After stepping out of the car, she attempted to double jump. She jumped into the air and attempted to jump a second time while airborne. Nothing happened. Okay, what about Sprint? She invoked Sprint and started running. This time the ability kicked in, and she ran at high speed down the block. Five seconds later, she came to a stop, slightly out of breath. She'd run a good distance in five seconds, but nothing that she wouldn't have been able to do normally.

It seemed that only certain skills carried over. An ability would only carry over if it didn't break the laws of physics and was something that a person would normally be able to do.

She realized that she'd already spent too much time fiddling around with her new abilities. It was time to return to Etheria. She'd wasted enough time on earthly concerns.

After returning to her apartment, she grabbed a bag of cheesy corn snacks and went back to the couch in the living room. She was about to pick up the controller when an idea struck her. Opening the closet, she fished around until she found her video camera. Her mother had given it to her as a gift last Christmas, but she'd not had the opportunity to use it, what with cell phones also being able to record video.

She put in a fresh SD card with lots of memory and set the tripod up behind the living room couch so that it could record both herself and the TV. She wanted to know what the game looked like while she was playing it and what her body did while she was away. Upon pressing the record button, a small red light appeared on top of the camera.

The time was 63:18:04. Returning her phone to the safety of her pocket, she made her way to the couch. Sinking into the cushions, she took the controller in her hands.

She pressed the rubbery start button and was overtaken by a momentary sense of vertigo as she returned to Etheria. Her earthly body was gone, replaced by stat-augmented strength, agility, and charisma. Tasha felt lighter and stronger once again. Maybe she could think of this as the real world and Earth as the dream. That might actually be preferable.

Less than a second after Tasha's return to Etheria, a multitude of dwarven voices rang out in chorus with the word "Zero!"

"What do you mean, you need to stop the universe?" Kiwi asked. "Are you returning to the world of players?"

Realizing that Kiwi was referring to something that Tasha had said before pressing the start button, she answered.

"I already did, just now. I've been gone for over fifteen hours."

The sound of confused murmurs could be heard from the reveling dwarves. They must have noticed that something was amiss.

"You're joking, right?" Ari said. "You haven't left this spot. I was watching you this whole time."

"I'll prove it. Check your menu clock."

Ari opened his menu. His jaw dropped open. "The clock says 63:18:01. It was at eighty just a few seconds ago. Then it's true, you really did stop Etheria."

"And the clocks show the countdown from the world of players," she said.

Over the night chill and the sound of confused celebrants, the shrill cry of a dwarven woman rang out. Another panicking voice spoke up, "What the hell is that!??"

A dwarven man was pointing into the air. "Up there, in the sky! It's..."

His voice was cut off by a shrill high-pitched sound coming from the jar strapped to Tasha's waist. The fairy-in-a-bottle said, "Holy crap, what's that thing in the sky?"

"T-Tasha's jar is talking," Pan said.

"Oh, hi, Trista," Tasha said. "I forgot about you."

"Well, screw you too, human. Just hurry up and look where I'm pointing so you can start panicking like the rest of us sane people!"

Lifting her head to follow where the fairy was indicating, Tasha immediately saw what she was talking about. Suspended in the sky, fully visible, was a small sliver of light spinning and winding into patterns. What was it? A long thread that coiled and danced in the air? For a moment it disappeared behind some clouds, but once those passed, it could be seen clearly.

"Pan, would you let me borrow your spyglass for a moment?"

Tasha looked through it and saw the object with slightly more clarity, though it was still small and blurry. She could almost make it out its form. It was like a serpent or snake, just floating there in the sky.

"I think it's a snake. A sky serpent?"

"It's Entropy!" someone shouted. "It's the destroyer god, come to end us all! Entropy comes! Entropy comes!"

"He's right," said Kiwi. "Entropy must be getting closer as the clock winds down. In another twenty hours, I would bet that we'll be able to see him clearly. When the time runs down, the contract keeping him away will nullify, and he'll coil around Etheria, squeezing all life out of it. I didn't truly believe in the threat until just this moment."

"Then we'll have to stop him," Tasha said. "We'll get the elemental orbs, open the Hallowed Chapel, and I'll get rid of the contract. Let's finish this part of the quest and find the Orb of Life."

"Agreed," said Ari, "but let's start tomorrow. We're all tired and need sleep."

"Not me. I just got fifteen hours of sleep while on Earth."

"Really?" Kiwi said. "And you're not tired? That's interesting, but the rest of us need sleep."

"Stupid trans-universal jet lag," Tasha grumbled, and the party went off in the direction of their inn.

Maybe Tasha could have Kiwi cast a sleep spell to overcome her insomnia. And then tomorrow they could get more pancakes before setting out.

CHAPTER 37

The Dragon and the Dwarf

Kaze's return trip to Brightwind took longer than he'd anticipated. He found it difficult to remain airborne for extended periods of time. Sometimes the wind would push against him, and often the upper air pressure would gradually lower his altitude. Kaze could only assume that it was the effect of the Orb of Air. It seemed that the orb was resisting his attempt to carry it away from its master.

His journey consisted of short low-altitude hops from one point to another. It was still faster than walking but not by as wide a margin as he had hoped. What should have taken days of flying was extended into multiple weeks of travel.

The mobs that spawned while airborne were different than the ones that spawned while he was on the ground. There were drakes, condors, beholders, exploding balloon creatures, and other such monsters of the air. Normally he would either fight such creatures or fly away from them, but given his inability to remain airborne for extended periods of time, his only option was to prevent air-based mobs from spawning in the first place. Whenever mist would begin to form around him, he quickly returned to the ground before it could form into an air-based mob.

In the end, it took him several weeks of travel to return to the outskirts of Questgivria and several days beyond that to reach Brightwind Keep.

When he finally made it through the capital city that surrounded Brightwind Keep, people moved to one side or the other as he passed. As a general rule, one did not get in the way of a dragon when one could avoid doing so.

"Lally ho, dragon!" said a gruff dwarven voice over the murmuring of the crowd. Kaze bent his neck to find the source of the sound and finally discovered his friend Hermes mixed in with the crowd. The dwarf closed the distance and embraced the dragon in a big one-armed hug, which wasn't actually so big given the comparative statures of the two adventurers. It was embarrassing for all parties involved, so the dwarf kindly pulled away before it got weird.

Hello, friend Hermes.

"Kaze, what are you doing here? Don't tell me you died."

No, actually, I'm here on a mission from the princess. I have the Orb of Air with me. Much has happened since we parted ways. I meant to thank you for saving my life, by the by. Nobody has ever saved my life before.

"Bah, forget it. It just worked out that way. I'm sure you would have done the same for me."

Will you accompany me to the castle? I must meet with the king as soon as possible.

The dwarf looked at the ground and fiddled with his beard. "Well, the thing about that is, Penryth the red dragon is in the castle, and he's none too happy with me right now. I'm trying to give him some space so he doesn't incinerate me."

What? Why is he angry with you?

"I refused to give him your location after I respawned. It seemed like a good idea at the time."

We shall see about this. Come with me.

The dwarf reluctantly followed Kaze through the city and toward the castle. The guards let the pair through without incident. They were directed to the war room, where they found the king meeting with several elven nobles as well as the dragon Penryth. The war room was large enough to accommodate all of them, though Penryth did take up a sizable section of the room.

Everyone was understandably upset about the appearance of Entropy in the night sky just days earlier, their fears now realized. There was no longer any doubt about the nature of the threat.

Hermes and Kaze had to wait outside for several minutes until they were given permission to enter.

The elven lord stood at the head of the great mahogany table. The table itself was a rare monster drop that the scan identified as an Exquisite Mahogany Table. Nobody in Etheria had the faintest clue as to what mahogany was, only that it was of a particularly high quality.

Penryth focused on the smaller steam dragon as he entered the room.

Kaze! I am overjoyed that you have returned to us. You should not have followed the bipeds.

Kaze lowered his head to the ground. *Are you very angry with me?*

No. I understand why you wanted to go with them, foolish decision though it was. It is enough that you are returned to us. The large red dragon sniffed at the air. *Why do I smell dwarf? Hermes, is that you?*

Hermes, who had been hiding behind the door and hadn't entered, stepped into the room. "Penryth."

I thought I had made it clear that I would slay you if I ever saw you again. It is fortunate for you that you are in the high lord's castle.

"Hey, I didn't want to be here either." Hermes indicated the little dragon. "It was his idea."

Kaze, why have you brought this dwarf into my presence?

Kaze raised his head from the ground and thought-spoke, *This dwarf died to save my life. We were fighting an enemy many levels above us, and he sacrificed his life to save my own. His final moments were spent recovering my health. I owe him my gratitude and respect.*

The red dragon stomped across the room, very nearly damaging the mahogany table as he went. He lowered his nose until it was inches from the dwarf, who tried to back away, but he was already against the wall.

Is this true, dwarf?

"I... er... that is to say, I suppose so. I didn't think it was that big a deal. He needed health, so I fed him a potion. The Jabberwock killed me a few seconds later."

The dragon drew his head back, and a thoughtful look crossed his face. *It appears I misjudged you.*

"It's no big deal. Forget it."

This is impossible. No dwarf has ever given his life to save a dragon. Your folk have shown my kind nothing but hate and disgust. Not since the days before King Dourmal's rule.

Hermes looked uncomfortable. "Well, I'm glad you're not angry at me anymore. Does this mean that you won't kill me after all?"

Indeed. Tell me, Prince Hermes, if you were to become King Under the Laundry Mountain, would you let us back in and return our eggs to us?

"Well, yes, I suppose so. I don't think it's especially likely that I will ever become king, however."

At that point, King Iolo Questgiver stepped forward. "Kaze, what is that box tied around your neck? I sense a powerful energy coming from it."

The steam dragon approached the elven king. *Take it. This is the Orb of Air. The player took it from Captain K'her Noálin, and your daughter send me to deliver it to you.*

The elven king took the small box from the dragon's neck and placed it upon the table. When he opened the box, a glowing orb lay nested within. Eddies of wind played in patterns within the globe.

The elf spoke to a male attendant, who left the room and returned minutes later with a thick metallic box etched with intricate designs. King Questgiver put on a pair of gloves before removing the orb and placing it into the box. After shutting the lid, the king turned to Kaze.

"Well done, Kaze. You have done this kingdom a great service. I wish to hear about my daughter. How does the princess fare?"

Kaze spent the next long while relating their adventures. About the flying monkey attack and how he'd joined her in the bizarrely rabbit-themed dungeon. He spoke of their travels together, the pirate attack, and how he single-handedly took down three pirate dirigibles before the rest could get away.

The following morning, Penryth and Kaze left the castle on their journey to Dragonholm at the North Pole. They had much to do and not much time to do it. The Dragon Kingdom was joining the quest for the orbs. Their days of idleness had passed.

The time had come to amass an army.

CHAPTER 38

The Bog of Most Likely Death

I t was early morning the following day, and the last remains of breakfast was being cleared away. The inn's continental breakfast didn't offer pancakes, unfortunately, so Tasha had to settle for French toast. Tasha sighed a pancakeless sigh. *Life is so hard when you're me.*

Henimaru had stayed in a different room than Tasha, but he had still joined them for breakfast before departing on his own journey into Zhakara.

"And now, my wife, I must take my leave. My journey leadeth me to the south, toward the human lands. Though the rescue is yet a daunting task, thanks to thee, I now have hope. If I am successful, I promise to annul our marriage as soon as I returneth with my offspring to more civilized lands."

Henimaru took Tasha's hand and kissed it before leaving through the swinging bar door.

The group drank their caffeinated beverages in silence for several minutes. "He wasn't such a bad... toad-person," said Tasha. "So, where do we head from here?"

Princess Kiwi set down her soymilk vanilla chai latte. "Belcross is less than a day's ride from the perimeter of the Bog of Most Likely Death. There's an outpost right outside the bog. We'll use their save point before venturing into the bog.

"It will take us several days of travel through the bog to reach the Spiral Tower. At the top of the spire lies the Orb of Life. It is protected by an impregnable field that can only be crossed by a person that the orb has allied with. The Orb of Life was once allied with my father, King Questgiver. With luck it, will ally with me as well."

"So, there's a *chance* that we won't be able to retrieve the orb at all?" Tasha asked.

"There's always been that possibility. We'll need to climb the interior of the Spiral Tower to reach it. Father said that the interior is a dungeon, so we'll need to fight our way to the top floor."

Tasha didn't look very pleased. "So once we cross the Bog of Most Likely Death, climb the tower, and retrieve the orb, we'll be two-sixths of the way done with our journey, right? There are six orbs and even getting this one has been a considerable challenge."

"Pfffpt... pppft, pffpt," suggested Slimon.

"Okay, Slimon's right," Tasha said. "I'll bet this one is the hardest to acquire and the rest will be easy by comparison."

"Well," Ari said, "there's no time like the present. Let's head out as soon as we finish our drinks."

The fairy Trista knocked on the side of the jar from the inside. "Listen, how about you idiots just let me go? You don't need to drag me with you all the way to whatever certain death you have in mind."

Tasha picked up the jar and held it at eye level. The fairy balanced on the bottom of the slippery glass jar. "If we let you go, you'll just try to murder us and kidnap the princess again."

"That's right, exactly!" the fairy said, then she clamped her hands on her mouth. "Uh, wait. No, I meant that I won't do those things. Honest."

Kiwi took the jar and held it up. "Why do you want to kidnap me? I've never done anything to you."

The fairy put her hands on her hips. "I couldn't care less whether you get kidnapped. You're just another contract to me. The only thing that matters is the honor of my ninja village, and that means fulfilling our contracts. It's nothing personal."

Kiwi looked angry. "It's nothing personal? You want to take my freedom away and turn me over to a madwoman. Do you know what she'll do if she captures me?"

"That isn't relevant to my contract. Listen, if you jerks aren't going to let me go, could you at least add some air holes? It's getting pretty rank in here."

"Air holes?" Tasha considered. "I guess we could do that."

"Or"—Pan giggled—"we c-could leave the jar... ajar! Get it? B-because it's a jar, and the lid would also be ajar."

Tasha gave her a dry look. "Pan, we can't be friends anymore."

Pan looked like she was going to tear up.

"Oh my god, bad joke! Sorry, it's just a saying in my world!"

Fortunately, even though the jar itself was unbreakable, the lid wasn't. Tasha used her utility knife to poke a few holes in the jar's lid. She even stuffed a small piece of French toast into the jar with her before leaving the inn.

The rest of the day was spent riding southward toward the bog across the open terrain. Since they'd left Slime's Row, they had been attacked by various assassins, but they were surprisingly weak and easy to take down. It was almost as though the queen wasn't really trying. Still, not being attacked by flying monkeys and evil queens was a blessing whichever way you looked at it.

With luck, the ninjas wouldn't cause any additional trouble. Their ninja boss wouldn't be able to order her minions to attack, what with said boss being imprisoned in a glass jar.

The journey south was largely uneventful. On the other side of a lake, a pack of brontosauruses was grazing, and it was fun watching them do their thing. Back home, nobody would believe her, so she snapped a few photos with her phone.

The mobs were fairly tame in this area. They encountered some level 14 gelatinous cubes that Kiwi was able to take out using fireball spells. At their level, the XP wasn't worth much, but Tasha did receive a notification that Trista had leveled up twice. It was never Tasha's intention to help her enemy level up, but at this point she had little choice in the matter. The only way she could ensure that the fairy wasn't a threat would be to take her with.

The outpost was a small settlement that bordered the bog, bordered by a wall composed of wooden pikes that jutted out from the ground. As she entered the small settlement, a bored dwarven guard let the group through without looking up from his trashy romance novel.

After registering at the save point, Tasha spoke to the stable master about arranging lodging for Denver and the riding chickens. It was painful for Tasha to part with her friend, but it was for the best, and only for a little while. Kiwi had cautioned her that the Bog of Most Likely Death was no place for a chicken or a velociraptor.

They spent the night at the inn before setting out. That evening after eating, Princess Kiwistafel gathered everyone together.

"Tomorrow we are going to pass through the Bog of Most Likely Death. It will take us about three days to pass through it and reach the Spiral Tower."

Pan raised her hand. "Pan, you don't need to raise your hand," Kiwi said. "If you have a question, just ask."

Putting her hand back down, she asked, "Why is it c-called the Bog of Most Likely Death?"

"Well, let me explain. It used to be called the Bog of *Certain* Death, but then somebody made it through to the other side, so they had to rename it to the Bog of Most Likely Death. The person who made it through the bog was my father, which means I do have some information that will increase our chances of surviving it."

"We're all ears," Tasha said.

Kiwi blinked. "What does that mean?" She touched her ears. "Are you teasing me?"

"What? No! It's a figure of speech. It just means we're listening."

Kiwi seemed to simmer down, but she still gave Tasha an odd look. "Yeah. Okay, as you might have figured out from its name, it's a bog. That means we'll be waist deep in bog water. You might want to wear galoshes. Since Lord Designer is constantly changing monster spawns, I have no current information about what kind of mobs we'll be up against. Since we'll need to slog through water, we'll be at a tactical disadvantage."

"Pfffpt!" said Slimon, whose body gyrated in time with his words.

"Yes, dear. Because slimes are aquatic, the terrain will actually give you an advantage."

"This doesn't sound too bad," Tasha said. "Are the mobs super high level or something?"

"No, as far as I know, the monsters won't be higher than level 30. There might be some zones with higher-level monsters, but we can avoid them. The mobs aren't the real danger in the Bog of Most Likely Death.

"The entire bog is covered in a miasma that causes a confuse debuff. The effect only lasts about ten seconds, but every breath you take restores the debuff. The confuse effect can cause you to lose your sense of direction, mistake friend and foe during battle, and will destroy any semblance of battle strategy. The reason travelers nearly always die in the bog is because the confuse debuff causes them to become hopelessly lost and attack one another."

"Do you have some sort of plan to get us through?" Ari said.

Kiwi tapped at the air in front of her, and a bracelet appeared in her hand. "This is a bracelet that nullifies the effect of confuse. The kingdom's armory only had one in stock. There are many that block 80% or 90% of confuse debuffs, but they would be useless in the bog since every breath you take causes confusion. I'll wear it so that I don't waste all of my MP attacking you guys in combat.

"The miasma only reaches about a dozen feet above ground level, so Slimon can reach a tentacle above the miasma when he needs to breathe. Slimes can go for hours between breaths if they need to."

"Pfffpt!" confirmed Slimon.

"Is the confuse debuff anything like being drunk?" Tasha asked.

"No," said Kiwi, "being drunk causes you to lose your inhibitions and make irrational decisions. Being confused causes you to lose your understanding of what is real and what is illusion. You may do or say absurd things while confused that seem reasonable at the time."

"As Slimon and I will be the only ones unaffected by the debuff, we'll lead the way to the Spiral Tower. Any questions?"

Pan raised her hand. "C-can we just wear really tall snorkels?"

Kiwi thought for a minute. "That's crazy enough that it might actually work, but we don't have any twenty-foot snorkels. For now, let's just go with my plan."

The next morning, they set out into the bog. Tasha had never actually seen a real bog before, so she wasn't quite sure what to expect. Turned out, walking through a bog was essentially walking through waist-high muddy water. Sometimes the water only made it up to her knees, though. Movement was much slower than it would have been on dry land. There was the occasional area of comparatively dry grass set upon a hill they could stand on.

Each step involved wading through a cold swampy liquid, and when Tasha's galoshes found purchase, it was not on firm ground. Every so often her legs brushed against some kind of bog vegetation.

And there were bugs, loads of bugs zipping around all over the place. The bog was awash in insect life, and they all swarmed around Tasha, their potential foodstuff of choice. The bug bites were annoying but didn't deal more than one heart worth of damage every half hour. The bites itched and stung like hell, though. Slimon even cast recovery spells on the party every so often. Tasha was constantly hounded by insect life, and in addition to them feeding on the party, they were loud. The sound of buzzing and chirping was so overpowering that it made conversation difficult unless they were standing right against one another.

As she continued to travel further into the bog, a dense miasma drew in around the group, making it hard to breathe, and just as Kiwi had warned, the "confuse" debuff appeared on Tasha's HUD next to her hearts. Visibility was severely limited, and she could only see a few feet in front of herself.

Tasha didn't feel confused, despite what the debuff said. Everything seemed totally normal. She followed behind Kiwi for a while, but then decided that it would be more interesting to go off on her own. There was a caterpillar wearing a monocle that she wanted to strike up a conversation with. Maybe they could share a spot of tea. It was a bit off in the distance, so she started to move toward it. Just as she got close, a tentacle wrapped around her and brought her back to the group.

"Pfffpt," Slimon said.

"Yeah, whatever. You're not the boss of me."

They continued in this fashion for the better part of an hour. Sometimes one of the party would go off on their own, but Slimon kept bringing them back. At one point he suggested tying ropes around the confused party members so they wouldn't wander off. Before he could put that plan into effect, though, there was an attack.

There wasn't any warning. The thick miasma caused the gathering mist to be all but invisible.

"Something grabbed my leg!" said Kiwi as she moved back toward the group.

"It wasn't me," Pan protested.

"I didn't think it was. Everyone gather into a circle."

The group moved together into a circle, facing outward. Actually, Ari and Pan were both facing *inside* the circle, but to be fair, Kiwi had not specified that they should be facing outward.

"What is it?" Tasha asked. "Did Mr. Caterpillar come back? Is he inviting us over for cocoa and biscuits? I *love* cocoa and biscuits."

"What? No, I think we're being attacked, but I can't see any monsters. I'm telling you, something grabbed my leg."

"And I'm t-telling you," Pan said, "it wasn't me."

"Pan, Ari, turn around and face outside the circle. Keep an eye out for monsters."

For nearly a minute, the group watched the bog. "There's nothing there," said Ari, "nothing but dry sand as far as the eye can see."

"Okay," Kiwi said, "let's start moving again. Stick together, though, just in case."

They moved together as a group. After a few steps, Tasha felt her feet crunch down against something. It happened again after her next step.

Tasha looked at the bog water apprehensively. "Guys, I think there's something crunchy under the water. I suspect tortilla chips. The crunchy kind, not the lady-friendly kind."

"If it's tortilla chips," Trista said, "can you slip one of them into my jar? Maybe some salsa too."

"Slimon, can you see what it is from under the water?" Kiwi said.

The sound of burbling coming from the water was the only response. Since Slimon was underwater, his normal method of conversation would be ineffective.

Tasha continued moving. Each step sounded like she was walking on hollow eggshells. Less than a minute later, Tasha felt something grab her leg, and she was pulled to the bottom of the bog. Being hit by any attack removed the confuse debuff, so she instantly came to her senses.

The glowing image of a skeletal wraith appeared in the water before her. Blue flames hovered in the apparition's otherwise empty eye sockets. It was wreathed in a glowing tattered white cloak.

Ghast (Level 25)
Remnants of the once living, made animate by spite and envy.
ATK 33   Mag ATK 41
DEF 8   Mag DEF 18

It wasn't attacking her, but it was holding her under the water. Along the bog floor were countless skulls that Tasha had been crushing beneath her feet. Why had she ever thought they were tortilla chips?

Most of her breath had been expelled when she gasped as the wraith pulled her under. She tried to equip her gunblade but couldn't see the heads-up interface properly.

Finally, after several seconds of failed attempts, she was able to hit the equip button, and the gunblade appeared in her hand. Swinging it at the ghoul under the water ended up being futile. The water resistance pushed against the sword, slowing its speed. The sword did penetrate his ghostly cloak, but it passed right through it, dealing no damage.

The rest of Tasha's breath left her, and panic began to set in. She waved her arms and legs wildly. At some point her gunblade fell to the bottom of the bog. She must have dropped it while struggling against the monster. She tried swinging her fists at it wildly. The third strike connected against his skull but only did one heart of damage. Tasha wasn't a hand-to-hand fighter, and her strikes were clearly ineffective.

Just as she was about to pass out for want of air, she saw lines of distortion pass through the water, one after another. Pan must be firing at it with her machine gun. It was lucky for Tasha that the gun seemed to work underwater. Some of the bullets impacted the skull, which shattered into pieces, and the flames that were its eyes vanished into nothing as the bones and cloak dissolved into mist. Ari's hand grabbed her and pulled her above the water.

"Now is no time for a swim, Tasha. You should change into your swimming suit first."

Tasha coughed out some bog water that had entered her lungs and drew in one breath after another. The confuse debuff returned as air entered her lungs. She was down to four heart containers, but Kiwi was already casting a healing spell. Tasha felt the healing effect wash over her.

"I... think I left my swimming suit back on Earth," Tasha said. She reached under the water and retrieved her gunblade. The battle menu said that seven of the ghast enemies remained.

Once she knew what to look for, the battle wasn't too difficult. The only advantage that the ghasts had against her was the element of surprise. She took out several ghasts as they were ganging up on her by stabbing them in the glowy bits where their eyes should have been. Sure, she might have accidentally attacked Ari and Kiwi a few times, but they couldn't in all fairness expect her to get everything right.

When the battle ended, their party had killed thirty ghasts. Slimon actually did most of the work since he could move swiftly in the water, and the ghasts were not easily able to grasp his slippery surface.

They took several minutes to recover from their near-death encounter. After a moment, Kiwi walked up to Tasha. "Tasha, we need to get going. We have a long way to go before it gets dark."

Several hours later, they were attacked by a new type of insubstantial translucent ghostlike monster that glided through the air.

Bog Wight (Level 27)
Swords won't work. You can't slay something that is already dead.
ATK 0   Mag ATK 50
DEF 20   Mag DEF 38

They were insubstantial, so their weapons did little more than pass through the creatures. Fortunately, Slimon and Kiwi were able to use recovery magic on them. Since they were undead, recovery magic had the opposite effect on them. Healing spells caused the wraiths to receive damage and become substantial and momentarily vulnerable to physical attacks.

Although the creatures looked fearsome, once their patterns were revealed, defeating them was fairly easy.

Finally the party defeated the enemy wights. The confused party members had dealt more damage to one another than the enemy, but every time Pan accidentally shot someone other than a wight, Slimon would heal them up right away. The only real danger was of Slimon or Kiwi running out of mana.

They encountered one more set of bog wights before the sky began to darken. It was time to find shelter for the night. Finding a large hill that was above the water level, Kiwi activated a portable campsite and set up a large tent. Since they were just above the miasma, the group returned to their normal levels of sanity. The campsite spell repelled both mobs and wild animals, but Tasha was especially pleased to discover that it repelled insects.

For the first time in her travels in Etheria, Tasha was able to make out the shape of the campsite's influence. The sphere's surface was made visible by a mass of insects that were buzzing right on the surface, trying to get in. It was like a dome composed entirely of bugs.

As Tasha watched it, fascinated, she heard a sharp squeaky voice. It was coming from the jar that she had tied to her waist. "Hey, morons! Hurry up and let me out! The jar that you trapped me in is full of bog water."

She looked at the jar. Some of the water had leaked through the air holes, and it was about three quarters of the way full.

"Oh, and by the way, your jar lacks basic bathroom facilities. This is a violation of my rights as a prisoner of war. We let the princess go to the bathroom when she was our prisoner."

Tasha wasn't buying it. "If I let you out, you'll just try to escape. You might even try to kill us in our sleep."

"No, I won't! I mean, not necessarily. Not right away. I need you idiots to help me survive this bog of death that you've dragged me into."

Tasha thought for a moment. "I suppose we could give you a thimble or small box or something to go in. Maybe a smaller jar?"

"I don't think we have any of those things," Ari said.

"Listen," Twinklebottom said, "for the time being, I acknowledge that I'm your prisoner, and I promise not to run away from you kidnappers. I'll even go back into this jar... after you've cleaned it up a bit. Ninja's promise, okay? I just really need to use the bathroom."

"Just let her out," said Ari, "her whining is getting annoying."

"Okay, fine," Tasha said and opened the lid of the jar.

"So long, suckers!" the fairy cried in triumph as she flew into the distance.

"Did any of us not see this coming?" Tasha asked aloud. Nobody answered.

They spent the next half hour enjoying dinner together. Just as she was chewing a mouthful of beef wellington, a high-pitched sound rang out over the bog. It was getting louder. Tasha stood up and opened her inventory.

From out of the darkness, Trista Twinklebottom flew directly at her screaming, "Help! They're going to kill me!"

She was being pursued by a large number of bog wights swarming behind her in the air. She slammed through the campground area, causing a disturbance in the bug dome that surrounded the campsite. While she was flying toward the group, Tasha removed her bug catching net from her inventory and swiped it through the air, catching the fairy in the net once again.

The wraiths impacted the surface of the campground effect, exploding into purple clouds of mist. Tasha grabbed the fairy through the net and pushed her back into her bottle, securing the lid on top.

"I hope you had a nice bathroom break."

"I hope you rot in hell," was Trista's reply.

"I do have some good news."

"Really? Did you all catch some incurable illness and you only have minutes to live before you die painful, agonizing deaths? Oh, please tell me that's the good news."

"Even better! We found a smaller jar after all. Princess Kiwi had one; don't ask me why. You can use it to go to the bathroom from now on, and we won't have to let you out. Here you go."

She opened the jar lid slightly and tossed the tiny jar in. It rolled to a stop on the jar's surface.

"I hate you all," said Trista, "just in case you didn't know that already. It's just nice to say that every so often. Some things shouldn't be left unsaid."

"Good night, Trista," Tasha said, setting her jar against the side of the tent.

That night Tasha played *The Neverending Story* on her enlarged smartphone for the group. That turned out to be a big mistake. Pan started crying at the point when Artax died in the Swamp of Sadness. It was fortunate that they had left Denver behind.

The second day was much like the first. Tasha kept trying to chase down bemonocled caterpillars. It was only thanks to Slimon's eternal vigilance that they were able to keep moving in the right direction.

Whenever Tasha was in the confuse state, she was unaware of her condition. She could see the confuse icon, but it never really registered. Her nonsensical actions always seemed perfectly rational.

The most notable encounter on her second day in the Bog of Most Likely Death was with the giant bog toad. The battle was going about as well as could be expected. Half of the party's attacks ended in friendly fire, but Slimon continued to heal them up and gradually, the toad's hearts were winding down.

Once the toad reached ten hearts, it unleashed a new attack. It snapped out its tongue, which stuck to Tasha's spidersilk armor. It then sucked her in and swallowed her in one gulp. Luckily, the party was able to finish the toad off before it completely digested her.

"Why does this keep happening to me?" Tasha sobbed as she tried to get the toad's digestive fluids out of her hair.

At the end of the second day, they set up camp on a hill that overlooked a clearing set against a cluster of trees. Tasha stood outside the tent, watching the movements of Entropy in the night sky. He was a tiny flowing thread that spun and twisted in patterns.

She was all set to enter the tent and start up a movie, but just as she was about to move from her position, Entropy froze. Tasha could feel his gaze, and a sensation of impending dread overcame her. It was as though her mind had been shattered into thousands of fragments, each focused on the sky snake in primal terror.

She remained captivated in his glare for nearly a minute before he averted his gaze. When he turned his attention away from her, Tasha shuddered involuntarily and entered the tent as quickly as she could. The eyes of a malevolent god had been cast upon her, and she didn't like it one bit.

On the third day, the bog opened up into a flatland. Plant life no longer surrounded them as they had before. For the first time, Tasha laid eyes on the destination. In the distance, the Spiral Tower was a thin needle that impaled the ground. As they continued their march through the flatland toward the tower, the poisonous miasma diminished.

By that evening, they'd cleared the bog and reached the base of the tower.

CHAPTER 39

The Spiral Tower

The adventurers stood at the base of the Spiral Tower, gazing at its form in the crimson sky. The last slivers of evening's light vanished under the horizon.

The screw-shaped tower ascended high above, intersecting with a circular metal plate on the ground. Waves of blue energy circled the outside of the tower along the spiraling protrusions, ultimately feeding into the ground.

"Creative Director, that thing's enormous!" said Kiwi.

"That's what she said," Tasha replied automatically.

Ari looked at Tasha, confused. "That's what who said?"

"Oh, crap. I just introduced 'That's what she said' jokes to Etheria, didn't I? Just pretend I didn't say anything. What are those bits of light that circle the tower?"

"It's raw healing energy from the Orb of Life," Kiwi said. "The energy travels through the coils and into the planet. Lines of energy carry it from here to save points across the globe."

Tasha stepped onto the metal plate and circled the tower. The spiral protrusions seemed to be ascending as she circled around it.

"Look," said Pan, pointing.

A larger-than-average save point rested on the edge of the plate on one side, and there was a large wooden shack next to the save point. Smoke was coming out of the chimney, and there was a wooden sign with an engraved image of a bed set upon it, indicating that it was a hotel. Tasha approached the save point. The floating floppy diskette faded away as she set foot on the save point platform. Her health was restored, and she received the familiar notification that her progress had been saved and the new save point had been registered as her continue point.

She approached the inn and opened the door. Just inside the building was a counter with three NPCs, each with the telltale words floating over their head. The bearded man was a merchant NPC. Tasha spent what little GP she had saved up on consumables while Pan resupplied on ammunition. The lady next to him was a hotel NPC. They booked a room for the night.

The third NPC was a dwarf wearing a chef hat as tall as he was. This NPC sold prepared meals. The cost of the food was lower than the cost of consumables, but it had to be eaten inside the hotel or it would vanish. This fell in line with the video game conventions that she was familiar with. They ordered various dishes and drinks before retiring for the evening.

After they had all awakened and been fed, the group approached the tower. There was a single small door into the tower facing the save point. Though Tasha couldn't make out any hinges, the door vanished as she approached, allowing ingress into the tower.

They stepped through the doorway into the portal interior.

> **Now entering dungeon: The Spiral Tower**
> **Recommended levels: 29–33, parties of 3–6**
> **Caution: Some higher-than-usual-level mobs exist within the**
> **dungeon. Avoidance is recommended.**
> **Floor 1/35**

The air was cool and damp against her skin. There were no torches to provide illumination, instead the walls were covered with a luminous moss that permeated the tower's interior. The sound of insects and wildlife filled the tower. Butterflies fluttered to and fro. A squirrel dashed into view around the corner before fleeing into the distance.

Tasha didn't know what kind of a dungeon to expect. The dungeons that she'd visited before had a distinct theme. First there had been the Temple of the Player, which had followed a temple theme, albeit a poorly designed one. Then there was the grotto dungeon, which followed a rabbit theme. The Spiral Tower housed the Orb of Life, and there was animal and plant life all around her.

Tasha wondered whether the insects and wildlife were mobs as well. Would the squirrels and rabbits attack if she got too close?

The entrance faced into a corridor that extended to the left and right and circled inward, following the outside of the tower.

"Left or right?" Tasha wondered aloud.

Aralogos pointed to the left. "Let's start mapping out the dungeon. Keep on your guard. Everything here is probably a product of mist, so we should assume that anything you see is out to kill us."

Ari wasn't that far off the mark. Five minutes into their exploration of the dungeon, a saber-toothed squirrel jumped out of the shadows and bit her on the neck. Fortunately, Pan was able to dislodge it with a well-placed shot from her handgun at point-blank range. The squirrel faded into mist as it died. This, if nothing else, was proof that the wildlife in the tower couldn't be trusted.

The rest of that morning was spent mapping out the first floor. It was a labyrinth, the hallways curving circles around the center in angles that increased the closer they were to the center.

Over time, Tasha had begun to notice spiral imagery everywhere they went. There were glowing spiral patterns on the walls and floors, and the general layout of the maze could be described as a spiral, the symbol for life and rebirth—at least that's how Kiwi explained it. Since the tower was where the Orb of Life was kept, it made sense for the dungeon to be based around that element.

The monsters tended to be around level 30, which was matched up with Tasha's own level. Pan and Ari were both higher level than her at 31 and 33 respectively.

Their enemies varied by level, the highest of which was at 38. Fortunately, level progression in Etheria seemed to be linear rather than exponential. A level 10 fighter could kill a level 30 spawn, although doing so would be a time-consuming, difficult, and dangerous feat. RPG systems which used exponential stat growth would make such victories near impossible.

As such, the party was able to take on the mobs of the tower. Pan tried to pull one at a time with her handgun, but more often than not they had to fight multiple enemies at once.

The most dangerous enemies were those of significantly higher level. As they were exploring the first floor, they spied a level 140 tree monster patrolling a corridor.

Elder Treant (Level 140)
It might be best to 'leaf' this guardian of nature alone.
ATK 133   Mag ATK 229
DEF 98 Mag DEF 100

Such a fight would have been over before it started. Fortunately, there were plenty of shadowy areas to hide in that allowed the group to bypass the tree without engaging it. The level 140 creature seemed out of place in a level 30 dungeon. Lord Level Designer often placed higher-level monsters in lower-level dungeons, just to keep the delvers on their toes.

Treasure chests were common in the dungeon and offered moderate loot, ranging from a small amount of GP to foodstuffs to common household items.

The second floor was much like the first, except that there were more trees and butterflies than before. It was like the entire dungeon was an indoor arboretum. Tasha would have described the dungeon as beautiful if it hadn't been trying so hard to kill her. This floor took them only an hour to clear—they got lucky and took the correct passages that led to the stairway to the third.

The monster spawns tended to be either animals, birds, or plants in nature. Tasha had lost count of the number of giant butterflies that she'd killed on the first few floors. Fortunately, she had managed to reach level 31 as a result of the nearly nonstop combat. She increased her mana by 1 and her strength by 4, bringing it up to 29 points. She already had a very high agility at 46 points but wasn't doing as much damage with her attacks as she would like.

The entire party was exhausted by the time they reached the fifth floor. Although there were no windows in the tower, Tasha's internal clock told her that it must be reaching bedtime. Fortunately, on the fifth floor they came across another NPC inn. The inn was a large shack housed in a clearing in the maze. It wasn't the elaborate NPC town that they discovered in their travels, just three NPCs who sold food, items, and managed the hotel. This seemed to be meant as a rest stop for adventurers and nothing more.

Days passed in this manner. They fought monsters while exploring the dungeon, mapping out the circular maze as they went, always looking for the elusive staircase to the next level. Every five levels there was a rest stop—an inn with a place to purchase consumables, rest, and recover their strength. Often the team needed to backtrack to the last inn when they didn't make sufficient progress to reach the next rest stop. Besides the dungeon bathrooms, the inns were the only location in the dungeon where the mobs wouldn't hunt them.

The higher-than-usual enemies were rare but ever present. So far, they had managed to avoid any direct confrontations, but there were several close calls. By the time they reached the end of the nineteenth level, Tasha had lost track of the days. How long had she been in this strange twisting maze of monsters and wildlife? Death lurked around every corner, hid in every hidey hole, and dripped from the ceiling above. If not for the comfort of her friends, she could see how the dungeon might have robbed her of her sanity. Even Trista's nonstop jabbering about being stuck in a jar helped to keep her grounded.

There were numerous treasures in the dungeon. When she had entered, her GP was all but depleted. Now, these many days later, she'd already collected over 23,000 GP. Dungeon exploration was dangerous but certainly lucrative. The NPC merchant didn't sell any gunblades, otherwise she would have upgraded.

She had leveled up two times since the first floor, bringing her to level 33. This time she elected to take two hearts and focus all eight points on agility. With an agility score of 54, she could easily put Olympic gymnasts to shame. She could probably outrun a speeding locomotive, even without invoking Sprint. Tasha imagined her couch-potato, out-of-shape self at home, sitting on her sofa with a controller in her hand. How much had she changed since then, not only in terms of her body shape, but also as a person? When this adventure was done, would she ever be the same?

She was wrapped up in those thoughts when the staircase to level twenty finally came into view. At the end of a glowy-moss-filled corridor sat the staircase leading upward to the twentieth—the halfway point of the dungeon. Unfortunately, blocking their path was another out-of-depth mob. This one was a mid-sized rabbit with glowing red eyes that radiated malice.

The Omnihare (Level 240)
The ultimate rabbit-themed enemy. Second in speed only to the Omnitortoise.
ATK 333   Mag ATK 221
DEF 177   Mag DEF 229

The Omnihare wasn't patrolling. It simply stood by the edge of the staircase, staring forward with ever vigilant eyes. There were alcoves that they could hide in while it passed, but the creature never moved on its own.

For a long time they watched it, trying to devise some way past. Finally, Ari offered a suggestion. "I have a plan for how to get past the Omnihare. Tasha, Pan, Kiwi, and Slimon can all hide in one of those shadowy alcoves. I'll get the rabbit to follow me down the hall, and once it passes out of sight, the rest of you make a break for the staircase."

A look of concern appeared on Tasha's face. "You mean to want us to use you as bait? I don't think you could outrun it. I have the feeling the Omnihare will move quickly. We would be using you as a sacrifice."

Ari grinned. "It doesn't matter. In case you've forgotten, I'm not real. If it kills me, I don't suffer an experience penalty or resurrect as a new person. Pan's summon ability will cool down after half an hour, and she'll just summon me again. I'll admit that dying isn't pleasant, but sacrificing myself for someone I care about isn't that bad."

"You are real," said Pan.

"Sweetheart, I'm well aware of my transient nature. As much as I'd like to believe otherwise, I have no existence outside of your mind. I'm just a storybook character playing out his part."

"Pffpt!" Sir Slimon contributed helpfully.

Kiwi nodded in agreement. "Slimon is right. Now is no time to discuss existentialism. Whatever the case, Aralogos can be summoned again—he won't be lost. I say we go with this plan."

Tasha and Pan reluctantly agreed, and the plan was put into effect. Watching the Omnihare for any sudden movements, the team slowly made their way into one of the alcoves and hid behind a protruding wall. Once the rest of the team was in place, Ari moved toward it and tried to get its attention. The trick would be to pull it from as far a distance as possible, then he would have to take off running. A level 240 mob would almost certainly kill him with either one or two hits, and it would probably outrun him. He would need to lead it away from the others before that happened.

As soon as he was as close to the mob as he dared to get, Ari picked up small pebble from the ground and threw it at the rabbit. The rabbit came to life, its rule-based mechanical brain perceiving him as an aggro target. Aralogos took off down the corridor, running at a fast clip, but his speed was nothing compared to the rabbit's. The rabbit followed Ari around the corner.

Without wasting any time, the team dashed toward the staircase. Tasha watched as Ari's hearts began to plummet in her combat HUD. He was barely alive but hadn't died yet.

They reached the stairwell, and the team began to climb, but Pan paused. There was a chest in a second alcove by the staircase that hadn't been visible from a distance. It was emerald green and lined with jewels. The thief within her couldn't bypass such a treasure.

Without pausing, she changed direction, darting into the alcove toward the chest. As she undid the latch and opened it, light glowed from within. She grabbed the small object that appeared without looking to see what it was. All she knew was that it was a floppy black circle. She would inspect it later.

As she was about to turn back, she noticed the flashing red indicator on her HUD that indicated that Ari was dead. A lump formed in her throat as she turned back toward the stairwell, but just as she was about to run toward it, she saw the Omnihare only a handful of paces from her. It was staring forward absently, once again guarding the stairwell. It had killed Ari and returned in record time. Tasha, Slimon, and Kiwi made it to the next floor, but Pan had allowed her greed to overcome her.

Fortunately The Omnihare hadn't seen her. She lifted up the hood of her invisibility cloak, vanishing into the darkness. Could she sneak past the Omnihare while using it? There was very little space around the rabbit for her to squeeze past, but she was very small and had high agility. She took a single step forward, and as soon as she planted her foot on the ground, the rabbit's ears popped up, and its head turned to stare into the alcove, straight through her. Pan froze. The rabbit continued to stare through where Pan was for several minutes before giving up and turning to face straight forward.

Carefully, Pan inspected the object that she had taken from the legendary chest.

Portable Hole
Artifact-tier item, indestructible
A portable hole can be resized by the user and creates a hole of extra-dimensional space twenty feet deep. To use the portable hole, place it on any flat surface, either horizontal or vertical. Cannot be added to inventory while objects are stored inside.

Now this was a useful item, but could it help her out of her current situation? Slowly she brought her foot back and quietly placed it on the ground. She took the hole with both hands and pulled it in opposite directions as far as her arms would stretch. It expanded as she pulled on the edges but retained its floppy circular form. Pan then slowly crouched on the ground and spread the portable hole onto the floor. She extended her hand into the floor and found that her invisible arm met no resistance.

She backed away a single pace and removed her hood, making herself fully visible. "Hey!" she cried out. The Omnihare's eyes perked up, and it looked directly at her, baring its fangs.

The absurdly overpowered bunny hopped directly at her, and just as it was about to reach her, it fell into the portable hole, disappearing from sight. Without wasting any time, Pan gathered up the portable hole, reduced its size, folded it up, and stuffed it into her pocket. She then walked past where the rabbit had been and joined her friends on the next floor.

It was a foolish risk, she couldn't deny that, but now she had a powerful artifact that she couldn't dare again use given its extremely dangerous occupant. Perhaps she would be able to dispose of the mob at some point in the future. The mob might even despawn once they left the dungeon.

After rejoining her friends, they stopped at the inn. Once an hour had passed, Pan was once again able to use her summon ability, and Ari rejoined the party. They had made it more than halfway up the tower, but they still had fifteen floors above them.

The continued to climb the dungeon, one level after another, carefully mapping out the maze to find the proper route, every hour hoping to find that elusive stairway to the next level.

They were on level twenty-four when everything changed. The circular maze was gone, and in its place the floor was filled to the brim with water. There were bubbles of breathable air scattered throughout the floor.

Tasha walked to the edge of the bubble that encircled the stairway and extended her arm into it. Ripples of water emerged from the point where her arm intersected the water. Tasha likened the surface of the bubble to the event horizon of a stargate. When she drew her arm away, it came back dripping wet.

Ari pointed at another air bubble some hundred feet away. "I think we'll have to swim for it." He turned to Tasha. "How long do you think you can hold your breath?"

"I dunno. Maybe twenty, thirty seconds?"

"Really?" He looked doubtful. "That should be barely enough to reach the next air pocket."

Tasha always tried to hold her breath when watching TV shows where the stalwart protagonist swam for long periods of time. She always ended up exhaling before they reached the surface.

"Aren't there any spells for water breathing?"

Kiwi scrolled through her menu. "Probably, but I don't know any of them. I could cure you partway. That should oxygenate your blood cells, giving you more time to make it through."

Tasha nodded slowly. "And you know about sciencey stuff like oxygenating blood cells, how exactly?"

"There are scientists in Etheria. Even if most of our technology is magic-based, it doesn't hurt to have at least a basic understanding of the universe."

"Pffpt," Slimon said, offering to test the waters.

"Be my guest," replied Tasha.

Slimon hopped through the air bubble's edge and formed eight tentacles behind him. He was able to move through the water quickly in much the same way as an octopus. A small school of carnivorous guppies swam up.

School of Murder Guppies (Level 33)
Weak individually, but deadly as a group.
ATK 50 MATK 0
DEF 61   MDEF 21

The collection of murderous rainbow fish attacked him, but he knocked them away with his tentacles. Finally, he reached the next air pocket.

"I'm next," said Pan. She swam to the next air pocket with little difficulty.

"I hate water levels," Tasha grumbled as she took a deep breath and stepped into the water. Halfway to her target, she was attacked by a shark. She let out a gasp, which came at the cost of air. She started swimming faster toward the next air pocket, but it was slow going. Pan tried to shoot the shark, but the bullets slowed to non-lethal speeds only a few meters after hitting the water's surface. It seemed that Pan's firearms wouldn't be of much benefit in this situation.

Should she use her gunblade? Maybe she could try a lightning spell... Her extensive experience with Pokémon battles led her to understand that lightning attacks were super effective against water creatures. Of course, in this close range, it would affect her as well. She was running out of options, and out of breath.

Just as she was about to try casting a lightning spell, Aralogos was there. He punched the oncoming shark in the nose, knocking it away. That might have been enough to discourage a real flesh-and-blood shark, but it only drew further ire of the ethereal construct. The shark came back, and Ari punched it another two times, killing it. It dissolved into mist that was absorbed into the water. Ari grabbed hold of the oxygen-deprived Tasha and carried her to the next air bubble.

When she awoke minutes later, she was fully healed.

The rest of the day was spent exploring the water level. They located the stairway to the next level right away. The problem was that it was behind a set of locked doors. The trick to this level seemed to be to find the three keys that unlocked the water gates. They found the first one being guarded by a school of murder guppies. The second one was on a pedestal behind a series of flaming fire pinwheels. The fact that the fire persisted underwater wasn't lost on Tasha. That appeared to be a function of video game logic. Her own fireball spells wouldn't work, but dungeon's obstacles seemed to possess some special quality.

Slimon did most of the precision swimming and fighting. Pan and Tasha were nearly useless underwater, but Ari was able to help out. Kiwi found that she could use lightning attacks on the water from the safety of an air bubble. The trick was to lure the enemies close enough for it to have an effect.

The final key ended up being a drop from a kraken monster. It wasn't easy to bring that creature down, but fortunately there were air bubbles that they were able to attack from.

The twenty-first through twenty-fourth levels were also water levels. It took several days to clear all four water levels, but finally they made it to the twenty-fifth.

Levels twenty-five through thirty-four were combined into one vertically designed level. Huge trees wound upward, creating a climbing maze. Fortunately Tasha and Pan had high agility scores, allowing them to move from branch to branch with relative ease. Slimon was able to use his tentacles to climb the trees. Ari wasn't able to jump nearly as far, but he could climb a rope with the best of them. Slimon carried Kiwi from one branch to the next.

Mapping this level out was more difficult due to the three-dimensional nature of the maze. They found the door without much trouble, but like the water levels, it was locked behind three doorways. The tricky part would be in finding the keys.

After two days of exploring, they finally found the last key to unlock the door. It was set upon a glass platform at the end of a vertical corridor. They could see it but lacked any way to reach it. They tried everything. Pan tried using Steal, but it was out of reach. She tried shooting it off, but it was fully obscured by the transparent platform. Slimon wasn't able to reach it, and the edges of the walls were too slick to grab on to.

"If only one of us had the ability to fly," Kiwi mused.

Tasha's bottle started talking again. Or more accurately, it was the small captive fairy ninja who started talking. "Hellooo... Did you idiots forget about me? Let me go, and I'll fly up there and get the key for you."

"Yeah," Tasha agreed. "If only one of us was able to fly."

Pan nodded her agreement.

"Come on, morons, just let me out! You can't leave me in this bottle forever. Just let me out already."

A thoughtful expression took root on Tasha's face. "I have an idea."

"Does it involve letting me out?"

"First," Tasha explained, "I'll get on Ari's shoulders, then Pan will get on my shoulders. Finally, Slimon will throw Ari as high as he can straight up. Once we get as high in the air as we can, I'll jump from his shoulders and perform a double jump, then Pan will jump from my shoulders and reach the key."

"Are you sure?" asked Kiwi. "That sounds kind of insane."

"I've played video games before where that worked. Let's give it a try."

And so, Tasha climbed up on Aralogos's back and onto his shoulders. Slimon lifted up Pan and placed the girl on Tasha's shoulders.

"Are you sure you want to go through with this?" Kiwi said.

"Umm... yes?" she said uncertainly.

Slimon lifted himself off the ground with three tentacles so that his center of balance was high in the air, giving him the leverage that he would need. He used another tentacle to grab Ari and hurled him up as high and as fast as he could. Ari was about halfway up the vertical corridor when his upward momentum died, and he reached the apex of the throw.

"My turn!" Tasha declared. With Pan still on her shoulders she leaped off Ari's shoulders into the air... and instead of jumping straight up, jumped at a slight forward angle, slamming her face into the wall. She double jumped anyway, which changed her angle to be straight upward.

Pan jumped from Tasha's shoulders, directly toward the glass pedestal holding the key... and slammed her head right into it. The key vibrated and moved a few millimeters but gave no other response. The trio tumbled down the vertical corridor, hitting walls and each other on the way down. Princess Kiwi winced as the three of them slammed into the ground.

Trista Twinklebottom was laughing like crazy, rolling on the bottom of her jar with mirth. "Do it again! Do it again!"

Once everyone was healed up, Ari turned to Tasha and said, "This has to be one of the worst ideas you've ever had."

"No! It'll work! My aim was just off. Besides, it helped me gain another level in my Double Jump ability. We need to practice this until we get it right."

"N-no more jumping," Pan insisted.

"Okay, fine," Tasha said grouchily. "Does anyone have any *other* ideas about how we can get the key?"

"Yeah," said Twinklebottom. "You bozos could let me out the jar, and maybe I can get it for you."

"Anyone at all?" Tasha asked. Nobody else had any ideas.

"Fine. It's not as though you can send your ninjas after us now anyway."

Tasha unscrewed the lid from the jar, and Trista flew out. "So long, suckers!" she cried as she flew off into the distance.

Tasha facepalmed. "Did anyone not see that coming?"

Slimon was the one who finally came up with a plan, which was actually a modified version of Tasha's plan. Tasha held on to Slimon as Ari threw her as high as he could. Once at the apex of the throw, she threw Slimon, who used his tentacles to grab on to the platform and pull himself up. He collected the key and slid down the walls to the ground without incident.

They made their way to the staircase that led to the top of the Spiral Tower. Trista was there waiting for them.

"It took you jerks long enough to get here. Hurry up and open the door. I want to get out of this damn tower and get back to trying to murder the lot of you."

"Fine, fine." Tasha opened the doorway, and the stairway to the top of the Spiral Tower was revealed. Light shone through the doorway. It must be daytime. Tasha had been in the tower so long that she'd lost track of whether it was day or night.

With her friends in tow, Tasha ascended the staircase to their ultimate destination. The end of their mission was at hand. In minutes, the Orb of Life would be in their possession.

CHAPTER 40

Fire and Life

The uppermost floor of the Spiral Tower was an immense metal circular platform. There was a single hatch built into the metal floor to allow access from within. A translucent blue force field surrounded the structure and prevented access by air. It was reminiscent of the protective field around Brightwind Keep.

In the center of the platform was an altar built into the tower, and upon it lay a small white globe that pulsated at repeating intervals. Within the globe were glowing spirals of white and blue light. As it pulsed, waves of energy ran through a spiral circuit in the floor toward the edge of the tower's rim. Surrounding the altar were four metallic spiral pillars.

Tasha walked to the edge of the circular tower. There were no handrails to keep people from falling off, but she wanted to see just how high she was off the ground. Far, far below was the great metallic base of the tower in which the Spiral Tower was embedded.

The save point was a small circle at the bottom of the tower. She remembered how large the save point was close up, but now it was little more than a small circular dot. For some reason, she briefly wondered if it would make a good base-jumping target. What a strange thought. Would these sorts of thoughts be normal for her from now on? She backed away from the edge and approached the Orb of Life.

As she began to walk toward it, the princess held her back. "Do not approach the orb. It has defenses to keep intruders from taking it."

As if sensing the presence of intruders, a field of lightning sparked to life between each of the metal pillars that surrounded the altar, like a net composed of strands of lightning.

"Then how do we retrieve it?" Tasha asked. "I suppose we could try poking it with a stick. We could knock the orb from its pedestal and pick it up on the other side."

"That won't be necessary," said the princess. "I'll get it. My father was once its bearer. Maybe it will accept me as well."

"What if it doesn't?" asked Pan.

"Then we'll find out soon enough." She walked toward the field of lightning and extended her hand.

As her hand touched the lightning web, her flesh became darkened and charred. She screamed in pain and drew her hand back. Slimon quickly cast a healing spell, bringing her back to full health.

Tasha was shuffling through her inventory, looking for a suitable stick, but before she found one, Kiwi got back to her feet and once again approached the altar.

"I... have to do this. One more time."

For a second time, she extended her hand into the lightning web. Her hand was instantly charred, but she pushed her arm further into it. The part of her hand that reached beyond the lightning mesh was healed. She put one foot into the lightning web and forced her way through. Her entire body was fried and then instantly healed. Soon enough, she was standing within the lightning web, mere feet away from where the orb sat on its pedestal.

Her sorceress robes were in tatters, but her body was unharmed. She reached out and grasped the Orb of Life. She held it in her hands, wonder reflected in her eyes. Without any effort or pain, she stepped back through the lightning mesh.

The moment she took the orb from the pedestal, a luminous pillar of light shone forth into the sky above. Moments later, the light was gone, and the spiral circuitry at the base of the tower had gone dark. The force field that had once surrounded the tower had gone dead.

Tasha joined her friends as they gathered around the princess.

"It... accepted me," said Kiwi. "The orb... I can almost hear it speaking to me."

Princess Kiwistafel rejoined her friends and held out the orb. It seemed to be a clear glass globe. There was a light glowing from within, spiral patterns of energy emitting outward, fading as they approached the outer extent of the globe.

Kiwi held the orb into the air, and a globe of power rushed forth. A large number of buffs appeared in Tasha's HUD.

Life Aura effect applied.
Buff added: Greater protection, DEF + 60
Buff added: Health regen, 1 heart per second
Buff added: Greater shield, MDEF + 60
Buff added: Haste, speed + 30
Buff added: Resist enchantment, added 50% chance to resist debuffs
All debuffs dispelled.

Tasha stood with her friends under the umbrella of power that Kiwi wielded through the Orb of Life.

"We've done it." Kiwi lowered the orb and held it to her chest. "We've done it!" she repeated. Slimon took her hand.

"Let's go home," said Tasha.

Ari walked to the edge. "One issue. I don't want to be that guy, but how are we going to get down?"

Tasha looked back at the entrance that led back into the tower. She really didn't want to go back through the tower. Though it would take less time going down than up, there had to be a faster way. She might be able to use the gravity shift ability to run along the tower's edge, but she hadn't leveled it and might not make it all the way down before the effect ran out. She could just jump and then reverse gravity at the halfway point, but that plan was dangerous to say the least. Besides, she needed a plan that would get everyone to the ground, not just her.

She looked over the edge and saw the outline of the save point on the ground far below. The beginnings of a horrible idea began to take root in her mind.

"What are you thinking?" Ari asked nervously. "I know that look. That's the look you get when you have a horrible idea."

"N-nothing," said Tasha. She didn't want to admit that she had actually considered for the briefest of moments base-jumping the save point. She reasoned that it would heal her the moment she touched it, so landing on it would be safe. It was a dumb idea, though.

Pan removed her parachute from her inventory. "Parachute," she suggested.

"Good idea, Pan. That's a much better suggestion than what I was thinking."

Fortunately, they all still had their parachutes from their earlier encounter with K'her Noálin. Tasha tapped at her menu and was about to remove the parachute from her inventory when she spotted a bright point of light in the distance.

It was a brilliant blue fireball shooting toward the princess from the sky above. Queen Murderjoy floated downward slowly from where the fireball originated. Before Tasha could cry out, the fireball fully engulfed Princess Kiwi, but the flame effect rebounded off of an invisible dome surrounding her. When the intense blue flames from the fireball died down, Kiwi was unharmed. The circular outline of charred metal surrounded the ground where the princess stood.

Tense violin music began to play in Tasha's mind. Queen Murderjoy's eyes stopped glowing, and she approached the princess. "I'm so very pleased that you were able to retrieve the Orb of Life. It certainly took you long enough. Now, I'll be taking both you and it with me."

Far above the tower, flying monkeys filled the sky. They kept their distance, leaving their mistress to handle the princess and her friends on her own.

"You were just waiting to ambush us?" Tasha said.

"Yeah, that's right. Don't worry, though. I only care about the princess and her orb. They will both come to serve Zhakara."

Tasha scanned the queen.

Queen Aralynn Murderjoy (Level 108)
Class: Mage

The queen of Zhakara. Cunning, amoral, and insane. Master of the Orb of Fire.
Strength: 20
Agility: 14
Dexterity: 18
Intelligence: 316
Charisma: 60

There were five rows of heart containers above her with ten hearts each. There were many damage and defense buffs on her. She had come ready for a battle.

"That fireball didn't damage me at all," Kiwi said. "You've miscalculated. The level difference between us is nothing compared to the power of the orb."

The queen raised her staff, and the Orb of Fire at its end blazed to life. Dozens of fireballs arced through the air and impacted an invisible sphere around the princess.

Tasha's hearts began to drain from the heat alone but were restored instantly. Tendrils of life energy emitted from the orb in Kiwi's hand into each of the party members.

The background music was rising in intensity. The violins were replaced by orchestral music, indicating the start of a final boss battle.

Kaze circled high above the ground. In the distance to the south was the great ocean, and to the north was the Bog of Most Likely Death. The tower was too far to see, but Kaze knew that it was there.

The sun was just beginning to set, turning the cloudless sky into a brilliant crimson. High above, the serpent god flew in patterns and circles along its orbit. Kaze had often gazed upon the terrifying apparition. There had been rumors amongst the elves that if you gazed upon it and were unlucky enough, it gazed back upon you. Those who experienced this were overcome with paralyzing fear. It was as though an ominous voice spoke wordlessly in their minds, telling of pain and death.

Kaze didn't like looking at it. The snake god in the sky frightened him. Though he hadn't understood the quest when he joined, he had a much clearer understanding of the threat now.

His background music switched to rapid violins, telling of a coming conflict. Kaze looked about in confusion. He returned his gaze to the direction of the tower and witnessed a pillar of light appear, stretching into the heavens. The effect only lasted for a moment. He might have even missed it if not for the report of the background music.

Kaze continued to circle but lowered his altitude. Minutes later, he landed.

Penryth! Come quickly. It is time. I saw an omen from the tower. Violins are playing in my brain! I think the princess is in combat.

The red dragon stood and approached Kaze. *Then it is time.*

The battle between Queen Aralynn Murderjoy and Princess Kiwistafel had begun. One on one, they appeared to be an even match. Murderjoy's flames could not reach the princess, and Kiwi undid any damage that the queen dealt out. There were attacks that brought her down to half health, but her damaged state lasted but for a moment before being healed.

Kiwi's Orb of Life afforded her perfect defense, but it didn't allow her to actually damage the queen. Tasha, Ari, Pan, and Slimon attacked the queen with everything they had, but they only ever did quarter hearts of damage at a time, and then only when they got in lucky shots.

Kiwi held the orb in one hand and her staff in the other. "Everyone, attack her. I can heal you up with the orb. Maybe we can wear her down."

As Tasha rushed toward the queen, a cord of blue energy continued to flow into her from the orb. She quickly closed the distance to the queen and slashed at her with Grasscutter. Unfortunately, Grasscutter dealt earth-based elemental damage, which the queen was strong against. She had numerous fire-based defense buffs.

Tasha returned Grasscutter to her inventory and equipped Namaka, which would deal water-based damage. That was marginally more effective, but the actual amount of damage was still pitifully low.

Tasha slashed at her crosswise, and as the hit connected, she was able to deal half a heart of damage. The queen hit her at point-blank range with a fireball, dealing fifteen hearts of damage, nearly killing her. Tasha's hearts were instantly restored. This battle was heavily lopsided against her.

Tasha stabbed at the queen, but some magical buff prevented her sword from penetrating the queen's flesh. Murderjoy only took another quarter heart of damage.

The queen smirked. "I don't know what you plan to accomplish. Even if you bring my health down, I'll just drink a health potion. You can't defeat me. I am like a goddess before you."

Tasha jumped back as tracer fire shot through the air toward the queen. Pan had opened fire, but each bullet impacted an invisible magical shell around the queen. The few bullets that made it through only did quarter hearts of damage.

Ari closed the distance, used his Stone Fist ability and punched the queen in the face. She fell to the floor, having received an entire two hearts of damage. She shot five fireballs at him in rapid succession, killing Ari. He vanished.

Pan held out her hand toward the queen and shouted "Steal!"

The Orb of Fire detached from the queen's staff and flew toward the girl.

"No!" shouted the queen, holding out her hand. Murderjoy's eyes began to glow, and the orb stopped its midair flight and returned to the queen's outstretched hands. Her staff fell to the ground.

"Almost," mourned Pan.

The queen frowned. "This is growing tiresome. Your levels are nowhere near mine. You have no chance to win."

"Maybe I can level the playing field," Kiwi said.

Additional buffs began to appear in Tasha's HUD.

Buff added: Master Strength buff: ATK + 40

Buff added: Master Defense buff: DEF + 40

The queen was down to forty-six hearts from her original fifty. Tasha again rushed toward her and slashed at the queen with Namaka, this time dealing an entire heart of damage. The queen shot five fireballs at her, charing her skin and internal organs and destroying her spidersilk armor. The damage to her body was instantly undone by the Orb of Life, but her armor was gone for good.

Slimon grabbed the queen in his tentacles and threw her toward the edge of the arena. The queen shot a blast of fire from her outstretched hands, propelling her back in. That was the closest they'd come so far to anything resembling victory.

Tasha kept on attacking her until the queen's health was at thirty-nine hearts.

Queen Murderjoy held out a hand toward Tasha, her eyes glowing a brilliant white. "Greater Charm Person!"

Tasha felt a strange sensation wash over her. For just a moment, she no longer saw the queen as an enemy. That moment passed as her debuffs were washed away by the Orb of Life's healing light.

The queen took out a red potion and drank it, restoring herself to a full fifty hearts.

"Just what do you think you are accomplishing? You can't win this. I have literally hundreds of health potions."

Tasha returned to Kiwi's side.

"The queen is right. This isn't a winnable fight. At best we're at an impasse. We need to go."

"What do you have in mind?" Kiwi asked.

"We could jump off the edge of the tower and use the parachutes."

Kiwi shook her head. "She would shoot us down from the sky. That or the flying monkeys would capture us before we reached the ground. Even if we escaped, she would just follow us."

"Where are the giant eagles when you need them?" Tasha muttered. But of course, there were no giant eagles. There were never giant eagles when you needed them. It was simply too convenient a plot device.

The fight continued for what seemed like hours, but in actuality it amounted to about forty minutes. As the fight drew on, neither side gained a significant advantage.

Finally, the inevitable happened. The queen got a lucky hit in and killed Slimon in a single shot. After that, the tide of battle turned to Murderjoy's advantage. Pan tried to steal the Orb of Fire a second time, but this time the queen kept a strong grasp on it. Flaming lances appeared in the air above her and struck the girl in the heart, killing her. Ari, who had no existence outside of Pan's imagination, vanished into mist.

The only remaining fighters were Tasha and Kiwi. The fight belonged to Queen Murderjoy; it was only a matter of time. The queen's level was just too far beyond them.

Gradually, the light from the Orb of Life began to diminish. The life spells were not as potent as they had been at the beginning of the battle.

Queen Murderjoy approached, a flaming dagger appearing in her hand. Tasha slashed at the queen, but her gunblade was deflected by the queen's shield. Murderjoy stabbed Tasha in the gut, bringing her down to four hearts. This time her hearts didn't recover, and the defense buffs were no longer in effect.

The queen sneered at the princess. "So, you've reached your limit. Foolish princess, you used too much power too quickly. Your weak elven body can't keep up with the orb's power. It takes years of training to master the kind of control needed to wield orbs as I do.

"Your friends lie dead and defeated at my feet. You've lost, completely and utterly."

The queen retracted the sword from Tasha's gut and plunged her flaming sword into Kiwi's chest. The princess coughed up blood, the Orb of Life falling from her hands and dropping to the ground as her body fell limp.

Tasha was the only party member left alive. The queen was at full health and the player had only four hearts remaining. There was a bleeding debuff in effect—in minutes she would be dead.

"Huh. I hadn't meant to kill her," said the queen, "but it doesn't matter. I assume she registered at the save point at the base of this tower. I'll just capture her when she respawns."

Queen Murderjoy turned away from Tasha and made to leave.

"Aren't you going to finish me off?" croaked Tasha.

"There is no need," said the queen. "I only came here to collect the princess and the Orb of Life. I couldn't care less what happens to you."

The fairy Trista Twinklebottom flew up at the queen from where she'd been hiding. "Hi, boss. So I caught the princess for you like you asked. Our bill will be in the mail. Do you suppose you could give me a ride out of here? This place sucks."

A look of momentary surprise appeared on the queen's face. She hadn't realized that anyone else was present.

"Ah, yes. I remember you now. You're that ninja we hired to capture the princess. Your hidden village failed me repeatedly. I'll have it burned to ashes. As for you, you can share the princess's fate. Fairies go for a premium on the Zhakaran market. We'll drain you of your levels and make you someone's pet. How does that sound?"

"But that wasn't part of our contract," said the fairy.

"Zhakarans are not bound by contracts or any other form of obligation. I've decided that your only value to me is as a slave. If you are unsatisfied, feel free to curse whatever gods you believe in."

This was a troubling turn of events for Trista, to say the least. She looked at the player where she lay on the ground, beaten and defeated. Her companions were all dead and lay scattered around the top of the tower.

Trista Twinklebottom hated each and every one of them. First the princess had the nerve to get rescued after all the trouble Trista had gone through to capture her. Then that human had the audacity to spare her life as though she wasn't even worth the effort of finishing off. Finally they had captured her and kept her in that damn jar for months. She hated that jar almost as much as she hated the player, and she hated the player almost as much as she hated the princess.

Trista considered her situation. On one hand, she was glad that her enemies were all lying dead at her feet. On the other hand, she really didn't want to be captured by the mad queen and turned into someone's pet. Trista had a hard decision to make.

In all of Etheria, there was no magic that could bring back someone from the dead. There were no revive spells. At least that's what everyone believed. Her kind, the fairies, knew of a secret art that could resurrect an entire party and bring them back to full strength, but at the cost of the fairy's own life.

If Trista wanted to escape the queen and the dark fate that was in store for her, she had no choice but to use her ace in the hole.

Trista Twinklebottom began to laugh. It started as a soft chuckle but rose in intensity and ended in a bout of maniacal laughter.

"Why are you laughing, little bug?" demanded the queen. "Stop it at once!"

"You foolish human. You would burn down the Hidden Smog village? You couldn't even find us. Do you even know what 'hidden' means?

"And I won't be your pet or anyone else's. You think you're winning, but you're not. Though this detestable human may be the one who defeats you, your defeat will be by my hands."

A fireball formed in the queen's hand. "You silly little insect. What possible power can you wield against me?"

The fairy rose into the air, her eyes luminous in anticipation of her racial ability. She spoke her final words to Tasha the player.

"Just so you and I understand each other: I hate each and every one of you bastards. PRETTY FAIRY GLITTER MAGIC!"

The fairy's body exploded into glitterbugs, which flew into the bodies of each slain party member. Light filled their eyes. Tasha's health and mana were fully restored.

Elven hands grasped the Orb of Life. Kiwi got back to her feet and looked at the queen. She put one hand out and shouted, *"Tuathá sûm!"*

The queen flew back far away from the party, landing at the far end of the arena but otherwise took no damage.

"What happened?" said Pan.

"Wasn't I... dead?" said Kiwi.

"I saw what happened," said Tasha. "It was Twinklebottom. She sacrificed herself for us. Well, actually, for herself, but the end result is the same. We have another chance to win."

Queen Murderjoy got to her feet. "What foolishness. The end result will be the same, no matter how many times you attack me."

"Okay, everybody, turtle formation!" Tasha said.

Pan, Slimon, and Tasha moved into Kiwi's spell of protection.

"The queen is right," Tasha said. "We can't win. Her level is just too high. We need to change our strategy."

"What do you have in mind?" Kiwi asked.

"We have to stop trying to win. In this situation, escape is the same as victory. Our objective has to be to protect Kiwi and the Orb of Life."

Ari appeared beside Pan. "How can we do that?"

Tasha thought for a bit. "We stay in a turtle formation around Kiwi. If we can make it to the ground, we could lose Murderjoy in the bog. Kiwi can resist its confusing miasma, but the queen can't."

Ari smiled. "That's actually a good plan borne of clear thinking. I'm impressed. How do we get to the ground, though?"

Tasha thought back to that terrible idea. "Maybe we could base-jump the save point? If we land on it, we would be healed instantly, right?"

Kiwi looked doubtful. "I'm not sure that would work. I mean, it might, but it's never been tried before."

While they were debating this, Queen Murderjoy was shooting fireballs, one after another, at Kiwi, but each one impacted the invisible dome around her, fizzling into nothing.

"I don't think we could make it down using the parachutes. Not unless we had a way to distract the queen for a few seconds."

Pan raised her hand. Kiwi turned to her. "Pan, you don't need to raise your hand. If you have something to say, just say it."

"I... have an idea... for a d-distraction"

Tasha turned to her. "What kind of distraction?"

Before Pan could offer any reply, a missile impacted the queen's fire shield, knocking her to the ground. A jet of ice struck her, followed by a ball made out of lightning.

Tasha looked to the sky and gasped. The sky was full of dragons. There were hundreds of them, with more arriving each second.

"Yeah!" Tasha cried. "This is even better than flying eagles!"

Ari shook his head at her with an amused look on his face.

The largest of them was a great red dragon who wreathed Murderjoy in flames, blasting her for a good ten seconds before relenting. When the flames let up, there was a circle of melted stone around the queen, who was herself unharmed. As the bearer of the Orb of Fire, it was doubtful that any amount of flame would be able to harm her.

The red dragon landed beside the princess. He lowered his head to the ground, and a single dragon rider dismounted. Hermes leapt to the ground and ran to the princess. Kaze landed alongside the red dragon and joined Hermes.

"Hey, Princess, I thought you might need a hand, so I brought a few friends of mine."

Kiwi turned to the newcomers. "Hermes! Kaze! I don't understand. Where did you come from?"

It was Kaze who answered. *We knew that you would eventually reach the top of the Spiral Tower and waited nearby to offer you aid.*

"I'm glad you did," said Kiwi. She looked Hermes in amazement. "But why did the great red dragon let you ride him?"

Penryth approached the princess. *Through his actions and sacrifice, he has proven himself a friend of dragons. Now quickly, get on. Just this once, we will allow ourselves to be ridden.*

"You have my thanks."

There are 430 dragons in my company. With the short amount of time we had to prepare, that was the best we could arrange. Most are levels 20 through 40, with nine of them being of levels 55 and above. I am level 83. Despite our numbers and levels, we cannot hope to prevail against an orb bearer.

A battle raged in the skies above. Some of the dragons were engaged in aerial combat with flying monkeys, who themselves were no longer idle observers. The remaining dragons were engaging the queen directly, either pelting her with projectile attacks or diving at her, swiping at her as they passed.

Queen Murderjoy got to her feet. There were jets of flame and ice striking her from all directions, most dissipating on the translucent red shield that surrounded her.

"Enough!" she yelled. "You think you are a match for my power? Not one of you is my equal. I'll destroy this pitiful army."

She launched dozens of fireballs at once, each finding a target. Some dragons died, others fell out of the sky, injured and unable to fly. Every one of her fireballs hit their mark.

Get on, quickly!

Kiwi started to climb up on Penryth, but a blast of fire struck the giant red dragon. The fiery projectile penetrated the dragon's chest and came out the other side, flying off into the distance.

It would have been the dragon's end, but for the power of the Orb of Life. Kiwi healed Penryth and started casting buffs just as another fireball impacted him.

The queen was dividing her attention between the dragons in the air and the princess. Every second that passed, another dragon fell from the sky, struck by one of the queen's attacks.

"This isn't working," Tasha said. "We won't be able to get away as long as she keeps attacking us." She turned to Pan. "Pan, I don't know what kind of distraction you had in mind, but now might be a good time to use it."

Pan nodded and threw on her cloak of invisibility. She ran toward the stairwell that gave ingress to the tower below. From her pocket, she removed the folded-up Portable Hole. Ignoring the intense sounds of the battle which raged less than a few dozen feet away, she pulled the hole apart, expanding its size, and placed it upon the wall.

Moments later, the Omnihare that she had encountered and trapped in the hole hopped out, its red eyes glowing with malevolence. The level 240 out-of-depth mob had joined the combat arena.

Something in its rule-based brain caused it to recognize Queen Murderjoy as the preferred target of aggression. Maybe it was from all the spells she was casting. Whatever the case, it ran straight at the queen and bit her on the neck for ten hearts of damage. The queen screamed, and her absurd headpiece fell to the ground, destroyed.

Blood was flowing from the wound, but she had the presence of mind to shoot it with one fireball after another. The mob's health decreased by about five hearts per second, but the queen was clearly outmatched. She might be the most powerful mortal alive, but there were still monsters far more powerful than her.

It attacked her another two times, bringing her down to half of her original health. The rabbit wasn't faring well against her continual onslaught of fire, however. It had been reduced to 30%. The power of the Orb of Fire was enough to make up the significant level difference.

"Let's go, quickly!" Hermes yelled, having already gotten on the dragon.

"Just one moment. I'm going to buy us a few more seconds," said Kiwi, who extended the orb toward the Omnihare, healing it and casting health buffs upon it. She quickly mounted up along with Tasha, Ari, Pan, and Slimon. The dragon dove off the tower and flew off into the distance.

As the dragon flew away, the battle between the Queen of Zhakara and the high-level rabbit mob continued. The battle HUD had disappeared, and Tasha had no way of knowing whether the queen survived.

Several dozen dragons joined them for the return journey. Of the original attacking force of 420 dragons, less than fifty had survived. The rest had fallen either to the queen or to the flying monkeys.

The return trip to Questgivrian territory was much faster than traveling by foot, the journey measured in days rather than months. The dragons were forced to engage intermittent mobs, but there were no attacks of Zhakaran origin.

From her place atop one of the dragons, she could see another dragon ahead of her carrying a small cage that contained Denver. She waved but wasn't sure that her dinosaur companion could see her.

By the morning of the fourth day, they had crossed into Questgivria, and by midafternoon, Brightwind Keep was finally in view. The dragons who bore the princess and her party landed. It had been over five months since Princess Kiwistafel had left Brightwind Keep, but at last she had returned home.

EPILOGUE

A major incident occurred late last Moonday evening atop the Spiral Tower, located deep within the Bog of Most Likely Death. According to our witness, who prefers to go unnamed, Aralynn Murderjoy, the Queen of Zhakara, engaged in a battle with the Princess Kiwistafel Questgiver. Also involved was the now infamous Tasha Singleton, best known as the good twin of the perpetrator of the Marketplace Massacre those many months ago.

The battle was joined by an army of dragons, who assisted the princess and her party in their escape. Since then, we have received confirmation that the Spiral Tower has gone dark and no longer emits its own light.

Eyewitness reports confirm that Queen Murderjoy respawned at a save point deep within Zhakara. When asked for comment, Queen Murderjoy incinerated our correspondent, who has since been resurrected. The Questgivrian crown confirms that they are now in possession of the Orb of Life but would not comment beyond that.

Tasha Singleton had this to say about the incident in question: "Get away from me, you paparazzi bastards!" Her strange otherworldly vernacular confirms the popular rumor that she is, in fact, the player of legend. More on this story as it develops.

The Brightwind Tribune, *Snickerdoodle 14th, 3205 3E*

Tasha set the newspaper aside and took a sip from her afternoon coffee. She was sitting at a pub with her friends Ari and Pan. "Pan, are you done with the funnies yet?"

"Nope."

Ari was drinking a local ale while Pan indulged in a strawberry milkshake. The pub wasn't crowded—there were only a few other patrons.

Pan was no longer wearing her thief outfit. Her cloak and baggy clothing had been replaced by the blue-and-green robes of a summoner, complete with a floppy hat and a beanie on top. When Tasha had scanned her earlier that day, Pan was revealed to be a level 5 Summoner.

Tasha asked the question that had been on her tongue. "So, Pan, what made you want to switch classes?"

Pan took another drink of her milkshake, still reading the funny pages. "I... wanted to see how far I c-can get." She looked at Ari, who finished her thought. "She means that she wants to level summoner as much as possible with the short amount of time that we both have left."

Ari took a sip of his drink. "No summoner in history has ever reached a level higher than 23. We don't know what kind of abilities can be unlocked at the higher levels. Maybe there's something that can grant permanence to figments like myself.

"But even if there isn't, even if I stop existing one day, I don't have any regrets. It was enough to be part of your grand adventure."

Tasha set her coffee aside. "Well, I think leveling summoner is a great idea. I'll help you power level as soon as possible. After that, we still have four more orbs to find. Murderjoy has the Orb of Fire, nobody knows where the Orb of Water is, King Dourmal has the Orb of Earth, and apparently the Orb of Death is on the moon. Unfortunately, I have this dumb war meeting to get to after lunch, so let's meet up later on."

They finished their drinks in silence. The pub had grown less crowded as patrons finished up their meals and left the establishment. Soon the proprietor would start prep work for dinner.

Ari and Pan both excused themselves and left. They had training to do, and Tasha had business back at the castle. Everyone was busy deciding what they should do next, and as the player, she had some part of that decision-making process.

Prince Hermes was in negotiation with the Dragon Kingdom. It seemed as though he had come to an agreement with them. It was time to liberate the Laundry Mountain from his father. Hermes hadn't wanted to seize power in this manner, but their need for the orbs had grown desperate. His father, King Dourmal, had outright refused to turn over his orb, even after Entropy had become visible in the night sky.

The waitress came over and gave Tasha a beer. "The lady over there ordered this for you."

Tasha looked in the indicated direction. There was an elderly woman sitting alone in the corner. Tasha thought that there was something familiar about the woman, but she couldn't place it. The ancient white-haired woman approached. "May I join you? You and I have something to discuss."

Tasha racked her memory, trying to place the woman, but nothing came to mind. She'd met many people since arriving, however, so it was possible that she had simply forgotten.

"I'm sorry, ma'am, have we met?"

The woman took the seat opposite her and leaned forward. She swiped her left hand over her face, which changed to reveal the woman's true form. Tasha recognized her instantly. It was the face of Queen Aralynn Murderjoy. The woman swiped her hand over her face in the other direction, restoring her earlier disguise.

"You!" Tasha exclaimed, jolting back. "What are you doing here? How did you get into the city?"

"How did I get in?" Murderjoy repeated mockingly. "You ask like getting into the city is hard. I just put on this disguise, and they let me straight through. I'm just an old apple seller going about her business. Brightwind's security is hilariously bad. But you already knew that, didn't you?"

Remembering how she had convinced a guard to make an abrupt career change, she realized that the queen had a point about Brightwind's lackluster security.

"Why are you here? You must be angry from before. Are you here to for revenge? Do you intend to kill me?"

"No," the queen said, "I'm not going to kill you. In fact, I'm counting on you to gather the remaining orbs. If that damn elven king is to be believed, that might be the only way to deal with that snake in the sky and terminate that blasted contract.

"To that end, I wanted to let you know that when the time comes, I will allow you to borrow the Orb of Fire. So long as you understand that it belongs to me, I'll let you use it to summon the Hallowed Chapel. When the time comes, I'll be there."

Tasha frowned. "That's unexpectedly reasonable of you. It makes our quest seem that much more achievable."

"I can be reasonable. You can't get far as a queen if you can't display reason when absolutely necessary."

The queen signaled the waitress to bring her another drink.

Tasha picked up her beer and took a sip. "Even so, why tell me in person? Why not just send a letter to King Questgiver or tell him yourself?"

"That brings me to my second reason for coming here." A smile crossed the queen's face. "I needed to see you in person. You see, I need you to bring Princess Kiwi to me."

Tasha laughed out loud, though she later realized that it may have been unwise. One should never laugh at an insane evil queen who wants you dead. In the days that followed, she would often think on that simple piece of wisdom.

"You're kidding, right? After the lengths we've gone through to keep her safe, you think I'm just going to turn the princess over to you?"

The queen just smiled and nodded. "That's exactly what I expect."

"I wouldn't do that. I'm her friend."

"Her friend?" Murderjoy sneered. "We Zhakarans understand that friendship is weakness, and love is the ultimate form of subservience. You would be wise to take that lesson to heart."

Tasha got to her feet, pushing away from the table. "I don't have to listen to this. Love and friendship fills us with purpose. It gives us something to strive for beyond our own petty desires. Love makes us stronger, not weaker."

"Is that what you think? Then I'll show you just how weak your so-called 'friendship' can make you." The queen's eyes glowed white, and she pointed at Tasha with her right hand. "Greater Charm Person!"

Tasha was momentarily surrounded by a light glow. For a single terrifying instant, she understood what had happened, but then her mind was overcome by a rush of confusion and unclarity. That confusion passed. She absently noticed the "charm" debuff marker that appeared on her HUD, but she paid it no mind. She felt perfectly fine.

What had she been doing just now? That's right, she was just talking to her very best friend in the whole world, Queen Murderjoy.

Tasha took a seat. "Aralynn, you look troubled. Is everything okay?"

"Hello, Tasha, my good, dear friend," Queen Murderjoy said. "I'm concerned about Princess Kiwi, you see. I'm afraid that her enemies might get to her, and I wouldn't be able to protect her."

Tasha was deeply concerned by this news. "Is there anything I can do to help?"

"Well, yes, there is. I'd like you to bring the princess to me. Have her leave the Orb of Life behind. I'm afraid it would just serve to draw out her enemies."

That seemed logical. Tasha would happily follow her dear friend's instructions. Queen Murderjoy was only concerned for Kiwi's welfare, after all.

"I'll go get her right away, Aralynn."

"I'll be here. By the way, don't let her know that I'm the one who sent you. Let's let that be our little surprise," the queen said with a smile.

Tasha got to her feet. She was lucky to have a friend like the queen. She was simply the best friend a person could have. Murderjoy was bae.

Not wanting to waste any more time than necessary, Tasha ran for the castle. The guards let her through, as the princess had instructed them to. Tasha took the main elevator. The princess was probably in one of those endless meetings about whether or not the elves should assist with the attack on the Laundry Mountain.

Tasha walked through a hallway and passed right by Snickers the Bumble, who was balancing upside-down on one hand. The clown winked at her as she passed. Tasha didn't trust that man; in truth, he unsettled her. She walked past toward the war council. When she arrived, she met Kiwi standing in the hallway.

"Kiwi, I'm glad I found you," said Tasha. "Can you come with me?"

"What's wrong? I'm kind of in the middle of a strategy meeting."

"There's a danger to your life. I'd like you to come with me. There's no time to lose."

"Are you sure about that? What is the danger?"

"There isn't time to explain. Just come with me."

"Okay, Tasha. I trust you. We're friends, after all."

The two made their way back the way she had come through the castle. They passed right by Snickers, who was chuckling to himself about something. Kiwi tried to pry more information from Tasha as they walked, but Tasha wouldn't explain. Finally, they passed through the gates, and Tasha led the princess by the hand into the city. They reached the pub where her friend Queen Murderjoy was still waiting for their return.

"You brought her to me," said the queen. "I'm so very pleased."

The princess turned to Tasha. "Tasha, who is this? Why did you bring me here?"

The elderly woman waved her left hand over her face, and her illusion vanished completely, revealing Queen Murderjoy in her regal splendor.

A look of combined horror and shock came upon Kiwi's face, but Queen Murderjoy held out her hand. "Sleep."

The princess fell to the ground.

"Why did you put her to sleep?" asked Tasha.

"So that I can take her with me to Zhakara, of course."

"And she'll be safe there?"

"No, of course she won't be safe in Zhakara. Come and stand closer to me, Tasha."

Tasha approached her oldest and dearest friend, the queen.

"You know what? Forget what I said earlier. I'm afraid that I've changed my mind. I've decided that I'm going to kill you after all."

The queen drew a dagger from a sheath at her side and plunged it deep into Tasha's heart. The charm spell was instantly broken, and as Tasha bled out on the floor, she knew what she had done. The queen stabbed her twice more, and the remainder of her health vanished.

The last vision of Tasha's third life was of the queen binding the princess and carrying her away.

To be continued...

CHARACTERS

Ally

An infamous cat burglar and member of the thieves guild. As a cat-person, she has a stat boost to her speed and stealth.

When she isn't robbing banks, kidnapping affluent citizens, and stealing national treasures, she likes to spend her time napping in the sun, playing mahjong, and drinking mai tais. She's kind to those she considers her friends, though her sense of personal morality ends there.

Ari (Aralogos) Branford

A martial artist who travels with his daughter, aiding her on her quest. Though Pan isn't his biological daughter, he has taken on the role of her father and has known her from a young age. His travels led him to the Temple of the Player, where he met Tasha. They quickly formed a close friendship.

Ari is the level-headed leader of the group. He tempers Tasha's impulsive nature by keeping a cool head and making rational decisions. His character class is Pugilist, meaning that he fights using unarmed martial arts.

Although he appears to be a simple traveler, he has a mysterious past and hides a dark secret. Specifically, the way his hair self-organizes into anime-style triangular spikes without the use of hair gel. He claims it's his natural hair style, despite the fact that hair simply doesn't work that way.

Billy Belly

The youngest of Farmer Belly's three children. Wants to marry the princess when he grows up.

Bobbi Belly

Farmer Belly's daughter. Wants to travel the world as a barbarian when she grows up.

Borgrim Deathhammer, Prosecutor

The district attorney who is assigned to prosecute Tasha's case after the Marketplace Massacre incident. He is feared as a prosecutor not only for his ability to find weaknesses in the defense's arguments, but also for the magnitude of his shouting voice.

After his defeat in court, he swears to bring the villain Tash-AH to face the iron hammer of justice.

Bubba Belly

One of Farmer Belly's three children. Wants to become a beastmaster and train a horde of warrior chickens.

Catalyst

The eidolon of change who takes the form of a thunder cloud. Catalyst was the being responsible for bringing Tasha into Etheria and reconstructing the Temple of the Player.

Charlotte

A spider woman who sells armor in the capital city of Brightwind. She's married and has a family of 341 children, most of whom live in the Webwood Forest with their father. Though she did kill and eat her husband after mating with him, he still maintains that the experience was worth it.

Dourmal, King Under the Laundry Mountain

Dourmal is Hermes's father and lord of the mountain kingdom. During his administration, he oversaw the exile of the dragons from the mountain and has closed the mountain off to outsiders. Dourmal is an orb bearer, master of the Orb of Earth. He uses the orb to dig deeper and more greedily than any of his predecessors. He rules the mountain kingdom with an iron fist and keeps the dragon eggs as hostages to hold off the dragons.

Recently, rumors have begun to spread among the hill dwarves that the Orb of Earth no longer answers to Dourmal. The king is rarely seen in public, and his staff handles most of the day-to-day operations of the mountain kingdom.

Entropy

The eidolon of destruction. He hates all forms of creation, including speech. His ultimate goal is the destruction of Etheria.

Entropy appears in the form of a floating snake high above the planet. After striking a deal with the former elven king Lorien Questgiver, he agreed to stop taking the lives of those who died, allowing them to resurrect at the save points. In exchange, he would destroy the world 3,000 years later. This event gave rise to the third age of Etheria.

As the mysterious menu clock ticks toward zero, Entropy inches closer and closer to the planet of Etheria.

Ernest Belly

The portly owner of the Belly Acres farmstead. He lives with his wife and three children, raising livestock and managing the fields. Every week after slaughtering his inventory of chickens, he cons some poor adventurer into rounding them up after they respawn.

Gelkorus

Chief among Queen Murderjoy's trusted advisors. Gelkorus does most of the actual governing of Zhakara. He has learned to manage the queen's random nature to a greater degree than anyone else.

Henimaru the Toad

A samurai toad-person who is on a quest to recover his children. Through a bizarre sequence of events, Tasha finds herself accidently married to Henimaru, though he promises it is only a marriage of convenience in order to get him into Zhakara without being taken as a slave.

Hermes

Prince Hermes is the son of King Dourmal and rightful heir to the mountain kingdom. When he was born, his father tried to kill him but only succeeded in cutting off his right arm. Since this happened before Hermes could be registered at a save point, his arm was removed permanently.

Iolo Questgiver

The current king of the Questgiver empire. He has been grooming his daughter, Kiwistafel Questgiver, as his successor. During his administration, Iolo opened the borders to the other races in an attempt to dissuade Zhakaran invasion and restore Questgivria's dwindling population.

He is married to Queen Kiwano Questgiver.

Jak Singleton

Tasha's father, who died a decade before the events of *Couch Potato Chaos*. He was the one who sent her the game cartridge that brought her to Etheria. As a gamer and couch potato, he raised Tasha to follow in his footsteps.

One of the previous players held the name Jak, Slayer of the Lich Queen. Tasha suspects that this other player was also her father.

K'her Noálin

K'her is a dark-elven sky pirate and master of the Orb of Air. He uses it to dominate the skies and conduct slave raids for Queen Murderjoy. He loves GP more than anything else and aspires to be the richest individual in Etheria.

Lakuriel Questgiver

The second king of Questgivria and father of Iolo Questgiver.

Libra

The eidolon of information, who appears as a fortune-telling puppet encased in a box of wood and glass. He appears here and there at unpredictable times and vanishes just as quickly. He will answer any single question posed to him and has never been known be provide inaccurate or misleading information.

Lord Hempledon of Wilmarth

The feudal lord who rules over Wilmarth. The title of lord is honorary and has no actual authority. His authority is derived from his superior level and wealth.

He allows citizens to hunt mist monsters within his territory in exchange for 80% of any GP dropped. He has also instituted a charge for access to the city's save point and NPC merchants and quest givers.

Lorien Questgiver

The first elven king. who led his people from the undying lands to Etheria, heralding the second age. For many centuries. he researched death and how death itself can be defeated. Only by striking a bargain with the eidolon Entropy did he find a way to end death's hold over the elven people.

Kiwano Questgiver

King Iolo Questgiver's wife and Kiwistafel's mother.

Mad Marina

The mad elderly witch who resides in Wilmarth. She is a master of lightning magic, though her adventuring days are far behind her. The matter of her actual age is a matter of some debate, though most people are wise enough to have that debate when she isn't within earshot. She takes in Ari and Pan when they first arrive in the city.

Magus Savik D'hagma

The high magus of Gothmër, land of the dark elves. He serves as Princess Kiwistafel's magic instructor.

Pan (Panella) Branford

This young thief girl travels with her father on a quest which leads her to the Temple of the Player, where she meets and Tasha, who becomes her best friend.

Pan has a number of debilitating conditions that she has learned to overcome. She's autistic and has trouble making normal conversation. It's sometimes easier for her to write what she wants to say in her notebook.

She's also nearsighted, anemic, and has congenital muscular dystrophy, all of which contribute to her weakened physical state. She has managed to overcome her physical weaknesses somewhat through stat allocation, and the class choice of thief allows her to move quickly and silently.

Princess Kiwi (Kiwistafel) Questgiver

The crown princess of Questgivria, she has acquired a nasty habit of being kidnapped at the most inopportune times. After being rescued by Tasha, the two become close friends.

She's highly skilled at offensive magic, but her ultimate goal is to unlock the Sage class, which can cast both offensive and defensive magic.

Queen Aralynn Murderjoy

She is the mad queen of Zhakara and wielder of the Orb of Fire. She also bears the honor of being the highest level person in the whole of Etheria. She seeks to enslave the entire elven race and spread her own version of freedom throughout the world by force of arms. Her sanity is come and go at times, and many of her decisions are questionable at best, but her mastery of the Orb of Fire is beyond question.

She leaves most of the work of governing to her trusted lieutenants and spends most of her own time on side projects.

Ramon

The elven proprietor and craftsman of the armor shop in the village of Bray. He lives with his beautiful but lazy dark-elven wife. He crafts armor that covers as little of the body as possible. He does this party because it increases the armor's durability, but mostly for the sexiness factor.

Sally Belly

Co-owns the Belly Acres farmstead with her husband Hubert Belly. Likes to trick unsuspecting adventurers into doing farm work.

Sir Not-Appearing-In-This-Novel

Verily, never has there been such a heroic figure as this. Legends spread far and wide about this Adonis of a man and his varied exploits.

Sadly, he doesn't figure into the story, so his madcap adventures remain untold and unremembered.

Sir Slimon

Sir Slimon is a knight of the realm. He grew up with Kiwi, and the two of them became infatuated with each other.

As a slime, Slimon is unable to vocalize human speech. He communicates in English using a combination of "pffpt" sounds and body language.

Snickers the Bumble

Known to the people of Brightwind as Snickers the Bumble, his real identity is the eidolon of mischief. He serves as King Questgiver's royal mage and is known as something of a trickster. Whenever he speaks, it is always in rhyme.

Tasha #1 (Tasha Prime)

Tasha Singleton, daughter of Jak Singleton, is a couch potato. When not vegging on the couch, you can find her at work, programming the latest in a long line of meaningless pay-to-win mobile games. She's incredibly lazy and actively resists any kind of change. When presented with the opportunity to become an adventurer, she resists her cowardly nature and accepts. That decision changes her life forever.

Tasha #2 (Warrior Tasha)

After Tasha Prime died, Warrior Tasha was born. She has a bit of a bloodthirsty streak. After meeting Ari and Pan, the trio become fast friends.

In a way, Warrior Tasha is the person who Tasha has always wanted to be—strong, brave, quick to make decisions, and willing to sacrifice herself to help others.

Tasha #3 (Impulsive Tasha)

Tasha's third iteration is more emotional and less logical than her earlier iterations. At times, this leads her to some unfortunate spur-of-the-moment decisions, such as marrying a toad-person in the midst of a drunken adventure. Her emotional and spontaneous nature often causes trouble for her. When brought to anger, she sometimes lashes out at her friends when she doesn't really mean to.

Unlike Tasha Prime, Impulsive Tasha is an early riser and is much more assertive.

Trista Twinklebottom

The mischievous and murderous fairy ninja known as Trista Twinklebottom is the leader of the Hidden Smog village. Her small form makes the class ideal for her, improving both her stealth and attack speed. She focuses exclusively on stealth attacks and hitting weak points. During her off hours, she enjoys relaxing in glasses of booze.

TASHA'S STATUS

Tasha Singleton (Level 33 Couch Potato)	
Race	Human (Player)
Subclass	None
Weapon	Grasscutter (ATK 31)
Armor	Light Spidersilk Armor (DEF 25 Mag DEF 5) Sturdy Travel Shoes (DEF 2)
Heart Containers	0/18
Mana Containers	0/16
Amusement Index	Not applicable
Strength	29
Intelligence	20
Agility	54
Precision	14
Charisma	22
ATK	57
MAG ATK	18
DEF	51
MAG DEF	19
Active Debuffs	Dead

Unlocked Skills (This is only a partial list and only refers to relevant skills of at least level one):

Stat Shuffle (level MAX)

> **When invoked, all earned stat points may be reallocated. 15% of earned stat points are lost for the duration of this effect.**

After five minutes, all stats are returned to their original state.
Cooldown: 12 hours

Rapid Leveling (Level MAX)

Player-specific ability. Player and all party members gain
experience points and learn abilities at ten times the normal
rate. Only applies to the first six party members, including the
player.

Gunblade Weapon Proficiency (Level 21)

Represents your experience using gunblades. When using
gunblades, accuracy is increased by 23.1% and damage is
increased by 10.5%

Sprint (Level 12)

When invoked, you can run at 312% of your normal speed for
13.4 seconds. Higher levels will increase sprint speed and
duration.

Bullet Time (level 9)

When projectiles are flying toward you, you become aware of
them and your perception of time slows down subjectively to
35% speed, allowing you to react.
Duration: 8 seconds
Cooldown: 11 seconds

Spell Design (level 5)

Represents your ability to program spells. Spells that you
design yourself receive up to an 18% power bonus and 3.4%
cost reduction as a function of the spell's originality. This
bonus does not apply to unmodified spells copied from
spellbooks.

Double Jump (level 5)

Grants the ability to jump once while already airborne. Ability resets when you touch the floor. Height of second jump is increased by 25%.

To the Pain (Level 2)

Improves aim by 35% when attempting to slice off an opponent's limb.

Wall Climb (level 2)

Improves your ability to climb vertical walls. You are 8% more likely to discover usable handholds.

Gravity Shift (level 1)

Allows you to change the direction of gravity subjectively, enabling you to walk on walls.
Cost: 1 mana per 10 seconds

Pretentious Jerk (level 1)

People whom you belittle are now 8% more likely to question their self-worth

AUTHOR'S NOTE

Thank you all so much for reading my book. I hope you enjoyed reading it as much as I enjoyed writing it. Tasha and company will return in the next installment of the Couch Potato Chaos trilogy.

After reading the works of authors in the genre such as Charles Dean, Blaise Corvin, Andrew Seiple, Rick Scott, Taj El and many others, I became inspired to write my own. I've always enjoyed comedic takes on fantasy by authors like Piers Anthony, Terry Pratchett, and Robert Asprin and felt compelled to write a more light-hearted take on the LitRPG/Gamelit genre.

Though the story is less stat-heavy than other books in the genre, I tried to ensure that each stat is meaningful and that actual combat damage is calculated in one-on-one battles. The style of the game is patterned after action RPGs such as Seiken Densetsu and Legend of Zelda. Concepts like DPS don't apply to games like that, though I did also integrate some features from MMOs such as the ability to manually set stat points.

The concept of "death" in works of fiction and gamelit in particular, often leads to the author creating the impression of plot armor because the story wouldn't be able to progress if the protagonist were to die. I attempted to avoid that by creating a form of death that has long-term consequences but allowed the hero to come back to life. When Tasha dies, she becomes a dramatically different person than who she was before. This allows characters to die in a meaningful way beyond the mere loss of stat points.

The "Rapid Leveling" and "Stat Shuffle" abilities might appear to be overpowered at first glance, but I don't really think they are. Stat Shuffle comes with a penalty and long cooldown that makes it very difficult to use in combat. The Rapid Leveling ability allows the player to become strong quickly, but it also has a critical weakness. In Chapter 17, Magus Savik D'hagma refused to allow Kiwi to level up because although leveling would give her stat points to become more powerful, she would lack actual experience. The muscle memory needed to cast spells wouldn't be there and her stat points would serve as a crutch. The same applies to Tasha. She has no training as a swordswoman or spellcaster and has to learn these new skills as she goes. As a result, her practical skill is less than someone of equivalent level.

Please take a moment to leave a review. As an author, reviews are incredibly helpful. If you wish to contact me, I can be reached on facebook or at couchpotatogamelit@gmail.com.

Thank you so much for reading! To find similar stories to this one, check out these pages:

Gamelit Society on Facebook at
https://www.facebook.com/groups/LitRPGsociety

LitRPG Group on Facebook at
https://www.facebook.com/groups/LitRPGGroup

GreatLitrpg at https://greatlitrpg.com/

Printed in Great Britain
by Amazon

55911931R00305